THE
MAKING
OF
YOLANDA
LA BRUJA

THE
MAKING
OF
YOLANDA
LA BRUJA

LORRAINE
AVILA

LEVINE QUERIDO

Montclair | Amsterdam | Hoboken

This is an Arthur A. Levine book
Published by Levine Querido

LEVINE QUERIDO

www.levinequerido.com • info@levinequerido.com

Levine Querido is distributed by Chronicle Books, LLC

Library of Congress Control Number: 2022945156

ISBN 978-1-64614-243-9

Printed and bound in China

Published in April 2023

First Printing

To the youth. To the Bronx. For those of us who don't bite our tongues.

PROLOGUE

Mamá Teté has a saying: "Al que no le gusta el caldo, que le den dos tazas." I guess I grew up thinking that was the only way. That if I didn't like something, I should keep at it, until the habit of turning up my nose at whatever it was, was gone.

I wish I would've never internalized the need to put the needs of others over my own. Force-feeding myself the things my body wants to say no to is exactly what has got us all in this mess in the first place.

The incident is not on Mamá Teté, my parents, or on the violence and abuse the world shows me. Trust me. This mess, it's on me. I'm the victim and the perpetrator of this story. I wish this wasn't the case. This mess is forcing me to deal with parts of myself I didn't even know existed.

1

THE CARDS DON'T LIE

I am panting, sweat accumulating at my edges, hands eagerly searching for the water bottle inside my Telfar bag. Thank God, I put on that edge control that keeps my baby hairs laid no matter what. I pat the small crown of cornrows on the front of my hair as I gulp down some water. Victory did them just yesterday after school, so they're still a bit tight. The bright lights turn on as we step into the small school bathroom.

"Come on girl, just read 'em for me," Victory says. She looks at the old deck of tarot cards Mamá Teté handed down to me two months ago in preparation for my sixteenth birthday. "Is this white boy sus or nah?"

Although we can't be in the bathrooms during lunch, we've snuck to the third floor of our school building again. The cream, glossy paint has long been chipping off of the bathroom walls, revealing the old brown color the walls used to be. There are messages written on the walls in Sharpie.

Taking another big gulp of water, it hits me that I've been giving myself a reading every morning, but this might be the first time I've brought them to school. I play with the water in my mouth before swallowing. I can't think of another time I've brought the cards outside.

But this morning was kind of a hot mess. Papi called early, which they never let him do in prison. Before he asked to speak to Mamá Teté, he sang me happy birthday, and then said he had good news: his lawyer told him he's on a list of early releases due to good behavior and overcrowding. It was the only birthday gift I needed, and I spoke with Papi way longer than I should've. I had no choice but to plan for my daily reading at school.

"Girl *bye!*" I say playfully, turning my back to Victory's request. "How I'm supposed to be reading you when it's *my* birthday?" I hang my medium, dark-olive bag on a hook. I touch it with pride. Then, I place my black and red North Face puffer jacket down on the cold bathroom floor. Victory sits on her knees in front of me. I grin wide sitting with my legs crossed.

"OK, you love your Telfeezy, we get it," Victory smiles. I nod. Mami gifted me the lightly used bag two days ago, saying she purchased it from a houseless person who comes into the supermarket selling things sometimes. "So," she says. Victory knows better than anyone that I don't bother the Bruja Diosas for nonsense—especially not about no boy.

"Why don't you just watch how I do my own reading? Then, you can read for yourself," I say, noticing her eyes are hopeful. "WITH YOUR OWN CARDS, that you can easily purchase, and ask whatever unnecessary questions you wanna ask."

I twirl on my bottom and face her. In this friendship, Victory is always in the teacher position—helping me through my struggles with chemistry and algebra—and reading tarot cards or la taza to her is kind of my thing. Pero not today, especially, because I'm not about to potentially ruin it just for that new kid. I dig into the secret pocket at the bottom of my jacket and retrieve the red satin scarf holding my deck, small lighter, and a stick of palo santo. Lighting the palo santo, I pray the smoke detector doesn't go off. The sweet aroma of burning wood envelops us, and I close my eyes.

"May all past energies be removed from these cards, for the clearest reading today," I whisper, starting my reading. I run my hands over the cards. Many of the cards are folded, bent at the center, and worn at the edges, while some have even been taped back together. But I hold them to my chest as if they are a gift the Gods have left for humanity. Mamá Teté does not like that I praise them like this. The cards are simply a tool, she says, and they should not be idolized, especially because they were given to us by a dead white man. "I'm sure he was as good as they'll ever be, but he was still a colonizer and a businessman. Selling the cards as the only tool people could use to divinate and erasing the fact that many of us had been doing it very well without any tools at all," she likes to remind me.

"After clearing the energy, I start off with a little prayer," I look at Victory. "It can be anything you want, and to whomever or whatever you believe in." I close my eyes again. "Thank you Bruja Diosas, Guardian Angels, Goddesses, Gods, good-hearted Ancestors, Unknowns, Universe, and all that is wiser and greater than humans, for another day of life in this body and for the messages you will deliver." I begin to shuffle the deck. These cards have been in the Alvarez family since the Europeans started settling in Ayiti, and it sends chills up my spine to think of the voyage they have taken through space and time to be in this stuffy, small, paint-chipping girls bathroom. At first, the momentum of my hands is timid, but then my shuffle is quick, almost hasty, as if the Bruja Diosas have been trying to communicate with me all morning.

"Let me know, Bruja Diosas, let me know."

I flap open my eyes to see the Tower fall out.

"Ooooh!" Victory reacts. I playfully roll my eyes at her.

The Tower is just that—a large tower on top of a mountain that doesn't seem that stable. It is in flames, and two people have dove out of its windows to meet their death. There is lightning and flames. "When Mamá pulls this out for clients, it almost always points to a sudden redirection 'cause of surprising or new information," I say.

What will I learn today?

I shuffle again, deciding today will be a three-card pull. "May the reality of what is to come be revealed for the highest good of all involved, Bruja Diosas."

The Devil jumps out.

Hmmm, well that's not good. The Devil is a hairy creature with horns and a five-point star at its head. This card hardly ever comes out for me, and although I know no card is "bad," my stomach knots up because—thanks to Hollywood and the Church—the image of anything related to the Devil gives me the creeps. The man and woman shackled together underneath the creature look like they are OK being submissive; the woman dangles a vine of grapes and the man holds fire. I take a deep breath. "Mamá Teté"—I clear my throat—"once told me, this card can be interpreted by highlighting unhealthy attachments people might have to the material world that do not serve our highest good."

"Well I hope it's just that. The Devil, however way we put it, scares the hell out of me, no pun intended, girl," Victory says. Her eyes are wide as she stares at the card.

The shackles stand out to me, and I wonder if the cards are trying to communicate that I am some sort of prisoner. *But to what?*

I shuffle again. *Please Bruja Diosas, come through and be straight up—*

The Death card spills onto the inside of my leg.

"Oh shit, girl, these cards just don't look too good," Victory says.

"OK, Ms. Obvious!" I snap quickly. I look at her apologetically and turn to focus on the card.

The Death card is that of a skeleton in full armor sitting on top of a white horse. It holds a black flag. The flag has a waning white flower.

"Hmmmm, well, death can mean a lot of things: rebirth, new beginnings, and actual death, but what I am feeling is this flower." I take a deep breath. "We fall, but we rise again," I say, smiling nervously. "When it's upside-down like this, it means a change must happen, but we might be trying to avoid it leading to chaos," I say. *Bruja Diosas, speak to me. I am sorry I was in such a rush this morning that I did not have time to reach out, but right now, I need to know—*

Your ideas about your role in the world must change. Your don cannot always keep you safe in this physical realm.

The words ring gently inside of me like a soft bell.

"Alright, so I'm walking from this reading feeling like there is some sort of change that needs to take place due to the Death card. This is connected to someone or something toxic I might be attached to. And there's about to be a huge shift—for multiple folks," I say.

"Girl, I'm all the way good. I don't need no more readings today," Victory laughs nervously. "Especially not about that white boy."

Loud banging coming off of the radiators connected to the school's old heating system startles us both.

"Be quiet! You mad silly," I say, standing up. I unhook my bag and step towards the sink. Right above the mirror is the Julia De Burgos quote I've learned to love: "Don't let the hand you hold, hold you down." Setting my bag down on the sink, I look at my face in the mirror and reach up into my ears. Other than the cornrows in the front, my curly afro stands proudly in all directions of my face, ending under my breast bones. My hair is a shield on days when it's out, without the front cornrows, because it makes my sound processors invisible to the world. But today all the external parts of my cochlear implants show. I'm not ashamed of having the implants—I know my parents worked hard for me to have them—but sometimes I don't want to be treated like the pretty smart-and-basically-deaf girl.

"It's damn near the end of fall anyway, Yo. Plus, who transfers their senior year? It makes no sense why he is even here." Victory has asked these questions fifty eleven times in the last twenty-four hours.

"It's the end of Libra season, girl. We still got two whole ass signs to go through before it's the end of fall. Stop exaggerating," I laugh.

"Have you seen some people swooning over him?! I mean he's kinda eye candy if you're into the quiet and mysterious kinda dude, but I am not buying the story that his daddy wants him to be in a 'diverse school.'" She ignores me.

"I mean—" A bit of my curls have looped around the wire between the transmitter and the processor and I pull on it to free it up. *Ouch!* When I finish, Victory repeats herself:

"No kid goes to boarding school their whole, entire life and then is transferred to a public school in the twelfth grade."

It's a heavy time right now. Black and Brown folks being killed or harmed by a racist person, or police—at the supermarket, at a festival, in a church, at the movies. Plus, I saw on CNN that so far this year there has been at least one school shooting per week. It makes perfect sense that it feels like there is nowhere we can go to be fully safe anymore. So, I get it. It doesn't feel good to have random kids put into our safe spaces out of the blue like that. I'm with Victory on this one. But, I can't be letting her run with some of her ideas sometimes. If she runs with them, I run with them, and that's a whole lot of anxiety I'd rather not deal with. At the end of the day, if we become tense balls of anxiety, who is that going to help? It's also my birthday, and I just don't want to deal.

"Maybe his dad is clout-chasing, I don't know," I say. Victory sucks her teeth at me, and goes into her bag.

"You know how I live my life, Victory: give everyone a chance until they prove you wrong. And even if they prove you wrong, Mamá says that's why we gifted with community and spirit for—to be able to deal with it. Also, remember what Mrs. Obi taught us about community justice just the other day? If the person wants to change, people have to give them a chance, right? Maybe he is here for all the wrong reasons, but maybe he's trying to start over fresh? Let's give him that for now." Learning about community justice had me thinking of the way our communities would be different if justice was left to us, and not to all the systems that try to categorize us into "bad" and "good" from the moment we enter schools.

"But he isn't part of our 'community,'" Victory makes air quotes. "You think *they* got spirit, Yoyo?" she whispers. We look at each other like we're scared of who is listening, and then we burst out laughing.

"They don't got our spirit, but shit, if it comes down to it—for the greater good of humanity, I'd be willing to include *some* of them, you know?" I shrug.

Victory shakes her head. "I swear to God you be reckless sometimes. Why would we share the one thing they've tried to take from us but can't?" But I know enough to know that she don't want my answer. I don't even know if I believe my answer truly.

"You right, we'll keep the sauce to ourselves," I say.

"The sauce and the juice—all ours, OK?" She takes out her new Fenty lip gloss and brushes her lower lip before pressing her lips together. "Girl, this lip gloss is EVERYTHING! Look at this brush," she says, passing it to me like I never seent it myself. As I reach for it, she snatches it back. I roll my eyes with a joyous grin.

"Guess what? I'm tired of sharing everything with your ass," she continues, going into her bag. "So we not sharing lip glosses anymore!" She takes out a small Sephora bag. I hug her as she hands it to me. The new Fenty lip gloss Holiday set and a small perfume. There is a birthday card too. I throw my hands around her again and hug her as hard as I can.

I open the first lip gloss, Fu$$y. It is a light-toned medium pink with a jewel finish—so fire! I brush my lips with the gloss wand. The brush is wide enough to completely apply gloss onto thick lips, like ours, in one pass.

"It's like Riri knew it was gon' be us buying this, you know?" Victory smiles at me, her hazel eyes beaming through the mirror.

She takes out her phone and opens up the camera app. I apply some more gloss on my upper lip and pose, blowing her a kiss. She snaps the picture and hugs my shoulders from the back. "Happy birthday. Keep getting older for the both of us 'cause I cannot live without you, Yoyo," she says. Her eyes fill with tears. "You my mejor amigaaaaaa in the worlddddd!" she sings, shaking off the tears and clearing her throat.

"Best frienddd," I sing back, "for ever, ever!" I go in for another hug. "On God. Thank you, V, forreal." I smile.

We quickly put everything into our bags and open the bathroom door. I poke out my head, looking to the left and the right first. My heart rate accelerates. I'm not trying to get caught up in nothing on my birthday. Seeing nothing, we tiptoe out of the bathroom.

☾

"CRC coming up, ladies," a voice says, just a few seconds later. I don't gotta look to know it's Mr. Leyva, the school dean. His voice is warm even when he's calling people out. That's why students, most especially me, respect and love him. He's one of the adults in the building who just gets us.

When we turn, Mr. Leyva comes out of the stairwell door. Damn, he's good. He leans against the hallway wall, his left foot up. He picks at his nails with one of his hundred and one keys. CRC stands for Conflict Resolution Conversation, but it's literally just detention. Victory begs a little, lying and saying we had some girl business to take care of. Usually, Mr. L lets us off, but today he is not budging. He's holding a light brown folder, which complements his off-white sweater and his red jeans. Mr. Leyva has to be at least fifty-five—he's older than all of our teachers and even the principals—but he is the only person I know who can still rock red jeans like that.

"Come on, Mr. L. I can't go to CRC," I say as he walks us to the stairs leading downstairs. "I'm the leader of the Brave Space Club, and it's *legit* my birthday today, you really gonna do that to me? You haven't even said happy birthday or nothing to me." At this, his face softens.

"Happy birthday, Yo. I wish you a long, long life," he says. I nod gratefully his way. "Alright, Yo, you want a break? How about you take Ben Hill on a quick tour of the building—"

"Oh nah, I'm good," I respond.

"You what?"

"I. AM. GOOD."

"Ms. Alvarez, you coming out your neck a lot since you found your voice," he begins. Mr. L has seen my come up. In ninth grade, I was dique shy and came out of my shell to fight or yell when I was not heard, or when clowns tried to come at me over my processors. "Listen, you a whole sixteen-year-old now. I ain't got the time to play these games with you."

Last year, when my dreams became vivid, my anxiety got real bad. I had this recurring dream that I was walking from school to the train, and when I boarded the train, it just went on forever. It didn't make no stops. When I tried to talk to people on the train, they couldn't hear or see me. After the fourth time I had this dream, I started to walk home in my dreams, but then I was walking forever down empty streets, never getting anywhere. I told Mr. L I had a feeling something strange was going to happen to me on my way home. We walked to the train together for three whole weeks—me, him, Victory, and a bunch of other first-year students.

"Make a choice: it's either the tour or CRC. You choose. Make it quick, I have to run and go get my lunch and my hot chocolate. I'll get you something from the store too if you want. A birthday present."

Julia De Burgos High is in a building shared with two different other schools, so getting around when you're new is complicated. The tour, although not official, is given to first-year students every year on the first week of school by Mr. L. I look at Victory as we go down the stairs. Mr. Leyva's keys make their own song as they jingle off his pants. *Just do it*, she mouths.

"Right now?" I ask.

Mr. L nods. "He should be in the lunchroom."

I open the heavy double doors of the lunchroom, and the heat from the boiling water they use to warm up the nasty school lunch immediately fogs my glasses. I take them off and the students who were as clear as day are now a compilation of burgundy, gold, and black, our school colors. A bunch of classmates walk past smiling or nodding. I return the greeting and continue towards the back of the lunchroom.

"Yolanda, hey!" I feel a tug on my arm. I look up and my stomach immediately drops. José is holding three birthday balloons and a gift bag.

"Happy birthday," he says.

"Thank you," I respond, looking at my arm, and then back up at him—communicating with my eyes that he should let go. Regardless of our kiss at the park last week, José must've lost his damn mind to think he has the right to demand my attention by putting hands on me in public. I repeat my staring process again

when I find his hand still on my arm. I make sure to roll my eyes
deep into my head this time.

"I just wanted to give you a birthday gift and talk," he says,
letting go. "You've been straight up avoiding me." José is a senior,
good-looking, and captain of the basketball team. It seems like
the entire Bronx is praying on his success in the sport. In other
words, in this school, he is used to getting what he wants. He's
been trying to kick it to me since I was a first-year student last
year. Although I like him, I don't want to be something else he
could just have. To complicate everything, up until September's
back-to-school night—when parents were invited to come in—
neither of us knew that our mothers were low-key friendly.
Apparently his mother worked for a couple years at the supermarket where my mother does the books.

"Listen, I haven't," I look up at him. The butterflies immediately start doing their thing as I look into his soft eyes. I suck my
teeth to shake them off. "I haven't been ignoring you. I'm just
busy, José," I lie. The only place I've seen him lately is Brave
Space Club. Other than that, I take the long ways to avoid him
because the feelings are so overwhelming. "Thank you for the
gift though."

He bends down and hugs me. He's wearing his basketball jersey over his school uniform shirt, and I suddenly catch a whiff of
his cologne.

"I have to go do something for Mr. L. We can talk later," I say.
I peel my eyes off of him before the urge to kiss him becomes
unbearable. Maybe this is what the Devil card was hinting at. But
I don't feel scared—I feel seen by him. That's scary, too, but not
the Devil card-type scary.

I turn towards the tables lined up against one another in the cafeteria, but I can't spot where Victory went. I look and look but nothing. I take a deep breath, knowing that I have to find her first; I'm not about to go give a tour with a bunch of balloons.

"Yerrrrrrrrr!" I hear the call. I turn and it's all of my friends from the Brave Space Club, including Mrs. Obi, with a cake and a gift bag.

"Happy birthday to ya! Happy birthday to ya! Happy birthday! Happy birthday!" They sing loudly and the rest of the cafeteria joins in. As I look at all the faces around me, my heart feels big in my chest. The people I know and love at this school are filled with joy, like my birthday isn't just a birthday, but a whole moment. I can't help but smile widely. Victory is cheesing too, and I know it must've not been easy for her to keep this secret away from me. I spot José shuffling over quickly, leaving his friends behind. Cindy is clapping mad loud and a couple other students are snapping in unison. Yeah, there are faces of students I don't really talk to too much, but I couldn't imagine a school experience without seeing them. Deadass. Even though they don't do anything for me, per se, them being alive and present does something for the school. Their voices are so loud, my head hurts a little, but I'm OK with this loud. I love this kind of loud— an overflowing noise of good things. I feel so special, and it causes every part of my body to have its own heartbeat. Mrs. Obi walks up to me with the birthday cake; she lights up the candles with a lighter.

"Hurry up and make a wish before I get fired for using fire outside our science class," she whispers, smiling mischievously. I close my eyes.

I hope this next year of my life brings me closer to being the person I was born to be. If I have to fold, may I never break. May I remember everything is leading towards the making of me.

I blow and open my eyes. Mr. L is now next to Mrs. Obi, clapping along with everyone else.

"Of course I knew it was your birthday, Little Miss Libra Sun, Aries Moon and Gemini Rising," Mr. L says, handing me a small giftbag that I know he didn't just get from the bodega.

"You didn't have to, Mr. L," I say with a smile.

"Now you open that up when you're by yourself. I don't want nobody saying I got favorites again."

"But you do, and it's me," I laugh, hugging Jay, who nods and is wearing dope ass lime-green eyeliner in lines, the spaces between them filled in with red eyeshadow, and baby blue dots under their eyebrows.

"It looks so good!" I tell them.

They step back, opening their arms around their jersey. "To celebrate you," they say.

As soon as everyone who was gonna hug me is done, some folks disperse, and mainly the club stays put. I set the balloons and bags at the center of the table near Victory.

"You still gotta go do that thing I told you to do," Mr. L winks, taking the cake from Mrs. Obi, who has a meeting.

"Go," Victory says. "I'll start cutting the cake," she says.

I nod, turn from my friends, and start looking around the cafeteria for Ben.

CHANCES

Ben's perfectly ironed and lint-free blazer catches my attention before he does. I mean, the thing is impeccable. I have zero clues as to why some people are thirsting over him though. Maybe it's the blazer. I get that it's catching some attention. Even though they're on the uniform purchase website, no one really gets them around here. It suits him though, so good for him, I guess.

I fast walk towards him, saying thank you to the first-year students who didn't come to the table but say happy birthday now that I am walking past them. The accumulation of voices sends static into the processor. Although I have had these for most of my life, my doctor claims my brain hasn't gotten used to too many noises at the same time. I rub my ear a bit to alleviate the tension.

Ben is sitting at the edge of a long lunchroom table, his shoulders tense, too close to his neck as he reads. One of his hands is under his chin and his legs are extended under the table. I can see the top of his head; the hair on it a bit spiky, like it's just been freshly cut, and I wonder if he went to a barbershop in preparation for coming to Julia De Burgos High. Despite the people sitting on the other side of the table, Ben is alone.

Lonely, I hear a voice correct me. As I get closer to him, I begin feeling the loneliness like a knot underneath the skin before it bruises.

"Hey Ben," I say, sitting across from him.

He looks up at me with a coldness that only warms up to sadness after a moment or two. "Hi," he replies. His cheeks grow red, and his ears seem to be burning out of nowhere. He shifts his green eyes back to his Kindle.

"Can we step outside real quick?" I ask.

He shrugs, puts his Kindle away, and follows me. He takes wide steps to the double doors and I try to keep up, bringing the straps of my new Telfar up to my shoulder. Everyone's eyes are on us, and I have to look down at the floor to avoid José's glance as we walk out.

Outside the cafeteria, I tell Ben about the tour, and he agrees to it with a shrug. His eyes look towards the school entrance dazed and unbothered. I let him in on the fact that we share the gym, cafeteria, auditorium, and courtyard with a charter elementary school, and they're to the left side of the main entrance. We walk into the right side of the school entrance, where Julia De Burgos begins. Silence buzzes at our ears as we tour the first floor. I point out the library, the computer science room, the offices, the mental health first stop, and the math classes.

"The first floor is basically the floor that has all the things any of the grades would need access to, plus every grade's math class. Math classes, as you can tell, are separated into these two wings." I stretch out my arms from the main hallway and point towards the other two. "On the left side, you'll find ninth- and tenth-grade math, and on the right side, you have eleventh- and—"

"*Twelfth*-grade classes. I know. You don't have to be a genius to figure it out," he chuckles. I quickly look back and watch as he rubs his chin.

I turn around, hold the door to the staircase open for him so that we can go up to the second floor, and roll my eyes. I am not doing this for him, but for myself, so he can be an asshole all he wants. On the second floor, I point out bathrooms, and then move to the first wing towards our left.

"Do you want to show me your schedule so I can tell you what classes you should definitely know?" I ask. He takes out a neatly folded paper from his back pocket. His hands are clammy as I accidently touch them to get the schedule. "OK, so you have Ms. Kaur for AP Literature and Composition," I say, pointing to her door.

He doesn't look towards the door, instead, his eyes are now fixated on my hair or my cochlear implant.

I take a deep breath. "This entire wing is English classes for all grades because we have this program that lets us choose the topic of our English classes, plus some of them are AP. Basically English classes—"

"Don't just have one grade," he cuts me off.

"OK, Impatient," I say, laughing a little bit, even though I want to remind him I'm the one giving the tour. He doesn't smile or laugh back, and I wonder if it's because he's straight up being rude or because he's as sad as I felt he was back in the cafeteria. I walk towards the next wing.

"This is the writing wing. For writing, you have Mr. Miles." I quicken my pace as we walk down a narrow hallway that brings us towards the next wing. I meant to explain why the school has an extra writing course—because we wrote letters to the administration last year to ask for a class that was strictly creative and had nothing to do with test prep at any given time of the year. But now, I just want this entire tour to be over. "Science wing. For chemistry, you have Mrs. Obi. I'm in this class too, by the way," I say, hoping he'll quit the bullshit since he'll have to see me every day.

"Oh, I hear you run the Brave Space Club. Is this teacher a Social Justice Warrior, like you?" he asks, looking at the laminated poster with Audre Lorde's quote. His eyes hold a coldness in them again as he reads through the poster. It says something about how the tools that oppressed people find in the master's house will never break down the master's house. While oppressed people might think they changing something with those tools, for whatever reason, at the end of the day, it actually isn't no real change.

"Excuse me?" I've heard the term before from the stupid social media videos trolls put up on YouTube, and a few problematic memes Victory has showed me. Plus, one of the last shooters left a manifesto talking a whole lot about "social justice warriors."

"Nothing," he laughs, "nothing." I take a deep breath, and even though I am mad irritated, I close my eyes for a second. *Guide me, shield me,* I pray.

"Well, I'm sure you know all the reasons why saying something like that is violent," I say. The words come out of my throat and slip out of my lips before I can even fully digest what I've snapped back with. I look back up at him, and I swear he is low-key giving me puppy eyes now—like what?! I take a deep breath and purse my lips.

"What school you coming from, Ben?" I ask, folding my arms.

"Butler Prep," he responds. I must have lost the tough glance because he quickly adds, "It's a boarding school in Connecticut."

"So this is a change, huh?" I release my arms, feeling like maybe he's having a hard day and this can be an in to him opening up. I walk towards the staircase leading to the top floor, waiting for his answer.

"I haven't seen much, not that I think there's much more to see." He looks around our hallways as if maybe he's lost, out of his comfort zone. "But I can tell you it's worlds apart." He looks at me. "I mean, at least for me. I know I'm different and have a lot of privilege compared to people here in the South Bronx."

"I can only imagine it's different for you. And yeah, at least you recognize the privilege you carry here," I reply. On the third floor, I point out the classrooms for electives: Drawing and Pottery, Music, College Readiness, Life Readiness, and Performance. We have a wide range of electives compared to other public schools in the Bronx, but suddenly I feel low-key ashamed pointing them out to Ben, who must've had dozens of elective choices.

Once I went on a visit to a private school with Victory. Her grandmother was willing to pay for the remaining portion of tuition if she received a scholarship. The school campus was enormous and felt more like a small city. They had all kinds of classrooms and equipment. On the tour, we counted five Black or Brown students, and when they spotted us, it was obvious they would've been hyped for Victory to join.

"Why the change of schools?" I ask.

"Well, there's two versions to that. My own and my father's."

A puzzling feeling comes over me. I remember Victory's

questions, and I squint my eyes with a question of my own, but I quickly shift to a fake smile since it's none of my business right now.

"The truth is somewhere in between that," Ben reads me. "My take on half of it is my dad is a dick. He wants to gain the trust of communities like this one to gain his seat."

OK, so he's fully aware that we know who he is and who his father is. I look at his fingers; his cuticles have been forcefully pulled off, and there's dried blood dressing the tiny wounds. We don't expose our parents around here—I would never speak about my people to strangers. I want the conversation to end swiftly. My heart beats furiously like it knows something I do not. My pelvic area contracts. My period must be coming.

"Well, this is it," I mumble. "If you need anything, let me know, OK?" He nods, and I turn towards the door. Looking over my shoulder, I see he is lingering behind, studying other posters on the walls. I know he's just studying this place, my place, my folks' space, what our minds and desires have pushed out around us . . . but something in me feels protective. Mamá Teté comes to my mind: "Our powers exist so we can preserve our power and take back and protect what is ours." I take a deep breath. I want to make Mamá Teté and the Bruja Diosas proud, and I want to make sure my people are aight—more than I fear being made uncomfortable by any type of mortal.

"Hey, Ben," I say. He turns on his heels, his hands behind his back, his entire body facing in my direction. His eyes are haunting—somewhere lost between a deep misery, the one I first felt and saw, and anger. I feel too exposed. I forget what I called out to him for.

He moves his gaze from my eyes to my head again and speaks

as if he's the one that called back out to me. "It's your birthday today, right?"

"Yeah," I answer. Forgetting what it was I was going to tell him.

"Well, happy birthday. And I'm sorry for what I said earlier. I didn't mean it," he states with an awkward smile. I nod, and the words I called him back for come back to me.

"Listen Ben, this might not be the bougiest school," I tug on the strap of my bag, "but welcome to Julia De Burgos. It's all some of us got, and TBH, most of us like it here. Hopefully, you will too."

BLOOD PULLS

What wakes me up is the muggy wetness I feel underneath the sheets. It's six in the morning, and the sun hasn't revealed itself entirely, but it sneaks up through the clouds enough for me to see the arte de rebeldía when I lift the sheets. Violet red has escaped me and seeped into the white threading of my sheets again. I once saw a piece of art at the MoMA that looked similar to this. I've created abstract art again. Mamá Teté will be annoyed with me, yet she will find purpose in cleaning the stains. I grin in the darkness of the morning and rub my belly. It's warm and plump. I am not worried because blood is the most natural element of me. Although I don't like the pain that comes with the cramps, getting my period mostly feels like a celebration of my humanness.

Mamá Teté won't think so. It's not my birthday anymore, so no more special treatments, plus she wouldn't stand for it on my birthday anyway. She stomps into my room already aware. The sheets are off my body before I have a chance to say something.

"You are a haragana!" I read Mamá Teté's lips. Her kinky afro is covered by a purple leopard-print satin bonnet. "Why aren't you using your calendar to figure out when it'll land?! Why won't you just pay attention when you start to spot?!" She asks these questions every month, so I've been learned not to answer them 'cause she's not looking for an answer. She's looking for me to change.

Mamá Teté strips my bed of its sheets, and I have no choice but to get up. She brings the white sheets into a ball underneath her arms and leaves for the kitchen. In less than fifteen seconds, she'll become an accessory to my rebeldía. She'll mix a little Clorox, baking soda, and water in a bucket, praying over them as she mixes. It's as serious as if she is casting a spell. *Bruja Diosas, may the white of these sheets not stain,* she'll pray as she sinks them into the bottom of the bucket with gloved hands. She's tired of rebuying these white sheets I insist on having. The white linens represent a clean slate for me. I like waking up every morning knowing I can start again.

Mamá Teté deals with me because other than that, I'm on top of everything else. I'm a good student, a respectful hija, and most of all, I am her only granddaughter, her first grandkid. She waited for my arrival ever since her only offspring, my dad, made it clear he was uninterested in the voice and power of the higher beings and instead chased women and money. Everyone is born with their connection, but it is important to keep at it, to cultivate it. Papi, like most people, chose not to.

I sit up on my naked bed and reach for the tarot cards on my nightstand. It's been part of my morning routine to pull a card since Mamá gave them to me. Before that, I just sat at my altar and meditated. Reading the cards feels like an active meditation.

"Spirit was clear—you were ready for the cards," I read Mamá's lips as she walks into my room again. She strips the pillowcases from my four pillows as I spread the cards across the bed. "My great-grandmother gave them to me, and her great-grandmother passed them down to her. These cards have been passed down for centuries," she states, like I don't know this story.

"Your great-great-great-great-great-grandmother worked for a Criolla, a white woman born on the island, after her Spanish parents arrived. La Española found them underneath her teenage daughter's bed, y pa que fue eso? She held them with a white cloth and ordered one of her Black servants to burn them since they were in a Christian home. It turns out her daughter never told who she got the deck from. But it was our ancestor who kept them under her skirt, and instead burned a book she had read dozens of times already." I look at Mamá sluggishly. I just want to read my cards and get on with my day.

"I tell you that story again so that you can remember you have the capacity to be more responsible with your body, Yoyo! If Spirit said you were ready for the cards, then you sure as hell can be ready to get up off your culo and put on a pad instead of staining these sheets every month! Your initiation is about to begin soon, you should be doing better than this!"

"Sí, Mamá," I say. With that she's gone again. I turn back to my cards.

Thank you, Bruja Diosas, Guardian Angels, Goddesses, Gods, good-hearted Ancestors, Unknowns, Universe, and all that is wiser and greater than humans, for another day of life in this body and for the messages you will deliver. I begin my morning prayers every day with these words as I touch the tarot deck. Bruja Diosas was an umbrella term I made up when I was five. It was supposed to encompass all those I name in my prayer until the Unknown who ruled my head came to me. Mamá's Bruja Diosa (Unknown) is

Culebra. My Unknown has not chosen me yet, so here I am still using a term that to other believers might seem childish, but feels good to me.

I take a deep breath and shuffle. Papi taught me how to shuffle playing cards when I was a little girl, on the days he took me to work at the car dealership. Going to work with him was like going to another kind of school. Papi made it his business to teach me everything from drilling a hole, to fixing a tire. He claimed the more a girl knew, the less shit she'd have to take from the world. The Ten of Wands card falls out. The card shows a person struggling to carry a load of ten sticks.

I get up only because I have to shower again, since the blood has now stained the inside of my legs. Why do we get our periods? I understand the biology, pero when did the Bruja Diosas decide it was those with this body who have to bear the weight of waiting on an unfertilized egg to drop? The worst part is that my body feels sad when it's time to give up the egg. Like, I missed its only chance to have a baby. I am a young person, but my body knows no different. I become sluggish and sometimes just downright depressed overthinking things, like my parents' divorce, and what Papi must be going through in prison. Sometimes I'll just watch a show and the minimal thing will happen and BAM! I'm crying. I try to remember that when my mood fluctuates around this time.

In the bathroom, I look up from the sink into the mirror. I have to get on my tiptoes to see the full reflection of my face. The light coming off the electric candles sitting on the sides of the bathroom sink illuminates my eyes while they cast their shadow on my neck. I use the old toothbrush to set my baby hairs into swirls, and I brush down my thick eyebrows. I put my processors on. As a toddler, I remember not liking to take them off; it felt almost magical to have devices that gave me my full hearing. But at around five, when Mami and Papi started fighting, I started taking them off on my own to keep from hearing too much. I close the medicine cabinet and finally stick them onto the sides of my head and the back of my ears. Suddenly, it's not just the white noise in my head, but the gloop, gloop sound of the little bit of water that always leaks from the bath faucet, the screeching of the 1 train arriving at the 225th Street station from a distance, and Mamá Teté's house slippers swish, swishing against the kitchen floor.

I rub my eyes, which are swollen with sleep. I yawn and open my eyes to look at my reflection. My nose is wide like Mamá Teté's, and I wear it proudly because she passed it on to me. She says it's a stamp from our ancestors, a stamp that will never let us forget that we are because they existed. My lips are thick and plump, like Mami's, and when I smile they spread to show all of my teeth. I see the two bottom teeth that grow crooked—Papi recommended I get braces, but I will be fine. Mamá Teté says I come from a line of strong and gorgeous women, and I can see it in this mirror. But trust me, I'd rather be unseen sometimes.

The minute I got my first period, Mami told me there was a power in me now that every person assigned this body was given. She said I was coming into it strongly, so I had to be really careful. She claimed I had to think twice about what to wear and how to sit. I was nine, and Mamá had already brought out the mujerista in me, so I told Mami that my body wasn't about to be a cage. In middle school I started to understand where she was coming from though.

Sometimes, I'd catch people on the street, classmates, and even teachers looking directly at my face or my body for too long. Through Mamá, I figured that it was more than what Mami thought. If I spoke to those who gazed during those moments, I figured out I could get what I wanted. It felt manipulative until I used this power to control a distant cousin in Dominican Republic, who was known to be handsy with young girls like me. I entered him through his eyes and still have enough control on him to force him into fighting his urges to touch bodies that are not his own without permission. I feel like doing the same thing to every man that looks at me or other people with malicious and brute-like energy, especially on days that walking anywhere feels like hell on Earth. But Mamá Teté says that controlling too many people takes a toll on the soul. I am too young to carry all that, she reminds me.

In the shower, I watch the blood wash down my body, into the tub, and down the drain. The human body is such a beautiful and strange place to be. I wonder when I chose this body. These bodies are so powerful. Whenever I forget that and complain about getting my period, Victory says, "Do you have a problem with being one of the baddest and most savage animals? We were chosen for this."

But it hurts so very much most of the time, to the point that I think it's cruel menstruating bodies don't get a break from school or work or life. I have to hang on to this power, even when it feels like a lie, to get through the first few excruciating days.

I get out of the shower, dry off, get dressed, and put on my school uniform. A burgundy shirt with gold letters that say Julia De Burgos on the upper, left side; black high-waisted straight-legged Levi's; and black Yeezy 500s.

"Yolanda Nuelis!" Mamá Teté shouts. She always adds my middle name when she wants to add a kick to her voice. As I spray my Kimberly New York Diaspora perfume Mami gifted me for my birthday, I realize Mamá probably found a stubborn stain that won't leave the fibers of the sheets. I've been sleeping in Mamá Teté's house ever since I can remember. I try my best to always be here Tuesday to Friday, but most of the time, I just end up being here the entire week. She's getting older, and this feels like my home more than any other place. Plus, I'm her only granddaughter. She says all of her wisdom and traditions won't die with her because she's making sure to pass them on to me. I don't ask her why she doesn't teach my younger brothers, Noriel and Nordonis, because I know she'd just answer: "The magic only opens up to those who want it."

As I walk into the kitchen, she looks up at me, "Can you believe this!?" She has the bucket to her left sitting on the kitchen counter and the sheets on her right hand. "De verdad, I can't believe you're lazy over this ONE thing. The ONE thing that you can get ahead of," she repeats. I look down at my sneakers. I want to tell her that this one thing reminds me that I am just a simple mortal who makes mistakes too. I want to admit that my dreams are too deep, and I don't like to interrupt them by getting up in the middle of the night.

Although in the last week, my dreams have been nightmares again, like the ones from last year: of finding objects I don't want to find, like baseball bats, ropes, and machetes. Sometimes I even feel awake in them. I can fly around the entire globe. I want to tell her about my dreams today so bad, because she always understands. But there is sweat on her brow now, and I know I'm messing up her morning routine, so instead, I say, "Cion, Mamá."

"Que todo lo bueno te bendiga," she replies. I grab a banana and a reusable plastic ziplock bag filled with grapes from the fridge, and fill up my bottle of water before I run out of the apartment for school.

"No te olvides, we have a reading today!" Mamá yells, as she watches me stand by the elevator.

I nod with a smile and step in behind the closing doors.

I swipe my neon-green Metrocard to get on the Bx1 up the street from the housing projects that Mamá Teté calls home. It's where my dad grew up. He's asked her mad times to move, but she refuses, says she left San Pedro de Macoris in Dominican Republic to create a home, and she created it already on the twenty-third floor of this building. The project building is gray and thirty floors high; there are at least three hundred families living within the walls. The building was built in the 1970s, but the city pays so little attention it might as well be a century old. Mamá doesn't mind the smell of sixteen-day-old urine or the constant police patrols walking up and down the stairs, 'cause we got community here. Most of her clients live there, and we never have to worry about anyone or anything bothering us, because everyone knows each other.

Although the bus is convenient, it's bumpy, and that is why I always attempt to secure a seat. I've lost count of the times someone has rubbed up on me "by accident" on an overcrowded bus. When I got my period for the first time, I cried and begged for a shot the pediatrician mentioned could take it away for a few years. Mamá Teté advised Papi and Mami against it, saying Mother Nature knows when a body is ready. So here I am, sixteen, with a body that, since I was eleven, sometimes feels like it should belong to someone else who is much older.

I walk straight to class when I get to Julia De Burgos. Our

lockers were sealed and considered out of use at the end of last school year, when school shootings across the United States hit an all-time high. Boys all over the United States done lost their minds; somehow they consecutively decided that taking guns to school during a mental breakdown was a good idea. That kind of stuff don't happen here in the hood. We got parents that'll pop us just for speaking back, but the rules of the burbs still travel to this side when it's convenient for those in power like the Department of Education. The Brave Space Club organized a protest to get our lockers back, and, as of this school year, we have been allowed to use them again. But I don't have time to stop at mine this morning.

My first class today is Physical Education. Mr. Jorel looks at me and nods towards the water bottles. I know he is telling me to help fill them up. The rest of the class is running a mile to warm up around the gym. People don't even scoff at it anymore. Everyone knows. If I run, period or no period, my back will ache all day due to the size of my boobs. I'd have to go home early to set heat pads and dunk my body into one of Mamá Teté's baños. I got a doctor's note and everything, so my only job in PE is to do stationary workouts, fill up the water bottles, and take the gym uniforms to the dry cleaners on Friday nights for Mr. Jorel. I pick up the crates with the empty water bottles and walk outside to the water fountains. The scent of pine smacks all the tiny hairs inside my nose, and I know one of the janitors, Ms. Elvira or Mr. Roan, has just passed through.

The hallways are always filled with hallway minglers, kids who don't want to go to class, but today there is no one. Something has changed. There's no way the entire student population decided to start the week on the right foot. Something's gotta be up. The squeakiness of Mr. Leyva's basketball shoes against the hallway floors announces him before he appears. His hands are holding the thick binder he always carries and a large number of lanyards with hallway passes.

"Alvarez, what you doing outside of class?" he asks.

"Filling up these bottles." I lift the crate holding the water bottles up to face level.

"Well let's make it quick," he says, slowing down his pace. Two tall white men in dark suits walk with our school principal, Ms. Steinberg, behind him. I bring my glasses off of my shirt and put them on. A man with a video camera mounted on his right shoulder and a young woman with a camera hanging from her neck rush in their wake as they all step into the gym. I roll my eyes, making sure Mr. L doesn't see me. "Who is that with Ms. Steinberg?" I ask.

"Mr. Hill, the man running next year for representative of New York's Twelfth Congressional District," Mr. L says.

"You mean Ben's dad?" I ask. I look away before he sees me roll my eyes again.

He nods.

I shake my head and go back to focusing on filling the bottles.

"How was the tour with Ben?" he questions me.

"Honestly?" I reply. Mr. L nods again. "It was aight. I mean the kid don't wanna be here, Mr. L. And it shows."

Mr. L sighs. "He's coming from a very different world, Yoyo, give him a break. I mean it isn't like the Bronx is welcoming at first glance."

I stop pressing down on the button expelling the water and shake my head. I don't understand adults sometimes. Like, really, is that the best he can come up with? "Mr. L," I clear my throat.

"We *are* trying the best we can. Most of us have never, ever had a white kid at our school. Never mind, a kid that clearly comes from money . . . and power. His father is running for a political seat! And now he's using us a token, putting us on TV like he's doing us a favor?" Mr. L opens his mouth to speak, but I bring my hand up.

"I'm not judging him or his dad. I believe everyone deserves a chance. But Ben kind of wasn't completely nice yesterday. He just wasn't and I'm not going to tapar el sol con un dedo like Mamá says." Mr. L looks confused at my Spanish—he's been learning. "I won't attempt to cover up the sun with a finger, in other words—I will not ignore what my gut felt. He was rude because he's sad, OK, but that isn't enough of a good reason for me. And then he kind of low-key tried to change it up too? Like don't play mind games with me, boy."

Mr. L chuckles and touches his chin. "Listen, Yoyo, I'm glad you know how to name when people are not being their best. But I have a good feeling you're going to have to take him under your wing."

"Nu uh. What you mean by that?"

"You're one of the student leaders at this school, Yo. You know how that goes," he says, walking away. I bite my tongue. Why do I have to be the one? Before I have a chance to ask that question, Mr. L is gone, out of sight.

CLAIRVOYANCE

The hallways are narrow and long in Julia De Burgos. On top of that, there are 352 of us in our tiny school building. The school was created just four years ago, and Principal Steinberg never lets us forget about how lucky we are to be a small school in the Bronx. Yet, we are always packed like sardines. It takes all of us four to five minutes just to transition into our next classes. The stuffiness is almost unbearable sometimes.

I take deep breaths and remind myself that all the energies I'm picking up on are not mine. On the walls there are posters for a bunch of clubs, but the Brave Space Club posters are the most aesthetically pleasing. Victory designs them and gives a whole Solange, clean, vibe to them. My favorite one has a tan background and dark gray circle in the middle. The wording is in a warm red, and the font is simple but edgy. I know it took Victory hours to design. *Care about your community? Join the Brave Space Club. Do the work.* The posters always urge students to join and process the social reality we are in.

School is what it always is. For the most part, everyone here plays their part. Many of us come from middle schools that had very few or no clubs, teams, and programs, so this place feels special despite its size and it not being wherever Ben came from. People know me for the most part because I run the Brave Space Club, and because I came in with a bang last year: putting everyone in their place if they tried it over my processors. To be honest, other than Victory, I have to put on a front to protect my truth with the Bruja Diosas. Mamá says it's part of the gamble—the one you have little to no choice in—when you open up to the Unknowns. Victory holds me down though. I've known her since forever, and she knows the truth: that Mamá Teté and I have been able to preserve and cultivate our connection to the Unknowns aka the Bruja Diosas. Her kinky coils announce her a few feet from me, before I see her face, and like always when she meets my eyes, right away I feel like someone sees the entirety of me—not just the parts I show them.

She raises her left eyebrow as she turns to look at Ben, who I see now directly behind her. His piercing green eyes look baffled at the sight of the crowded hallways. *What's up with his vibe?* her eyes ask. I shrug my shoulders. I really have no idea. I squeeze into the wing with Mr. Ruiz's class for US History.

Despite the class being called US History, the classroom has flags of every Latin American country, and a green, black, and red one with a black panther in the middle of it. Mr. Ruiz wears a brown turtleneck unzipped to his chest with a red-and-white-checked collared shirt underneath. His hair is cut low on the sides and his very soft curls at the top are shiny and wet with gel. Secretly a bunch of folks have a crush on him. On the first day, he told us he was born in Queens and raised in Ecuador when his mother was deported. For high school, he came back to Queens to live with his Colombian father.

After everyone is settled down in their seats, Mr. Ruiz says, "Buen día, mi gente, creators, doctors, activists, entertainers, writers, researchers, artists, engineers, and intelligent folks. This young man, Ben Hill, is going to be our newest community member. Please make sure to show him the ropes if you see him around a little lost." Everyone chuckles. I am glad they do. Yesterday was awkward. When he first stepped into other classrooms and spaces around the school, people seemed to constrict into themselves. Like the space around us was no longer our own. "Don't worry, Mr. Hill, we got you. Feel free to introduce yourself." Mr. Ruiz puts up his fist, a sign used throughout the school that reminds us to bring back our power to center. The talkers in the classroom bring down their voice right away, something that never happens.

Ben stands up. "I don't know," he starts, "I'm Ben." The way he hunches makes him appear shorter than he did in the hallway. "I know very little about anything around here," he grins nervously, his voice shaking a tiny bit, "so I'll probably need your help as Mr. Ruiz inferred." With that he stands up straight, his chest elevating with him. His blazer opens up a bit to reveal the burgundy uniform shirt underneath. I fight not to roll my eyes— he sure wasn't appreciative of my help during the tour and now he might need it? Puh-lease. I look around the room; everyone still holds their silence. Everyone's looking forward, but not really looking at him. I shake my body a little bit in my seat, attempting to shake off whatever is happening to me—this sudden feeling this boy has over me. It's not really like me to not give people a chance. But I did yesterday, didn't I?

"What you be doing after school though?" Jay breaks the awkward silence from the back of the classroom. Mr. Ruiz signals for them to cut it out. A line of neon-orange eyeliner runs below their eyebrows today, and their jersey is flung over their right shoulder.

"I play a lot of video games . . . right now . . . Fortnite."

"What's your tag?" someone else calls out.

"Yo, add me MaskofDagoat183rd," another voice says.

"My tag is Jibara174th. I'll be on at 5 p.m.," Cindy says.

Ben smiles and blushes. I watch his eyes scan the room. Curiosity sits at his forehead. I shake out my shoulders a little. He could just be curious, just be acting brand new, right? No, no, he said what he said. And that poem we read by Maya Angelou, about believing people are who they are, the first time, is true. Still, I wonder what it's like to go someplace and be the only one. Sometimes I feel like that when Mami takes me to fancy dinners upstate for my birthday or something, but at least I feel safe with her around. I keep hearing Black and Brown people are the minority, especially now that we thinking about college. It's a scholarship for minority students, this or that. I guess I never been far enough away from home for too long to see it be a reality. There are almost always white people on the screens and in books but never too much directly in front of me.

"All right," Mr. Ruiz says, "let's go back to noise level zero, folks. Ben, you can sit at the empty desk behind Yolanda." The desks are in rows facing Mr. Ruiz's desk and the whiteboard because we just had an assessment yesterday. "Oh, hey Yolanda," Ben says. He walks towards me and throws me a quick smirk, waving at me like we're long-time friends or something.

I look out the window and see the cars zooming by. A black Lincoln Town Car, a BMW X5, a Toyota Camry. My dad worked at a dealership that also operated as a taller, so I know most car brands and types. When I make it one day, I would like a Tesla. I read that it's better for the environment, and they've just come out with a less expensive option for folks who can't pay like a gazillion dollars. We don't see much around here, but once when I was nine, Papi took me on a road trip in a camioneta that he was going to leave wherever we went. I don't even remember what state we went to, but it was much warmer than it was here. We were driving there so he could pick up a Tesla to bring back to New York and sell at a profit. Papi only took me on these trips, never my brothers or his wife. He let me sit up front sometimes. He drove for long hours, and I napped or read or ate whatever we picked up from a drive-through. When I woke up from naps, Papi always asked me about my dreams. I miss him on a daily. I think that's why I let down my guard with Mr. L last year—he cared about my dreams, too.

I can always tell when someone is looking at me. It's like the skin isn't really dead, it's just observing, like a wise tree. I feel him burning my leaves. There is heat on my back and my spine feels weak. I look back and there it is: his green eyes meet mine. He smiles, in a way that moves his mouth more to one side of his face than the other. It makes him feel friendly. Maybe I am over-reacting. I smile back. He's a new presence; the cards might be off—hell, it might be just me.

My cramps begin to kick in and I take deep breaths and work to shift my hips in my seat.

"We are going to practice academic discussions today. You are all excellent at talking. You talk about who is messing with who and who is coming for what," Mr. Ruiz says. Everyone laughs, knowing it's true. "But what we are having difficulty with is carrying a conversation about the things we are learning in class, the content. Based on the reading you had for homework, we are going to work to have a thirty-minute whole-class conversation. This is a new practice we'll have every Thursday. It'll give us an opportunity to read texts that often are not taught in high school from Americans who were often unseen, and it'll strengthen our ability to have discussions. That might sound like a break from test prep, but during the conversation we are adding on, we are elaborating, we are coming with facts to back up our claim." A slide with sentence starters flashes up on the screen with questions to get us thinking. But all I can think of is the burning of Ben's eyes still on my neck. I close my eyes, and there it is: a vision. Cloudy at first, as if I opened my eyes under a pool of milk, and then it slowly clears up—a movie just for me.

The ceilings are high, and the windows overlook Central Park; there is a plump, comfortable, thick white rug underneath my feet.

"I apologize, headmaster," Mr. Hill says into his phone. "Of course. I'll consider that." He nods a few times. "Thank you, and my apologies once again."

Ben's father sits on his desk and looks over at Ben as he folds his arms. Ben is wearing black slacks, a white button-up, a gray vest, and a red trucker hat. The words Butler Prep *in white under an oval gold logo. "You've done it again, son. Made a name for yourself." He pauses and stares.*

"Take that hat off in my house!" His dad snatches the red trucker hat from his head. Ben's hair falls over his eyes.

Ben laughs. "You prefer I wear it outside?" His father shakes his head, his gaze now fixated on the ground before him.

"What do you need, son? Speak to me. You weren't always like this." Ben's father looks up at him.

"You weren't always this busy trying to save everyone but your own. I need you to open your eyes, Dad! Our country is being taken

from us. The American thing to do in your position would be doing something about these people, but instead you are—"

"Your great-great-grandparents would be so disappointed in you, Ben!"

"Why don't you just say you're *disappointed?" Ben responds. Fury circling around his heart. I feel a cramp in my chest and turn to look at my own body, and there is a gray cloud circling and circling. I look up and the same cloud is wrapped around Ben. More than anything, Ben feels unheard, unseen, unliked by his own father.*

"I've failed myself, but most importantly, I've failed you and clearly this country."

"Oh fuck off, Dad. The country will be just fine no thanks to you," Ben yells. He wants to cry, but he pushes down the need.

"Go to your room," Mr. Hill whispers. "If this is the mountain you're going to die on, I am disappointed and done with you!" Ben gets up as he curses his father and picks up a crystal Christmas ball on his father's desk. He flings it towards the window, and it shatters on impact, the window still intact. His father doesn't look surprised.

"We have to take back our country, Dad! Wake the hell up. If you don't do something, we will!"

Mr. Hill grabs Ben by the arm and pushes him out of his office.

"You sound like trailer trash, Ben," he grunts. The minute he closes the door, he grabs his phone and sends a text.

I follow Ben to his room. He paces around in his bedroom. From one side of the room to another. He wishes he could call someone, anyone. But none of his friends will understand. They are like him, but different . . . Ben says and acts on their collective thoughts, but they don't. They blend in like sheep, Ben thinks. At this thought, he begins to feel lonely; a mass of deep, dark, dark red spheres, like old

blood, shines from his chest. He sits at his desk and opens up his
Macbook. It is opened to Chrome, and I watch as he types into search.
I want to see what he is searching for, but my vision goes milky again.

I'm being pulled back into the darkness of my eyelids as if the
vision hadn't sought me out in the first place.

The vision drops into my consciousness like goo, and I feel
drenched from head to toe in it. I turn to face the window and
blink furiously, only to meet a concrete wall. What was that
about? Why is he so in his feelings about "our country"? It's his
first week here. But why that vision? For the first time in my life,
I, Yolanda, nieta de Teté, do not know how to deal with or what
to do with the divine information sent to me. But it's my first
vision since I was a little girl—of course I don't know what the
hell to do. I'm going to have to lean on the Bruja Diosas and
Mamá Teté to figure it out, right?

"Yoyo, build off of Miriam's thoughts," Mr. Ruiz calls on
me out of nowhere. My mind is as blank as I imagine my eyes
to be as I am still coming down. But I read last night. "On Du
Bois's double consciousness," Mr. Ruiz adds, scratching his palm
a bit, embarrassed for me. I hadn't been present to listen to
Miriam's thoughts, but I know enough about duality, and I did
my homework.

"I think he was trying to say that oppressed people are always
split internally," I begin. "There are many ways to be oppressed,
so there are many splits among most of us in this room happening
all at the same time. This is something those with more privilege
don't have to experience, I think," I add. Mr. Ruiz nods. "Or
maybe they do? No, because this country supports their consciousness, their thinking, their way of life."

I hear Ben clear his throat. The sound he makes is enough to make me shiver. I look back at him, but there is the smirk again. Dique friendly. The clearing of his throat landed like it was sarcastic though, and based on what I just seen, I can assume it was.

"Going off of Yolanda's definition and what Du Bois said, I do think it's necessary to have a double consciousness. Like we have to have different sides and switch between them according to where you are and who you around. We don't switch up because of all these respectability things, we do it to keep what is ours, ours," Adzo, a sophomore, says. I nod and so many more of my classmates do too.

"You right, Adzo," Lilian, another sophomore, says. "My mom took me to a resort in DR in the summer. Me and my cousins was dancing, making TikToks to new dembow, and why this group of people who were clearly not Dominican tried to tell us we weren't doing our own dance right? It's because we let them in too much. You see how Rosalia is doing a bunch of music that don't even belong to the Spanish? But she's the one making money off of it."

"You don't invite everyone to the cookout," Jay adds in a low voice.

"Some will say code-switching between different consciousnesses isn't always fun or easy," Mr. Ruiz adds.

Mariela raises her hand, after flinging her straightened black hair, and says, "I'd like to disagree with Yoyo's definition and with Du Bois period. I mean, I feel like if you, as an oppressed person, just decided to—I don't know, follow the rules, do what you're supposed to do, like work hard, focus on yourself and God, then maybe the splits won't have to happen. And it isn't so bad to share our things and what we know, Lilian. We're all humans."

"Girl bye," Cindy, who is sitting right behind her, says. She pops the Puertorican flag pendant that hangs from her necklace into her mouth, and sits back and slouches on her chair, opening her legs wider.

"Right!" Lilian scoffs.

"You know Du Bois probably was straight, had a wife, and went to church and all that, right?" Dayvonte, a junior, says, flicking his pencil in the air. He leans into his desk, his strong shoulders more apparent.

"Yeah," replies Mariela, "but what I mean is now people just want to be—"

"Du Bois was known to be an absent father and husband," Ben says. The entire room shifts towards him.

"And what does what Mariela just said and what you just claimed have to do with double consciousness?" Dayvonte asks, squinting his eyes like he can't understand Ben at all—but the tone of his voice tell us he don't want no answer.

"I am just saying many leaders don't practice what they preach," Ben adds. A friendly smile on his face again, like what he said is just a thought, and not an insult.

"I know that's right," Julissa, a sophomore, says, snapping her hot-pink manicured fingers. I shake my head a little because she just the type of person who just be agreeing to agree. I swear she don't have not one confrontational bone in her body, but be trying to add flames to heat for no good reason.

"Nu-uh," someone says from the back. And I'm glad for it.

"What we not finna do is change the subject," Jay starts. They uncross their legs and fold their hand neatly over the desk. Jay is not the one. "Ain't we talking about double consciousness or not, Mr. Ruiz?"

Mr. Ruiz looks at us blankly. He always pushes us to these conversations but hardly ever has the backbone to move us through difficulty. "I'm going to stop us right here. This is what I mean by academic conversations. It's OK to disagree, but we must listen to one another *with respect*," he states, looking at Ben and Jay, "while also not trying to erase or deny other people's experiences, mi gente." I hate that he decides to do it before answering Jay. Their question was valid, but Mr. Ruiz goes on to the next slide and poses the next question like it's nothing. I look at Ben from the corner of my eye and shudder. It's so ironic that we are talking about Du Bois on his first day in this class.

Bruja Diosas, all that guide, love and protect me, I ask that you come through. Why did I have this vision with Ben? Am I giving him too much of my brain space, is my mind just doing too much? I feel a tap on my shoulder.

"Hey, you've got a pencil?" Ben whispers. I hand him mine. Wait, what the fuck I just give him a pencil for? Now, I don't have anything to write with. Shouldn't he have writing utensils? I take a deep breath. I'm doing too much. I usually don't. I get up and walk to the back of the class where Mr. Ruiz has a few extra materials folks leave behind. I pick up a nasty, chewed-on half pencil. *Bruja Diosas, what's wrong with me?* I walk back to my desk thinking about the vision and feeling his heartbeat like a loud base at the middle of my palm.

It's not that they would discredit me if I talked about having a vision. I mean, yes, I guess they could do that, or call me crazy, or strip me of my bruja ways. I wish I could just hold onto what I know deep down inside: that no one can do that. Back on the island my parents come from, everyone's a little brujita. Everyone has the potential to unearth their powers and trap a lover, create a child, heal the sick, end their enemies, and even transform their life. Not everyone taps into that knowing, but it is always there at their disposal. People understand that while some are sprinkled with a little magic, others are born with the don, with the gift, with the full force. It is what it is. My people believe deeply even if they wear their Catholic cloak on a daily basis for safety. But when shit hits the fan—and shit always hits the fan—they turn to the soil, to the skies, and the leaders of the other side.

But this isn't the island. This is not a place with an open vein of magic. This is a place where an entire race has oppressed and sat above the rest. On this land, the blood-spills always bubble back up to the surface, and instead of cleaning it, the oppressors constantly cover it up with cement. Entonces dime, who here would believe my vision?

5

BRUJA WAYS

The click-clack of Mami's long nails on her computer keyboard tells me she is home when I open the door. Mami's house is uncluttered compared to Mamá Teté's—the air smells and feels different because of it—but it has never quite felt like home. The same way Papi's house that he purchased with his new wife, before he went in, never quite felt like mine. I close the door behind me.

"Yolanda, is that you my love?" Mami says from the living room.

"Sí, Mami!" I say. My voice is different with Mami. Singsongy. Mami has been through some real stuff in her childhood. For starters, Mami's real mother had nine children, and she ended up giving her and another one of her siblings to two families who had more opportunities back when she was six in DR. Not that she shares those stories with me, but Mamá Teté says sometimes Mami's wounds show up in me. That's how blood works. On top of it, Mami doesn't have an hija, not the way other parents do, and I know that triggers a lot of abandonment and inferiority complexes in her. I try my best to be as much of her daughter as I can when I am around.

After my parents officially separated, they ended the lease in the apartment I was born in. The separation brought up the shadows in Mami and Papi. They were mostly at odds and badmouthing each other when they did happen to be around me. I was already attached to Mamá Teté, and I was getting up at the crack of dawn whenever my parents had to drop me off at her house before they went to work. Eventually Mamá Teté and I came together to tell them I wanted to live with her. Mami tried to fight it, but eventually gave up. Her only condition being that I spend a few days at her house, too.

I drop my bookbag on the couch and hunch over to kiss Mami on the cheek. "It's nice to see you here unexpectedly. I've missed you," she says. I didn't go to Mamá Teté's after school because the vision has got me shook. I went to the only bookstore in the Bronx—The Lit. Bar. It's owned by a Black Boricua woman who grew up in the Bronx. Usually, I go with Victory, but I needed some space. I ordered a hot chocolate at the bar and read through the first few chapters of Junauda Petrus's *The Stars and the Blackness Between Them* for a bit. As I walked out of the bookstore, I realized I didn't want to go home to Mamá Teté, so I came here.

Also, I really missed Mami. Despite it all, she loves me and tries her best to show it when I'm around. I've never missed a reading—I've been too excited to read to do that. For years, I've been waiting to help Mamá with them. But it was only earlier this summer she allowed me to step in and help. It's part of my training. I know I'll hear it later from Mamá, but I would be no good today. One thing I've learned is I cannot do readings when I'm caught up, because it will cloud what comes up for the person. And the Bruja Diosas haven't answered me at all.

"This paper me tiene loca," Mami sighs. "I have to deliver it dique tomorrow, and it's been on the syllabus since the beginning of the semester." Mami is working to get her Bachelor's at the community college before I graduate high school in two years. She says she is doing it for me, and I believe her and all, but I also think she's tired of serving as an accountant at the kosher supermarket in Riverdale. She's been there since I was three, and she hates the way two of the owners talk at her, although she can mess with some numbers. She's almost thought of quitting before, but the owner she feels the most loyalty towards raised her pay and checked his siblings. She's studying accounting now. I can see the stress that leaves dark circles under her eyes, and on the dry spots on the top of her hands. Her curly hair is tamed with gel up into a tight, high bun, exposing the same arched cheekbones I have. She takes deep breaths and looks at the paper next to her. I see the prompt: *Write an informational essay on the benefits of consumerism.* I want to tell her it's simple, if she knows anything about consumerism and the big, old, wack capitalist world we live in. I mean, they basically forced us into consuming everything because it's of "benefit." I want to offer my help, but the last time I offered didn't go so well.

"You got this, Ma," I say.

"Go into my bag," she says, not looking up from the screen. Her faux black leather tote hangs from the shoulder strap on one of the chairs beside her. "In the little pocket with the zipper." I unzip the pocket and reach in, feeling a tiny velvet square bag. She looks at me now with urgency. "Well open it!"

I unbutton the bag and turn it over on my palm. A white and

yellow gold chain falls into it. I lift the chain and examine its thick bottom. It's my name, with a tooth in the middle of the o.

"You remember how that came out?" Mami smiles.

"Of course I do, Mami!" I say. "Papi tied floss on a doorknob then slammed the door. Trust me, I remember!" Mami and I laugh. She mimics a young version of me, crying. She ends up laughing so much tears come out her eyes. I go over to her and hug her.

"Bueno, here. I found that tooth," Mami says. "You're getting older and wiser, but this little tooth reminded you were once just my little girl"—Mami squeezes my cheeks—"the other day."

Her phone rings, and the name blinks: Anthony. Her new boyfriend. She's been dating him for at least a year now. He's nice enough, I guess. Every year or two since my parents separated, it's a different guy. I get it now, but I hated it before. It was Mamá Teté who helped me understand.

"Your mother had you young," she said. "Just 'cause it didn't work out with your papi, she shouldn't have to be a nun." I got that, but what bothered me was that Mami would change our schedules and plans around for men. When I added this point, Mamá Teté said, "Mi vida, what's bothering you is that she's making herself small for these men then. That's a whole different problema." But Mamá Teté never told me how to help Mami fix the issue.

Mami picks up and goes to her room. When I see her hustling, she's grand even at a supermarket, but when I see her doing this—walking away from what she has to do—I can't help but think I want to be nothing like her. I want her to have love, but she's always pursuing her search for it like romance is the most important thing in the world. What about friendship?

She hardly has friends. What about our relationship? It's like since I decided to live with Mamá, she just let it be. Didn't even fight me much on it. It all annoys me. I scroll through my phone. I don't have any social media because from what I've seen, it's a huge distraction, so I go straight to my messages. There's a message from José.

Hey, I just got out of practice. Wanna grab a slice? I blush thinking of seeing him alone again. I'm flattered he keeps pursuing me. And then catch myself ready to ignore what I have to do to see a boy I really like. Mami comes back to her chair and begins typing furiously. I look at her and I know her time crunch has been expedited.

"He invited you out?" I ask, putting my phone down. She nods, half-excited and half-embarrassed. They're going for dinner, so now she has to rush through this paper to see him.

"I can't wait to have my degree," Mami says, looking up at me from her laptop and changing the subject quickly. "I don't want to keep counting pennies. This is why you have to keep doing the good work you're doing in school. You don't want to be like me at my age." She extends her hand and holds my cheek before turning to type again.

Mami has crucifixes all around the house. Even though she doesn't go to church every week, or pray every night and day, she keeps them up believing it brings us the protection of God. I can't talk to her about the things I see and my gifts too much. She jokes around and calls it brujería, like it's a bad thing, and I just end up irritated. She says I'm too much like my Mamá Teté.

"Mami," I start, "before you go, can you make me that tea you used to make me?" I ask.

"What tea?" she responds, keeping her eyes on her computer.

"The one you used to cut apples for," I try to remember. She smiles.

"Claro que sí, Morena." There's a hint of gratitude in her eyes, but also she looks pressed, and I know it's because she doesn't want to make Anthony wait downstairs when he arrives. I don't ever really ask her for much.

After I shower, I remember that the Bruja Diosas ain't really being direct with me. I sit in my bedroom upset, looking at myself in the mirror. My jaw is flexed. I've been holding so much tension, it hurts. I'm wearing a white T-shirt that reflects a rainbow onto the glass window with the help of the lowering sun. I touch the darkness of my cheek, reminding myself to be gentle with the insight that was given to me. Mamá Teté says the Bruja Diosas don't like to be pressured, like us, that they like doing things at their own time. And still I go back into my memory, trying to figure out what the hell I have done to make them change up the chord of communication right now. I need them to speak to me, so I can tell them I have no idea, no clue what to do—or better yet, I have no idea what to do with the information they've provided in the vision.

As I light the white candle I bought at the bodega after school, I pour a prayer to the Unknown Luzangel. *Bring me clarity. Let me see what my duty is regarding what I saw this afternoon. All that came before me, guide me. Bruja Diosas, protect me with your love, shower me with the wisdom of the Universes inside and outside me. Please see me through.* There's a knock on the door then. Mami.

"Mi'ja, aquí tengo tu té," Mami squeezes the cup and her hand between the doorframe. Normally, she doesn't come into my room to stay for too long, but today I just want to be heard.

"Come in," I say. Mami kicks off her nude pumps at the door

and walks in. She kneels in front of me, bringing up her hands to offer me the té de manzanilla. I smell the star anise and the cut-up apples she soaks in cinnamon. I lean in and try to drape my hands over the cup and my mother's hands. Looking at her, I flush.

"What's wrong, Yoyo?" she asks.

"I had a vision today, and they won't clarify it for me . . ." I can't produce the words to say more. I fight back this immediate anger I feel towards the Bruja Diosas for being silent. I am usually not the type of girl who cries—Mami and Papi found strange ways to shame me out of it when they were at their worst—so I am more comfortable leaning on anger. But fear arrived with this vision, and it won't leave me. It sits between my stomach and my throat like stone. *Why?*

Mami bites the inside of her cheek.

"Mi niña, la vida es un proceso. And I am sure this, too, is a process because everything is. Maybe something has changed. Try another way." She leans towards my forehead and plants a kiss. Mami loves Chanel Nº 5. The strong hints of jasmine, coriander, peach, and orange invade my nostrils, and I inhale deeply. It surprises and soothes me to know she is leaning towards acceptance.

Despite how much Mami doesn't like the bruja ways of Mamá Teté, she respects them. Las Dimensiones is an old religion. It's how a lot of enslaved people on both sides of the island of Ayiti remained connected to their original African Gods, when the enslavers forced them to accept Christianity. It's gotten a bad rep because the oppressors labeled anything they didn't understand as "black magic" and evil, but Mami knows better than to diminish it to that. Each Unknown within Las Dimensiones holds narratives, characteristics, and protection spells to guide its people.

"You know when I was pregnant with you, I had a feeling about your father, but I didn't want to accept it," Mami says. "So I prayed and prayed for a child that was wiser than me. When your grandmother announced that you, the child of her eyes, had the don, I gave thanks and accepted, even if it isn't something I necessarily believe in for myself."

Mami truly figured out her prayers had been answered when I was five. It was a perfect lazy Sunday morning. I remember stretching my little arms, feeling Papi's beard on one side, and Mami's soft cheek on the other.

"Buen día, morenita," Mami kissed my cheek. I closed my eyes and the vision came into my head like a late dream. In the middle of the navy-blue sky, I saw a baby boy growing inside a pool. I jumped inside the pool to get him. He felt like something that belonged to me. When I came back up from the water, Papi had him in his arms, and I started drowning. I fought to stay up, to float, but the infant had a voice, and he said, "Papi." I yelled for my dad to reach for me. The more I yelled, the more distant they became. Then, there was a woman who hugged Papi and the boy. And she wasn't like Mami or me, not even her voice. When I opened my eyes, Papi was shaking me.

"I'm right here, morenita," he said. I have always been bruja.

"A little boy?" I cried. Papi didn't even bother to lie. He cried with me.

"I love you, baby girl. I love you," he kept saying. Mami looked at him fiercely, like a lioness without territory to truly fight for.

"Explain it to me," she demanded. And he did. My brother was set to be born within a few weeks.

She looks at me now as if it is true that I am wiser than her.

I have always been a bruja. This was never a secret to Mami, and even though she manifested it for me too, she struggled with it. Hated that sometimes this don had caused me to grow up faster than she wished.

"I don't like brujería and stuff, not in this house, as you know," she says. I roll my eyes, get ready for the speech telling me I have to be careful with who I invoke. "But," she continues, "I love you, and I am trying my best," she says. Her phone rings from the kitchen. "That must be Anthony downstairs," she says. "I have to go, my love, pero call me if you need me." She kisses my forehead as she zooms out the door.

"Love you too," I whisper. I wish she tried better to understand that I cannot be my whole self while splitting myself in pieces for her to accept, but I also know it isn't totally her fault.

After Mami leaves, I say the same recitations and prayers that usually always deliver. But nothing comes. I shuffle the tarot cards—shuffle and shuffle. And shuffle some more, and yet the canvas where the universe paints what I need to see remains blank. I wonder if it is time to ask my grandmother for help. But I'm afraid Mamá Teté will force me to tell the principal—to call the police and tell them what I saw, without telling them how I saw it. And how am I supposed to do that? Plus, something inside of me, something I can't name, tells me I can't tell her yet.

I scroll through my phone. *Bring me a slice to my mom's building,* I text José back.

He's at my door in less than half an hour with a whole pie and my favorite passion fruit juice from the corner restaurant.

"Thank you," I say, opening the door for him. My phone buzzes in my back pocket, and I am relieved I don't have to look at him as he enters.

Yolanda Nuelis, where are you? ¿Todo bien? It's Mamá Teté.
My heart rate accelerates, and I swallow. I forgot to tell her I
wasn't coming over, or maybe I forgot intentionally, so I did not
have to go and tell her about this damn vision that got me all
twisted up? I guess it's a little bit of both.

"Wow, this apartment is really clean or kind of uncluttered?
Your mom a Dominican Marie Kondo, huh?" José laughs.

We sit on the couch, and I turn on *Chilling Adventures of
Sabrina.* I've watched this show with Victory, and she hates to
love it.

"It's difficult to say what it is I feel about this show," I told her.
"On one hand, I love that there are new shows about witches,
you know? Pero like, I'm pissed white girls are always the main
characters in shows about magic, and even 'black' magic seems
to be OK for the world just as long as a pale girl is the one doing
it. It's as if the world can't handle the unseen if Black girls is
moving it."

Victory agreed. "Have you watched *Siempre Bruja*?" she
asked. I shook my head. "Girl, the main character is dark like me
and that's a win, you know? But the moment it was revealed that
she risked her life for her master's son, I couldn't watch the shit
anymore! Mom and I were trying to watch it for Spanish practice, but the minute she started following white folks into the
future, we turned it off. It's so sad."

"Do you believe in brujas?" José asks now. I look at him suddenly. Does he know? Can he sense it now that I've let him into
one of my houses? This is why. This is why I shouldn't do anything out of impulse. I take a deep breath. Whenever people
speak of magic or brujas anywhere in the world, it seems it is
assumed to be dark and bad-intentioned, so that is one of the

reasons Mamá Teté has taught me to protect our don, like our ancestors had to.

José has a strong jawline that accentuates when he chews down on the hot pizza. There's a gloss of oil from the pizza on his lips, and it makes him look softer.

"I do," I say.

"Sameeeeeee," he says. He swallows gently. "I didn't really believe in all that crazy shit before, but yo, YOOOO!!!" I know he's just saying "yo," but I imagine he is calling me. He puts down the slice on the paper plate in front of him. "Something crazy, crazy went down, and I changed my mind." I've never seen him this excited about saying anything. I laugh and tell him to go on.

"You know my moms sends me and my sister back to El Patio every year," he turns to me. "We have never really gone to my dad's side of the family because his family is still like dirt, dirt, dirt poor. Like I'm talking about my aunt and uncle's house had plastic curtains as a roof in some part of their"—he takes a deep breath and shakes his head—"home, I guess, but it was basically a shack. But whatever, my sister was like, 'Oh yeah, they're poor and that's more of a reason we should go.' So we go to Dajabón. It's so far that it takes my dad like four hours to drive there, it's basically on the border next to Haiti. Halfway there he says we will probably spend the night and leave in the morning 'cause it's dangerous and whatnot. I'm tight 'cause I wanna go back to Santiago, but what imma do? I hear about the crazy shit that happens to drivers at night." He takes a breath and I nod because it's true. There are stories about police stopping folks at red lights just to get money out of people traveling. That's what happens when a government doesn't pay people enough to live and the country has been exploited though.

"We get there and they kill a gallina. My cousin, Carlotta, is like twenty and she is cooking on this stove she made out of stones and sticks and shit. She's pregnant with twins, so my sister is helping her. Her little siblings don't even have fucking shoes. It's nuts, and I tell my dad that Mami has to start sending at least half of the cajas she sends her family in Santiago to his family because dime? It only makes sense." He taps the side of his head like his mother and father don't really think, and it warms my heart for a minute.

"Can you get to the point of the story, José? It's DR, an exploited country. A lot of folks are poor. Don't you know this?"

"NO! In Santiago my family is struggling for sure, but not dirt poor like that. When I'm there I see people, I guess on the road, who are poor, but it's different when it's personal. That's fucked up, I know," he says.

"Anyway, we have a good time. My dad pays for a bunch of their debt at the colmado, and the sun starts coming down. We stay outside drinking Presidentes and stuff. My sister is doing Carlotta's feet, and the kids are playing with my DS. Carlotta's chair is leaning against the house because my sister wanted to make sure she didn't tip over. She's like nine months pregnant, and she's huge. Out of nowhere my sister looks up and she screams. She says she saw a big ass bird on top of the house with long hair that made it look like a woman. But everyone is drunk and they laugh at her. They say she's just seeing things. That she never been to the countryside before and she probably got confused between the shadow of the trees and the shape of a woman." He reaches out for the Sprite and takes a gulp.

I know where this story is going. In Bonao, where Mamá Teté is from, it is said that back in the day pregnant women were guarded day and night around their last trimester. Family members would take turns staying up while the women slept. Today, people rush to baptize newborns, hoping that will spiritually protect them.

"So my sister says she's not going to bed. She's going to break night. I stay up with her as long as I can but by las dos en la madrugada, I am tired, and I fall asleep on the mecedora beside her. I feel her hand tapping on me. 'José, wake up!' she whispers. When my eyes are open, she says, 'You hear that?!' The house has a tin roof in the bedrooms and you can hear it creaking like something is walking on top of it. It could be a chicken or a little lizard, you know? But I look at the ceiling and nod. We tiptoe to Carlotta's room, she's sleeping with her two younger siblings. She's sleeping belly up, and from the roof there's like a thin yarn of spider web. When we turn on the flashlight on my phone we see there's blood in it that's coming from the belly. I run outside and on top of the house there it is: a big bird with the other end of the web going into her belly button. Everyone wakes up and my uncle and Carlotta's neighbor climb on top of the house and try to fight this bird, because it literally doesn't even try to run or fly away—that's how much it wanted the baby's blood. Apparently some witches turn into these big ass pájaros to cover up their identity. Anyway, Carlotta is so nervous, her water breaks, and we have to drive to the nearest hospital like two hours away. One of the babies was born dead. The other one is fine but she almost died too. They named her after my sister, Penelope."

"Wow," I say, pretending to be amazed. There are so many of these stories and occurrences in DR. I grew up on Mamá Teté telling me about them until I saw something like it myself on one of the summers we visited. "That's wild."

"WILD. Witches are real. It's not just a show."

"You think they're all bad, like the witch you saw on the roof?"

"I don't know. They had to get another mujer con 'dones' from another campo to come clean up the place. So who knows? Maybe they're all born with a different purpose? Yo no sé. It's just una locura. Crazy, crazy." His hands are shaking.

I know Mamá Teté has taught me to be protective of what we have. But José believes. He wouldn't shut me out. I know it. I have to try and see how he feels about it, about people like me.

"Mamá Teté has dones," I say. As soon as it's out, I feel exposed. But there's also a part of me that wants to tell him I also have dones—specifically the one of sight.

"That doesn't surprise me at all. It's part of who we are. Again, I just think it's messed up when people use it to harm others or get things by force," he responds. I nod. The silence stretches out, but it's comfortable.

I look at his pumped arms and his vascular forearm. They are full of goosebumps. I run my hand through his forearm, and as I look up at him, I realize I like him way more than I thought, because my stomach feels empty and my body feels full. I look at him and smile, and he puts his hands in my hair. I put down my own slice, and he laughs as he leans into me and kisses me. His mouth tastes like cheese and spearmint, but his tongue is so warm and heat runs up and down my body, alleviating the cramps I've been feeling all day. He pulls away from me, and I open my eyes only when I feel him staring at my lids.

"Why do I like you so much?" he says, and kisses my nose. I shrug. The reality is, I've wondered that too. At our school, everyone wants José. He's legit the star of the basketball team, maybe even the high school basketball star of the Bronx, and was raised mainly by his mother and sister, so he is respectful, he's smart, he isn't the type of boy who tries to hide his emotions. When he's upset, he shows it, and when he has a lot of joy, he is eager to share that, too. He's dated quite a few girls at school, and it's one of the reasons why I never paid any real attention to this feeling until weeks ago, when we saw each other at the supermarket. We were both with our mothers, and while we just waved at one another, our mothers embraced each other, telling us they knew each other from the neighborhood. The Bruja Diosas started pushing me towards him.

I climb over him on the couch and kiss him again. He runs his hands up and down my back like maybe he'll find a zipper to open me up. I wait for him to clutch my boobs like others have before, at the first opportunity, but he doesn't. "Why do I like you so much?" he repeats into my mouth every time he pulls back for a breath, but I have no answers except, "I like you, too."

His phone begins to ring in his pocket, and I get off of him so he can reach into it. "MAMI" is calling, it says. He looks at me with an apology.

"It's all right," I say, suddenly embarrassed that I am actually a bit upset. He kisses me again, his scent piercing my pores, and then I walk him to the door.

6

JUSTICE CALLS

You *what?!*" Victory squirms on her bus seat. Laughing, I playfully cover her mouth.

When her parents are running late, Victory takes the bus with me. I'm grateful today was one of those days.

I haven't had a romantic interest ever or anything close to one. Yes, I've made out with people here and there, but only because I develop crushes when I go back to the island with Mamá Teté, and it's always a relief when I know it'll only last for a couple weeks. Also, the person I liked the most was Zainabah, I've known her for as long as I've known Victory. We had our first kisses together when we were in fifth grade. We took to exchanging letters during recess, and then responding to one another throughout the day, exchanging again on the school bus. Everything inside of my chest fluttered when I saw her pastel-colored hijabs in the mornings, midday, and in the afternoons.

We had so much fun exploring what we felt towards one another. One night, I had a dream of us: we were older, holding hands in public; I could smell flowers on her and everything. On the first day of sixth grade, on the way home on the yellow bus, I told her about it, and she freaked out, out of nowhere. She called me a liar, claimed that what we were doing was not OK, declared that my dreams were evil and dirty. We haven't spoken since. I told Mamá Teté about it and everything, because it did break my heart, the way she pretended I was gross for having liked her the way I did. As life would have it, we ended up at the same high school. This year she's in my AP Literature class, and while we acknowledge each other, we just don't vibe at all anymore, and Victory pretty much hates her for having hurt me. Since Zainabah, I just don't have expectations for anything romance-related. Maybe I'm scared of hurting like that again, or I just don't have the energy to heal from that right now, or maybe it's that the only relationships I've known always end badly? Maybe I'm a little bit like my father, or my mother actually, who knows?

"Yeah," I smile, "yeah." I remember his hands in my hair, his fingers ignoring the knots—the parts other people would find difficult—and caressing my ears with care.

"Did you feel," she looks around and winds her body in her seat, "you know?"

"I guess I did, girl," I say, shaking my head, knowing she's talking about the heat that sits between my legs more often than ever. "But I'm not ready for all of that."

She sucks her teeth at my response.

"I'll live my best life through you for now."

Victory had sex for the first time last year with a boy from Brooklyn. He had swag, licked his lips, and wore folded beanies with fire ass kicks. He was good at styling himself, I'll give him that. But he tried too hard. He knew Victory was way out of his league, to be honest. She basically wanted to see what it would feel like, and she hated the hype and the anxiety that hung around sex for her. She told her mother, who simply told her it was natural for her to be having thoughts around it, and signed us up for a course on safe sex. The boy's older brother died from cancer shortly after they went all the way, and Victory stopped talking to him altogether. His brother's death changed him, and she said she had to be honest about the fact that she didn't have the capacity to help him grieve. But I know Victory—if she's into you, or she loves you, she'll put in the work. I think she didn't want it to become serious with him at all. And that's OK, better than choosing to string him along, I guess. Since then, she's focused on herself in classes and graphic designing club.

"There's something else," I tell her, not sure if I should or shouldn't, but the Bruja Diosas wouldn't speak to me this morning, not even after my morning rituals. Maybe this will help. It can't hurt, right? No, it won't. This is my best friend.

"Tell me," she says, looking up.

"All right, listen," I begin. I look around and realize we're almost at our stop. "I want you to chill. I have it under control, and I will take care of it." She gathers her stuff and turns to face me. "I saw something, I mean . . . I had a vision yesterday . . . in class." I struggle to find the words.

"OK?" Victory nods. "So you started having visions. That's a BIG ASS deal!" The last bit she screams in excitement. I'm surprised until I realize I haven't even celebrated the fact that the visions have started, which means maybe my initiation is moving along.

"Yeah! I did, which—you're right—is exciting. Pero it didn't feel that way until now. I feel anxious because the visions were with Ben. About Ben," I say. V sucks in the air around her. "He was upset and extremely lonely," I go on, feeling the dark spheres again. "Basically, it was a fight he was having with his dad." I laugh nervously.

The bus comes to a stop and we get off behind a group of students from our school. We slow down, letting them walk ahead of us. "Girl, say what you gotta say," Victory replies.

"He got kicked out of two other schools before coming here. His dad is mad embarrassed and disappointed, but basically Ben doesn't agree with his political viewpoints."

"Isn't his dad pretty progressive?" Victory asks as we walk towards 138th Street.

"Yeah, supposedly," I say. I look at Victory.

"Don't tell me that boy's a white supremacist!" Victory says, as she connects the dots.

"He said some wild shit in the vision, so it feels that way. I mean, he's really not fucking with his dad, even though he actually just really wants his attention." I don't tell her about the fear it has left in me, to keep down our anxiety levels.

"Oh hell naw! What did I tell you?" Victory moans. "I knew that white boy was trouble! He is *hella obvious*! How many times imma tell you: like who the hell transfers at the end of senior year?" I begin to respond, but she cuts me off, and we start walking again. "Maybe you should tell someone, Yoyo." Her eyes widen as they always do when she's expressing her fear. One thing about Victory is that her intuition is strong AF, even if she doesn't dabble in what I'm able to see. "He sounds like a safety transfer or something. Think about it. When do seniors get transferred months deep into the school year? When it's a safety transfer," she adds.

I thought telling Victory would be easier than telling Mamá

Teté, but my body feels contained by her response, by what she is telling me to do right now. "He said he and his dad had different reasons for his transfer," I say.

"Well of course his daddy ain't gonna tell none of us the truth. He's trying to win trust. You've got to tell."

"What exactly am I going to say, Victory? Not only would adults feel as if he has a right to his opinion, but who would believe what I saw, other than my own folks?" I take a deep breath. I try not to think about Zainabah and what she claimed: that I lied about my dreams. In the past, I have told people I trust about the things I see. Sometimes it works out well—they make some money, study a little harder, or go to the doctor and get ahead of a health problem. But sometimes my dreams, and now my visions it seems, make reality really sour. A whole ass mess. Victory knows this.

"So why should I tell them this?" I ask.

"Because when you feel anxious and shit—which you do—about what you see, it always comes true. You know this. I don't have to tell you this, Yo," Victory responds matter-of-factly. I run my hands over the side of my head, feeling the processor. Sometimes I be thinking this deafness is a gift from my ancestors, from the Bruja Diosas. I don't have clarity of hearing, and that allows me to cut down on the things I don't want to be part of, so I can focus on my power and what I am being shown.

Victory learned not to doubt the things that show themselves to me long ago. The first time I proved my point was in sixth grade. She was having stomach pains and had been out of school for multiple days. The doctors said everything was well. We had a sleepover one Friday, and I dreamed of a woman telling Victory's mother she was moving. The next morning, I asked her if anyone she knew was sick, and she nodded saying her father's mother was. I told her to prepare herself, but she lashed out on me telling me I had no idea what I was talking about. Her grandmother died the next week, and her stomach pains became heartache.

"Admit it," Victory says, then stops walking as we cross over to Morris Avenue. She folds her arms across her chest and stands in the middle of the street. "Admit it!"

"Admit what?!" I try to encourage her to cross the damn street by waving my hand.

"You're protecting him." She looks me in the eye and then starts walking again. We walk in silence towards the school. I want to say something, but I'm not trying to fight and I want to actually process what she said.

As we arrive at Julia De Burgos, we see Ben exiting the back of a Lincoln. Of course he takes cabs to school. How else will he make it from the Upper West Side to here? I bet he probably wakes up mad late too, and still manages to get here on time. The window to the backseat rolls down, and a lady with brown hair pokes her head out. "Ben, please remember what got us here!" The lady's lips become tight as she quickly glances around us. Ben doesn't look back at all.

"You heard that?" I whisper to Victory. Despite the prior uncomfortable moment, she's my best friend, and the only one that knows what I could be thinking. We shuffle a little faster into the school building.

"I did, girl, I did." She shakes her head.

Bruja Diosas, build an armor to protect me from my own negative energy right now. I hate that I am being negative, but I feel so blocked. I face my wallet down on the ID machine and walk into the school after it beeps.

"Hey," Ben calls out to me. I wait until he's let in. "I'm sorry about the other day."

I'm clueless.

"I called you a 'social justice warrior'?" Ben reminds me with a smile. A kind smile. He runs his fingers through his hair.

"Oh, that's right. You did have an attitude," I say.

"It was my second day," Ben shakes his head lightly. "Everything is just so new here, you know?"

Doesn't give you the right to be a dick, I want to answer, but I nod anyway. A slight ball of tension begins to collect itself on the left side of my head. I bring my pointer and middle finger to my temple and rub in circular motion. I am letting whatever energy Ben carries affect me, and I don't like it one bit.

"I have some Advil if you need," he offers.

"No, no. I'm good," I answer.

"You run the Brave Space Club, right?" My entire body stiffens. He knows damn well I do. A ball of energy feels as if it is coming out of my chest, creating a shield around the club.

"Ms. Steinberg says you're the person to talk to about getting involved in school." I open my mouth to respond, but he continues talking. "She told me about some of the clubs around here, but the Brave Space Club seems to be most interesting. My parents are actually helping fund a few more clubs, and attending your club would help me get involved, but also to be honest with my parents about the needs of the school."

"Mmmmm," Victory looks at me.

"I know you apologized," I say. "But you called me and Mrs. Obi social justice warriors though, point blank, period, so it's funny how now the Brave Space sounds interesting to you." I squint my eyes in faux curiosity and then shake my head and tighten my lips to try and communicate what I'm really feeling: it's most likely crap.

"Right," Victory says. I know she's been listening, but is pretending to mind her business to let me handle my stuff.

"I'm sorry," he drops his head. "Again, I shouldn't have said it the way I did. It was just different to see that poster. We didn't have big statements like that at my old school. I'll have to adjust."

See? He's just trying to be helpful, friendly, I tell myself. The tension in my head intensifies.

"OK, cool," I manage to say. Victory continues walking.

"When does the club meet?" he asks, keeping up with our quick strides. I want to direct him to the basketball team or something. He's tall enough for it. Plus, the Brave Space is a *brave place*. We never called it a safe space because we knew we would be uncomfortable—talking about the events and feelings we bring up invites anything but safety sometimes. Would bringing somebody in mess up the vibe? *Fuck.* I mean, of course having him there is going to disrupt it some way, somehow.

"Today," I say. I raise an eyebrow at Victory. Someone would end up telling him anyway. Immediately I hate myself for telling the truth. "It's usually Thursdays after school."

"Can I sit in?" He reaches into the side of his head and scratches his brown hair. "I'm just trying to feel things out." He rubs his chin. Sometimes people simply need community, love, to feel welcomed. Maybe this vision shit is just all in my head. What would it hurt for me to be on a good terms with him instead of letting all these emotions bubble up and take over? But I know what I felt and I know what I saw. This is all hard.

"Yeah, of course. Just as long you ain't scared, you know,"

I chuckle, awkward as fuck. Why am I being mad corny to help this kid feel comfortable?

"Of what?" he raises an eyebrow.

"To become one of us—a social justice warrior or whatever," I laugh sarcastically. He opens his mouth, but now I do the talking. "I mean, I accepted your apology, but I ain't forget what you said."

"Mr. L, I need your keys to open up Mrs. Obi's room," I say. Mr. L is helping a first-year student open up their locker.

"Ya'll in Ruiz's class," he says, his eyes still on the dial on the lock. "And stop acting like imma just give you my keys, fool." The first-year student chuckles.

"That's why you don't even got a room though," I snap back, turning around and fast-walking towards Ruiz's room. Immediately I know I've gone too far. "My bad, my bad," I yell down the hall.

"You good, Alvarez," he yells back. "You see, this whole school is mine."

Mrs. Obi is out. It's been happening more and more these days—Mrs. Obi taking a day off here, a day off there for the last two months. Mr. Ruiz stands at the door at 4:00 p.m. as I walk up, expecting us with an obnoxious grin on his face.

"Welcome señorita," he guides me into the room with an extended hand. Clearly taking his subbing of the club way too seriously. "What's today's meeting about, Ms. Alvarez?"

"We're gonna have a circle to process the latest." I take out my school laptop and link up today's slides to Mr. Ruiz's projector. In the last two weeks, a boy of fifteen was shot when he called

911 for help over his chest tightening. In Florida there was another school shooting, and a mother was shot multiple times in the back in front of her son after they stopped her car.

Mr. Ruiz takes off his glasses and holds the bridge of his nose. "It's never ending."

"Feels that way for sure. But if we don't have hope, we have nothing," I say. The words come out of my mouth out of practice or routine. But the truth is: I am tired, and my hope is dwindling every time these things go down again and again and again. I feel like ever since I took over this club, one of the main things we've had to do is hold space for our feelings around violence towards Black and Brown bodies, out there in the world we are supposed to confidently enter.

Club members start rolling in. Cindy and Marcus, both juniors, begin setting up the chairs into a circle as I set out snacks I got from the cafeteria: Cheez-Its, string cheese, small cartons of milk and apple juice. I look around, take a deep breath, and smile proudly. I started this club in seventh grade. Walking around the school cafeteria, the hallways, and even the library, I realized so many of us were having the same discussion in private. There was fear, confusion, sadness, and deep rage at what was happening to Black and Brown people on a constant basis. Sometimes teachers let that happen in the classroom, but most of the time, we had to move on to stay on top of academic schedules before we were collectively ready to. When I got to Julia De Burgos, Mrs. Obi stepped in, and even though she wasn't my teacher yet I'd been dying to get to know her because she is legit, till this day, the dopest teacher. All the upperclass students had only good things to say about her and she was always kicking it with a group for lunch, or taking her classes on cool trips. She helped me recruit students by spreading the word and throwing in incentives here and there. I didn't imagine so many students, from every grade, to show up. When Mr. Choi, the vice principal and the adult in charge of club funds, saw the student turnout, he was happy to support us.

My phone buzzes in my back pocket and I pull it out. *Yolanda Nuelis, te espero en la casa hoy.* My heart drops. I forgot to answer Mamá's text last night. *Cion Mamá,* I reply immediately. *OK, I'll be there. Sorry I forgot to answer last night. I stayed at Mami's.*

"I played with the white boy last night," Cindy tells Marcus. I put my phone away.

"He good?" Marcus asks.

"Nah, he straight up trash. Or maybe he was letting me win 'cause I whooped his ass." Cindy laughs. "He trying to fit in though. His last school was basically mad bougie and shit. He was telling me he geeked to be here, didn't want to be at his school anymore." I roll my eyes to myself, but a part of me wants this to be true. Ben should be feeling comfortable here. If he feels comfortable, then maybe the weird feeling I got from the vision is nothing to be concerned about.

José walks in and removes his thick headphones; his basketball jersey hangs off his left shoulder. He nods at me with a slick-ass smirk as he grabs an apple juice. I turn away from him as Julissa and Amina, both in my sophomore class, take a seat. Hamid and Jay grab snacks and ask others to move back, so the circle can widen. Mariamma, Lucia, Frances, and Bryan, all first-years, join in. Autumn, another junior, gets the attendance sheet going, and Victory rushes in and finishes what seems to be some homework. Taslima, a senior, who has a side hustle doing henna at school for people's birthdays or special occasions, rushes into the class fixing her hijab. Last but not least, Ben walks in. He gives me a small wave, and I return it. The smell of cigarettes low-key floating off of him.

"Hey," he greets Cindy, and she daps him. I have to keep from laughing at how uncomfortable he looks as she pulls him in.

As the circle fills up, I take a look around and notice that the demographics have officially shifted. In the past, the only white person has been Amina. She's Albanian, and her family has lived in the Bronx since they migrated to the United States before she was born, like many of our own parents. We don't even consider her a white girl to be honest—we consider her a girl who happens to be white. Her folks came from Albania a few months before she was born. Plus, she's mad aware of the white privileges she still has, and calls it all the time, even calls herself in when she realizes she's overstepped or is taking up a lot of space. So, I don't know, sometimes we forget.

OK, so she's still white. I know. She wouldn't be stopped by the cops for no good reason. She doesn't know anything of the sweat produced by your body when a cop car gets too close. She isn't followed around stores downtown. But her experiences vary from good ol' "White Americans." Her parents are immigrants, and they know what it is like to leave home for a place of broken promises. They know what it's like to not be able to defend yourself in English. Amina knows what it's like to be a kid being asked to translate paperwork or stumbling over two languages, so a part of me feels that level of connection with her.

Ben is the last to sit in the circle, and most of us do a double take as if we can't believe he's actually rolled up in here. Mr. Ruiz clears his throat to break the staring.

"Let's start with an ice breaker," he says, rubbing his hands together. "That's what ya'll do, right?" He looks at me for approval. I nod.

"If you could be a candy, what would you be?!" Hamid calls out from his chair. People all over laugh. I decide to stick to it, even though today feels like more of a serious note. But we need joy, right?

"I'll start," Victory says, walking to the center of the circle and picking up Penny, a stuffed version of Lady Liberty.

"I, of course, would be chocolate," she says, extending her arm to the light and turning it as if she's a gem. Her skin actually shines with shea butter. "'Cause look at this deep skin. Mmm. I'm going to go to the left," she says, handing off Penny to Julissa, a senior, who has cousins in every grade and who changes the color of her hair every month. This month it's green at the ends.

"I would be a Milk Dud," she says. "Hard to chew on, but worth it." Some of the boys shake their heads, attempting their best not to say some perverted shit.

"I would be one of those Hershey's Kisses with the caramel in the middle," Yasheeda goes next. She's the head of the drama club and only drops in when she can. "Ya know what I'm talking about." She holds her moisturized hand in front of her face and fans down her finger. She hands Penny down.

"I would be Toblerone," Hamid says. "You can't find me in the bodegas without the lotto machines," he rolls his hands through his hair. Everyone laughs. Hamid's hair is mad shiny and thick and he never lets us forget it. He was born in Yemen, and although he likes to act like he's a class clown, he is usually the mediator of the group.

José takes Penny from Hamid and he looks at me, "I think I'd be a Sour Patch Kid. Sour then sweet." My entire face is on fire. God, don't let anyone notice. Victory looks at me and smirks discreetly as Penny goes on to Ben. The second Penny lands on Ben's hands, it's like everyone holds their breath, trying to stay loyal to something unknown.

"I don't eat much candy. But my dad gets these chocolate truffles from DeLafée every few weeks or so. There's edible gold in them. They're really good, but to be fair, they have to be. A box of four hundred and fifty grams is pretty expensive," he chuckles. He hands Penny off by the leg and her small fire torch lumps downward. Amina takes out her phone, types something quickly, and then grabs Penny.

"I would be a Banana Laffy Taffy," Amina says, typing into her phone. She's about to hand Penny off to me, but she stops herself. "You know, Ben, it says that chocolate bar is like five hundred dollars?"

Ben shrugs. "I think so."

"OK baller!" Cindy jokes.

"I mean I guess, but most of our parents haven't seen five hundred dollars in one shot, unless they're paying rent. It's something to think about when you eat *candy* that costs that much," Amina says.

"That's true," Frances whispers. People nod in agreement with Amina.

"I know that's right," Yasheeda says. "But Ben, you better bring some of that delicacy for us to try one day." Everyone laughs, including Ben.

I am grateful to Amina that none of us had to say it, and she took that on herself. I am also grateful that Yasheeda breaks the tension with her humor. Amina hands Penny to me.

"I would be a Blow Pop. I really like hard candy and gum, so it's a perfect mixture." I look down at Penny, a brown replica of the Statue of Liberty. A bunch of the textbooks say she was a sign of freedom for immigrants. Mamá Teté says it was for her too at some point, and I can't help but think of that time being so distant from now. Freedom costs so much now, so much. I hand Penny off.

"Alright, connection circle is done," I say when everyone has had a turn.

Mr. Ruiz goes to our next slide. On it are article titles and headlines from just the last two months. Victory helped me put this slide together at lunch. We decided against images. The truth is, the media is a gift and a curse. A gift because of communication, but a curse because the way folks show images and talk about violence ends up numbing our feelings. An image that might've made us hit the streets to protest ten years ago probably don't hit the same anymore. Media normalizes the violence, so we get tired of the fighting and demanding of change.

Some people look away, others reread the headlines carefully, others shake their heads. I glance at Ben, the corner of his mouth trembling slightly. The vision nudges some part of my brain.

"These headlines are the normal things for us to see now," José says. "I think it's all part of a plan to dehumanize us."

BLACK TEENAGER KILLED IN HIS OWN HOME AFTER CALLING 911.

FOUR FATALLY INJURED IN SCHOOL SHOOTING IN FT. LAUDERDALE.

BLACK AMERICAN KILLED IN SACRAMENTO

ON HIS GRANDMOTHER'S LAWN AFTER A TRAF-
FIC LIGHT VIOLATION.
    A SCHOOL SHOOTING FOR EVERY WEEK OF
THE YEAR.

"Was it always like this? The headlines?" Marcus asks.

"Feels like it for us," Lucia says.

"Mr. Ruiz, you lived through times where there wasn't so many of these?" I ask.

"There has always been violence against Brown and Black people," he says. "But now, something that would've taken a couple days or a week to circulate, takes just an hour or two thanks to technology."

"You lucky," Hamid whispers. "Or not."

We sit in silence for longer than any of us feels comfortable. My skin feels like it's overexposed, even though it's dressed in a school uniform. The floor is messy. The spot I stare at has rolled-up gum wrappers and an empty Cheetos bag. I know for damn sure had Mrs. Obi been here, no one would've dared. I lift my eyes only to see others staring at their own hands or at the same floor I've examined. We obviously do not want to meet each other's eyes no matter what—it's a lot to take in. Every time we process events like this, our response is different.

"Hmmmm," Ben remarks. He rubs his pointer finger and thumb on his chin. My body stiffens. He just got into the club, no way he's trying to show his ass on the first day. "Interesting." I look at him, and when he meets my eyes, I turn-tilt my head with a question I do not mean for him to answer at all. Everyone notices him, but not much gets said. The room feels encircled by a discomfort that can't be seen, so it's difficult to say what needs to be cut, attacked, or examined. But something ain't right. *Bruja Diosas, it ain't right at all.*

"*Mmmmkkkmmmk,*" Mr. Ruiz's clearing of his throat breaks the silence. "What do we make of all the perpetrators?" he asks. He places his hand on his chin as if he is thinking, too. Like he doesn't know what he's just unleashed. A chill runs up my spine, making me tremble in my chair. I zip up my black hoodie.

"I don't make anything out of it outside the obvious," Autumn whispers. "They're always male and white."

"That's the way it's always been, isn't it? The beginning of these countries we call 'developed,' it's always been at the expense of Black and Brown people," Amina shrugs.

"What difference does it make to notice that? It ain't like nothing is about to change. Honestly, I am tired of talking about this," Jay says. They sit up in their chair.

"You tired when Black people, that look just like you and your family, dying left and right?" Victory asks, but we all know she not really asking, she just wants them to feel silly for saying that aloud.

"I am, I really am. We can't spend this time just chilling and talking about some fun shit? Culture, our cultures, ain't just about pain, Vic."

"I feel you," Marcus says.

"Same," a bunch of people say. "That's real," I hear another voice agree. Victory shakes her head, disappointed, but a part of me is sick of all this talk too. Victory has a lot of capacity to deal with discomfort and confrontation compared to most of us. We not built the same, she always reminds me.

"OK," I start. "I get it. We are tired, and how can we not be? It's a miracle to go through a few weeks without these kinds of headlines. That's not normal at all. But the fact that we tired, we sick, we sad, we whatever—it shows we still feel, we still here," my voice cracks.

Bruja Diosas, come through. Speak through me if you must.

"We still here, and we not alone. Like Mrs. Obi always says: we are standing on the shoulders of all of those who came before us. There have been way, way too many before us. You think we here 'cause people gave in to the tired? Come on, y'all, we ain't reinventing the wheels to figure this out. We are just continuing the pushing through 'cause we the youth right now, and that means we got the energy, technically we are fighting for our future. And throughout all of this we gotta hope all this changes, even if just a tiny bit. We got this and if we wanna take breaks, we can do that, too. We can rest. We need rest. But yeah, we fighting, we swinging, we throwing hands, 'cause our future depends on who comes up on top." I take a deep breath. "And we won't have to fight forever. There will be another generation of young people just like us coming up that will take on this work, too." Victory smiles at me—her teeth all wide and white—and I know I just put my foot in that little speech.

"Great speech," Mr. Ruiz winks at me. "All right folks, you heard her. What do we do now?" Mr. Ruiz leans forward, his forearms on his knees.

Ben's eyes don't move from my cheek. I feel him all up on my face, but I don't look.

"We can have a circle, get it all out? We can pick up the graphic novel we put down last week?" I suggest. Last month a nonprofit organization donated a class set of the graphic novel version of *Kindred,* by Octavia Butler.

"I vote for the second option," Hamid says. More than half of us raise our hand in agreeance. And Amina stands up and gets the books. She starts handing them out, and when she gets to the last copy, Mr. Ruiz and Ben don't have one.

"You OK if I share with you?" Ben asks, looking straight at me.

"Yeah, sure," I say dismissively. The tension in my head begins again. *What else was I supposed to do*? He moves his chair to my side of the circle and everyone shifts to give him space.

I crack the book open ready to jump in.

"Hold up, Yo," Marcus says. "Let's get a refresh 'cause some of us weren't here or some of us just forgot by now."

"We all know *you* forgot," Frances says quietly, but Marcus still hears her and sucks his teeth.

José explains that Dana, the main character, saved Rufus, the little white boy, from drowning. His mother comes to get him after Dana saves him, but there was a click sound, meaning a gun, and it's what triggered us into stopping the book last time.

"You think they got her?" Autumn asks.

"Hell no, she's the main character. That's the only way they keep Black characters alive," Jay answers. Everyone laughs.

We get into the book taking turns reading each page aloud. Everyone's reading voice is different, but even when some people struggle through the dialogue, we are eating up the story. Octavia Butler was truly one of the GOATs.

"Oh nah!" Cindy says aloud as Victory reads. Rufus has just confirmed Dana is his descendant!

"That's weird, but why it always gotta be Black women saving everyone? Like can we just exist and rest, please?" Yasheeda says.

"Right," Victory responds.

"Like now what? What is she supposed to do? Of course she's

going to save him from all his own mess 'cause she wants to survive," Amina adds.

"Right."

"I would save him, too," Ben laughs. "He's just a kid, you know?"

All of the sudden the same feeling of him grabbing up the air around him comes over our classroom. Everyone's eyes turn to Ben, who has been quiet the entire time we read.

"He's doing wild things tho," Mariamma says, and the minute she breaks the silence, it's like we can all breathe again. "Like who burns down a house 'cause your dad punishes you for *actually* stealing?"

"His dad didn't 'punish' him, he beat him," Ben responds.

"Good point, I guess," Mariamma says. "I wouldn't beat my kids. But my parents? They would punish *and* beat me if I took something from anyone without asking, OK?"

"Girl, same," Yasheeda affirms her. "But I ain't about to burn down my house over it." The rest of us nod in agreement.

"I mean, I do think that some kids rebel because of the abuse," Autumn adds.

"No, no, no. My thing is, why is getting 'abused' an excuse? We get beatings, but we don't use that as an excuse to be more violent," Taslima adds. "At least not at the same rate. I just feel like kids like Rufus get to use any little thing to do something like burning a house, and then on top of it, they're excused or saved."

I look around, trying to figure out if the conversation continues, or we drop it and get back to the book.

"Right like we are deadass going to victimize this kid? Like, I get it, you mad at your dad, but also you a baby beast just like him," Jay says. "He uses the n word with a hard er at the end, like lil mans, what?"

"Not that he can be saying the other version either," Cindy points out. The other day, when Fat Joe was defending J.Lo and him saying the n word because they grew up in the hood with Black people, and maybe have African ancestors like a lot of folks in the Caribbean, she was the first white Latina I heard checking whoever was defending them.

"Rufus is an upcoming little racist, and I'm not about to act like just 'cause his dad whooped his ass, now Dana gotta be out here risking her life for his," Jay finishes. They cut their eyes and stare at the ceiling as if asking for patience from the Gods.

I nod my head. I mean, yeah, he's just a kid, but he was going to burn everyone to the ground including the enslaved people who had nothing to do with that. And Jay is right: I am also weary, real weary about the way we jump to feel bad and empathize with white folks, but not with Black people. It took us less than two seconds to collectively forget what Dana was going through—literally jumping through times, thrown into a super dangerous period in time, and given the job of saving this little boy in order to keep her family and self alive.

"Let's keep reading?" Mr. Ruiz offers.

We continue reading. The entire club enthralled in the pages. Even Ben seems to be into *Kindred*. This is the first time we've been this close, and I can smell him although I can't place what it is he smells like. When we get to page forty-one in the book, I fold myself in a little bit. The same feeling of being exposed hovers over me again and I know a lot of us feel it in the room, too. Dana has walked in on a white man beating a Black enslaved man and ripping the clothes off of his wife.

Victory takes in a long breath and exhales heavily and completely as Amina reads. Mariamma starts biting her nails. Cindy
sits up in her chair. The air gets thick and breathing gets a little
harder. Even though we know what it was with slavery and the
way white masters pillaged through spaces and bodies, it is still
hard to read, difficult to see—but it is what it is. And trust we'd
rather be reading *Kindred* than reading *Lord of the Flies* or *Of
Mice and Men* like we were forced to all year in ninth-grade ELA.

"This is graphic," Ben states the obvious towards the end of
the page.

"But it's the truth," Victory responds, annoyed that he has
interrupted Amina's reading.

"Isn't this fiction?" Ben looks at Mr. Ruiz, who offers no
answer. "I don't know how much truth this author used."

"Excuse me?" Victory says. I swallow. "It's historical fiction,
Ben. And I am sure you've already learned about what went
down to create this big old country."

"And Octavia Butler was everything. I'm sure she researched
a lot before writing this book," Lucia blurts out. She uses her left
hand, where a bracelet with a charm with a Mexican flag rolls
down her wrist, to push her glasses back to the top of her nose.

"I'm just playing devil's advocate here," Ben says. He shifts in
his chair, and the scent he carries gets a little stronger. A faint
smell of cigarettes and a super light musky smell, maybe a
cologne, and spearmint from the gum he's chewing. "Doesn't
this feel like a lot of violence to place on some of these characters
from the very beginning?" he adds. I cross my legs at the ankles
and sit up. Does he mean the violence the enslaved people had to
endure, or the violence on the hands of their white masters?

"Nope, we ain't about to do that, Ben," Victory shakes her

pointer finger. "You are not about to criticize the book because YOU are uncomfortable."

José looks at me and arches his eyebrows. I shake my head.

"Everyone's uncomfortable. Are we not?" Ben looks around, but no one answers him. Loyalty is airtight in these parts. It's how we survive.

"We are uncomfortable for different reasons though," Amina points out.

"Can we just get back to the book, y'all? Damn?" Yasheeda sucks her teeth. "It's just about to get good!" Again, so grateful for Yasheeda.

Victory looks at me and arches an eyebrow at Ben—signaling: be careful. I bring up the book between Ben and me. The page shivers as he exhales.

"Imagine if we could do that though," José says. "Time travel back to the past though."

We take a collective breath, imagining. I would love to go back to the past and meet all my ancestors who gathered all the wisdom Mamá Teté learned to pass down to me.

"I would've had Trujillo in a chokehold," Marcus says, whose dad is Haitian. At the beginning of the year, he schooled a lot of us on the Parsley massacre, when we had started talking about dictators as if they had only been a thing in Europe.

"Shit, I would work for Saitama's Serious Punch just for him," José laughs.

Some of us laugh, including me, even though I don't get the reference one bit.

"I mean I would be cool with traveling back to the past only if I could take back what I know now," Bryan says. "Like I would definitely want to go back to the post-colonial world with some gunpowder knowledge. I feel like that's the only real reason shit went south."

"That, among other things," Mr. Ruiz adds.

☾

The sun is low in the sky by the time we get outside the school building at 6:00 p.m. Outside, club members and other students from other clubs say bye to one another or group up to take the same route home. José, Victory, and I walk together towards the bus.

We don't speak for a while. And when José open his mouth, it's to make a joke that softens up all the tension of the day for the three of us.

7

CAFÉ RITUALS

The strong scent of urine smacks me as soon as I step into the project building. I can't even blame folks. Bladders have proven themselves weak in my personal opinion. I step into the elevator, and I greet one of my grandmother's friends, a Honduran woman who goes to Mamá Teté from time to time for card readings.

Mamá Teté texted me to come home, and truth be told I can't ignore the dark cloud that keeps showing up when Ben is around any longer. Maybe if I just tell her a little bit of what's going on, she will be able to help.

"Cion, Mamá," I say entering the door. Mamá Teté is in front of the stove making café.

"Que todo lo bueno te bendiga mi'ja," she responds. She tightens her thick lips when she catches my eyes, so I know she's feeling some type of way.

"It's late for coffee, Mamá." I sit down on the chair squeezed into the kitchen.

"It's never too late for coffee or coffee readings."

"You've got a reading?" I ask.

"No, Yoyo, WE'VE got a reading." She tells me she had to postpone the reading from yesterday to today since I didn't come home. Then, she looks into me as if she is trying to stop the night from invading the light of my soul. God dang she's pissed. OK, so I didn't call yesterday or respond to the text to say I was staying at Mami's, but what's the big deal? She pours a coffee without sugar. Without cream. And walks into the living room. I follow.

"Mamá—" I try to explain. But she turns around and hushes me.

"You don't have to tell me anything, Yolanda Nuelis. You had a vision. I already know, no thanks to you." So she called Mami? Great. I try to explain that I was going to come by today to talk to her about what's been going on, but she stops me from explaining again. I haven't had a vision like that since I was five. I have my dreams, but this felt stronger, and came to me out of nowhere. After some silence, I try again.

"Mamá, that was the first time that happened to me since I saw Noriel. I was nervous. And what I saw, maybe it is not a big deal," I say.

"Why do you say?" she turns to me.

"Because," I think about today. Yeah, Ben was problematic, but there are problematic people everywhere. Yeah, I felt some things, but can it be that alarming? What can he really be trying to do? "It just scared me a little. I felt like I was right there, and I just needed some time. You should know that." She looks at me like I'm being wildly disrespectful or something, but smirks understandingly. She points to the couch.

"I've told you fear is a tool before, we don't always have to avoid or run away from the feeling," Mamá takes a deep breath. "Siéntate, Yolanda Nuelis," she demands. So I'm not off the hook? OK. I follow her instructions and sit on the couch she still has covered in plastic, while she pulls out a folding table from behind the couch and sets down the coffee.

Finally we are sitting across from one another. She has the cup of coffee over a small plate. She pushes it towards me. I take the coffee cup up to my mouth and begin to slowly sip. It's no use fighting her. She has these premonitions that are wiser than mine.

Mamá is guided by Culebra, and I don't really play with her too much.

When she lived through her bodily form, Culebra was a Black woman from the West Coast of Africa. She is one of the ten daughters of the Unknown, Tierra. Culebra is strong and powerful. On Earth, she was devoted to the liberation of women in her community. Whenever she was called upon to help fellow women, she came with a hoard of serpents and snakes to free the women and dominate whoever stood in her way. When a powerful dragon attacked the neighboring lands, Culebra was called upon as backup. When colonization and slavery began, Culebra traveled to the Caribbean in order to protect her people. Her spirit remained grounded in the Caribbean when her earthly body passed, and since then she lives through her faithful followers.

My Unknown, or Bruja Diosa, has yet to choose me. Mamá is guiding me through the journey there because Mamá is powerfully chosen. The story goes that when Mamá was pushed out of her mother's womb, there was a snake by her feet, just watching her birth. That's powerful to be chosen upon entry to the world. All that to say, I don't play with Mamá Teté, but I was nervous and confused and damn, can't I catch a break?

Mamá's eyes don't come off me until there is a minimal amount of coffee left in the cup. The heat rushes down my throat. I hate that I had to drink it so quickly, but finally I turn it over on the small plate.

"Mamá, ya," I say. I really hate when she looks at me like she knows something I don't. She puts her glasses on, then turns the coffee cup over. She pulls her face away from the cup like it's venom. She looks, observes, and puffs air in and out of the wideness of her nostrils.

"Mi'ja, what lio have they gotten you into?" she says. She now looks up at me, and I don't know which look makes me feel most uncomfortable. I want to ask her to elaborate, to tell me more, to just say the things that are being highlighted by Culebra in her mind and heart, but I don't really want to know. I have already been forced to know so much with this gift: Papi betraying Mami, predators' disgusting thoughts, and now it seems like whatever Ben is going through. I want to know no more. Imagine that. A kid who doesn't want to know more shit before they're ready. They exist, because it's me right now.

"You have to give servicios to your altar. With your allowance money, you also have to buy Culebra a purple or dark-green candle, so I can light it up on my altar—for the reading," Mamá says.

"But you didn't tell me anything," I protest.

"I read you, and it seems the Unknowns are keeping me from seeing what's going. But if there's one thing I know: when the

Unknowns want to say more, they'll say more." She points towards the door. When I turn from her, I roll my eyes and step into my sneakers. I walk towards the door, put my keys back into my pocket, go into my wallet for the only five-dollar bill I have left, and I'm out.

I take the elevator down to the seventh floor and exit from the backside of the building. The local bodega always has tons of candles on deck. A whole lot of us in the building use them on rotation for the dead, the sick, the saints, the Gods, the spells. I walk towards the back of the bodega, come across the gray kitty, and rub its back. It follows me to the dark corner with the candles. I get a purple one and two white ones. As I'm about to turn around, to walk towards the counter to pay, I feel this need to turn around.

Red. Red candle. I pick up a red candle. At the counter, I pay my five dollars.

"You're missing $1.75, Morena," the man says.

"Can I come back and give it to you? You know me, Ramon. I'm good for it," I say. A group of three men who hardly ever leave the bodega pretend not to be listening. Ramon points to the handwritten sign that says "AQUÍ NO SE FÍA."

"OK, I'll leave the red one," I say.

"I got her," another man, standing behind me in line says. He's older, wears jeans, and an oversized red T-shirt. Instantly I feel every wall in my body rise. People sometimes expect something for even a tiny favor. *Take the help.* The goosebumps take over my flesh. There you are. You're back. I take a breath of relief.

"Thank you so much," I force myself to listen. "What's your name? I'll make sure I pay you back."

"I'm Michael. You won't see me around here too much, so it's all good. You light that candle," he says. I smile and say thank you again before heading out.

At the entrance of the building, men stand around smoking Newports and playing dice. Boys and girls sit on the wall, on their phones. They mostly all live in this building. I've basically grown up with them, used to play tag in the building together, used to ride bikes in the park together, used to throw water balloons at each other in front of the building, but one way or another after high school started we just all went our own paths. Some of them still hang out here together, others were sent to Catholic schools, others moved out of the projects. At first, I sometimes felt the tension for whatever reason. Mamá says that's how we are when we hit puberty. Start getting territorial or whatever. Now, I smile politely or greet them with a head tilt or just do nothing, and they do the same. One of the men, Moses, from the seventeenth floor, walks towards me, his hands going in and out of his pockets taking out money.

"Hey, you Teté's granddaughter, right?" Moses asks. He damn well knows I am.

"Yeah," I say.

"I owe her. My grandma got her to make me one of her baths and a mix of waters for the floors," he says. "Give her this for me." He hands me fifteen musty twenty-dollar bills. The humidity coming off the bills makes me imagine he legit had to sweat for this money.

"Baths are only—"

"She told me. It's donation-based, right?" he asks. I nod. "She also told me to get her a purple or green candle. I gave that to her a few days ago. I didn't have the money then, but now I do. Tell her I said anything she need, I got her."

"Not a problem. That's what we here for," I say, knowing that's how Mamá always closes off when someone thanks her.

I run back to the bodega. I try to ask for the man who lent me the money, but he's gone.

When I get into the apartment, I give Mamá the candle for Culebra and bring out the money. She sits in front of the TV watching the novelas, the coffee cup still in front of her. The characters in Latin American telenovelas are always white Latines. Never is the protagonist a Black or Indigenous person. If there's even such a character, they are minor. Indigenous folks always have clown-like, servant, or insignificant roles. But it's all we got. And it's all Mamá Teté can watch without getting too lost.

"Mamá?" I say. She turns towards me. Her face has shifted, she looks softer, and yet her eyes look darker too. I know the spirit has reached her. "What did you do for Moses?"

"Made him a bath to keep his enemies away."

"What was the floor water for?"

"Our building. These pendejos forget that when they do things while living here, we all need protection too."

For every floor? I think to myself.

"Teté heard it took him a week to mop every floor with the water. But that's what I needed from him," Culebra says. Her voice is belligerent, but I know there is no harm. I lean into her to give her the candle. In a quick flash, she grabs my arm. I flinch knowing it is Culebra and not my Mamá entirely. With her finger, she marks the back of my forearm in an S-like form. *Que la Culebra siempre te proteja.*

I take a deep breath. Feel a wave come over my body.

"Thank you, Culebra. I'm going to my room now," I say,

yanking my arm back. Mamá crosses her legs around each other tightly. Her head hits the back of the couch with a thud.

☾

I wish I could speak on when I noticed that I was connected to the Unknowns and my ancestors—the honorable and the not so good too. But there was no beginning, and who knows about the end? Not I.

I have always known. It was the reason I grew with almost no close friends, outside of Victory. At a hug, a handshake, a glare, the messages came to me just like they came to Mamá Teté.

Her jealousy is dangerous.

His rage is not healthy for you.

Stay back—they aren't ready.

I was five when Mamá Teté sat down and explained the messages were a privilege—that everyone had them, but they didn't ring as strong for just anyone. The Unknowns affected everyone on the island, but they *worked* for a select few. The saints had to choose you: unlike other religions, faiths, or practices, you didn't come into it because you chose to do so. It is a gift really, but in reality compared to other people my age, I would say my life sometimes is lonely. With the exception of the Bruja Diosas, my parents, Victory, and Mamá Teté, talking about how the "supernatural" mixes up with our physical world can't really happen.

When I was in middle school, I did try to fight it. Simply because I wanted to fit in. But the more I ignored the whispers, the louder they became, and the more frequent they came. It helped that Victory showed me how to view it all as an extra tool, instead of an end-all be-all, and I know it's what Mamá Teté has always been saying.

I sit on the floor because its coolness and sturdiness makes me feel grounded, as if nothing can move me or shake me up. Today, though, Mamá shook me up—the look on her face. She has been a human with the same gift as I for so many decades, and I would've thought she couldn't see something that would surprise her into fear. But she did. It's why she called on Culebra for answers. It's why Culebra mounted her.

My daybed is the same twin-size one I have had since Mamá installed it herself for me, long before my parents divorced. She says she knew they would divorce since they married, but sometimes people just gotta live and learn. Next to my bed is a white bureau with a small mirror. Next to the door is the shelf I use as a small library. Unlike Mamá Teté, I like the neutral, basic colors of black and white, so when I open my closet door, those shades are the main ones you see, with the exception of the red on my puffer coat, and another few items only. I spot the white candle I didn't use last week, and I remember the okra I have soaking in the kitchen.

I sit with the white candles in front of me. I never really have color candles because no Unknown has chosen me yet. So, this red. The feeling to get it was dense and yet felt like a light breath. I say a few words: "Thank you Bruja Diosas, Archangels, Guardian Angels, Gods, Honorable Ancestors, Lwas, Unknowns, Orishas, Saints, Universe, Mother Earth, Father Sky, and all that is good and greater than humans. I ask that you deliver answers to me. That the gates of communication be open."

I light the candle. The flame comes up quickly. It is relatively long and the oranges and yellows thrive together. I run to the kitchen to get the okra. When I settle back on the floor with the tin container between my legs, I thank the waters for their willingness to help me with this okra bath. Okra baths were something Mamá did not usually do but she learned from a friend when she traveled to New Orleans to meet with other Black and Brown diviners. She said the okra baths were made to take in and drown out energies that keep people from clarity. The Bruja Diosas know I need all the help I can get. I begin to squeeze the twenty-two pods that have been soaking for days in freshwater until they rupture and the spine with its collective seeds appears. I then take the spine between my three-inch nails and the back of my fingers, to split them into expelling all of their goo. The goo is what is needed when making these baths.

After working with the okra for forty-five minutes, I turn around to wipe sweat off my forehead, and I realize the trance coming in. It starts with a heaviness at the top of my head, as if the heavens have chosen my mind as its foundation, and then there's heat with an inner coolness that softly applies pressure.

I am asleep before I know it.

Her back is kissed by the sun. Her thighs are soiled. She sits on a straw mat over the Earth. I am her. I know I am. She is working on the same pot of fresh water and okra. She looks to the other side and there is her home—round and made of mud. Smoke rises from the top and she knows it is the man she calls her father making food while she makes medicine. A toddler runs and climbs onto her back, and he feels as cool as a shield. I have never heard the language he speaks, but I understand him as he laughs, "Sister, she's going to catch me!" She moves the basin and brings the toddler to her legs. The baby's eyes shine with joy. He looks like her, his lips pronounced, his nose wide and flat.

"Babu, get back here," she hears the voice of her mother yell from the house.

"What do you have, baby? Come on, give it to big sister."

She takes his small, warm hand, and pries it open to find a rock. Although she's never seen it, she knows it's valuable. Warm rose and cool aqua lines gleam on its surfaces.

"I'm going to take this, Babu, OK? Go back inside with mother." The small boy runs off disappointedly.

"I've got it," she yells back into her house.

She leans back, and her back aches. Stretching, she remembers the many requests of okra baths she has to meet. She feels hands on her shoulders. She turns back to see her grandfather. Out of all her cousins and siblings, he now only remembers her. She was trained by him, since she was Babu's age, on the power of plants and how to make medicine. They smile at one another. The blue-and-gray edges on his irises remind her that their time is now more limited than ever. Grief washes over her.

"We can feel sad," the old man chuckles. "But we must always remain grateful for having been given the time we've spent together." She nods.

"You're such a hard worker, little fire," the old man whispers. She smiles and works faster, as if his words make her hands more potent for the bath.

"Who is this batch for?" he questions.

"For us," she says, the smile falling from her lips. She shakes her head trying to remember who the requests came from. "For us," she whispers. And then it hits her that the requests have come to her from herself through her dream.

Fear crawls up the soles of both of our feet.

☾

These are the dreams I have often. The ones I am used to, to some degree. They assure me there were many before me. Many people who saw, who made, who cured. It assures me that humans weren't always vessels of ego. That their natural state had been to aid the connection between the divine and the human. That there's always a way back.

PERIOD

The first bell rings. I've been looking for Victory all morning to apologize about yesterday in person, but I can't find her.

I'm sorry about Ben yesterday I text her as I walk to first period. She didn't really want to talk about what went down yesterday, so I know she was big mad and needed space.

Mr. Leyva stops me. "Yoyo, come on, girl. You know better than to have your phone out in these hallways."

"PUTTING IT AWAY!" I announce. Mr. L shakes his head playfully. I continue walking. Before I get to class I go into a small corner and take out my phone.

Girl, y r u apologizing FOR HIM? she replies.

U right. I kinda feel like I welcomed into Brave Space +I could've helped w checking his problematic ass :/ I reply

Ben was definitely out of pocket, and for whatever reason it felt like I was tongue-tied. For the first time since I took over the club, I couldn't get a word in. I don't know if it was that he was so close to me, that it was his first time at our meetings, or the vision. Maybe it was a little bit of everything. I quickly put my phone back in my pocket.

Mrs. Obi stands at the door of her classroom giving us high-fives as we go into class. She is probably the only teacher who does it, and at the beginning we thought she was extra for it. After all, we aren't in third grade, but it makes you feel wanted even though none of us would admit that aloud. She has a red cardigan and has just installed her fresh, new box braids. She's holding a blue bin with folders, meaning we're picking new lab partners.

"Good morning, Yoyo. I am so happy to see you. I heard ya'll went into layered terrains yesterday," she says. I nod.

"Yeah, some of us weren't ready for all that, so we picked up *Kindred*," I reply.

"I'm sorry I wasn't here to help you navigate that discomfort, but you did good! I heard you listened to folks and met others where they were at," she adds. "But I didn't get the full download, so you must fill me in later." I shrug OK. I reach into the bin and open the folder to see my lab partner's name—Ben.

"Nah, let me switch, Obi," I say. After having spent all of our meeting yesterday beside him, I'm good on spending more time like that. He was doing too much yesterday, and . . . I still get a vibe I can't necessarily name or place. But I know I definitely do not like it.

She leans over my shoulder. "Ben, huh? I know from his parents, who I met during his onboarding process, that he needs all the help he can get to catch up with chemistry," she says.

"Really? I mean he went to private school. I am sure he has what he needs to catch up. Mrs. Obi, with all due respect, I am doing excellent with Bianca."

"You're excellent with anyone. Think of yourself as O-type. You've demonstrated to me you're compatible with all types of folks in this place. And to your last point, I think you're making an assumption that all kids who go to private school are academically great, and that's just not the case."

I stare at her like I couldn't care less, 'cause I really don't.

"I'll throw some extra credit points," she says. I want to tell her I don't need them, but she knows I don't. Plus, I swear teachers be making extra credit stuff up. "Come on, Yo, IOU."

"Fine. If it all goes to left, it's on you, Mrs. Obi."

"I got you, Yo, I got you," she smiles, leading me into the classroom.

Since Mrs. Obi and I started the Julia De Burgos branch of the Brave Space Club, we have had many, many, many ups and downs. But most importantly, I have learned a lot from her. She teaches me to be patient and always be curious before jumping to conclusions. But this feels odd, even though I trust her. I wonder if she's trying to push my thinking or something teacher-y like that by having me work closely with someone like Ben. I know she doesn't know him at all actually, so she doesn't fully know how dangerous he can maybe be.

I started the club in seventh grade with Victory's help, as always. Also our seventh grade ELA teacher, Ms. VanNorden, who sponsored the club. It was right after when we'd learned who the forty-fifth president of this country would be, someone who has proven to be hateful and honestly racist. But he showed to the world that there are more of them than many of us cooped up in big cities thought. After we moved to Julia De Burgos, Ms. VanNorden heard I was having a hard time in high school, and she connected with Mrs. Obi to bring the club here.

I drag my feet to my lab table and sit down on the stool. I look over at Bianca who has been moved with José now. Although he's a senior, he's trying to take the chemistry regents for an extra rope at graduation, so he's using his free period to retake chemistry. She plays with her curls as she shows him her notes. I've worked with him before, and I know he doesn't have to look at her notes. I'm annoyed and honestly all up in my feelings. To be clear, I am jealous. I try not to stare too much.

The door slams. Ben's eyes are irritated like he hasn't slept. The top button of his uniform shirt is undone.

"Yo, you good, Ben?" a student calls out. He smirks as he walks towards a table without paying any attention to Mrs. Obi's extended hand attempting to redirect him to my table. I look at her and raise my eyebrow; she takes quick nods like "OK."

"Where am I sitting?" he asks once he is in the middle of the classroom. A bunch of us turn to him and stare at him like he's silly. Yesterday, he walked into Mr. Ruiz's class pretending to be humble and whatnot, but clearly that's gone out the window.

"Right here," I say. Mrs. Obi continues taking attendance. "All right, scientists. Now that y'all are feeling comfortable using the periodic table as a resource, we are spicing it up—"

"What did you say?" Ben calls out, sitting next to me.

"The period—" Mrs. Obi begins.

"I am not at all comfortable with periods," Ben cuts her off. "Blood just makes me queasy. I don't see the act of menstruation as a cycle. Quite frankly I think they're gross." He smiles, leaning back while holding on to the table. He looks around waiting for an entourage, for others to join and laugh with him. But the class clown role is taken and people don't fuck around on Mrs. Obi.

"What?" Bianca says, squinting her eyes, and looking at him like Ben's clueless. Students all over the room suck their teeth and scoff, aggravated by his interruption.

"Bruh," a bunch of kids say, shaking their heads and keeping their glances away from him.

"You corny for that, dawg," Marcus says from the front row.

"Mr. Corn Dog!" Dayvonte blurts out. In typical underclassman fashion, everyone in tenth grade in this class joins in. I cover my mouth to keep from laughing and look at Ben. His nostrils flare as everyone laughs. Mrs. Obi walks up to him, whispers something in his ear, and pats his shoulder.

"My bad, Obi," Dayvonte whispers to Mrs. Obi as the laughing dies down.

"All right, all right, let's see how prepared y'all are. What's the atomic number for . . ." Mrs. Obi rubs her hands, like she's deeply thinking. "Krypton!" she smiles. "Yeah, I like me some Krypton. Turn and talk."

All of us look to the left wall because that's where the periodic table is normally plastered, but it's still covered since our last quiz. The class bursts out in discussion. People really like Mrs. Obi around here, so they're really trying to figure it out, taking out their notes and looking for clues in their textbooks.

Mrs. Obi walks to our table and crouches down to our sitting level. "Ben, I am really happy to have you in class," she starts. "One thing I loved that you did when you came into our classroom was try to orient yourself in this space by asking where you should sit. That shows me you are aware of new territories and how rules must be used for survival. One thing I think you may want to work on to be successful in this classroom is not speak over me or others, especially when it is off-topic and quite frankly silly. I can guess you have questions about menstruations, and we can talk about that after class if you set up an appointment." She smiles. Her dark, shea butter-dressed skin shines under the bright classroom lights. "I know you'll do better, Ben."

Ben is bright red, as if he'd rubbed his face on snow for long minutes. The whites in his eyes are glossy and the lining of the green within is highlighted. In a matter of a minute, his features have changed. I wonder if anyone would think of him as eye candy looking all scary like this now. It's as if all the blood he has in his body decided to visit his face. He clenches his fists under the table. He's irate, and the energy sticks to me somehow. I shift in my seat to remind my body we OK. I've never seen a white person look this upset. Around here we yell, scream, talk shit— basically we let it out—but he is holding on to it, and it hurts me to watch.

"You good?" I ask, remembering yesterday when he apologized for having been weird like this. *Why didn't he pop off like this with Mr. Ruiz?* Ben looks at me, breathes deeply, and looks aware. I take out my phone and Google: "Is social justice warrior positive or negative?" A Wiki explanation pops up first: "The term *social justice warrior* became negative in 2011. The term refers to those who adamantly support progressive views such as cultural and racial inclusivity and feminism." I feel affirmed because I already knew what was up. *But how does something like standing for humanity become a joke?*

It becomes nearly impossible for me to look at Ben and not think about the origins of racism. Mr. Ruiz started off our Thursday discussions in US History by teaching us about the construction of race. He got into the ways in which those in power used racial myths to justify the ruthless ways in which they oppressed Black and Brown people. He mentioned how even in Latin

America, racism was used to build social classes. According to him, colonizers always met Natives and the enslaved with war and bloodshed, and I wonder if that's because they didn't try to talk about what was really bothering them. If they kept it all bottled in like Ben, I can see how people like his ancestors ended up raping, killing, and enslaving us. It was the only outlet they turned to. There's so much hate in his body, I can feel it in the pit of my stomach. *It won't lead to anywhere good,* I hear.

I fake cough just to interrupt the quiet. "Soooooo, I think the atomic number for krypton is thirty-five or thirty-six from what I remember," I say. "No, thirty-six, thirty-six for sure. What do you think?" I truly don't care for his response. He doesn't respond; instead, he scribbles circles in his notebook. His face turns directly to it, leaving me looking at the top of his ashy brown hair.

"Why are you so angry? You were the one who said something . . ." I begin, ". . . foolish." I really wanted to say dumb, but I'm not about add heat to this fire.

His eyes are even more irritated than when he walked into class, as he looks up at me like I've lost my mind. "Leave me alone," he says. He shakes his head and looks away. "Sorry," he whispers. "Just, just . . . don't speak to me right now." He shakes his head, and then looks at me again. His eyes are filled with anger and now softness. "Please. I can't believe I'm really at this shitty school," he pushes through his teeth.

I look up at the smartboard, astonished at him being honest. No one's ever come out their face to me like that. He testing me. I take a deep breath . . . just testing me—that's for sure. Mrs. Obi is explaining our objectives for the day, but through the corner of my eye I try to observe him. Mami says she tries to see the good in people at all times even when they've proven her wrong, because it's what good Christians do or whatever. When I learned about the Crusades and told her about it, she said there is sweetness in all people, even when they cause harm. I search his tight, clenched jaw, and the small, red arteries running around his cheek. But there ain't shit sweet here.

"What are you looking at?" he spits in a whisper through his clenched teeth. I roll my eyes, and I catch José staring at us to my left.

"You should take a breath and chill, dude," I say. For the rest of class, his fists remain clenched under the table, and I move on working like I have an invisible lab partner. Mrs. Obi tries to intervene a few times, but I signal that I'm good. I know what's really good with Ben now. His tactic is being flip-floppy, and that's not genuine at all. So imma trust what I've been feeling and do what I have to do to protect me and mine. 'Cause he's not about to fuck Julia De Burgos up for us at all. Not if I can help it.

The bell rings announcing the fifth period, lunch. He grabs his heavy-looking bookbag and is the first to the door, even though we were at one of the farthest tables. I try to follow him to his locker, but he goes straight to the staircase. *Keep your friends close, but keep your enemies closer,* the Bruja Diosas whisper—a reminder or an instruction? He runs up the stairs like he knows where he's going. I look towards my locker, and José is leaning against it. He meets my eyes, but I open the door and follow Ben.

"Hey!" I call out.

"What do you want?" he turns around, his tone softer than before. Wow, this kid is *mad* flip-floppy.

"Are you officially in my Mrs. Obi's class now?"

"It's a requirement, isn't it?" he responds, as I catch up to him. I nod. *Think, Yolanda, think.* The vision flashes in front of me for a second. I press my lips together as the uncomfortableness settles. *Bruja Diosas please come through!*

"I'm down to do the best we can as lab partners right now," I say. He stops and looks back at me, a question in his eyes. "I think it'll help both of us learn from one another." I have to swallow my own saliva to keep from throwing up in my own mouth. Since the communication with the Bruja Diosas is so minimal right now, I don't have a plan or direction right now. I have to make it up as I go.

"I'm OK. I don't do group work," he says.

"It's not a group. It's a team," I reply. I get chills up my spine as I think of this school and everything it's taught me. Julia De Burgos High is our home. If the vision makes me feel as fearful as it does, maybe it's because Ben's fury will eventually enter this space, a place that is low-key sacred for a lot of us, myself included.

"What's the difference?"

"A group is random and a team has a shared goal," I answer.

"My goal is to get the fuck out of that b—," he takes a breath, "out of her class."

"You just met her," I say.

"Do you think this is easy for me? It's not!" he says, turning around and going up the stairs. For a second, he's not a grown ass senior, but a small boy who doesn't know where to place his anger and hurt. He stops at the top. "Leave me alone." He runs up the next flight of stairs. I take a deep breath. *That's his stuff, not mine.* His energy is heavy, dense, and he uses it like an armor.

I could feel him, and I saw that he simply couldn't accept the connection between things. He doesn't get how different organisms react to one another. He doesn't think in groups, in teams, and he truly believes everything is singular. But that isn't who we are here. We are in a school in the middle of the Bronx. All we know is how to stick together. All we know is leaning on each other to push through.

When I get to my locker, José is waiting. He smells like expensive cologne, and my stomach grows arms that urge me to lean into him. He leans against the wall and licks his lips when he sees me. For a second, he looks at me like he's hungry for something more than food.

"You babysittin'?" he asks after a second, looking towards the door I just came out of.

"What?" I say. He leans his head right next to the locker. "Just looking out for him. He's new. Wouldn't you want to be helped?" I walk towards the lunchroom and José comes after. We pass by Mr. Leyva and both acknowledge him with a pound. Mr. L nods at me, and I know he picked up on what José and I are talking about. José opens the double doors for me, I walk through, and he follows. No one has seen us together, and we're just flowing with it. I try to backtrack in my mind when I told him walking together in public was OK, but I have definitely not given him the green light. Do I care though? Not really, so I don't fight it. I've done enough pushing back today and it's only 12:30 p.m.

When we walk in, it's as if every student decides to halt their breath and turn their face towards us. I feel naked, observed.

Other seniors from the basketball team, Ezekiel and Guy, run towards us and give José a dap. They look at me out of the corner of their eyes, and I know they are giving him some weak congratulations about being in the lunchroom with me. José has been trying to get my attention for over a year, and it's not like it's been a secret.

"It's not even like that," I hear José tell Ezekiel. I sit at the edge of an empty table, and he joins me.

"Why is it your job to get this boy used to our school?" he continues, sitting down across from me. I shrug my shoulders.

"Ain't you gonna get lunch or something?" I ask, and he shakes his head. No one eats the nasty ass school lunch. Not unless you're starving or they managed to cook something that's edible. I open my sandwich and slide half his way. He looks down, embarrassed.

"Thank you," he says. It's a Salsalito turkey, jack cheese, lettuce, and tomato sandwich: my favorite. My dad got me hooked on it the last year he was out of prison, when he was too busy to cook, and instead would stop by the bodega and ask the man behind the counter to make me something good.

"You not gonna tell me?" José asks as he chews.

"Tell you what? You pressing me for some answer I ain't got."

I pray Victory appears out of somewhere, but I know she's probably making something up for one of her classes.

José nods as he goes in for his second bite. And then it hits me like a warm wave. "Are you jealous?" I laugh. He doesn't say anything. I laugh some more, bringing my hand to my mouth. I'm not laughing at him; it's just I never had a boy show jealousy at this level over me. He takes out his math homework, dusts off his hands after the last bite, and crouches over it.

"Oh, so you're not gonna talk to me now?" I ask, sliding my hand onto the worksheet. I see some of the girls in the table disimulando but looking at us. He looks up at me, and I want to slide my hands onto the side of his face and kiss him, but I can't. Not here.

"It's not like that. I just feel like I want him to fit in, so he doesn't feel like an outcast. You know?" I say. I wish I could tell him the truth: that I saw something, and I'm scared of what it could be. Wish I could be honest and say that what I am most terrified of is that his rage will spill into us.

"It's not your job to make sure he fits in though. Didn't they assign the valedictorians to do all that?" José asks.

"Yeah. But also we are a part of this community, so we should all be trying to do it. I think you right, it's not my job . . . it's all of ours."

"BUT WHY tho?! Why?" His voice becomes lower after a second, but there is still a bit of anger on his face. "Did you not see how he disrespected Obi? It's like his second day, and he clearly doesn't give a fuckkkkkkkkkk about being part of this community." I don't say anything.

"Say something, Yolanda," he demands.

"Listen, he said some questionable things in our club, and as the lead it's on me," I say.

"You think this white boy is unwell mentally or something? That's why you going so hard?"

This is the perfect opportunity to say something. The mouthful of words I want to speak suddenly tastes like acid. I take a swig of water and swallow. I really like José. Like he makes me want to lean on him, type of like. If I tell him I see things before they happen, that I am usually in conversation with the Bruja Diosas, and that my grandmother is training me for this—will he think that we are out of our minds?

"That's not what I'm saying."

"So what are you saying?"

"That she has a feeling he might fuck some shit up if he doesn't find his niche soon," Victory comes out of nowhere and sits next to me. *Thank you, Bruja Diosas!* I'm so grateful to see her here, and I hug her tightly. "And it's just a bunch of us around here, so who he about to mingle with, José?" She shakes her head sarcastically, and it cracks me up.

"Yeah, what she said," I smile. José looks genuinely confused. His eyebrows are furrowed, and he blinks and shakes his eyes, like he's trying to see clearer.

"Listen," he starts, "you can't be everything for everyone at this school, Yoyo, but if that's what you wanna do, do you. But imma just say, have you thought about what he would be doing for any of us if we had gone to his fancy school?" I don't say anything. "He wouldn't give a shit about any of our asses." He gets up and walks to the water fountain and then to his boys. Leaving half of half of my sandwich behind.

As I watch him walk away, there's a whisper in my ear. *He's on to something.* I roll my eyes because the Bruja Diosas is just chilling I guess. *Yeah, I know he is. Thank you for coming through and confusing me more though.*

"José's bugging, Yo, but not bugging, bugging. Ben was rude to you, he was rude to me, and he was rude AF to Obi. That's a pattern. You need to stop trying to save him, and focus on your own stuff," Victory says. She writes on the papers in front of her. Her red pen digging into the paper. Her letters are chubby and wide, so different from her.

"Yeah, you're right. I'm sorry," I say. She looks at me ready to snap my head off.

"STOP apologizing for him, Yo!" she exclaims. And I want to repeat that I'm apologizing for my actions, not for Ben's.

"Fine, my bad, it's a bad habit to apologize!" I say. "Why are you writing in red pen?"

"It's the one I found," she says.

"Weird, you know yesterday I was pulled into getting a red candle? I've been getting white and black ones for so long. And out of nowhere I was at the bodega and was like, I need to get a red one." I give her a look, raising my eyebrow.

She drops her pen. Looks at me. "It's really happening! First the vision and now the candle, the color, the symbols! I'm dumb excited for you to know who it is!" she says. I love that Victory gets excited about this stuff for me. Her parents have always upheld Afro-centered theologies and religion. Although they don't subscribe to any per se, they get that we have survived because of our faiths, and so they respect all of them. Victory picks up the pen again and smiles up at me. For a split second, I feel like everything will be OK. Like all this connected with Ben is not just about him, it's also about me and the work I've been doing all my life, to follow in my grandmother's tradition. Then, she continues to copy down definitions on her cheat sheet.

"You really trying to be the valedictorian, huh?" I smile. I take back the half José left behind and bite on it. Today, I am hungry.

"Hell yeah," she says, not taking her pen or eyes off the paper. Hell yeah.

"How about you? You have another vision yet?" she asks, looking back up at me.

Taking a deep breath, I shake my head.

"You not about to ask Mamá Teté for help?" Victory looks up at me.

"I told her a little bit. She read me, but says the Unknowns are basically making her wait for more information," I respond. I sit with it for a moment . . . maybe they're waiting on me to say it to Mamá Teté myself. A discomfort centers itself at the bottom of my gut. My brain struggles to look for answers. I take a deep breath and shrug again as I look for a path that lies somewhere in the in-between.

☾

"Why did you say I'm protecting Ben the other day?" I ask Victory. We're walking into The Lit. Bar to chill while we wait for a ride from her mother.

"Silence is protection, Yoyo," Victory says, opening the door for herself. She holds it open for me and I walk in. After we ask for hot chocolates at the bar, we sit down at one of the tables.

"I think you're protecting him without meaning to, but I do think you're doing it 'cause he's some white boy. I bet you money, money, that if he had been one of us, you would've been told," she says. She taps her orange, brown, and gold short nails on the top of the cup before bringing it up to her lips. Victory comes from a long line of activists. Lately she's taken to call them Resistors, because she says anyone can use the term activist now, without doing any actual work. Resistors, she says, lets people know her family fought, pushed back, and laid down their very own lives for change, even if they never made the textbooks.

"That's some bull—," I start.

"Oh, is it now?" she says. I roll my eyes. I should've been real with myself—Victory would push me like this. She has never been the type to be chill; instead, she is always ready to take action. "Listen, this is happening to you, so you have to do something about it. Tell Mrs. Obi or Mr. L or something. Maybe they can help figure out why this kid would even come to a school like ours, a place where social justice is always talked about. They could've sent him anywhere else . . . but here? He's gonna have a hard time if he's really not about it." I look at Victory, knowing she's right, but fuck, I don't have it in me right now.

Victory and I have constant conversations about race. After all, we are both members of the Brave Space Club, but more than that she's come with me to Dominican spaces, so she has seen the culture firsthand. She knows that a girl as Black as me in my family will be called Morena, while she will be called Negra, even though our complexions are nearly the same. It's like Dominicans are scared of language that will commit us to our Blackness. It's changing, of course. There are so many of us who have been reclaiming ourselves and our ancestors, like Mamá Teté. But all the other shitty parts the way they keep us apart, and disconnected—still feel heavy. Victory always reminds everyone that growing up in a world like ours—where whiteness is admired and Blackness is violently denied—makes us biased too some times. And that's for every avenue of identity the status quo upholds, Mrs. Obi has explained. We have so much programming, as Black and Brown people who have given in, in order to survive, that it's difficult to see your own shit. Even though Mamá Teté makes it a point to uplift our Black lineage, I've seen firsthand how racism and colorism works on the island and here. No doubt the prejudice has rubbed off on me in one way or another, like it does on everybody, and no matter how uncomfortable that makes me, I have to own it.

"Maybe you're right," I finally say. Victory makes a point that speaks to what I've been feeling though. It's not OK for me to protect Ben because he's the only white kid at school, but isn't it just as easy for people to claim I am seeing what I am seeing, because he's the only white kid at this school? "That's just it though. He's the only white boy here. What if they say I'm just feeling some type of way about him and it's not necessarily real? And what exactly are they supposed to believe? If I say anything, it's like I'm crazy, because I didn't *see* it, see it. I saw it," I say. I wave my hands around my head.

"Listen," Victory says. "Have you seen his father? They have pictures of them entering our school. His pops is waving at the camera, and Ben is crouching his head like he's being arrested. It's like he's low-key ashamed, and you can tell that man is trying to teach him a lesson or change him, I guess."

"So it is obvious to everyone that he doesn't want to be here and poses a threat?" I ask. Victory shrugs and says she hopes so. "This all fucking sucks," I continue. It sucks to think of how Ben's future is just laid out for him to win, and how I am here struggling with whether or not to say something that can shift the trajectory of mine. "You know, Ben most likely hasn't seen the worst of life yet. And here we are trying to write essays around the most messed-up thing that has ever happened to us, to sell ourselves to the highest bidder when those college applications come around."

"Girl," Victory says, bringing her hand to her heart. "That hit here."

"Did you catch what happened?" I say, trying to change the topic.

"Girl, I'm just about done with the news. They've always been after us. But now it has to be a daily thing to see Black people die?"

"That part," I respond. It does get tiring, sickening to keep watching how many of us die, so, so young, and on top of it, how many times people are basically allowed to kill us—with no real repercussions. What does that do to us after a while? We normalize it. We get to a point where we see it happen so much, we just let it be.

9

WHEN DADS RETURN

Papi wore a bright orange jumpsuit the first time I saw him dressed in confidence. It was the day Mamá Teté took me to see him receive his Associate's. I still have the picture of him on my locker. Him smiling, his Black body swallowed by the orange as if it were the actual sun.

And now, through the restaurant front's window, I see him dressed in jeans and a long-sleeved black sweater. He looks neither lost, nor elevated by the sun. Through the foggy windows of the restaurant, he looks like any other man.

"Go on, I'll be home," Mamá Teté says. She winks at me through wet lashes. She picked me up early from school and brought me to El Malecon. As I watch her walk away towards the bus stop, my heart begins to bang inside my chest. El Malecon is Papi's favorite restaurant, even though it's basic as hell and basically a chain at this point. I wish Mamá Teté had stayed to be a buffer if anything gets weird, but I am also glad she left. When I visited Papi, we never had any privacy. Between my stepmother, my brothers, and Mamá, I had zero time to update him on what was going on for me outside of the prison walls he called home. It's why I started writing letters to him often.

I open the heavy glass door and the wet heat, coming off of all the food being kept warm behind the long counter, hits me. I take off my foggy glasses and put them in my jacket pocket. As I walk towards him, his face gets clearer. He is looking down at a phone. Scratching his head with one hand and touching the phone on the table with the other. Touch phones weren't as advanced as they were when he first went in, I imagine. He is older obviously, but as I watch him, I feel like he feels younger in some way. From here, he looks a lot stronger, a lot leaner now. I guess that's the part that makes him appear younger. I look at how hollow his cheeks are above his oily beard. It's strange because even though he looks refreshed, I can still tell he's lived an extra life in there. I can't help but cry.

"My girl," he says when he lifts his head to catch me wiping away my tears. He picks me up and swings me around. I am as light as a feather in my father's arms and for a few seconds, whatever has weighed me down these last few days is gone. I am a little kid again and he's just a dad, not a man who has spent the last six years locked up, not an imperfect person in my eyes yet. His body feels more muscular as he hugs me in, but his face looks like he's been through it. My father's wet mustache is spiky on my cheek. Anything could happen today, and it would all be fine. Papi is here, in this world where we get to exist together, like it was finally meant to be. Finally out of a place where I know they treated him like less than an animal.

He pulls out my chair, and I sit still looking at his face in disbelief. I reach for him after we sit and squeeze his big hand between my own. The few times I went to visit Papi, I was never allowed to hug him. Sometimes I grew the courage to reach out and squeeze his dry hands, but we were always caught and reprimanded—as if holding each other was wrong. Just the thought of that makes me cry more, uncontrollably, my breath nearly cut off. It goes on like this for what seems like forever. Every time I think I am coming up from the wave of tears, I smile and apologize.

"Don't be sorry, mi'ja," Papi rubs my back.

By the time I am able to breathe normally again, the muscles in my cheeks hurt from all of the smiling and crying. He uses his thumb to wipe my tears, and then he stares out the window.

☾

The streets are particularly loud today. The sirens and chatter that take over the Bronx after school swarm into the restaurant like fruit flies, annoying and impossible to get rid of.

The last time I saw him was six months ago. When he first went in, he told me he was going away for some time. I was ten, and my little brothers were five and three. He had been sent away before that as well, but never for years like this.

"You're an entire mujer already," he says. I am not a mujer; I am just a girl who has missed her father even though my limbs have extended, and my chest has exploded. I want to tell him this, but I don't want to scare him or make him think he's saying the wrong things. The truth is, I hate when grown-ups call growing girls mujerones, because it forces this sense of responsibility on us that I frankly don't want just yet. It also on some weird level sexualizes us. "I missed so much, haven't I?"

"It's OK. There's still a lot of time," I smile. "Plus, I'm not a mujeron yet, Papi. Even though I've been forced to grow up, I want to enjoy what's left of my childhood."

Papi grows a bit quiet at this. I swallow. A few pounds of marijuana in a car. That's what got Papi thrown in jail. What got him the full six years was that as a nineteen-year-old he had been arrested for "resisting arrest," for hopping the train. He was given a public defender who was not on his side. The second time it was for a physical altercation at a bar when he was twenty-five, and again he couldn't afford a lawyer. The third time, Papi borrowed a car to drive me to school. It was the week I had gotten my period, and I was refusing to go into school. The school had already called and said if I had more than eighteen absences during the year, my guardians could be mandated to go to court. I refused. Mamá Teté didn't know what to do with me, so she called him. He borrowed a fancy BMW that one of his friends at the dealership had just gotten. He was speeding and then the siren started getting louder and louder. When the cops pulled us over, Papi instructed me like he knew what to expect.

He said, "The cops are going to walk over. They probably won't treat me too nice. That's OK. I don't want you to cry, Yoyo. Ya 'ta'te tranquila. Don't speak to them. Wait for your mother or grandmother." They told him to put his hand on the steering wheel and not move. The tone of their voices made me feel like he was in trouble already. One of the cops said, "Don't worry, sweetheart." But it was like the words coming out his mouth didn't match the thing behind his eyes. They stayed on Papi as the cop's partner moved to the trunk. I felt like an entire rock was stuck in my throat. He came back with a few ziplocks in his hands and said, "Get out of the car." The one who had called me "sweetheart" told me to get out and sit on the curb. Papi looked back at me and nodded, not saying a single word. I remained tranquila like he asked me to. But when the cops threw Papi against the hood of the car, like he was a rag doll, I turned to fire. I got up from the curb and kicked one of the police officers. When he tried to grab me by my legs, I dug my nails deep into his face and let my nails run through his cheeks. He pushed me, and I fell on the curb on my lower back. By the time they got us both to the precinct, the officer's skin was underneath eight of my fingernails and my lower back was killing me.

"OK, girly, I won't call you a mujer. You got it," Papi says. "What did I do to deserve you, tesoro?"

The waitress comes by, and Papi doesn't check her out at all. I am low-key worried. Has Papi been switched? Maybe he just changed? He orders a morir soñando and chuleta frita with rice and beans.

I look up at her. Her name tag is Wendy. "I'll have pescado frito with tostones. Y un jugo de chinola, por favor." Wendy scribbles in her notepad and says our food will be ready soon.

"No mondongo?" Papi says, his eyes widening.

"I'm a pescatarian, Papi," I remind him. "I told you so in one of the letters." Wendy stands nearby still scribbling into her notepad.

He smiles. "Remind me again: how come?"

"I read this book. You would be surprised what this country does to the meat we eat!"

"That doesn't surprise me one bit. Of course they'd find other ways to kill us. Pero, I'm happy to die con una buena chuleta." He laughs and leans back, finally relaxed.

"Don't play about death, Pa," I playfully punch his arm. And then it hits me: he was basically kind of dead, out of sight for sure, for the last six years. "I don't know what I'd do without you." My eyes water.

"It's OK, mi'ja. I'm back for good." He leans back to me and holds my hand.

"What happens now?"

"Your Tío Kelvin held down the dealership. So, I am going back to that."

"Just that, Pa?" I say. Fuck, that sounded accusatory. I don't be thinking before I talk sometimes. He digs into his lower lip with his teeth. He folds his arms over the table and nods.

"Just that, Yoyo. I promise," he nods again. Shame is spread across his face, and I feel like an idiot for having double-checked. With recreational and medicinal marijuana being legal in so many states, it feels like Papi was completely arrested due to racism, discrimination, and bias. I don't want to add to that.

We talk about the family—my brothers and my stepmother. He says they're going to Dominican Republic for the summer, and I tense up thinking of having to share Mamá's home, our family home, with that woman. She's OK, but just not my favorite person to be around. I haven't seen my brothers in about two months. Usually I only see them when they come over to Mamá Teté's, but my stepmother has been bringing them around less and less. I feel uncomfortable until he tells me they'll be mostly staying with her side of the family, and he cannot go due to parole.

When I ask about his experience, he tells me things I know already from our letters, phone calls, and visits. That it was hell, but it also allowed him to get a few certifications under his belt. It was the only way to keep him from going crazy. He says losing your mind there is easier than staying alive. He reminds me that he made a lot of friends—people who are good, but just made a mistake. He wishes prison were more like a recovery center than punishment.

"I read a lot, believe it or not," he says proudly.

When the food arrives he asks, "How's school?" *Bruja Diosas, please do not allow my brain to be clouded up by this boy.* I take a deep breath. Ben still fogs up my head.

"Good. I'm still getting decent grades, you know? I have some really cool teachers this year. And others who I could do without, to be honest. But I'm not complaining," I laugh. Some people I know outside of Julia De Burgos hate their school, and I just don't feel that way.

"Yeah, I hear you. We didn't have teachers we could relate to when I was coming up," Papi says.

"Most kids, at least in most public schools, I think, still don't." Most of my teachers were white when I was growing up, too. It wasn't until middle school that I had an Indigenous Ecuadorian teacher. And even though we have a lot of teachers of color at my school now, we are a very small minority.

"That makes no damn sense," Papi says. He takes a sip of his water. "You would think in the most diverse city in the world, school would be diverse." Ben flashes into my head again.

I swallow some of my food. The fish is so well-seasoned and the tostones crisped to perfection. As I chew, joy overwhelms me. I take a mental photograph, tell myself to always hold this moment close to me. A good meal, Papi talking to me like I am a whole person. I feel like I can tell him anything.

"Papi, there's this new kid. He's white. The son of someone running for a congressional seat, un politico basically."

"¿Qué, qué?" he widens his eyes, as he cuts into his pork chops.

"Yeah, and he's not . . . OK." I think back to Ben's complicated anger towards me yesterday in class. "I guess. I really don't
know. I get this feeling he's really angry, and lonely, but also super
hurt. Does that make sense?" I shake my head. I don't wait for Papi
to answer, because maybe I'm asking my damn self? "Like we
were reading this graphic novel, and he kept low-key defending
the white characters, who were wrong, period. And the other day,
he disrespected my favorite teacher who is legit the nicest teacher
so many of us have ever had. I guess we just don't live the life he
lives, like he don't live the life we do. But he's rude, point blank."

"MHHHMMMM," he chews his chuleta.

"That good?" I ask.

"I missed our food," he says, and closes his eyes. I imagine his
taste buds exploding and exploring the sofrito—the bell peppers,
the onions, the cilantro. He squeezes a few lime wedges on the
rice and chuletas and smiles as he chews. Everything inside of me
feels good seeing my father enjoy his freedom. Life is really about
tiny, happy moments like this.

"I'm going to have to cook for you one day soon, Pa," I say,
chewing on a tostone. Papi nods happily.

"You know in there it's the same way I guess," he starts. "The
way students are separated, especially here in New York. Public
schools are mostly just for Black and Brown kids, and you walk
into a private school, you don't see a lot of us. Well, in there it's all
of us. But we stick to ourselves, you know? The white ones in
there, got an inflated ego too, and sometimes they do make it
dangerous in there for someone like me who didn't want to be
involved in any more trouble and have my sentence extended.
Even when they might be in there for doing the same things as us,
and in many cases worse, they somehow look down on us and

make sure we know it too." He bites into the bone of the chuleta as if there can't be even a tiny piece left uneaten. I decide not to say much after that. I let him eat until the only sound left is that of the fork, trying to scoop all there had been off of the plate.

He takes a deep breath when he's done and he leans back in his chair.

"It's important to trust your intuition though," Papi says. Before I can say more about Ben, how he feels like a threat, he continues, "Pero enough of that mierda. Sometimes we have to talk about these things because they're obvious, and we aren't crazy for having our suspicions, my love. Yet, we have to step out of that sometimes y hacerse el loco because it'll rob you of inner strength, and get you to be just as miserable as a lot of them, too." He pats his stomach, and I nod profusely, 'cause he's right.

"Any love interests yet?" he asks. The question sounds so odd coming from him. He has a smirk on, but all I see is his dark gaze, hoping his inkling is wrong.

"I have none," I say, sipping my chinola juice.

"You can talk to me, Yoyo. Come on, you're sixteen. You are not fooling me!"

"Well, he's not like my boyfriend, boyfriend," I say, my palms sweating.

"Why is he even coming up then?"

"Papi, you asked," I blush. "His name is José. We aren't together, but I can tell he likes me."

"And you like him?!" He slaps his thigh in laughter.

"I guess."

"Is he respectful?"

"Yeah, he is. But I'm kind of not trusting of men too much, you know?" I shrug.

"Yeah, I wouldn't trust us blindly either if I were you." He looks down on his hands.

"Are you back living with Norah?" I ask. She's Mami's archenemy, my stepmother, and my little brothers' mother. Mami and her hate each other because once upon a time when I was being created in Mami's womb, Norah was the other woman, and she stuck, clearly. Mami threw Papi out after my vision, of course, even though he didn't want to go.

"Yeah," he nods.

"Are you happy to be back with her?" I ask. He looks up at me with a question, but undeniable sorrow. And I wonder after everything he's been through, if it'll ever truly be any other way.

"Sure, mi'ja. We've had happy moments," he replies, and wipes his mouth with a napkin. Mamá sometimes tells me, he never wanted to let go of Mami. "Pero quien lo manda, ese buen idiota," she always adds.

"Do you regret stepping out on Mami the way you did?" I continue. I sit up. I'm older now. I can ask the questions I've kind of always had. I want him to know I am not a chamaquita anymore. That I am well-aware of the repercussions of his actions.

"I do. I did. I guess I still do." He wipes the crumbs off the table. "That's just the way it was for men though. My dad, my grandfather, my great-grandfather—all had multiple women and secret families." He takes a deep breath. "I think it kind of pumps up our egos. Like we feel better about ourselves? Insecurity most likely," he shakes his head. "It's never an excuse though, Morena."

"¿Les puedo brindar algo más?" the waitress asks. I order a flan, and papi orders a coffee. I wait for him to say something about sweets when the waitress leaves, but he says nothing. I guess today is special. I ain't complaining.

"When I found out you were a girl, Yoyo, I thought I had been cursed. Mami was so happy, she said Culebra had blessed her. But I felt for a while that I would fail you, whether I became the best man individually or not. I didn't get rid of that feeling until I went in and you started writing me those letters. I noticed that I had been blessed. I don't get to save you or teach you how to avoid men similar to the men I have been. You're your own person, and it'll never be your job to change me or anyone else, especially no man. But you taught me so much with your letters."

My eyes grow hot as they fill with tears. My eyelids tremble as I try hard not to blink and control the tears. "Come here," Papi says, standing up from his chair and kneeling next to where I'm sitting.

I throw my arms around him and bring my face to his shoulders. He hugs me back tightly. He smells like dried skin and Irish Spring soap. I cry into the collar of his black sweater.

It hurt when they took him from us. It did hurt when they took him from me. It always hurts.

☾

Mistolin and coffee hit us in the face when I open the door to Mamá Teté's apartment. A scent I have come to connect with renewal. I can tell she's full of all the energy in the world when Papi announces he's come to drop me off. She basically glides down the small hallway and into the kitchen, telling him she's prepared coffee even when he tells her he just had some.

"Siéntate, siéntate," she shoos him away from the kitchen to the living room.

"Let me read your cards, Pa," I say, when he plops down next to me.

"Mami got you on it?"

"Spirit has her on it!" Mamá yells from the kitchen.

"Nah, mi'ja," he says. "I have always been into the element of surprise, you know?"

"What he means is he likes to live reckless!" Mamá yells again. He throws his head back with a little chuckle.

"I am still surprised by what I am shown," I try to argue.

"Saint picked you yet?" he changes the subject.

"Not yet. But I do think I'm in the process," I shrug. He smiles and plays with one of my curls. I want to tell him I'm almost certain I am about to be picked: the signs are all there. But I want to stay humble and not jinx it.

"You look just like me. It's so awkward to look at the female version of yourself." I laugh at his words. Everyone says I look like Mamá, but he resembles her a whole lot, too.

My phone buzzes. *Hi Yo, my sister got some tickets to catch Haunted Road downtown any day this weekend, but they called her in for work. You down to go with me? I know it's last minute.* José is really, really trying. My face gets hot.

"Who is that?" Papi says, fake leaning towards my phone. I crowd it away from him.

"Nadie!" I smile.

"Yeah right, that must be José, huh?"

"Shushhhh!" I say, "I haven't told Mamá."

"Oh she knows," he laughs. Mamá Teté comes out with a gold tray of coffee and brown sugar. She sits next to Papi and runs her hand down his knee as he pours his coffee. When he's distracted pouring milk, she runs her index finger below her eyes. She notices me watching her and rubs his back, then begins to cry.

"Mami, it's OK," Papi says, putting the coffee down.

"Oh, I know," she says. "I'm just happy you're home, Nelson. Estas son lagrimas de alegría."

I'm down, I text José back. "Mamá, I'm going to go to the movies," I say. I stand up, deciding to give them some time alone.

Mamá looks at me all crazy. "We have another reading, Yolanda." When we attended to the reading I missed, Mamá Teté watched me closer than ever. I hope this time she trusts me more.

"Now?" I ask.

"As soon as your father drinks his coffee and goes home to his wife," Mamá says. And now she's looking at Papi all crazy. I guess he's avoiding Norah, which makes sense to me honestly.

"Who are we reading?"

"Maria from the twelfth floor, her cousin," Mamá Teté says.

"OK, can I go tomorrow?" I ask. She nods reluctantly. *I can do tomorrow*, I text, hating to have sent two texts back-to-back.

As soon as Papi leaves, Mamá starts setting up the table.

"What are we reading her with?" I ask Mamá. Mamá either does the coffee or the white candle and glass of water technique. Sometimes when Culebra mounts her, she doesn't bother with techniques and gets straight to the readings, but that usually only happens during misas or days surrounding them.

"You choose," Mamá Teté responds. She winks at me, and I am hyped! She is going to let me do my thing with this one. Since my vision and coffee reading, Mamá Teté and I haven't felt this tight. At the beginning of my reading training, she used to just have me watch. But the more precise I got, the more she would let me do for a client. I clean my hands, pat agua florida on my shoulders and neck, and place an unlit white candle on the table. Mamá Teté nods. A knock on the door tells us our client has arrived. I hear Maria introduce Mamá and the client, Marte, to each other.

"This is my granddaughter and apprentice, Yolanda," Mamá introduces me to Marte. She's wearing her hair in a tight bun, highlighting her brown eyes and the deep bags under them.

I greet Maria and Marte and move them towards the living room. Marte removes their brown wool coat and folds it over their lap.

"Bueno," Marte begins speaking. But Mamá raises her hand.

"I don't like hearing too much before the reading begins, because they'll tell me what I need to know. Your spirit guides seem a little quiet though, so if we need your help, I'll ask."

"Can you please take this glass cup and fill it up to wherever you feel and bring it back to me?" I ask. Marte gets up and steps into the kitchen. The scent of deep earth arrives under my nose. Mamá looks at me curiously. "Something about earth?" I whisper to her.

When Marte comes back, the water settles to the middle of the glass.

"What is it you want to know today?" I ask Marte. Marte looks at Mamá Teté, who nods.

"There is some land back home, in Honduras. My father left it to me, and I don't know what to do with it. If I try to keep it, my brothers will make my life a living hell because they wanted it for themselves, but if I sell it, I feel as if I am letting go of something he worked so hard for." I turn on the white candle carefully and say my usual prayer under my breath. We watch as a spark flies off of the wick.

"Good news," Mamá Teté smiles at Marte. I continue watching the fire.

The flame grows quickly and tall.

She will not fail either way she decides to go. If she sells it, she will have some money now, and that's good. But the land has a lot of life to it, and keeping it will make her ancestors happy and her descendants will create even more fortune from it. The land promises to always provide, the Fire tells me.

I tell her what I see, and Mamá Teté pats my knee in approval. The pride in my chest grows.

The fire starts wavering. I look at the windows all closed. The flame starts dancing in a spiral violently. I pull back and so does Marte.

"¡Ay, Dios mio!" Maria shrieks. With her pointer and middle finger she taps on her forehead, chest, and shoulders. The holy cross. That's the thing about traditions from the people I come from: they are always tied to an organized religion to cover our bases.

And now I talk to you, the Fire says, *danger is coming.*

The fire crackles and sparks and continues dancing in circles. Mamá Teté stands up and ushers Maria and Marte to the door. She asks Marte to come back tomorrow and she will deliver another reading for free. As soon as they're gone, Mamá rushes back into the living room.

"Yolanda Nuelis," she cries. "Please tell me what's going on."

"The fire is talking to me." I feel the heat on my face as I look over at her. I take a deep breath, then continue:

"Something is going on with this boy at school. It's related to the vision I had. It feels serious." I bring my hands between my knees. "I don't know though. I feel like if I say something, no one will believe me." For years, Mamá Teté has been training me, so that when one of the Unknowns chooses me, I am strong, solid, and sufficiently ready to have such force on my side. She reminds me that every dream is a message from our subconscious to advise or warn, every feeling attached to a part of our lowest level of identity, and while feelings don't have to be totally ignored, they shouldn't be truly given into either. But there is a space in the gut connected to the Universe, the Unknowns, and the Gods—and that, she says, that must be paid attention to. Intuition.

Mamá Teté sits down next to me. Her red lip quivers. "Why are you doubting yourself, mi'ja?" The way disappointment leaks out of her voice punches my chest. I don't want to disappoint Mamá. The orbits around the flame circle and circle and circle as if making sure we don't avoid what it is telling us. "Remember what we've been training for," she puts her hand over mine. "You have to listen to yourself, to your Bruja Diosas."

"But are these just my feelings, which we know aren't always right, or is this *really* them, Mamá?"

I bring my head down to my hands and lap. I want to tell Mamá Teté, she is the only person who I can speak to about this, and still I do not know what to say because there is a knot in my chest. What if I share my full vision of this boy, and the way it kind of terrifies me, and she does the most and tells on him, and I'm not right at all? I'm tired of all the crying today, but this is too much. This wasn't even my reading. Mamá Teté blows out the fire.

"Why don't you take a step back, my love? Stop processing the external world for a bit. Feelings usually feed off of whatever is going on on the outside, but what's going on in here?" Mamá touches the space between my chest. "You don't have to carry this alone. You and I are an entire community because we are here together. Please share whatever it is with me, Yoyo," she rubs my back.

I pick up my head, look into her eyes, feel the burning in the pit of my stomach, and tell her everything.

"Well," Mamá Teté begins, "you continue to observe him, and I'll do my own thing, or at least as much as the Unknowns will allow me." She reaches a hand towards my face and runs it up and down my cheek. "I used to be a lot like you when I was your age, mi'ja. I thought, if I have this much help from all that is good and greater than me, then I can change the world, change people." There are tears in Mamá's eyes. "But we aren't saviors, and we don't always have to be the ones carrying the weight of other people's darkness." Mamá takes a napkin from the table and daps her eyes. "You may watch him to stay alert, like anybody else, but you don't even pretend to try and save him, oíste? That's on him, not on you."

I open my mouth to tell Mamá Teté that I am not really trying to do it for him, that it's for my friends and me, for Julia De Burgos High, but Mamá raises her finger.

"Above all, you cannot tell authorities how you see, Yolanda Nuelis," she says. "¿Tú me eta entiendo?"

"Sí, Mamá." I nod.

10

MORE TRUTH TO THE FIRE

New York City falls are basically winters, to be honest. The cold will pierce the pores of your face with its freezing temperatures and burn you for no good reason—all at the same damn time. I run up the stairs and exit the 59th Street Columbus Circle Station. I hate that Christopher Columbus continues to be celebrated anywhere, but mostly on this side of the world. All that white man really did was normalize colonization and the enslavement and abuse of all of our ancestors. I shake my head looking away from it. Imagine a protest in New York City that ended here, with the pulling down of this dumb ass statue. It's giving glorious revolution, and I laugh walking up to 67th Street.

I walk by the long lines and look over at the screens which announce in neon lights that all shows are sold out. I go in my pocket for the lip gloss I picked up at the beauty supply on the corner of the train station before I got on. I run the brush on my thick lips and smack them together to finish off. Placing it back in my pocket, I'm grateful José got these tickets in advance. I bring my hat lower on my forehead and crouch behind the collar of my North Face. My poor nose feels like it no longer belongs to my face due to these temperatures. Anticipation pumps through my body. This is our first official date, date, and I want to enjoy it. Plus, since I told Mamá Teté about the vision, after our last reading, something in my chest feels lighter.

A gloved hand touches my nose, and I look over to see José grinning at me.

"You look like a bundled burrito," he laughs.

"You look like a Slim Jim with a coat on," I bring out my lips to say.

"Oh, you got jokes now?"

"I got jokes!"

"Well, your momma is . . ." he smiles, "majestic because she made you." He leans into me and kisses me.

"Alright, imma let go of how corny that was," I laugh into his mouth. Our lips make so much warmth in just a few seconds.

When we get upstairs, a manager reminds us our show doesn't start for another thirty minutes and they won't let us in for another fifteen. I watch José as he takes off his hoodie, hat, and gloves. His caramel skin is red at the surface. He leans on the wall and brings me close, and my entire body electrifies. My lips shake as I force my poker face to be in full effect, but in reality I just want to smile. So, I do. I let myself smile and he kisses my forehead.

"I'm happy we're here," he says. And even though I want to ask if he means like here in the movies, or here in terms of the fact that I am finally letting him in, I just want to enjoy this moment. I've never been this involved with someone. Never really felt like this. Never leaned on someone's body like they could handle the pressure of my body.

"You want something from the stand?" he whispers into my neck. He burrows his nose there for warmth.

"Sure," I pull back, and kiss him. "Peanut M&M's and something warm."

"I think they have teas," he says, looking over me to the stands.

"That's perfect."

I take out my phone and text Victory. *Ahhhhhhhhhhh,* I send her, and an emoji with the heart eyes. I texted her on my way to the theater about my dad and my last-minute date with José.

My parents would call you sprung, she replies. I smile because I'm not even ashamed to say it isn't so. I feel all warm inside.

I know, I reply. *Also, guess what?*

Victory sends the eye emoji.

I told Mamá about the vision.

I love to see it! Proud of you, Yoyo, she replies.

"Yolanda?" I hear a familiar voice. I look up. *Oh no.* He rubs his hands together and blows into them. He has three friends behind him. Two who are white and definitely twins. And then there's a Brown kid with slick black hair.

"Hey Ben," I say.

"You catching *Haunted Road* tonight?" he asks, gesturing towards a poster of the movie. One of the twins examines me; the other boys stand behind him like they can't just go make the line, or at least bother to introduce themselves, so instead they just stare too. The twins' wool jackets, the Burberry pattern displayed on the cuffs. All of a sudden, I feel wack in my puffy bubble coat. But whatever, that's just a thought—not who I really am. I know that.

"Yeah, are you guys here to see it too?"

"Yeah," Ben says. The boys in the back don't answer, even though I am clearly also addressing them. "If you're here alone, you're more than welcome to sit with us." Ben is beaming at the opportunity. He looks soft again, not like the kid who was problematic, but tender instead.

"Oh thanks for the invite, but no—I'm actually just waiting for José to get back with some sna—"

"Oh." Ben wavers between a smirk and a sneer. "OK, well I'll see you around. Enjoy the movie."

"You too," I say. He turns his back to me.

"You were just REJECTED!" I hear the Brown boy say, his voice filled with an Indian accent. Ben punches his arm lightly as the other boys struggle not to laugh. A feeling, like a stone, settles between my throat and my stomach. The smell of crackling popcorn feels too thick now under my nose. I turn around and face forward.

"Hey," I hear from behind me. Ben is approaching me again. "I want to apologize for being off at school again."

"You don't have to just apologize to *me*," I say.

"I know," he smiles, looking at my brown faux leather combat boots. "I had a restorative with Mrs. Obi and Ms. Steinberg after school. I apologized to Mrs. Obi. But I am apologizing to you because you were trying to reach me, and I was being a total dick, so again I'm sorry." He looks up at me now.

"I mean all right," I shrug, my hands still in my pocket. He smiles again and shuffles back to his place in the line.

OK? He apologized. It's hard for some people to apologize. So, he's trying, I guess. Everything is fine. It's going to be great, I tell myself.

"I hope lavender tea is good. They had that and Lipton. Lavender sounded fancier."

I smile at José as he comes up and take the cup, which warms my hands instantly. He holds on to the M&M's.

"Ben is here," I say, taking a sip from my cup. He looks around, spots him, and raises his chin when they lock eyes.

"Here we go," he mumbles.

"It's not like we're sitting together, so it'll be fine." I look towards where Ben is as I brush the back of José's hand with mine. His skin is so soft, and I feel a slight tightening of my stomach.

"Out of all the theaters in this entire city, what are the chances we go to the same one?" He ignores me as we wait for the movie to open. "I know you're trying to give him a chance or whatever, but he's odd, Yoyo. I'm telling you. He just don't feel right." José goes into his pocket and brings out his phone. I'm not being nosy or anything, but he opens up a text from "COACH" with a basketball emoji right next to it. He quickly reads it and puts the phone back into his pocket without responding, then stretches his neck and looks in Ben's direction again.

"Is everything OK?"

"Yeah, apparently this basketball league that was giving me the option to leave high school two years ago. They were gonna give me like a hundred grand every year to play for them. I said no, I'll play for an actual college team, not for some league. What if I get injured? What if I just don't want to play anymore at some point?" He takes a deep breath. "They're still interested. Hitting up Coach nonstop. I'm not doing it though. If I go to college, at least I get me a degree out of everything."

I nod. "That sounds tough though. A hundred grand a year? Not everyone makes that type of money out here."

He raises an eyebrow, pursing his lips, and shaking his head in agreement. He tilts his head to look over at Ben again. "Man," he says.

A pressure arrives over my head, and it settles as if gravity wants to demolish my skull. The milkiness I experienced in Mr. Ruiz's class comes over my eyes. I rub my eyes and open them, only to be met with the same clouded view.

Fuck. Not here. Not right now. Bruja Diosas, all that guide, love, and protect me, I ask that you give me a moment.

I close my eyes. There are black, white, and red waves swirling in my head and blurring what's in front of me. I am so hot I take off my coat, swinging it between my thighs, and twirling my curly ponytail up into a bun. I fan my neck with my hand.

"Yo, you OK?" I hear José. An image starts constructing itself in my head. With my hand, I try to fan myself and whoosh away what I know is coming. I drink some of the lavender tea. It lands like acid in the pit of my stomach.

"Are you OK?" I hear José say from a distant place.

"I'm going to the bathroom," I say. As I speed into the restroom, I feel how much I hate keeping secrets. That I have to twist the truth in order to keep who I truly am away from him. Fuck, I hope he doesn't think I am out of my mind or just being recklessly dramatic. Pushing open a stall door and quickly closing it behind me, I swallow and shut my eyes. The vision takes over my mind.

Ben is crouching over his backpack on the corner of a staircase. The colors swirling around his head are vibrantly enraged. I step over to him as he zips up the backpack and looks up, but through me. Hello, I wave my hands in front of him, but he cannot see me. I reach for his hands. They are moist, heavy, and sweaty. But they quickly fall right through my own when he balls up his fists, the grip deliberate. I place my hand at his back, the back of his heart. His heartbeat is accelerated as if he has just run miles and miles without stopping for a breath. I begin to hum a quick prayer, but I am zapped away, like when I touch the fridge handle with my hands still wet.

I open my eyes, exit the stall, and wash my hands. As I lather them in soap, they feel heavy and like they aren't my own. I meet my eyes in my reflection and bring down my head to throw some water on my face. I am exhausted. The meat on my bones is heavy. I look at my forearm. All the little hairs on my dark brown skin are standing straight up. I hug myself as the fear of the vision creeps up the back of my ears. Someone pushes in a door loudly, and the bang wakes me up fully. I exit the bathroom and rush towards the line José was in. He's not there, and suddenly I feel alone. I fumble as I get my phone from my pocket.

I'm towards the middle row, my phone vibrates. *The movie is about to start,* José texts again. Relief settles and I open the door to the dark auditorium.

When I finally reach José, I feel some kind of peace, like I'm closer to my body and not stuck in a world that takes me into the past and the future. José lifts the armrest and lifts his arm, making space for me. I cuddle up under his arm. He smells like a place I'm safe in, especially after the vision. He laughs loudly at the previews and my heart gathers itself. He looks down and kisses me. "Yoyo," he whispers into my lips, "you're sweating."

I reach up and touch the cold sweat on my forehead. "I'm fine. I got it." I bring a couple of napkins to my forehead. What was Ben protecting in that backpack? Why was he so nervous? Technically, I didn't see anything . . . so there's no reason to trip, right? I close my eyes briefly, allowing the thing inside me that never fails me. I open my eyes. Come on, Yoyo, be real with yourself, you know what it is. My heart is beating so loud in my ear, I can follow along its beats. He's trouble. Should I tell someone? As I begin to settle, my lower stomach begins to cramp up, a pain shooting to my back. I bring my hands to my hips and stretch a little bit, settling again into the crook of José's arm.

I want to tell José everything. Would he like me less if he knew that I have visions, that my Bruja Diosas talk to me? Would he think I am similar but different from the witch he saw on top of the roof in DR?

"You sure?" he whispers.

I nod and turn to the big screen.

☾

Mamá Teté is waiting on the couch in her purple bata when I come in. Her hair is covered by a yellow satin bonnet. I take off my shoes and coat at the door and walk into the living room.

"It happened again," I say, plopping down on the side of the couch next to her. "Another vision. The boy is angry. He was crouching," I try to paint a picture with my hands as I talk. "Crouching over a backpack. He was so, so, so protective of it, Mamá. I couldn't even see into the bag. But he was fuming. What could he have in there?"

Mamá nods, placing her hand on my knee.

"I tried to help him," I say.

Mamá Teté sucks her teeth. "Yolanda, te dije you cannot save the boy."

"I just put my hand over his back and started a prayer, but I was pushed out," I say, looking Mamá in the eye. "And he keeps being super rude, but then he apologizes to me and seems as if he's actually sorry. It's confusing."

"What do I always tell you about apologies?" Mamá asks.

"An apology without changed behavior is not an apology at all," I chant. And then smile, feeling silly I haven't remembered.

"Give it a little time. I wish I could do more, but they won't let me. Don't doubt that you're being guided, mi'ja, even if what you're seeing gives you un chin de miedo," she says. I nod and look at the novela on TV. A white woman is yelling at her Indigenous housekeeper.

"And what am I supposed to do with that, Mamá?" I focus.

Mamá looks down at her chestnut-colored hands. The soft wrinkles of them remind me of how much she's been through. I look up at the wisdom of my grandmother against the navy-blue background of the sky behind her.

"I went to the Unknowns on your behalf. I tried to take on whatever it is you have to do, but they won't let me. That means one thing: this really is your initiation."

Mamá takes a breath, and her nostrils flare.

My heart plummets to the bottom of my stomach, plummets to the soles of my feet, and then rises. Pacing itself, pushing the weight of all my blood to reach the spaces above me. Then it floats back into my body and settles into the place it calls home in my chest.

"Consider this another level of your dreams. It seems the Unknowns might be upgrading your gift to see. You've been having such vivid dreams as a child," Mamá suggests.

I feel helpless. Yes, I dream vividly. The dreams are usually a warning or an offering, and that's great and all, but if I can't do anything to help in my waking life, then what are they for at all? No, no, I am blessed to have these gifts, this ability.

Mamá puts a hand on my knee, and I take a deep breath and shut my eyes. *Bruja Diosas, come through.* I bring all my focus to the fear settled between my throat and stomach. I reach into the bottom of my intuition. *How real is this feeling?* The tips of my fingers and the tips of my toes begin to feel a rush of static, and something that feels like a light forms and wraps itself around me from head to toe. *A protection.*

I sigh. I pray that the Bruja Diosas help Ben, that his family or whatever authority he listens to aids him. Because if they don't, I am afraid I will go against Mamá Teté—I will try to change the course of my visions.

11

BLACK BONDS

Victory's house is like a mini gallery of Black art. The biggest piece stands on the opposite side of the wall when you walk in: a woman, her afro reaching the heavens as she opens her arms towards the sky.

The living room is open and airy, except I've looked behind the couches and there are large plastic bins holding documents and photographs. Victory's mother saves everything, like her own mother. She says we must be our own historians, we must document our own lives. For such a big chunk of history, those in power have been including what they want to, excluding what they don't want the world to see. So, she always preaches about how we have to begin doing the archiving of our own lives, to pass down to future generations.

"Hi Yolanda!" Victory's mother, Pearl, says. She gets up from a small desk with an Apple desktop where she sits. She holds me close. "Girl, I haven't seen you around here in a while. How are your elders?"

"Mamá is doing well. You know nothing ever brings her

down," I laugh, thinking of Mamá. "My mother is writing papers and all that trying to get her Bachelor's."

"Bless her. Yolanda, going back to school ain't easy. That is very brave of your mother, you know?"

"Yeah," I whisper, "and my dad, he's back." I look at Victory with relief.

"When?" Pearl asks, squinting at Victory, who obviously hasn't shared.

"I was gonna tell you right now," Victory says.

"Well, now Yolanda can tell all of us. Dinner's ready," Victory's dad, Valentine, announces, throwing a dishrag over his shoulder. Recently he's let go of his hair, so now he's bald, and I'm still getting used to it if I'm being real. He gives me a hug before he and Victory disappear into the kitchen.

"Help me set out these utensils, Yoyo," Pearl says. I carefully place a spoon, a fork, a knife, a butter knife, and a small dessert spoon down. We never really eat this way at home. We usually eat whenever we have to, but in Victory's house, it has always been a thing. On the weekends, breakfast is also together—togetherness is a requirement to success, Valentine claims. And while my family and I bond in other ways, I try to enjoy this coming together whenever I can.

"Yolanda, why don't you say grace tonight?" Pearl says once everyone sits. I nod.

"Unknowns, Great Mother, Father Sky, Loving Ancestors, Santos, Orishas, Lwas, Guardian Angels, Universe, and all that guides, loves, and protect us in our Divine Purpose, thank you for the food we are about to enjoy and bless the hands that prepared them. Please protect our people. Please protect our spirits. Please hold us and never let go."

"And bless the person who shopped for groceries this week," Pearl says. We laugh.

"Ase," everyone says.

"So Yolanda, say more about your father being back," Valentine says, getting up to serve us. Oven-baked chicken and potatoes. Even though I've been a pescatarian for years, they always seem to forget. I decide to just eat the chicken. I am sure they got their hands on the best there is, and Mamá would call me a malagradecida if I turned down anyone's offering. It smells amazing. The herbs, dill and rosemary, flirt with my senses.

I tell them that my father came out a week ago and that we've been spending a lot of time together. They ask lots of questions: how is he doing, and how is he accommodating back to life. I explain that he seems happier than the last time I visited, obviously. I can't tell them much about how he is accommodating to life 'cause I truly don't know—it's only been a week. But what I do share is that he is ready to take this chance seriously.

"Ase!" Pearl and Valentine say. Then Pearl looks at me.

"The Devil creates spaces within us to poison our minds," she looks at me. "Your father, child, he's going to need all the love he can get." I nod and Victory asks how it feels to have my dad back. I can't lie to this family at all, because I feel like exposing my wounds here leads to feeling better.

"It feels a little different. He's now back to checking up on me regularly, so it's weird to have another adult to explain things to. But I'll get used to it. I know I will. I feel stronger now that he is back, so that's what matters, right?" I say. The urge to cry hits me, but I stop chewing and take a deep breath.

Valentine stretches his arm and puts his hand over mine. "Take your time," he reminds me.

When we're all done eating, Pearl and Valentine clean up the table, and Victory and I start on the washing of dishes. She washes and I dry.

It takes us at least half an hour to finish. When we do, we go to her room. The walls are white but covered with framed posters that have been passed down to her. My favorite is one that says "Make Love, Not War" in a curvy font against a yellow backdrop. At the bottom in bold letters it states, "We, The People, Oppose the War in Vietnam." Her grandmother gave those to her. There are others like the one announcing a free breakfast for children courtesy of the Black Panthers. The one above Victory's bed is The Fugees album cover, which she got from her father. Apparently, it was the first concert he went to as a young kid with his mother. Victory's bed set is a very light-white and gray cheetah print with a thin yellow trim. She has a white desk in a corner that also serves as her vanity space.

"How was the movie theater date? Tell me everything," she asks as I sit on the love seat by her bed. We haven't been able to catch up at school because I've been doing a lot of work with Mrs. Obi on Brave Space, and during the days I am not, Victory has been going over whatever they go over at the graphic designing club. When I get home, I've been trying to hop on the phone with her, but Mamá has been working me with the readings.

"We was basically making out the entire time on the train," I say. I cannot help but blush when I think about it. Whenever we took a break, I'd look around and most people were either minding their business, because it's New York City, or looking at us with a level of tenderness—but there were others who were straight up appalled.

"Also, it's starting to feel normal to be around him, you know?"

"So now y'all a couple, couple?" she asks.

"I don't know, neither of us has said or asked," I laugh. "But girl, he brings out all of these sensations in my body. Sometimes I forget to breathe when he looks at me. He opens his arms to me as if I were this puzzle piece he's been looking for for some time, and it just makes me feel BIG."

"Damn, girl. That's HELLA deep," she smiles. I wish all I had to talk to her was about José. What I do know is I have to tell her about my second vision.

"Ben was at the theater with some of his friends," I say.

"Of course he was. You and José just couldn't have one little uninterrupted date." She shakes her head. "What they look like, his friends?"

"Meh," I shrug. "One of them was Brown, so there's that," I say, low-key hoping that means something. We look at each other suspiciously, knowing it's not, and cackle.

"I had another vision," I blurt out. She looks at me crazy through the mirror. "On the date," I clear my throat, "before I went into the theater." I don't tell her the pressure it came with.

"He was crouching over his backpack," I start. "He's protective as hell over it, but I couldn't see into the bag."

Her eyes widen. "And where was he?"

"I think he was in the back staircase at school."

"Was it a weapon, Yoyo?" Victory asks.

I come from a place where anything can be turned into a weapon—a soda can, a toothbrush, a pencil. Victory presses her lips and looks at me.

"I said I couldn't see into the bag," I respond. I look out at the window behind Victory; the sun is sitting in the in-between of the sky. The oranges, reds, and yellows opaque the blue sky and make it appear like it's nothing, white. "I am certain it was a weapon though, yes. I can feel it," I say, "right here," bringing my fingers into a spot underneath my belly button.

"You scared?" She rubs her palms against her knees.

"A little, yeah, I mean. He was angry and high-key looked mad sus," I say. "You think it's tied to the first vision, right?"

"Of course it's tied to the first vision." She turns around. I bite into the cuticles on my middle finger. "Are you going to tell an adult at school, Yoyo?"

I shrug. I want to, but still it always comes back to: what evidence can I provide? Isn't that how everything works in this world? Evidence, evidence, evidence. Innocent until proven guilty. I get it and also it's stupid. People do messed-up things all the time, and there are no cameras rolling or any witnesses, except the person they're hurting. Sometimes people can't provide the evidence and it's like the thing that happened to them, never happened at all. What evidence can I possibly provide for knowing what I know about Ben, his past, and his future?

"You keep giving him grace," Victory rolls her eyes. "Why do you keep trying to give him the benefit of the doubt for?"

"It's not the benefit of the doubt. I am clear—he is bad news and he's going to do some fucked-up shit, Vic. I know that. I just don't want him to"—I wave my hands in the air—"do something stupid. Julia De Burgos feels like all we got sometimes. I have to find a way to make people believe me, and whoever I tell at school is going to ask for some sort of proof, and I have to be ready for that, you know? In the meantime, we have to keep him"—I run my flat hands in opposite directions—"calm."

Victory rolls her eyes and throws herself onto her bed. "It

feels like you care about him more than you care about yourself or us, tbh."

"WHAT!?" I stand over her in disbelief. I just explained myself. All the blood in my body rushes to my head, and it feels like my chest is about to pop.

"Girl, why are you surprised at me saying that?" She stands up irritated. "He's been super rude to you. And the other day, you saw how he treated me in the meeting—and you didn't even say anything in the moment."

I take a deep breath. "I'm sorry. I tried to apologize," I say, my voice still angry.

Victory brings up her hand and paces her room. "Then you saw him being dumb rude to Mrs. Obi. And you keep having these visions, but you ain't alarmed enough to do anything about it." Victory comes over and speaks close to my face, not moving her eyes off of mine. "When you finna tell someone, Yolanda?"

"I told you I told Mamá Teté and she said not to say anything to people in power who legit just won't understand."

"And did she say anything else?" Victory crosses her arms.

"She's doing her own work for it. But ultimately this is my own initiation, the visions. There's very little the Unknowns will let her do for me."

"So ya not finna tell no one *at school* or, I don't know, his dad?"

"Girl, what you mean—what am I really supposed to really say? That I have visions? Come on now. Please explain who you think will believe me off of that." I roll my eyes. I don't get why it's so hard for her to understand this. "So that's why I'm trying to find a way to get him to stop being so angry, at least until I have proof, Victory."

She rolls her eyes, walks away from me, but then turns and walks back. Putting her palm in mine, she sits and I do too. "You know fixing the world isn't on you, right?"

"I don't think I'm a hero or something—" I start.

"I've known you for way too long for you to lie to me, Yoyo. You are always trying to fix something or someone like it's your job to. It ain't your job," Victory says, standing up once again.

I take a deep breath as she continues talking.

"What you think you're T'Challa or some shit?" The anger somersaults and leaps out from my head and takes over my entire body. "I promise your silence ain't about to protect Julia De Burgos, or should I say Wakanda?"

I turn from her, close my eyes, take a deep breath to bring myself together. OK, Yolanda, you know she's just being extra, it's just a joke on her end. But no, she's really out here pushing it.

All the things I've ever tried to fix come like waves around my head. One: when Mami kicked Papi out after I woke up from the dream, after he established his relationship with Norah, I tried to fix my parents' relationship. Felt their comeback was on me. Two: when Mami has had her breakups and hits rock bottom, feeling like she isn't enough, I always go out of my way to cheer her up and get her back into dating again (even when I roll my eyes at it later). Three: when Mamá Teté misses my grandfather, the one I never met, so much she can hardly get out of bed, I'm the one that gets her up, reminds her who she is. Four: anytime Victory needs me, I am all in, ready to go to war to make sure she's all right. I don't think I'm a hero or any of that. I just care. I care a lot.

My brain comes back into the room as Victory starts again. "Now, I know for a fact you think you can fix Ben and his obvious problematic ass behaviors, but you can't and you have to be OK with that." I feel the adrenaline pumping to my veins, my knees beginning to shake. The anger in my body is now rage, and it rises to my throat. My ears are burning and ringing, and for a minute I swear I'm bleeding out my nose. I swallow. Still the rage pushes to be let out.

"You don't know everything about me," I say, smacking my hands against one another. "We can't tell anyone at school because no one will believe me without concrete evidence, Victory. I don't know how many times I gotta keep repeating myself. Don't you know what they've done with people like me for centuries? Burned us at the stake, hunted us, created a spiderweb of taboos to make it so that people think we are evil, point blank, period. My visions are not understood in schools or anywhere else for that matter. You might take me serious, you might believe in me and Mamá's tradition, but most people don't. You act like I'm the pope when I'm just a"—I lower my voice—"a witch. I'm only just a bruja. And not some New Age white witch, or a person throwing cards on a table and calling it self-care on Tik-Tok, I am a Black girl witch who sees things, and even in our own spaces, you see how people get the minute you mention any part of our beliefs or connections."

I start packing up my things. My hands are shaking uncontrollably. Victory is the only person I have in the world to truly talk about this other than Mamá, and now I have no one. My legs feel weak as I get up. She stands in front of me, blocking me from leaving.

"Get the fuck out my way, Victory," I growl. I feel so much

pressure pushing up behind my eyes as I see her stay in place. I want to cry because I am angry at her for not understanding, for pushing me to do something that terrifies me. But another part of me wants to punch her straight in the face. She holds my hands again. I have spoken before. I have voiced what I see, and it always leads to some Tower moment—like my foundations are burning, and I'm falling onto jagged rocks.

"You have something a lot of people have pushed away or haven't earned. You're acting like it's an extra burden put on you, and it's not. It's a duty. If you see something, say something—just like the train announcements say. You know, the MTA tries to use that saying towards us. Trying to get us to tell on each other, but how about you flip it and tell on Ben? We need to be telling on angry white men and boys. Maybe they search him and find something, and that's it."

"It's not that simple, Victory!" I yell. She lets go of my hands.

"They don't tell you to touch the damn package or to approach whoever left the package unattended. They don't ask you to take care of the damn thing. They ask you to tell someone who can help." She finally moves. "You need to do something, you need to *say* something!" she claps. I open the door, mumbling under my breath that she has never listened to authority anyway.

"You know what will be on you, sis?" she asks, as I walk out. "If he does anything? That. Will. Be. On. You."

12

MOVING THROUGH
THE HARD STUFF

The minute I open my eyes to rub the sleep from them, my mind rushes to the fact that Victory and I still haven't spoken. I look out my bedroom window and take in the sunlight bathing the Bronx. The buildings, even uncared-for project buildings like this one, look pretty with the glow. It's been a hell of a few weeks. I haven't even seen Victory at all these past few days, which means she's been taking on ways around the school to avoid me.

As I turn to my night table and reach for my cards, my chest feels hollow. I say a quick prayer asking my ancestors to assist in what I must see, and shuffle. The cards feel make-believe in my hands for the first time, and even the shuffling don't hit right today, like it hasn't felt right all week since our fight. I take a deep breath and pull out a card. Nine of Swords. Shaking my head in disbelief, I laugh. The cards aren't make-believe—I give them their power, and they've been super on point lately. The Nine of Swords is of a person in bed, waking up with their hands spread over their face. Above them, directed at their head, are nine swords. Yeah, I can see that. Dark and mixed-up feelings are weighing me down. I am focusing on all the things that can go wrong, instead of what can work to the greater good for all of us. Usually I pull at least three cards in the morning, but wow, this is more than enough.

As I get ready for school, Victory comes back to my mind again. We have reached a point in our friendship we have never reached before. We've never gone this long without speaking to each other. The entire Ben business is now seeping into my relationships, and that isn't right. The people in my life are what I cherish most. My stomach tightens up and nausea sets in like it always does when I am hurting badly. I swallow and breathe, focusing instead on laying down my baby hairs with edge control. Usually V and I would just send a silly meme or a simple emoji to get over little bumps, but this is going to definitely take more than a text.

I brush my teeth, have a glass of water, and grab a banana on my way out. Mamá Teté kisses me at the door and daps Florida water on my head, forehead, and chest before kissing my cheek. Stress must be resting all over my face nowadays.

If you see something, say something. It's all the train conductor wants to replay these days. The posters plastered on the tops of the train cars—it's all my eyes want to fixate on today. I didn't want to come into school, but the club members started a text thread in which they insisted on meeting.

"Hey, so I've been processing everything. From what I've heard about the first Brave Space meeting I missed—sorry about that again—to the moments and words you've exchanged with Ben," Mrs. Obi says, on my way out of her class. I stick behind.

When everyone else is gone, Mrs. Obi shuts the door and sits on a stool across from me at my lab station. "First of all, I'm sorry I didn't ask this first: but how's your heart?" she asks. I tell her I'm a little stressed. I put it all on my dad being out and say it's taking a larger toll on me than I imagined. And while that is true, it isn't the plain truth, but she accepts it nonetheless.

"In terms of Ben," I shrug, "I kinda don't want him back in the club, Mrs. Obi. Seriously." Mrs. Obi taps her nails on her laptop.

"I feel you, Yoyo, I really do. But as the leader of the Brave Space, how did you handle that difference of opinion between the members the day I was gone?" She sits down at her desk. I sit down on the desk in front of her.

I shrug. "I kind of let it happen, to be honest—let everyone take it up," I say. I go back to the day, see Victory, Jay, Mariamma, Hamid, and Yasheeda reacting to *Kindred*. "Eventually we just got back to reading though."

"I hear that. Do you think letting folks flesh it out was helpful?"

"Well yeah, because folks got to see everyone had an opinion, you know?" I say. "Plus, members should also have freedom to say things, too. I shouldn't always be the one jumping in. I don't have to take up all the space."

Mrs. Obi nods.

"It is my job to teach you how to be a leader and how to hold these conversations. I want to start by saying: Yoyo, I am sorry I was not there on the day that Ben entered our club. His arrival was quick, and overall it has been a sensitive transition," she says. My hands begin to sweat, and I feel self-conscious—hyperaware of the space my body takes up in the room. What did I do wrong?

"Next, I want to name that it is not your job, in the skin you're in, to teach other people about our humanity. However, as a leader, when someone makes comments that sound or feel like they negate someone else's lived experience, you must end the circle. A member was harmed by the fact that the conversation in the reading did not end when Dana's level of responsibility was up for debate. In those moments, your duty is to say: 'This circle is now closed.' Because like it isn't your job to educate, it also wasn't on your Black and Brown members."

Acid begins to rise like a thick battery up my esophagus. *Fuck, was it that deep? How did I miss this?*

"Look," she starts to explain, "remember that all-school circle we had last year about sexual harassment and assault?"

I nod.

"When some of the seniors started making jokes, Mr. L ended the circle. He did that because making jokes about sexual harassment and assault may imply that the harm isn't that serious, and someone among us, even if just one person, might be triggered."

"I understand," I say.

She touches my hand. "It's OK. This is a work in progress. You are a work in progress. And he is too, right?" She doesn't have to say his name for me to know she's talking about Ben. I nod. Wait, why did you do that? Nod. For what? Do you think he's a work in progress? I mean, shouldn't he have that right, but his work, his work is not . . .

"I don't think his work is leading towards our progress," I say. Ahh. As I speak it, they feel like the right words to name the discomfort in the pit of my stomach.

"What do you mean by that, Yolanda?"

"What if I told you I have visions, Mrs. Obi?" The world stops. I want to bite into the words I just said and swallow them, the same way I felt when I told José about Mamá Teté's abilities. Mrs. Obi folds her arms over her chest.

"I would tell you I have a great-auntie and grandmother who do as well," she says, rolling her head in circles. I laugh.

"But you're a scientist."

"Girl, who told you science and spirituality —for a lack of better word—are separate?" She laughs, taking a sip from her water bottle.

"True," I smile.

"Right," she says.

"I've had a few visions about him," I say, twirling my two thumb fingers around one another.

The bell rings. Mrs. Obi hastily checks her watch. She stands up frantically. "I have a meeting, Yoyo," she says, gathering her water bottle, laptop, and coffee mug. "Thank you for sharing these things with me. I'm sorry I have to go. Let's keep talking." She rushes out. And I feel some relief, even though I wished for a moment to tell her the full truth.

On my way to my next class, I keep my eyes on the walls to avoid meeting anyone. I want to tell someone about this first step, and not just anyone—I want to tell Victory I've started to tell Mrs. Obi. The hallways are buzzing. Everyone is talking, and my processors are working to process it all for me. A group of students sound really confused and upset. I hear a student tell another, "It's really just a joke." As I squeeze through the narrow halls, two first-year girls chat in the middle of the crowd, while the rest of us struggle to get through. Instead of annoyance, it brings a wave of sweet nostalgia over me. I miss Victory, and not

being at a good place with her has me feeling like a part of me
is missing.

"He's kind of cute for a white boy, ¿tu no crees?" I hear when
I finally get into the English wing.

"And generous, girl. Yesterday after school, he ended up paying Amin from the corner bodega for a bunch of our stuff. So you
know me, I got those good Grandma's cookies."

Whatttttttttt? I hope to God my face isn't thinking aloud for
me, but I roll the hell out of my eyes. I continue walking, still
keeping my eyes on the walls. Then, from a few steps away, I see
a bright yellow spot on one of Victory's posters. That is not Victory's color scheme or style, period. I rush towards the poster,
and the yellow spot says:

"Social Justice is Cancer."

I try to pull it off, but it begins to ruin the rest of the poster.
I let it go. It's a sticker. I yank off the entire poster. *Who the
hell would do this?* I feel a tug on my stomach. *You know exactly
who it is.* I run to another poster and there it is: the same bright
yellow spot.

☾

Although I bump into José a few times during the school day and
get a few hugs in, the energy in the school building hangs thick
like smoke. All day everyone's going on about the stickers, trying
to investigate who it could be, and sharing their opinions about
whether it's serious or not. All day I cannot focus on any classes.
By third period, the second time I saw José, he tried to mention
the stickers to me in passing, but I waved him off—wanting a
chance to talk to Victory first. But Victory doesn't meet my eyes
during passing periods, so I can't even try to tell her that I've

seen the posters, and that I'm sorry. I'm sorry I didn't listen to her, but mostly I am sorry I didn't listen to myself. For lunch, I use my pass to go outside and go for a walk, even though the freezing temperatures go through my black Timbs. I sit on a building stoop and shuffle my cards inside of my backpack. While I know that what I am doing is not wrong, I don't want to be seen. I pull out the Five of Cups and feel like my whole life is on the card. I am sitting here wallowing over spilled milk, when I have a whole two glasses and there's a bridge nearby I can use as a tool to get by. *But what is the tool? And where am I going?*

On my way back to school grounds, Ben spots me.

"Hey Yolanda," Ben calls out, walking behind me. "What did you think of the end of the movie?" The brick walls within me quickly come up. There's a darkness hidden somewhere around him that has nothing to do with my vision, and everything to do with who he is.

"It was fine," I say. I try to keep it pushing because I know for a fact he is the one behind the stickers. No one I know has the means to create stickers like that, and it's never happened before. People know better than to say shit like that out here.

"Did you see the end coming?" he asks. I pick up my speed because more than anything I want to be on school grounds now. At the end of the movie, the families who live on the road figure out that when the ghosts haunting them were alive, they lived through intense levels of trauma.

"No," I shrug. I speed up and cross the street into Julia De Burgos. But he meets my pace. "Not really."

"Me either," he says. "I thought those ghosts were all just evil for evil's sake, you know? No real reason for them to be haunting that neighborhood."

"I guess," I shrug. And look at him knowing damn well I am wearing my resting bitch face, but still he smiles at me. He lowers his eyes towards my black Timbs.

"You know I've been wondering if you'd like to get some—" he begins to say.

"Yo Ben, you getting on tonight to play?" Cindy yells.

"Yeah, I'll be on," Ben calls back with a smile. Pedro, a junior, greets Ben with a dap. And I am confused as hell. When did he start making acquaintances around here? But also what the hell was he about to *say to me*?

"Some of us are heading to the library for lunch," Pedro tells Ben. Ben replies he'll be there. Shit is wild quick, but as done as I am with him, I am grateful in some complex way. If he makes friends, maybe he'll feel less lonely, less angry. Maybe he'll stop doing all this fuck shit.

"Get ready for that ass whooping!" Cindy says, before Mr. Leyva pulls her aside to tell her to keep her voice down. Ben laughs walking towards his next class.

"Yo, yo," Mr. L catches up with me. I see Cindy moving towards her class too. "You good?"

"I'm fine," I say.

He pouts at me and looks me up and down. "Girl, you know you can't lie to me. You and V mad at each other or something? Is it the sticker business going on? I know how hard that girl work on those things."

I shrug. *Tell him.* I look over at Mr. L. *Tell him.*

"Something's happening," I say, and stop. Mr. L was one of the first adults I told about my dreams last year. He believed me. Escorted me to the train until the dreams stopped coming, and when they did, I wasn't scared of what they were telling me anymore. *Do I tell him, Bruja Diosas?* Mr. L looks at me, a question on his brow, and all the students, all the noise running up and down the hallway, stops. My mind races around the possibilities of telling him.

"Something is wrong," I say. "I feel it and I see it, Mr. L." I begin to walk again. "I don't know how to prove it, but imma try."

Mr. L tries to say something, but I walk into class.

◖

By the time it's time to congregate for Brave Space in Mrs. Obi's class, I am ready to go home. My body feels weak and my head is pounding. I have not caught a flu since I was in middle school, and here I am feeling as if I am drowning. Mrs. Obi tells me she doesn't mind running a circle today, and I give her the go-ahead. In reality she is doing me a huge favor. I sit on a chair as close as possible to the door, so while everyone arrives they see my back, and I don't have to do the greetings. It's petty, but I want to avoid all eye contact, and have direct access to an exit if this circle becomes unbearable.

Victory comes in looking like a total Queen. She's wrapped her hair in a gold satin scarf, one I did not notice earlier when I dodged her in the hallway. She sits across from me and arches her eyebrow at me. It's a peace offering I can live with for now, so I raise my eyebrows back at her. José sits next to me without saying a word. The tension between us feels dense, and I wish I could tell him I'm not necessarily mad at him. I just don't know how to juggle all that's going on. It has too many legs, too many people are involved.

Before we begin Mrs. Obi goes over our norms: one mic, one

voice, listen from the heart, speak from the heart, step in and step out, what happens in the room stays in the room, and double confidentiality. These norms are second nature to us at this school. Circles, open communication, and vulnerability have always been encouraged and lifted here. Reading the room though, it seems like no one wants any of that.

"I want to start off by apologizing to the whole group. I know I wasn't here last meeting, and last week was canceled. I had an important personal matter to attend to, but I want everyone to know I value this space and everyone's commitment to attend it." Mrs. Obi clears her throat. Ben isn't in yet, and I hope maybe he's quit. "We welcomed in a new participant, and that is great because our mission is to expand. However, it's come to my attention that there was harm caused in this group, due to things that were said that day connected to the content of *Kindred*, and today we must repair that if we are to move forward as a collective."

Amina nods, but for the most part, no one says nothing or looks like they agree with what is being said. I know Ben came out of his neck in our last meeting, and this sticker shit definitely doesn't help at all. I glance at the room again, trying to read it.

"I don't think anything is going to be resolved here," Victory says.

"Nope," Dayvonte adds.

"Not at all," Autumn says.

"I agree," José joins.

"I hear y'all. What's going on though? This isn't like any of you to enter a circle not ready to remedy," Mrs. Obi pushes. She offers Penny up to whoever would like to talk, and Victory reaches for her.

The door opens with a loud creak, and we all turn to see Ben. He apologizes quickly and takes a seat next to Amina.

José looks at Vic. Jay shakes their head as they cup their chin in their hand.

"Alright, ya'll, come on now. We can't just stay mad. Let's talk or something," Hamid adds.

"Someone is messing up my posters, and I am not with it," Victory says. "AT ALL, Mrs. Obi." She takes a big breath. "And TRUST, I am going to get to the bottom of it." Victory looks straight at Ben. He looks back at her blankly.

Amina goes into her bag and takes out one of Victory's posters. She passes it around. Those of us who have seen the poster already shake our heads and nod, while there are others who are surprised.

"Nu-uh! This is right here is wild disrespectful," Cindy says. "Ya think it was a first year or something?" I am surprised she hasn't seen the stickers for herself or heard from others.

"First-year students are not about to be out here coming after upperclassmen," Jay offers. "Let's be real, C."

"I am so sorry about this, Victory," Mrs. Obi says, when the poster gets to her. "This is not OK. I will support you in getting to the bottom of this."

Victory nods.

"All right," Mrs. Obi begins. "Let's take a few collective deep breaths." Even though some of us just want to wild out right now based on how angry we are, we sit up, and close our eyes. "Inhale deeply through the nose," Mrs. Obi models, "and exhale it all through the mouth." The collective exhale sounds like a deep AAAHHHHHH. After we repeat this a couple times, Mrs. Obi has us all open our eyes.

"All right, activists, I understand there's a lot on our brains right now, so maybe we can move this restorative to next week. We do have to finish this graphic novel and write that collective essay for the nonprofit. So how about we check that off the list, and I'll work with Victory to get down to this poster business?" Folks nod in agreement. Many of us share books, and Ben gets his own.

☾

Mamá is at the stove when I get home.

"¿Qué haces, Mamá?" I ask, kissing her left cheek. I hug her as she continues to stir a wooden spoon in the pot. The mixture in the pot is dark brown and pungent.

"A bitter bath," she says. She bends her neck at the side to kiss the top of my head. I take a deep breath and take in her Florida water scent. "Go shower," she tells me.

"For me?" I pout my lips playfully.

"Mmmmmhhmmmmm," she responds. "I know you need it. To clear out the stagnant, negative energy that comes with being clairvoyant." I close my eyes. Try to sit with the peace it gives me to be so close to Mamá.

"Being able to see is a gift, mi amor," she says. She pulls herself from me, holds my arms, and looks into my eyes. "Even when it is heavy, it is a gift, a privilege, a duty." I nod.

I go into my room, take off my school uniform, and wrap myself in a towel. Before I step into the bath, I put on my plastic bonnet, and lather an apricot scrub on my face with my fingertips. I wash my hands and open the jar of coconut oil that always stays in the bathroom. In the winter it is solid, but in the summer it is straight up liquid. I use my fingertips to scoop some of the oil onto my hand. I rub my hands together and massage my neck and shoulders. *It is important to love yourself. It is important to spend time on you,* I hear in my ear. I smile. The Bruja Diosas are always with me.

After I shower, I scrub the tub clean. I watch the oil and dirt circle the drain. I watch it all go. Mamá knocks on the door.

"You ready?" she asks. I pop a tub stopper into the drain.

"Sí, Mamá!" She walks in and pours the entire concoction that is her specialty-clearing bath. I turn the water on and let it run.

When the bath is half filled, I stop the water. Mamá comes in again. "Santa Culebra, Santa mía, me refugio para mí y a los míos a tu poderosa protección y me refugio en mi fe. Te ofrezco esta luz en tu honor," Mamá Teté lights a purple candle. "Te ofrezco tu café molido y tu miel," Mamá places two small cups filled with coffee and Malta India. "Santa Culebra, Santa mía, que derrotes todas las dificultades mías y de mi familia, como destruyes a todos tus enemigos."

I step into the bath. "Stay in there for twenty minutes. Make sure to dip your head from time to time," Mamá says, closing the door.

I lay back in the bathtub, close my eyes, and prepare to release. *Wash off all fears, Bruja Diosas. Show me to see what I must see,* I pray. I dip my head, including my fro, into the water. I hold my breath and allow myself to linger and take in all the colors behind my eyelids.

WHAT'S REALLY
GOOD THOUGH?

Welcome back, scientists," Mrs. Obi greets us at the door. The energy isn't as heavy despite the peace offering the Brave Space turned down. The whole weekend has come and went, days of the school week have passed, and Victory and I still have yet to say a word to each other. After the bath Mamá gave me, I fell into a deep sense of calmness. I lie. It was a numbness. Yeah, the kind of numbness that makes you believe you don't really care about nothing, just to make it through the hour. I spent the entire long weekend in and out of bed binging series and snacking on whatever Mamá bought me when she came from outside.

I step into class with José, who texted me all weekend and tried to get me out, but it was way too cold for all that. Also, it felt like I was betraying Victory somehow—in a fight with her, but having fun with José. Made no sense, I know, but I still held myself to it. He drops me off at my seat, and bows, sweeping a hand behind his back like a royal.

"You a clown!" I say. Low-key hyped and high-key embarrassed at the way he is doing the most.

"But I make you laugh though," he smiles.

The bell rings and we all settle into our seats. "All right, ya'll, announcements! Can anyone tell me what's going on this week?" Mrs. Obi says.

"Your birthday?" Bianca calls out. "Wouldn't be surprised if you a Sagittarius, Mrs. Obi, with yo fine husband."

"Not my birthday, and keep my husband out your mouth, girl!" Mrs. Obi laughs.

"A day off?" Marcus offers. Now, it's our turn to all laugh 'cause Mrs. Obi stay putting us to work.

"We just got back from Thanksgiving break! But no, not that either," Mrs. Obi says.

"A test," Ben says. Mrs. Obi points at him with her pencil and shakes it.

"You, Ben, are correct," she answers excitedly. A good amount of folks look at each other in confusion; others leaf back to the syllabus. "Our next exam is this Wednesday. Those of y'all who forget to study over the weekend, have two days to get it in. Can I have two volunteers pass out these review sheets?" I stand up and walk over to her, and so does Marcus.

Mrs. Obi gives us permission to take out our phones and put on our headphones to listen to music, and we spend the class period revising, reviewing, correcting, and chatting. I use my black pen to rewrite the question or the prompt and a blue one to write the answers. It helps me stay organized and focused. By the time the bell rings, I am halfway done with my review sheet. I throw the strap of my Telfar bag over my shoulder and walk out.

As I leave the science wing and walk towards my locker, I

look around for signs of Victory, but I can't seem to spot her. I see the back of Mr. L's head a few times, but I dodge him. I don't have the words yet to answer the questions I know must be coming from the last time we spoke.

"Yo, but look at all these new clubs though," Cindy says as she stands in front of the announcement wall across from my locker.

"A coding club?!" Amina covers her mouth.

"IN THERE!" Hamid says. "That's where the money's at." Suddenly, there's a crowd by the wall.

"A photography club?!" someone yells. "Ain't no way, bruh!"

"Self-care club?!" A group of seniors high-five each other. "That's the energy we need with all this stress these days," one of them says, moving the hair out their eyes swiftly with their pointer finger. Although the wall is filled with excitement, I can't help but notice the absence of Victory's posters.

I feel a tap on my shoulder. I flinch and turn. "Can I talk to you?" Ben says. His eyes dance between looking at me and looking at the space behind me. I low-key want to twist his fingers for having the audacity to touch me.

"What?" I say walking towards my locker. A part of me wants to tell him he doesn't have to tap me to get my attention, but I do not have the time or energy to get heated today.

"You seem to be really into chemistry class, and I kind of suck at it," he says. "Do you mind studying some time after school?"

I look at his hands—his cuticles are bleeding a little. The tone of his voice tells me he's desperate. I purse my lips and look around.

"Study where exactly?" I tilt my head. *Bruja Diosas, guide me, allow me to be the vehicle if needed.*

"My place," he says. Immediately, no, and taking a deep breath, I turn to face my locker.

"Why would I go to your house, Ben?"

"Technically, it's a brownstone," he says, standing next to me. Real smart. I roll my eyes. I mean, has he lost all of his senses? This flip-floppy shit he does is entirely out of pocket.

I touch the dial and begin turning it to the combination I know by heart. I expect him to move on, but he just looks at me, waiting for me to fold. "My driver takes me home every day, and he wouldn't mind bringing you back to the Bronx after we're done." He brings his thumbs around the bottom straps of his backpack. I click open my locker door.

The picture of Mamá blowing me a kiss with a vibrant red lip stares back at me. Under the picture there's my name in bubble letters written by Mr. L. And the Polaroid of me and Papi in his orange suit the day he received his Associate's. Right next to it is a picture of me and Victory side by side at the beginning of sixth grade, one of our arms wrapped around the other's shoulders. Our eyes are gleaming at the joy of starting the first day of middle school. My chest aches. *You need to do something, you need to do something!* repeats over and over like background noise in my head.

"Yes, no?"

I look up at Mamá's face again. *"This really is your initiation,"* she said. And it is.

Proof—I said I needed proof to be believed. Well, where better to find some evidence than his house? This move has fallen into my lap, and I have to take it.

I arch my eyebrows and purse my lips. *What is happening?*

He smiles and looks me in the eye. I pull. *Answers. You're getting answers.* His cheeks and ears grow red.

"When were you thinking?" I ask.

"How's today after school?" Ben says. *Go.*

"Sure," I shrug. I'll have to tell Mamá.

☾

Getting into Ben's car is a whole ass hassle. I make him wait for me on a neighboring street to avoid anyone seeing me get into his car. We take the highway into Manhattan and go all the way down into the city locally to avoid traffic, or at least that's what he keeps saying.

"What do you want to listen to?" Ben asks.

"The radio is fine," I respond.

"What station?"

I shrug. Ed, the driver, turns to Z100. "One Dance" by Drake plays in the background.

Half an hour into the ride, Ed's brown eyes meet my own through the rearview mirror. The dark liver spots on his desert-sand brown cheek line up like a small constellation. "How you doing back there, young lady?"

"Good. Thank you," I say.

"Let me know if the temperature is OK," he tilts his head at me. His voice has a British accent undertone. I nod. I wonder how it must be for him to have to bring Ben back and forth every day. What do they even talk about?

"Ed, you mind stopping at the grocery store?" I look around and we are still on 103rd Street. I look out the window and see the project housing and the ninety-nine-cent stores.

Ed comes to a stop and double-parks. "You want to come in

and pick out some snacks?" Ben asks. Ed opens my door, and we walk into the bodega. *This isn't a grocery store*, I think to myself, and roll my eyes as I step inside.

"My man," the Arab man behind the counter calls out to Ben.

"What's up, Abdullah?" Ben says as we walk past a few refrigerators.

"There's not many stores by where we live, and Kristina, our house manager, goes shopping tomorrow," Ben says, opening one of the fridges to grab a Mountain Dew and orange Gatorade. "Feel free to get whatever you want."

I take a big Arizona Fruit Punch, and I walk around the aisle and grab limon chips. I walk slowly towards the front, enjoying every second I don't have to be that close to Ben. What am I doing here really? If José or Victory found out, or anyone in the Brave Space Club for that matter, they'd be done with me. I exhale. *I trust you, Bruja Diosas. I do.*

"There you are, Ani!" I hear Ben's voice, definitely with a different tone. When I get to the front, Ben is on his knees in front of the refrigerator that holds ice cream and ice cups. I have to get closer to see he is stroking a gray cat.

"How come you didn't come to the door and greet me when I walked in?" he says in a baby voice. His hand softly and gently moves through the cat's fur. "Oh, you're definitely feeling thinner. Catching no mice these days, are you?" He brings his head and lets the cat sniff and lick him. It's like he's transformed. Ben looks up at me and smiles.

"Yolanda, this is Ani, Abdullah's cat," he says, standing up, the big cat now in his arms.

"You mean the bodega cat, Ben?" I place my things on the counter.

"I don't know what he sees in this cat. All that cat does is play with dead mice, but Ben doesn't care. Always kissing and touching it," Abdullah laughs. "Oh, Americans."

"Right," I say, placing my things on the counter.

"Yeah, yeah, how much?" Ben walks to the counter.

"$15.20," Abdullah says. Ben gives him a twenty and tells him to keep the change.

Ben walks up to the cat again and kisses the top of its head before we leave. "See you soon, Ani."

☾

When Ed drops us off in front of Ben's brownstone, my stomach feels like I'm at the very peak of a rollercoaster before it drops. A part of me wants to dip, but I have to remind myself that I am here because I was divinely guided. From the outside, the brownstone has three floors. Basically, Ben lives in a mini-building all to himself and his family.

"I'm home, Kristina!" Ben yells from the door. He sits down on a dark wooden bench by the door and takes off his shoes. He hangs up his coat. I follow suit. There's a small bathroom by the staircase and closed door. A fair-skinned woman with dark hair walks towards us.

"Welcome back, mi niño," Kristina says, coming down the stairs. I am almost surprised she speaks Spanish to him, but I'm not totally shocked. But who cares? Spanish is also a colonizer's language. Her black, thick hair is tied loosely into a low ponytail, and oil or sweat is dripping down her face. She must be a few years older than Mami. She arches her thin eyebrow at me and looks at Ben with a clear question.

"¿Usted tiene hambre?" she asks Ben, taking her eyes off

of me. I take a deep breath. She doesn't like that I'm here; I can feel it.

Ben catches on. "Kristina, this is Yolanda, my classmate. Yolanda, this is Kristina, our house manager." Not expecting that, I turn my head quickly to him in amusement. When she gets to the bottom of the staircase, Kristina looks at my socks. One is blue, the other one white. Mamá and I haven't been able to do laundry, but I don't say anything.

"Yolanda, I have a cousin with that name," she says, extending her hand to me.

"Mucho gusto," I say.

"Your Spanish is really good," Kristina replies, arching an eyebrow.

"Your English too," I bite back. Damn, I didn't have to do all that, but it really annoys me when people from other Spanish-speaking countries act surprised at the fact there are Black people in and from Latin America. There were way more Africans kidnapped and transferred to Latin America than the United States, but anti-Blackness makes it so they forget that.

"Yolanda is a—"

"Native speaker. I'm Black and Dominican. Not like a Black American parent—both of my parents are from Dominican Republic, is what I'm trying to say," I smile. Sarcastically. The silence becomes obvious and bothersome as it usually does when moments like this happen.

"We're fine, Kristina," Ben says. "We stopped for snacks." He starts going up the stairs, and I follow.

The first thing I notice is how spacious the home is. The ceilings are super high and I feel small, like when you're at a museum. My socks slide through the wooden floors, which make no creak.

"This is really nice," I say.

Ben shrugs, brushing off the comment, and I follow him into a doorway. "Well here's the dining room," he points out to his left. There are two huge windows overlooking the park. A long wooden table with eight chairs. And old art on the walls. I follow Ben to the doorway through the right. "This is the reading room, we can study here if you like." There's a big portrait of him, his father, and his mother in front of a white wooden house dressed by a blossom tree. Ben is laughing in his father's arms, the top row of his teeth newly grown and too big for his face yet. He must be nine or ten. His mother smiles, crouching above them like she has just walked in on the scene for the photograph. We walk back into the hallway and towards the back. "Here's the kitchen."

"Where the magic happens," Kristina says. I didn't even realize she was around. The kitchen is huge. Bigger than any kitchen I've ever seen. An island in the middle, and a very modern stove. The cupboards are all white with gold handles. There's also a small breakfast booth overlooking the park. I look at one of the closed doors. "That's a pantry and that door," Ben points to the door behind the steel fridge, "is Kristina's room."

I follow Ben back to the stairs.

"We have the TV room upstairs, my dad's office, and the bedrooms," he says as we go up. "I'm going to jump in the shower and change really quickly." He throws his backpack from the hallway to the TV room on the left. "That's my parents' room," he points to a white door. "My room," he points to another. "And my dad's office." The last door is ajar.

I walk into the TV room when Ben goes into his room. The TV is literally a projector screen across a wall to the left. I throw my body on the white sofas and feel so deeply held by the cushions. These are heavenly comforts. Even the lush throw is luxuriously soft to the skin. I close my eyes and open them quickly when I hear the water running from Ben's room.

Now's my chance.

My heart flutters in my chest as I get up and tiptoe as quiet as possible into the hallway again. The door to the office is still a bit open. I peek down the staircase and do not see Kristina; I look around and don't catch a camera in sight. I continue tiptoeing towards the door. I push the door as slow as possible. Thank God it makes no sound. At first glance, I see my vision took on some liberties, but the office is similar to the one I saw. I smile at myself and give my eye the freedom to wander. A large, dark desk, a leather couch, a coffee table.

"¿Todo bien?" The voice makes my entire chest contract. Kristina.

"Sí, everything's good. Just exploring," I turn around, grinning nervously at Kristina.

I walk towards the TV room again.

"If you need anything, I am just downstairs," she says as she shuts the office door behind me. Her steps are light as she goes back down to the kitchen.

Five minutes pass, and the water is still running. I take a deep breath, getting bored of the view and the silence. I open my limon chips and begin to munch on them. A chip falls on the couch and before I can see where it landed, I lean on it. *Fuck.* As I dust off the couch, I glance over Ben's backpack. *Ben's backpack!*

The water stops running.

I have time, I have time. The train has not yet stopped in the station. I tell myself the same thing I tell myself when I have to run for the subway. He still has to get dressed. I open the zipper to the small pocket. Nothing of interest. Second pocket, nothing of interest. I move my hand around the bottom of the backpack. My heart is practically galloping out of my chest as I keep my eyes on the door.

My hand bumps into a circular plastic object. I pull it out.

The stickers. A roll of them. A big portion of the strip is already used. I take out my phone quickly. Turn to my camera and record. I point the camera around the TV room; I zoom into a family picture, and then I pull back to record the entire roll.

A fire takes over me. I am heated. I tremble from anger as I put the roll of stickers back into their spot in his backpack and zip up the bag.

I stand up and put on my backpack and head down the stairs.

"Yolanda, is everything all right?" Ben asks, coming out of his room. I look back quickly and notice he glances into the TV room before he comes after me.

"Everything's good. I have to go," I respond, still moving down the stairs.

"You sure? Where are you going?" he asks, as I step into my boots.

"My grandma's calling," I lie. I can hardly breathe. His presence suffocates me. I look at him one more time as I put on my coat. He's just washed his hair and it is slicked back; he looks older, more serious. His jaw is tight as he waits for an answer. "She changed her mind, she wants me home," I say, opening the door.

He grabs my arm. "But are you all right? You look scared or angry or something? Did I do something wrong? You can talk to me." I aggressively pull my arm away.

When I open the door, the woman in the photograph is at the doorsteps taking off her running shoes. She is wearing black tights, a hat, and a running jacket. She lets go of the leash to a large Dalmatian.

"Buddy!" Ben pets the dog, and it stands up and licks his face. He becomes the boy at the bodega again. Soft, friendly, gentle. There's laughter.

"Six miles today! Not bad at all," the woman tells Kristina and me. "Hi, I'm Mrs. Hill, very nice to meet you," Mrs. Hill gives me her thin and bony hand. The Dalmatian starts to sniff at me, and my body becomes stiff. It's a beautiful dog, but no.

"Yolanda Nuelis. Nice to meet you, too," I say. "I was just leaving." Ben gently tells the dog to sit, and it does. Ben looks at me.

"You sure you don't want to stay for dinner or something?" He arches his eyebrows in a plea.

"I'm good. I have to get back to the Bronx."

14

WATER FOR THE SAINTS

I said what I said," I growl.

I look towards the door, and Mr. L waves from outside of it. *You good?* he asks. I stick out my hand and move it side to side, *so-so.* He nods and moves along.

I cross my arms over my chest. "I don't know why you won't believe me, Ms. Steinberg." My voice is deep and loud with conviction, and the tiny hairs on my arms are alert. The school office has never felt as cold as it feels right now, even though I feel like I am burning from within. And despite the bright colors coming off the bulletin boards filled with student work, it has never looked more gray.

"It's not that I don't believe you, Ms. Alvarez. I just want to get the facts straight," she folds her hands over the table. Even though I know what I saw, Ms. Steinberg's condescending tone makes me feel like a straight liar. She's the principal and—I get it—she's feeling a lot of pressure, but so am I. I feel the anger exit the internal parts of me and pile up on my face. Mrs. Obi nods at me as if to reassure me that she has got my back. I wish Mamá Teté were here—just the scent of Florida water and sage that comes off of

her skin would relax me, remind me that everything has a purpose. But she's been trying to facilitate whatever is unfolding.

"Again, you are saying you saw a roll of stickers with your
very eyes?" Ms. Steinberg paces back and forth in front of her
long desk.

"That's what I said," I repeat. "And that's what you saw in the
video, right?" We've now been in the office for half an hour, and
with every tick of the clock, it seems like she believes me less.
Somehow a part of me believes me less, too. *Stand your ground.*
My eyes did not fail me. I saw it. There's proof. The beating in my
chest, the adrenaline that rushed through my veins, the fear—it
was all real. I lived through it just yesterday.

"Tell me one more time just before I call Ben's family."

"Principal Steinberg—" Mrs. Obi begins.

"No," I say. I've repeated my story two times to her, and now
she's asking me to say it again? I take a blank incident report from
the filing desk and sit. "Give me an incident report. I'll write it
out instead."

JULIA DE BURGOS ACADEMY   **INCIDENT REPORT**

DATE: 12/3/2019
REPORTER NAME: Yolanda Nuelis Alvarez
DATE & TIME OF INCIDENT: 12/2/2019 @ 6:00 p.m.
OTHER STUDENT(S) INVOLVED: Ben Hill
INCIDENT LOCATION: Off School Grounds
IF OFF SCHOOL GROUNDS, SPECIFY: Ben Hill's house (Somewhere
in Upper West Side)

DETAILS OF INCIDENT (WHAT HAPPENED?): On Monday, December 2, 2019, I went to Ben Hill's house in the Upper West Side. He invited me over to study for our chemistry exam. A few minutes before 6:00 p.m., he had me wait for him in the TV room. He told me he was going to shower and change. I walked around the second floor a little bit. I had never been inside such a huge house before, so my curiosity led me to peek into his father's office. The house manager, Kristina, found me, and she redirected me back to the TV room. I ate some snacks and waited. But then I saw Ben had left his backpack beside me. I searched in it, and when I came across the stickers, I recorded it. I'll show the video to anyone who wants to see.

OFFICE USE ONLY

STUDENT TIER BEHAVIOR: _____

SCHOOL CATEGORY OR OFFENSE: _____

SCHOOL SAFETY PLAN PROCEDURES: _____

DATE & TIME OF CONTACT: _____

CONTACT LOCAL OFFICIALS (IF NEEDED)

DATE & TIME OF CONTACT: _____

SIGNATURE BY SCHOOL OFFICIAL: _____

DATE: _____

Ms. Steinberg reads over the incident report, leaning on the bookshelf next to me.

"What are the next steps?" Mrs. Obi asks.

Ms. Steinberg's eyes go back to the top of the page.

Mr. Choi, the vice principal, knocks on the door before entering. He greets me with a pound.

"Good morning," he says. Ms. Steinberg frantically catches him up on everything, hands him the incident report, and sits at her desk.

"What are the next steps?" Mrs. Obi repeats.

"I think the next steps are very clear," Mr. Choi states, looking intently at Ms. Steinberg. "We start by calling in his parents. It's important we get permission to look in his backpack ourselves." For a second I feel relief remembering what Victory said—if I spoke up, maybe it would lead to a searching of his things at the very least.

"Let's be calculated, Andrew—the new coding program, the clubs we've been able to start, and the spring field trips coming up that we've been able to fund. Make no mistake it's because of the Hills," Ms. Steinberg protests. My fists ball up on my lap, but I understand her. I understand having nothing and being given something and fearing it going away. Our school is one of the best public schools in the borough, and still we don't get the funding we needed. In just a couple of weeks, we have gotten the resources we needed to start clubs a lot of us had wanted for so long.

Mr. Choi turns on his walkie-talkie, "Mr. L, has Ben Hill entered the building?"

"No sir. Not yet," Mr. L responds.

"Please have him come into the office when he arrives."

"Heard you," Mr. L responds.

Bruja Diosas, may everything turn out OK for the highest good of all involved. Please protect the students and adults in this building.

A sour taste takes over my mouth and I suddenly feel nauseous. There's no going back now.

The late bell rings. I think of my empty desk in math class. It sure as hell isn't my favorite class, but I wish circumstances were different and I'd be there instead. Truly grasping trigonometry instead of winging it and hoping for the best. Did anyone see me come in early this morning, or do they think I am absent because I am sick or something?

My phone buzzes in my pocket, and I excuse myself to the bathroom. Ms. Steinberg reminds me not to talk about this with anyone as I open the office door.

The pressure feels lighter just outside the office. I take a deep breath and taste it in the back of my throat. The visions have told me I'd have to do this for so long, and still I tried to fight it. So much resistance for nothing—to still end up here.

Hey, I saw you in the office, everything OK? Victory. My stomach falls flat into itself. All the blood in my body rushes to my face.

I open the door in the bathroom, and the tears begin to surface. I swallow, fight them back in.

In the first-floor bathroom, I respond.

When Victory arrives, we don't say a word, she just throws her arms around me. Should I tell her I went to his place? A part of me wants to be honest. I can already imagine her saying I am being shady, choosing his side. Maybe she'll think I had other reasons to want to go to his house, like wanting to befriend him or something. But she isn't crazy! Right? Will she understand or judge me? I take a deep breath, taking in all the nut butters on her skin. I close my eyes. And wrap my arms tighter around her.

After a long silence, I bring up the video on my phone.

"We already know it was him," she says. She shakes her head. "You didn't have to do all that now. You could've just asked me how I felt about the stickers and seen what I was trying to do."

"What were you trying to do?" I ask.

"We found someone who recorded him doing it," she says. "I don't know why you would put yourself in danger, giving him the benefit of the doubt, if you already know what he feels." And the walls within me come out of the ground like shields.

"Mrs. Obi knows already," I ignore her. "She's probably going to call an emergency meeting and lead a restorative," I say. I want to let her know it's handled.

Victory shrugs. "That's not enough, and you know it."

"Victory, if *you* had bothered to ask me, you'd know I'm trying to come up with a strategy."

She rolls her eyes.

"I've tried to tell Mrs. Obi, I've tried to tell Mr. L," I continue.

She crosses her arms.

"I told them about my visions," I say.

"All of the visions? From beginning to end?" she asks. I wash my hands and get ready to leave.

"Alright then, that's what I thought," I hear her murmur.

☾

Mrs. Obi is not at the door offering pounds or high-fives. We don't normally meet on this day, but our club was brought together last minute, and the lunch lady had no snacks to give us either. The students who begin coming in start building the circle of chairs.

José walks up to me. "You good?" I nod.

"Yeah, my bad. I've been distant because—" I start. "Honestly, I have no good reason." I look down at my hands.

"It's like that sometimes," he says. He brings his hand to my chin and raises my face to his. "It's OK. I want to show you something." He pulls out his phone, but Mrs. Obi tells him to put it away. I smirk awkwardly.

"Coach let you out of practice for this?" He normally comes to our weekly meeting, but that's the only day he doesn't have practice.

"I told him it was quick, but yeah I'm going to hear it," he smiles.

Victory changed out of her uniform after last period. She walks in with denim overalls, a yellow turtleneck, and hoops. As per usual: best dressed.

When everyone is sitting, Mrs. Obi passes Penny to me.

"So we're here because we found out who has been messing up our posters," I say. Victory stands up, walks across the circle, and takes Penny from me.

"Well, this lil boy," Victory points Penny at Ben, "has tried the wrong one." Mrs. Obi tells Victory she wants to hear what she has to say, but essentially checks her tone. Club members look uncomfortable, some lost, and others somewhere between holding their breath and puffing it out loud.

"What you talking about, V? Am I missing something?" Cindy asks, and she looks over at Ben.

"He defaced ALL of our posters. The posters I PUT TIME INTO!" Victory's left leg begins to shake. I have never seen Victory raise her voice like this, and I know she's ready to say whatever it is to bring justice to her art. Mrs. Obi looks at Ben, who is reclining in his chair with his hand across his chest. He reaches for Penny, but Victory holds on to her.

"Innocent until proven guilty," Ben smirks. He sits back, and I feel stupid as fuck for not having cursed him out earlier. I mean really, what the hell is wrong with me? And where's the guy that was trying to get me to stay yesterday? I look at him, but he hardly catches my eye. This boy is really out here trying to play us. At the beginning, I sensed his sadness, his loneliness, but now it's all anger, bitterness.

"Ben, you did that forreal?" Cindy asks. She sucks her teeth loudly, shaking her head. My heart feels heavy for her. I can imagine a part of her is in disbelief, but I know deep down inside she just feels disappointed in herself for having trusted an outsider that would do this to one of us. He ignores her. And I swear to God, I just want to get up and smack him.

"Typical for you to say that," Amina says. I want to try to use the norms, use Penny as the talking piece, but everyone is hot. A part of me misses the rules, the structure, in this chaos.

"We got the evidence, Ben," José says, taking out his phone. I guess this is what he was trying to show me. I look over his shoulder and in the video Ben is pasting stickers over them. Acid rises up my throat again. I look over at Victory, and she arches her eyebrow. I hate that they had already done all of this and kept me out of it. Why? Because they were that tired of me trying to give him a chance? When did they even meet to do all this? I reach down for my water bottle, open it, and take a sip. *Damn, they knew about this.* I look at José, a part of me feeling betrayed. *I guess I didn't tell them about going to Ben's either.*

"The only reason we didn't give you what you got coming to

you is 'cause we got a lot more to lose than you," Jay says. They sit up in their chair and stretch out their legs.

Ben's face is flushed as he laughs. "It's a joke, you guys, just a little joke. Why are we being so serious here? Now everyone has an excuse to get back at me."

"All right so maybe it wasn't—" Hamid starts, but Amina cuts him off.

"NO!" She looks at Hamid like she will gut him right here, and he backs down.

"And what do you think we can possibly do to you without consequences, Ben?" Matumata, a first-year student, says, who is quiet as hell, but is always present. Her makeup stays on point, and the baby hairs coming out of her hijab are always laid.

"Good question. I think the entire world has chosen affirmative action, so there's a lot you can get away with now," he responds.

Victory gasps. Marcus gets up out of his seat.

"I wanted to be wrong," I say. Suddenly, there's a fire growing in me. I close my eyes. There's a circle of heat above my head. I am back in Ben's house.

I look down at my feet, the same socks, the same day. I can hear Ben's voice. Without knocking, I opened the door quietly. The room is large. The walls are white and at the center of them is a navy-blue line running along all of the wall space. On the far-left end from the door, Ben is at his desk, talking into a microphone connected to his desktop. On his desk right next to his arm, there is a black object. I squint my eyes to get a clearer vision. A gun. He is giving his back to me so he does not see me. I tiptoe back out of the room. As I am running down the stairs, he hears me. Kristina, the house manager, asks me what is wrong, but I do not answer. I quickly grab my bag,

step into my sneakers, and run out of the front door. He catches up
to me outside the door. Kristina is right behind him, and he looks
different besides her—younger, more innocent maybe? There's a
deep pain inside my chest. "I wanted to be wrong about you," I say.
I look all around me. Central Park West is packed, full of people. He
asks me to come back inside so he can call his family driver, and I
say I am good. I look into his eyes, and the pain becomes unbear-
able. It forces me to place a hand on my chest. "I wanted to be wrong
about you," I repeat.

José's hand on my knee brings me back in a flash. I open my
eyes, and I am looking through a glass of milk. I rub my eyes until
my clear vision is back.

"What did you want to be wrong about, Yoyo?" Mrs. Obi
looks out towards me. My eyes swell with tears.

"Him," I point towards Ben with my chin.

"It was nothing more than just a joke, nothing more than
that. I promise," he says. He buttons his blazer and smiles. A perfect smile. An all-American smile. Dude was definitely raised to
perfect the act of deceiving. My mind becomes clouded by the
fire, but also by the image of Ben petting the bodega cat and his
dog just yesterday. So much empathy, so much tenderness
towards a four-legged animal . . . and where is that for us? I rub
my eyes again.

It becomes clear to me that he's telling the truth: we are nothing but a joke to him. I look over at Victory and she's on the verge
of tears. Her leg continues to shake as if she can't contain everything moving inside of her. I've never seen her look so defeated. I
open my water bottle and take another sip, trying to collect myself.

Be like water, I try to tell myself, *gentle, calm, nourishing.*
Don't be fire. Not right now.

But it's only been a few weeks. A few weeks, and this kid has managed to turn a brave space into a difficult one. The fire loops around my brain.

"Why though?!" I yell. And I hate myself for even presenting a question. He doesn't deserve the benefit of the doubt right now. Then, the fire inside me is crackling. He smiles softly at me. With all the force in my arm, I throw the aluminum water bottle at him. After it hits the side of his head, it lands and explodes on his beloved blazer. He stands up, the water falling on the floor. I imagine the water to be an offering to my ancestors. *I call upon you, Honorable Ancestors, Bruja Diosas, all that love, guide, and protect me.* The fire inside me is now on the outside and encircles my body. I breathe deeply and exhale slowly, asking the fire to grow around the other bodies in the room.

Ben charges toward me, but José is already an entire shield in front of me.

"I know you lost, but you ain't stupid, pariguayo e' la mierda," José whispers. Their faces are so close that I am scared a single breath might force one of them to erupt. Mrs. Obi tries to squeeze in between them, but they don't allow for any space to exist for that.

"Use standard English when you're trying to insult me," Ben smirks.

"You better get your face out my face," José warns. His chest grows.

"José and Ben, please step outside!" Mrs. Obi urges. But it's too late to de-escalate.

"You better listen to her, boy," Ben snarls.

"Boy?!" Autumn shrieks. Everyone's voice says something, pumping with anger.

"You must've lost your damn mind," Cindy shrieks.

"Coming here like you run this school," Jay adds.

"Who the hell even let this kid into the club?" someone asks.

My brain begins to pound against my skull.

"I'm going to tell you one last time, get your face out my face," José whispers. And some spit undeniably escapes José's mouth and lands on Ben's face. Ben pushes José only to have José push him back so hard he flies out of the circle.

Everyone in the circle rises up, stands up, and surrounds Ben. No one says a word, but our eyes are all over him, as if we are trying to examine him, honor our rage, and decide what to do next.

Stand up for each other. Estoy orgullosa de ti. Protect one another. Self-preservation. Our ancestors whisper among us. I like to think that in this moment we are everything they wished for when they sacrificed everything they did.

We hear the walkie-talkies before the security guards come in. As Mrs. Obi explains to Mr. Leyva what went down, he looks at me, but then away quickly, as if to make sure I don't catch the disappointment in his eyes.

15

SHAKING MY HEAD

We are crowded into Ms. Steinberg's office—Papi, José, José's sister Paola, Mrs. Obi, Mr. Ruiz, and me. Mami was working all day and Mamá Teté had a reading, so this left Papi as the only person who could come to the restorative. He was excited, too. Over the moon even. He claimed he was proud of me for showing this kid I meant business, but most importantly for standing up for myself. Papi has always been an advocate of, "If they bite you, you bite back."

"Por tu estar de gallito," Paola says, "trying to get chosen." Papi covers his mouth to hide his quiet laugh. Paola has been avoiding my eyes, and I know she ain't feeling the fact that José defended me. I get it, it's her little brother, but it's not on me that our cultures raise boys to puff out their chest and fight for respect and to prove they're "men." It's dumb, I know, but it also felt good to be defended in that moment. That's ridiculous, right? No, I deserve to feel special, but I guess this shows that I have also been conditioned to want certain things to feel like a "real girl." Goddamn. We have a lot of undoing and unlearning to do.

"It's not even like that, Paola," José responds. Ben and his

father, Mr. Hill, finally arrive. The heating system hisses and
bangs as it automatically begins feeling the cold wrapping up this
building.

"Good morning. We apologize for the tardiness. I very much
want to be here, but I have no more than fifteen minutes before I
have to leave for a district meeting," Mr. Hill says, as he opens his
blazer and sits.

"Of course," Ms. Steinberg says. She begins by going through
the norms. Ben looks at me whenever no one is looking at him,
and my skin wants to crawl into itself.

Ms. Steinberg asks me, José, and Ben to name what happened from our perspectives. In each perspective, I am the one
who ultimately throws the water bottle at Ben.

"Yolanda, what was it that you felt the moment you swung
the water bottle?" Ms. Steinberg asks.

I look over at Papi. He purses his lips and nods. I want to tell
them the truth. That I had a vision and that I know no matter
what hope I had about changing Ben's mind, he isn't here to see
the good in us.

"I felt disrespected, like Ben wasn't being considerate of
the club or its members. Ben is new in this school. He doesn't
know the sacrifice it's taken us to have this club in the first place.
He thinks it's a joke, and to be honest, I am not sure why he even
tried to join it—it's clear he doesn't believe in social justice," I
say, "period."

Ben tries to intervene, but Ms. Steinberg reminds him he'll
have his chance.

"Ms. Steinberg, despite all the messed-up stuff happening
to Black and Brown people, kids, a lot of us would come in here
and forget about that. Ben's presence has"—I try to find the

word—"disrupted that." Mr. Hill's eyes look empathetic while he rubs his chin with his fingers.

"And Ben, what did you feel when you posted these stickers on the posters?"

His jaw is tight, and he stays quiet for some time, but eventually Ben starts telling his side of the story.

"This is a school, not a Black Lives Matter march."

There he is. Whatever front he was trying to put up for some of the teachers and students—it's all a game.

"Ben!" his father exclaims. "You've got to excuse Ben. You see, growing up the son of a politician has made him a rebel without a cause of sorts." He shakes his head, looking disappointed as hell. "Look," he puts his palm on the edge of the table in front of him, "as you all know, I am a Democrat, and we don't share the views presented by those stickers. And when I say *we*, I am including Ben and his mother. Again, he's a boy, just rebelling."

"No, I'm not some pretend liberal—" Ben starts.

"Ben!" Mr. Hill says. The silence becomes so loud, my ears ring. I touch my earpiece, and Papi asks me if I'm OK. I nod.

"Listen," Mr. Hill clears his throat, fixing his blazer. "My son has friends who are people of color. His godfather happens to be a Black man, who I went to Fordham Law with. What Ben is saying is simply coming from a place of immaturity, and we will work on it at home."

Paola looks at Mr. Hill as if she can't believe he fixed his mouth to say we-have-Black-friends-so-we-can't-be-racist. "You've got to be kidding me," she finally says. "With all due respect, I know you not coming in here and trying to tell us that your son is not racist because he has a Black godfather."

"No, of course not," he says. The blood rushes to his face.

"Oh OK," she says, clearly pretending to be OK with his answer.

Mrs. Obi purses her lips. "Mr. Hill, as the adult who was in the room, I want to share that the things said in the space are of great concern."

"Well, maybe you can tell me why my son was pushed onto the floor and surrounded by all of the students in the club?" Mr. Hill adds. Gaslighting, of course. I am a fool. Why was I low-key believing his dad was completely on the opposite end of the spectrum? He raised him!

"Ben pushed first," José says.

"Did that result with your body on the floor?" Ben asks.

"Considering the boys' different build," Mr. Hill begins.

"Listen, my brother pushed him with whatever force because your son pushed him first. My mother raised us not to hit first, and my brother didn't, but he's not a pendejo," Paola cuts him off.

"But the force," Mr. Hill adds. He looks at the other adults like they're supposed to help him out.

"My brother is an athlete, OK? And to be fair he felt some type of way about your son's ridiculous reaction to social justice. I mean, the audacity is out of this world!" Paola adds.

Ben takes a deep breath that feels sarcastic at its exhale. "How old are you? You don't sound old enough to be here for José," Ben says.

"You better go elsewhere with your respectability politics," Paola bites back.

We're silent waiting for the principal to say something or for someone to respond.

"Mr. Hill, I think students like Yolanda and José feel threatened by Ben's verbal remarks in our socio-cultural environment during these very difficult times for marginalized groups. I hear that Ben is in a very unique position, but it is one of privilege. I want to make sure we are not excusing the harm he has caused," Ms. Steinberg says. I am surprised; it wasn't the energy she was giving in the office the other day.

Papi nods, and Mr. Hill looks at Ben with grief and anger both sitting on his brow.

"Come on, what we're asking for here is an apology, not money. Why is it taking so long?" Papi points out impatiently. My jaw softens at the sound of Papi speaking up for me, but I don't want him to get too involved. I'm not embarrassed that my dad has been to jail—I am scared they'll use it against us.

"Your daughter attacked me," Ben yells. "She can't help being aggressive, clearly." Ben looks at his dad.

I can't see the boy in the cafeteria with a deep loneliness; I can't see the softness he showed with the bodega cat either. I can't see who he was when he read the room and realized Kristina was being rude. All I see is a sharp, cold anger.

"Dad, you know I can press charges," he says.

Please, Bruja Diosas, don't let him say I've been to his house. Mr. Hill shakes his head. Ben gets out of his seat, his fists full of himself and blood. "She assaulted me, not the other way around. She started this entire incident," he stands over the table. Mr. Hill urges him to sit. I look at Ms. Steinberg. It feels like this is the moment to stop this restorative.

Papi opens his mouth to speak, but José says, "You looked for it, didn't you?"

Ms. Steinberg asks us all to respect the talking piece which has been ignored the entire time, a triangle set in front of Ben's father who keeps looking down at his watch. He whispers into Ben's ear as if we're not all here.

"I'm not apologizing," Ben says. Paola rolls her eyes and says something about riquitos under her breath. The heating system kicks and bangs like an auditory protest to Ben's stance.

"If that's the case, this circle cannot conclude, and there's a three-day in-school suspension order for all parties involved," Ms. Steinberg announces.

"What?! This is some bullshit. My brother ain't ever been involved in no school drama. And now he's on school suspension because this little boy doesn't know how to say sorry?" Paola's voice gets lower and lower in my head. Their pressure settles into the seat of my brain. *No, no, not now, Bruja Diosas.* I take a deep breath. *Please not now.* As my vision becomes milky, I close my eyes.

"That *is* some bullshit," I hear Papi affirm.

It is muggy and humid in the back staircase. It's just me here, I notice quickly. Ben's navy-blue backpack is at my feet. I fall to my knees and take the zipper between my fingers. I take a deep breath. Clomp! Clomp! Clomp! There are wet and loud footsteps approaching from the bottom of the staircase and also from the top. I let go of the backpack and look in both directions, but there is nothing physical, just the sound of wet steps. I go back to the backpack, the zipper hot this time; I pull slowly, the zipper hisses. I put my hand in the backpack and keep my eyes on the staircase. My hand rustles through some pages, but when my fingers bump into a cold, heavy thing, I know exactly what it is.

But there's no convincing Ms. Steinberg. She says there are various parts to every story. That there were various parties involved without a doubt, and that everyone has to be held accountable. I want to throw up. Does this make it to the college application?

"Ms. Steinberg, this is my first offense, why am I being placed in in-school suspension?" I say. My voice cracks a little. I know suspension ain't even that big of deal, but I don't want to have it attached to me. The bangs from the old heating system come to a halt.

"There was violence all around, Yolanda. We have to be fair," Ms. Steinberg responds.

Papi places his hands reassuringly over the knot I've made with my fingers.

On our way out of the office, the members of the club are standing around, pretending they weren't just waiting.

"Don't worry about it, Yo," Papi says. "Mamá can make you one of her baños to get rid of toda esa sal." I nod. Yeah, maybe Mamá Teté can work her magic to make me feel better, because this feeling ain't it.

Mr. Leyva rushes the club members to their classes, and as soon as the hallways are cleared, we make our way out. Despite being in a rush, Ben's father stays behind in Ms. Steinberg's office. *Hmmmm*, I cross my arms. What are they trying to do to make this go away for Ben?

"Mr. Alvarez, I am Mr. Leyva," Mr. L catches up to us. "Your daughter is one of my favorite kids. And I'm not saying that because she's here." Papi and he begin to chop it up. I take the opportunity to go back to the office saying I forgot something. I tiptoe in. The office door is not totally closed.

"Mr. Hill, I have to be frank with you. He will serve the in-school suspension if he is to be here at all," Ms. Steinberg says.

"Is there anything that can be done in terms of a donation—"

Mr. Hill is cut off. "I'm going to stop you right there. I was trying to figure out how bad this was right before you arrived this morning. I contacted Butler Prep. They have informed me of Ben's prior situations," Ms. Steinberg says. By her tone, I know she's no longer standing on the side she was on earlier.

"Pushed out due to harassment and stalking, both motivated by hateful views," she continues. "Hanging nooses as an art project, wearing a Native American headdress for a presentation, *physically* injuring an Asian student with chopsticks? Butler failed to see how his views led to these incidents until it was too late. We won't make that mistake here," Ms. Steinberg says sternly. "One more incident with Ben, and I will make sure he never sets a foot in this school again."

A breeze comes in through a window, and the door closes.

What in the actual fuck? I close my eyes. *Honorable Ancestors, Bruja Diosas, all that love, guide, and protect me, I apologize. I am sorry that I really doubted myself and in turn you all.*

When I open my eyes, my vision is blurry. But I see Ben, through a cloud, in front of me. His face is a blur, but his eyes are cold and clear. I swallow to keep from choking on my own heartbeat.

Papi drives me home. Normally, he's been playing bachata while he drives these days, or we talk. But today it's only the sounds from outside the car keeping everything from being completely silent. My phone buzzes in my pocket. José. I ignore it. Quite honestly, I just don't want to mess with anybody. I feel heavy,

drained. I have never felt like this before. A part of me doesn't
care about a thing. I started my sophomore year on the right foot,
and now it feels like I've lost all the progress I made. There's a
hole inside of me so deep with pain, it is numb. Despite the fights
and talking back last year, Julia De Burgos has become the place
I go to be the best version of me. Now it is all crumbling.

The only person I want to talk with about what I heard is
Victory, but we're still mad at each other and whatnot. And
I'm not ready. But now with everything I heard from Ms.
Steinberg—can that help the situation at all? My jaw aches
from all the tension.

Papi reaches out and touches my face. It's his finger brushing
over my tears that force me to realize I am crying.

"It's OK, mi'ja. Cry," he says. And now I am really crying. Snot
and tears running down my face. I wipe them off with the back of
my sleeve. I want to believe him when he says it's OK. But the
first thing that comes to my head is him telling me not to cry so
many times in life. I remember it on the day of departure from
our home. Even though I had been the one to know about his
deception first, I cried when he packed, and I cried when he said
his last goodbye at the door before Mami got out. And when my
tears flooded my face and my nostrils during pickups and drop-
offs, he'd say, "Relax, Yoyo, stop crying. It isn't the end of the
world." Maybe he was hurting too, but when I cried out for him
as he went into the elevators, and screamed like a limb was being
slowly pierced off of me, he said, "Mira, mucha e' la mierda, get
inside. Ain't nobody died. Stop crying." It's hard to accept him
being this soft with me now, but people get to change, right?

"Look," he says, swinging an arm to the back seat. "I bought
you this." I tear off the red tissue paper, and Assata Shakur's

Assata: An Autobiography is revealed. The cover is glossy and shiny. "I read it in there. It was one of my favorite ones. She is a brilliant and strong woman. Like you."

"Thank you, Papi."

◖

When we are approaching Mamá's door, I wince. Mamá won't understand. She will think I failed. Before Mamá is a bruja, she is a Black woman, and then an immigrant. She is here to uplift my bruja ways in private, but in public she wants me to be the best girl I can be. She will say suspensions never go off records, and they're prison's distant cousin. It's something she says often when she hears about a neighbor's kid being suspended or kicked out of school. I was supposed to be the one who did things right by her.

"Mamá will understand, Yo," Papi says, basically reading my mind. "In her eyes, you can do no wrong, Yolanda." But that isn't true. I want to tell him that things have changed. That Mamá Teté has been shifting as I have. That she was already afraid when she saw the café the other night.

She is sitting on the couch watching novelas when we get in. I can breathe a little easier because this means she must be in a good mood. She points towards the kitchen to tell Papi and me there's food saved for us. There's chicken drums con arroz y hab-ichuelas for Papi and yucca and stewed cod for me. Papi serves us both a glass of Coco Rico, and we go sit on the couch with Mamá. I'm not hungry, but you have to appreciate the old lady's ability to cook twice out of love for us, so I eat. Plus, as long as my mouth is stuffed, I don't have to say anything.

"How did it go?" she asks. I drop my fork and chew the batata that's in my mouth before swallowing it.

"I have in-school suspension for three days," I say. She says nothing. Papi explains.

"OK," she says. "You'll complete your suspension then."

(

After Papi leaves, the novela is done, the dishes have been washed, and she and I are in our batas getting ready for bed, I decide to press her. "Whatever you're doing, Mamá, can you please make it work faster? He's ruining my life at school now, and I swear he is a threat to the community there," I say.

"Patience," she says. "Mostly with yourself, Morena." She takes off her glasses and takes a deep breath. "Cuando tu iba, ya yo venia, Yolanda Nuelis. When you're ready to take the next step, I will be here to defend you with everything in my body and spirit. I told you to wait, to not tell anyone of authority. But now, I know I cannot and will not force you into anything. You have to decide what to do on your own. This is part of your work, your initiation."

I nod.

"This is your process. The Unknowns won't let me interrupt your journey as much as I want to." Tears rush to her eyes, and she kisses my forehead. "I am only here to facilitate."

16

SUSPENSION, TIME-OUTS, AND THE WORKS

DAY 1

They have got us in different rooms. I was placed into a room that is hardly used and stores most of our broken computers. There are dust bunnies and trails of rat poop everywhere I look, but at least I am alone.

That's soon interrupted when Mr. Leyva comes by and says we are all going to be placed in the same room due to the fact that I can't be unattended, and the other two small rooms are needed by teachers who had to pull out a small group of students.

"But Mr. Leyva," I start. "I'm not about to do anything out of pocket. I can just sit here and read!"

"There's nothing I can do, Yoyo. It's out of my hands," he says, sucking his teeth and closing the door behind us. I hate that teachers and principals treat him like he is supposed to do everything around here except make and bend some of the rules.

In the new room, Mr. Leyva offers us some new books to read, but I've brought my own: *Assata: An Autobiography*. This morning Papi really texted me to remind me to bring it to school. He said so I'd have something to keep me company, and it made me sad to think, damn he really was lonely in there. He smiled when he saw it under my arm when I came into his car. Papi is making a habit of picking and dropping me off whenever he can. I appreciate it more than he knows—not that he would want to know all the reasons as to why I hate the public transportation system. He said reading *The Autobiography of Malcolm X* and this Assata book is what saved him from himself in jail.

I hope that it saves me from my own hell: staring at the back of Ben's head four rows from me, while José is in the corner, five rows behind me. Mr. L is supervising us, so they've gotten a substitute to cover his posts. The top edges of the wall are filled up with university flags.

Mr. L wants to talk so bad you can see it in his tic to say something any time one of us coughs ("You catching a cold or somethin'?"), or any time one of us takes a mind-break from a book ("That book got you thinking, huh?"), or any time the bell rings ("They must all be going to Period X.") I smile at this because I'm used to it, but Ben shakes his head every single time like he's interrupting him from some big old job. He rubs the top of his head a lot, and I wonder if this is the way he self-regulates. I mean in the last three hours he's at least done it sixteen times. I've counted as I notice out of the corner of my eye.

That's who I've become around Ben. He makes me self-conscious and hyperaware of what and who is around me. And no, I'm not saying I've changed because of him. But he's definitely changed the energy around here. I hate that he has that kind of power, but it's the only way I feel I can stay safe in the moment, especially after what I heard Ms. Steinberg say.

José coughs, and I look up from my book. He gives me a small wave and I give him one back. *Thank you*, I mouth. I haven't said it was everything for him to have stood up for me. I could have defended myself, of course, but it just felt good to know he was on my side at that moment. He nods at me. *Siempre*, he mouths back, and I have to bring my book up to cover my face so he doesn't see my dorky ass smirk.

"All right now," Mr. L says, and raises an eyebrow at the both of us. Of course, that only makes José and me look at each other and bust out laughing.

By the time lunch comes around, I cannot believe we still have four periods left to go. José is picked up by Coach to go over the disciplinary consequences of his behavior, and Ben is picked up by the school counselor, Ms. Peters. A first-year is sent with a lunch tray for me, and I am excited to see it's pizza, an apple, and chocolate milk. Three things the DoE can't seem to fuck up.

"You said something the other day I haven't forgotten about," Mr. L says, as I bite into my apple. I chew and the tanginess causes a burst of sweetness-overload in my mouth.

"I guess I did," I say. I know he is referring to the feeling I told him I was having of something awful happening.

"You having the same dreams you had last year?"

I take a calculated breath, put my apple down, and correct my posture. "I still have dreams, but now I have visions, too. That's what I told you about."

Mr. L takes a swig of his hot chocolate. "Say more."

"More like what?" I shake my head. I feel the walls within me rise.

"You don't got to do all that now." He places his cup on the table, walks over to me, turns a chair in front of me, and sits. "You want to talk about it?"

"I started receiving visions right after Ben got here," I start. My hands begin to sweat and I rub them against my black jeans.

"What kind of visions?"

"Visions like dreams, except I am wide awake. Little by little, it's all making more and more sense, because they explain who this boy is and how he came out of left field and into our school."

"Oh yeah?" Mr. Leyva asks.

"He's been kicked out of mad private schools for having racist views, Mr. L." By mad I mean two, since Ms. Steinberg said a couple and that's two.

Mr. L jolts a little. "You said you had a vision tell you that?"

"Well, yes, but then I heard it too from Ms. Steinberg when she was talking to Ben's dad the other day. And recently I got another one where he's super upset, crouching over a backpack. But I can't see what it is."

"Maybe it was the stickers?" Mr. L says, peeling a callous on his hand.

Oh my god. My world stops. All the anxiety I've had about not being believed disappears. I feel uncovered again, like I did the first time.

He believes me. He knows my visions are real. *He sees me.*

"You good, Yo?"

"You believe me," I whisper.

"I don't take you as the lying type of kid," he chuckles.

I smile. "But no, it definitely wasn't a sticker, Mr. L. I believe— no, I know—it was a weapon."

DAY 2

José writes a whole ass letter that he hands to me before we walk into the room they're holding the three of us in. We don't even bother to switch things up. We sit in the same order and places as yesterday. The room feels colder today, so I keep on my sweater and jacket. I place the letter in my coat pocket and take out Assata's book. I've finished a third of it because I read after school to avoid speaking to Mamá Teté, who looks like she's in pain all day since she can't help me in the way she wants to.

Mr. L goes into his bag and takes out a white bag and a brown paper bag. He walks toward me first and when I look in the white bag, I see it's a few egg sandwiches. In the brown paper bag, there are three hot chocolates. I smile up at him and take one of each, grateful for his good heart. He walks towards Ben, and I watch him shake his head without saying thank you. I swear to God these privileged kids got no manners. It makes me angry to just see Mr. L be disrespected like that. Sure, he has the right to say no. He could just not like eggs, right? But he doesn't even seem grateful; instead, he looks upset he was bothered with the question. Mr. L then crosses over to José who takes both of them and stands up to give him a pound. José's manners make him so much more attractive. He doesn't let being "popular" get to his head like others do.

I crack open the book to where I left off. Assata is describing arriving at Rikers Island. She describes being internally searched, and I press my legs together on instinct, as if in another life, another time, I had experienced that pain.

☾

DAY 3

Today feels like the longest day. The roof of my mouth begins to hurt by 11:00 a.m., and I have no desire to read *Assata*. I go into my pocket and take out José's letter, which I forgot to read. Papi picked me up, so I couldn't read it then, and by the time I showered, ate, and had tried to connect with the Bruja Diosas, I was tired AF. I unfold it slowly and bring the paper up to my nose. It smells like sandalwood and moss, and I giggle when I realize he really sprayed his cologne on it.

Yo,

I've never written love letters. You feel like a good first. I have written notes to girls I've liked if I am being honest, but they were just notes—the type you throw across a room when a teacher turns their back—not as long as this letter at all. I want to be honest because I don't want whatever this is to start with lies. I am sure you know how that can go wrong. I know we young and whatnot, but I don't want us to go wrong. Not yet anyway. Maybe not ever? I know that's crazy, but I'm just saying.

When you came into Julia De Burgos I was a junior, and I hated the fact that I felt pulled to a freshman. Remember your first day how I tried to help you find your class, but you just ignored me? I thought about that all night. And that time you swung at Marcus for yelling "you deaf or something?" because he was calling after you after I told him I thought you were cute. You was a little stuck-up and shit, but I also thought about the way the white hoodie looked against your nutmeg skin. The way you always came to school with your curls in different hairstyles, it got my attention. I ain't going to lie, it communicated you took care of yourself and I loved that. I decided then you were too good for me. I wasn't out here taking care of myself because I wanted to, but because I was forced to by Coach, by my mom, and definitely by my sister. So I continued doing what I was doing. The reason I am saying any of this is because I've been thinking about my parents. They ain't together even though my mom is amazing and she loved him like crazy. My dad wasn't good enough though and he broke her in a way I don't have the words to describe, I guess. My sister is so guarded because of it. She doesn't really fuck around with anyone cause of it. Anyway, I promised myself that when I felt strong for someone, like you know, romantically, I was gonna try my best.

This year though, I just couldn't help it, and I think God or the Universe, or whoever is out there, don't want it in any other way. Because you in one of my classes. I'm so happy Coach forced me to retake chemistry! You're so smart and you think for yourself. I love that. I can't ignore my feelings or you now. Plus, watching you take the lead in the club just makes me picture you in the future as someone important for our community, and I want to be right there with you when that day comes, maybe. I know we are just in high school. But this gotta mean something.

I like how your voice is mighty even when it's soft. How you try to escape people's eyes but you shine so bright. Yo, we need your light. I like how your hair knows no bounds, it stretches everywhere even when you try to tie it up. The last time we kissed I was scared to touch it because I know girls don't like that. I feel so needy writing these words, but I don't care. I'll take the L if I need to cause I want you to know. My sister tries to help talk about my feelings, so I told her about you. How I'm going to college and a part of me don't want to because I finally got you. I don't even want to go away, I want to stay right here. She wasn't with the no college part, but she says she can see why I'm whooped. I also explained why I stood up for you. I told her you hadn't asked me to or anything like that. It just felt like what I had to do in the moment. I would've done it for anyone in that club if I'm being honest, but for you: with eyes closed.

I am sorry I got us into this situation. I know you are blaming yourself for throwing the bottle at him, but we all know he high-key deserved it. Maybe if I would've stayed in my seat I could've avoided making the situation into a scene, but I just did what came to me: defend you. It's not the best thing to do and yet it's the only thing I got to give someone like you.

I know you don't need saving. I know you don't need me. I know you have the right to choose. So I'm asking you right now, putting my pride on the sidelines: Will you be mine, Yolanda Nuelis Alvarez?

XO,
José

17

WATER BE AS NECESSARY AS BLOOD

I t's dark when José and I walk out of our final day of in-school suspension. Instead of giving him an answer I kiss him and slip my hand into his.

It's only 4:45 p.m. and I feel like I have to go home to bed already. It's so dark. One thing I cannot stand about the winter is how it does not let us fully enjoy our days. Still, I appreciate that during this time of the year there is a natural need to be alone, to reflect, to go deep on all of the things the brightness of longer days keeps tucked away. I see her only when we get closer and I let go of José's hand immediately.

I do it instinctively, with no good real reason. It's always been just Victory and me, even when either one of us has had our little side things, and it feels awkward letting her see me with someone else. Someone who has been filling the time I haven't spent with her in the two weeks basically. Even space on my phone. In this time, all I've gotten are messages from José, not her.

"I'll take the bus home. Can I call you later?" José asks. I nod, satisfied at his social intelligence because boys sometimes, well, they don't catch any clues.

Victory is wearing platform Doc Martens and a long black maxi dress under her waist-cinched bubble coat. I imagine she's wearing long johns underneath because it's still so damn cold. Her faux gold double-knocker earrings move with the wind. Sometimes she switches out of her uniform when the last bell rings. Even if it's simply to take the bus. She says it's a moment to adorn herself with what she wants.

"So y'all out here just holding hands now?"

"Well, I guess we are," I smile.

"You don't have to be weird about it, you know?" she says. "If you like it, I love it."

I nod, grateful for all she is.

"You want to walk to the Dominican place?" she asks. Usually, we just go to the bodega and share a butter roll and soda or juice. No more than $3.50.

"Oh you got Dominican place money?" I laugh. She says her parents gave her a little extra since she mentioned she wanted to treat me to dinner on my last day of suspension, after everything that's happened. We still gotta share though, but I'm not complaining.

The perspiration from all the boiling platanos and turning, broiling chickens hits us as soon as we walk into El Malecon. The merengue playing reminds me of all the house parties Papi and Mami used to force me to go to as a kid. I always found friends though.

Although Victory and I are acting as if nothing has happened, there is a full cloud hanging over us. I want to talk about what we said, but I also don't want to ruin today. Victory and I met in kindergarten. We went to The Little Apple School on Dyckman Street, and she was the only non-Spanish-speaking girl in our class. Her parents, who knew enough Spanish to get by, believe in the importance of Black people sharing as many common languages as possible. They never fail to remind us that Black people, the descendants of the ones who were forced to this side of the world, were Africans first. And in that way we are united past nationalities, languages, and distance. At Little Apple, no kid seemed to want to take the time or effort to communicate with Victory, but when you're five, effort is practically a myth. One day during play time we both had to use the bathroom, so our assistant teacher took us. Inside the stalls, I started singing a pipí song with a simple and particular hum. Victory joined along. For the next week, Victory and I pointed at objects, and she said the word in English and I repeated in Spanish, or vice versa. We taught each other how to speak the other's mother tongue, and it secured this bond for us.

"So we all out of language now, huh?" Victory says. People have been reading my mind a lot these days. The waitress brings us complimentary garlic bread. We order two morir soñandos, and fried fish with tostones and salad.

"I'm so—" I start.

"Don't apologize. We said what we said," she smiles.

"And it had to be said." I take a piece of bread from the basket the second it's placed down.

"Listen, sis," she begins. "I am going to be here no matter what. But this Ben shit is getting out of hand. You just sat through a three-day suspension over him."

"Getting?" I roll my eyes. "The kid is officially out of pocket."

"That part," she points at me. "So what's your plan?"

"I am just watching him close for now. I am trying my best to stay vigilant about the things I dream about or whatever vision I get I will share with Mamá for extra insight."

"All right cool," she nods. I am not sure if she truly is OK with my answer, but we both let it be. "You don't have to carry this alone, and it's not on you to save anyone. Mom says it's time Black women hang up our capes 'cause it's never beneficial to us. It just drains us," she continues. I nod sadly because it's true. I cannot save anyone but myself. I'm not a hero or martyr. I don't want to be either, even if they're glorified everywhere.

"Yeah, I hear you. Honestly, first I told Mamá, and it felt like less of a burden. Then I told Mrs. Obi and Mr. L, and the weight of it felt even more lighter. Now I just feel like I need to sharpen up this strategy," I chew.

"You know I believe in your visions and in your powers. But there has to be a way to solve this physically, in real time," Victory says. She goes into her bag and brings out her journal. Although I know she isn't saying it with bad intentions, it burns a little. Even though no one else can "see" it, Mamá and I have got it.

"Mamá is doing whatever it is she can. Making me baths, pouring blessings upon us all, but she says she really can't push me to take action or do much herself until I'm ready. The Unknowns won't let her," I say.

"What you mean they won't let her?" Victory flips the pages in her journal.

"It's my process, and she can't intervene until I'm ready."

"I see," she flips through some more pages.

"Girl, please," I say. "I'm trying."

"What Mr. L said about your visions?" she continues flipping.

"He asked questions. Honestly, he believes me. He didn't say much, but watch us come back next week and something is different.

You know how he is." Victory nods over and over while taking a sip of water. She looks up and into the deepest part of my eye.

"There's something I have to tell you," she says. She takes a deep breath, nodding her head over and over, her eyes now on the table. "I've done some research on Ben while you were in detention." Her hands dig into her backpack.

"OK?"

"So, yes, your first vision about this kid was, as we all know, correct. He's been kicked out of two elite private schools in three years," Victory says. She mentions that during our time apart she went into a rabbit hole and did a ton of research, including sliding into students at Butler Prep's DMs through a fake Insta account. She opens up her journal and spreads her hands over the pages. She sits up. "And of course, his dad has flipped this 'inconvenience' to his advantage and used Ben being here to bring in some voters."

I tell her about what I overheard about what went down at Butler Prep. "But girl, what did he actually do to get kicked out the first place?" I ask. She suddenly looks overwhelmed with all the information. Like she's trying to connect dots.

"Ma'am, can you give me a minute? I'm getting there." She widens her eyes. I wave my hand, edging her to go on. "So after Cindy told me his username for Fortnite, I messed around with the spelling of the name, and, of course, I found him on the internet. All up on YouTube."

"Making videos?"

"No, but leaving these racist ass content creators comments like, 'Right on, brother. Bring back the America that works.'"

I practically throw up in my mouth.

"But that isn't even the weirdest thing," Victory continues. "His most common comment is: AYAK?"

"Girl, what that mean?" My mind begins rushing through potential acronyms and abbreviations.

"Are You a Klansman?"

"STOP IT!" I yell.

"Yup, I mean I don't think he's been initiated or whatever the fuck. I think he's just doing it to try to be down with those people. But some of these folks actually replied with 'AKIA' or 'A Klansman I Am.'"

"Even if he's not, it's dangerous."

"We already knew all this, right?" Victory asks. "We knew he's riding a white supremacist wave or alt-right or whatever folks wanna call hateful and racist people nowadays." Victory sighs. I'm silent for a while. We did know, she's right. We had gut feelings, I had the visions, and it all pointed to this. But having all this proof? Wild. Wild. Wild. I don't want this for us. I don't want it for *any* of us. I don't even want it for Ben, to keep it one hundred. It really does break my heart that the world is set up to be this way. Where did we fuck up? How do we undo all of this?

"Right?" Victory asks again, bringing me back from my thoughts.

"Yeah, we did," I say. I hate that for bits and pieces of time I doubted myself, the visions, and the Bruja Diosas. "Thank you for believing in me, Victory. Sometimes it's like you believe in me more than I do in myself."

She waves me off like it's nothing.

☾

He calls me at 10 p.m., when I am half asleep, but I pick up anyway. I try to cough out the sleepiness in my voice when he asks if he should just call tomorrow. "No, we can talk now," I say. It's the weekend, and I already miss bumping into him.

"Did you read it?" José asks. I blush when I tell him I did.

"So?"

I'm scared to say yes. To begin a pattern that looks like Mami's. Feeling like a man is a necessary detail in my life. But I like him. Really like him. Even keeping him waiting pains me.

"We can try it," I say. I hear and see him release his breath, and I can't help but chuckle.

"So you're my girl, yeah?"

"Uh, nope! We are together, that's it. I'm not yours and you are not mine." And I feel balanced after I say that.

"I can live with that, Yo."

I readjust myself on the bed and accidentally press on the camera option. When I look at my screen, his face is on it. He smiles, and we just lay there smiling through the phone. I take a deep breath as I feel the place inside my gut rise up to my chest.

"I like you, José," I say. "Like a lot. And I know you like me also, but you don't know who I am . . . not fully at least."

"OK. Do you want to tell me who you are then?"

"I can try," I whisper. I tuck my hair behind my ears.

"That's all you can do. I'm here for whenever you're ready." José sits up.

José feels so close to me. A part of me feels like these few months of school have low-key been years. Except he really doesn't know everything about me. How unfair is it for someone to have all these feelings about me when they don't know the entire truth? It's just not fair. I have to tell him.

"Remember the story you told me about your cousin and the witch?" I ask. I follow suit and sit up.

"Yeah, what's up?"

"What if I told you I carry that energy, too?" The flame of the candle on my altar flickers and grows into a straight, thick flame. A confirmation. *Thank you, Bruja Diosas.*

José purses his lips and shakes his head just once, bringing his face closer onto his phone like he's trying to understand. "Bruja energy?"

"Mmmmhmmmm," I smile.

He shrugs. "Don't all Caribbeans, all Black people, have that? My mom be saying she's praying for me, my grandparents too, but the way it feels and actually shows up in my life—all of that smells like a spell to me, Yo." He chuckles and so do I.

"Yeah, yeah," I nod. "Exactly." He isn't wrong, but letting him think that's what I am referring to would be wrong. It would be a way of continuing to deny and downplay my connection.

"You right, pero I have *BIG* bruja energy. My grandmother has been guiding me into the tradition since I was a little girl. Many in my bloodline have accepted the energy for what it is and called it by its name," I add. José looks away from the camera. His face angled towards a wall shows off his sharp jaw, as he thinks. Now I'm pursing my lips and squinting my eyes as I wait for an answer. "You understand?"

His eyes move back to the camera, back to me, and he smiles. "I might have questions later, but I respect that, Yo."

I smile, my lips quivering a bit. "Yeah?"

"Of course," he nods. "Thank you for telling me." He brings the phone closer to his face and blows a kiss that sends us both into laughter.

BEYOND LA BOTANICA

Mamá Teté wakes me up this morning by lifting the back of my shirt and scratching my back vertically and later in cir cles. I don't even have to look back to know it's her. The scent of coffee and agua florida that follows her everywhere gives her away. Her fingernails feel like a small bird gliding around my back. I used to go to sleep this way when I was a little girl, and if Mamá Teté wasn't around to do it, I'd make Mami or Papi do it.

I stand up, the white noise of the night still in my ear, the sounds of the world up in the early morning vibrating through my body. Mamá Teté plays with one of the curls that have escaped my bonnet some time during the night. She gently tucks it back in. I look at her. Her chocolate skin has grown more and more sun spots. Her eyelids are beginning to collapse. Mi vieja is getting older. I take her face in my hands and plant a big kiss on her cheek. She hugs me, takes my entire body in, squeezes, and then taps on my back three times with the palm of her hand. She looks at me, and I read her lips: "Vete a bañar." I point to my tarot cards; she knows my routine. She takes them in her hand, does a quick prayer, shuffles them, and spreads them for me to choose.

I shimmy out of joy. Mamá isn't always in a good mood with me anymore. I pull one towards the middle.

Ten of Wands. A person is carrying ten sticks to another place; however, they are clearly struggling and feeling weighed down by the task.

"You're doing too much, Yolanda Nuelis. Enough is enough," I read Mamá's lips. She crosses her arms in front of her chest. "You shouldn't have to carry this load alone. You have to lean on your Bruja Diosas. And I have to figure out how the Unknowns will let me help you. It isn't possible for you to do it alone, mi vida." Even though Mamá Teté is saying these things, I hear the Bruja Diosas loud and clear through her.

"Now go," Mamá points to the bathroom. My phone vibrates. "Your mother is calling you."

☾

Only because I beg does Mamá finally agree to taking an Uber Shared to la botanica. If it were summer or spring, I would've said let's walk—it's only thirty minutes. But it's too cold to walk right now. And every time Mamá and I get on public transportation, she gets into some sort of argument with a pervert. "She's sixteen!" she'll yell. She'll look at him and won't let go until the man is yelling right back at her. The Uber ride is nice. The driver has a yellow and red headwrap on, and the car smells like straight-up chamomile.

"Buen día," Mamá says, settling into the back seat.

"Ase!" the driver responds. There is a sweet melody in her voice, and her smile makes me feel like today will be uplifting.

"Ah, I see—Osun priestess?" Mamá says, putting on her glasses.

The driver looks at Mamá through the rearview mirror. "That

I am. Had my baptism a year and a half ago, and I am now hustling, but always working for Osun," the driver says.

"Where did you get initiated?"

"New Orleans, but most of the work I did in Puerto Rico and Cuba."

"I went to Haiti, Cuba, and Puerto Rico once in the same year," Mamá says.

I look at Mamá Teté. She stares out the window squinting her eyes a little. She goes into her pocket without taking her eyes off the window and she pulls out her dark glasses. She bites her lip a little. Mamá has never been one to think about the past too much, much less talk about it and to a stranger. Pero, I know Spirit must be calling for her to.

"I thought the Unknowns and my ancestors had abandoned me. The love of my life, my son's father, murdered while working in this taxi business. On top of that, my son refused to respect the connection we've inherited. I thought maybe there were different powers out there. Powers that would give me what I wanted when I wanted. I was young then. I didn't understand that Spirit delivers under divine conditions. Out in the islands, I met so many good people. People I wish I could call. To tell them I figured it out for myself: our ancestors and our saints all commune together. When I make offerings to one, I make offerings to all."

"Ase, sister, ase. Sounds like that was your process," the driver responds.

Mamá and the driver exchange numbers before we exit the car.

When Mamá opens the door to La Botanica Miel de Pie, the scent of sweet flowers and white sage wraps around me. Tía Dulce's daughter redesigned the place. By the entrance there are large glass bowls holding water. Another holds many coins, offerings from those who enter. Mamá places six quarters into the bowl.

"Esta súper bonito in here," I tell Mamá Teté, and she nods. It's my first time seeing it this way. There is a large bamboo chandelier hanging from the ceiling, making the botanica have more light than it ever had. In the past it was dim, like many other botanicas in New York City I have visited with Mamá. In the middle of the floor there are two medium, brown leather couches. In the center of the couches, a long bamboo table with candles and three different decks, quartz crystals on top of them. The two walls that surround the place are painted yellow and they are lined up with glass shelves that hold many herbs like sage and rosemary bundles, fixed candles and oils, and many differentiating crystals and divination decks. Further in, a wooden counter separates the front from the back of the shop.

Once at the counter, Mamá leans over it, picks up a bell by the register, and waves it to announce we are here. Tía Dulce walks out of the back door dressed in khakis, a yellow turtleneck sweater, and furry slippers. Her curly wig makes her appear more youthful. The red on her lips spreads into a smile as she reaches out her hands, dressed to nearly her elbow in gold bracelets and bangles.

"¡Comadre!" they shriek. Tía Dulce puts up the wooden counter and now the front and the back seem like one big room. They fall into one another's arms. Mamá Teté comes in here at least once a month, but they act like they haven't seen each other in years every time. They've been friends since soon after Mamá Teté arrived in the Bronx. Mamá even helped in Tía Dulce's second daughter's birth, automatically making her her madrina.

"Pero Nuelis, is that you?" Tía Dulce looks at me.

"It's me, Tía," I say. She pulls me into a tight embrace. All the sudden I am a child instead of a teenager. When I was young, I really didn't like my first name, Yolanda, so everyone called me by my middle name. It wasn't until I started ninth grade that I started reclaiming Yolanda. She pulls me off, and looks at me with so much joy before planting a kiss on my forehead.

"Miel has blessed you," she says, looking at me again from head to toe.

"Tú no sabes nada," I hear Mamá Teté murmur.

Tía Dulce waves us into the back. Walking into the narrow hallway, we turn right into a doorway to the small room where she keeps her altar. It is beautiful—flowers everywhere, a shelf with many glasses of water, pictures of relatives and friends who have passed, and statues. A large plate of food—covered up of course. The Miel statue that always takes me out is front and center as ever. It is a Black woman with a sweet and yet aloof smile. She wears a yellow head wrap, and a yellow shawl covers her body although all her curves can be seen. Her fingers each have rings, every wrist and ankle adorned in bracelets. Tía has large plates with white petals and honey at the statue's feet.

Tía throws her hands up. On the wall opposite her altar, everything is in shambles. There is a sink, a small electric stove, and dozens of mason jars. "¡Ay, perdónenme! All these baños, all these trabajos, all these things for the people. But I do it with love. Always."

Mamá nods and smiles. "Comadre, we need your undivided attention whenever you can." Tía moves from one unfinished task to another. She wipes her hand on her pants. Then Tía walks us out of the small room, and quickly shows us her new office before pointing us to the last door, the small bathroom.

"Wow," Mamá Teté says. She mentions that last month only the front of the botanica was done and she thought that was it. "Remodeling all of this must have cost a ton."

Tía Dulce walks us back out front. "You know there were many, many favors I had to check in," she winks.

"Oh yeah," Mamá Teté winks. "We know how those go." They laugh, and it is clear they share inside secrets.

Tía Dulce puts down the wooden counter, and we walk out into the botanica. Sitting on the couch, I see Tía has a public altar by the glass storefront I must've missed when we entered. There are many statues of Unknowns and others, flowers, cups of different drinks, and food. But what stands out to me is a huge statue, even bigger than Dulce, of a dark person in red pants smoking tobacco. I've seen this statue before, but not like this, not this size.

"The girl had a vision. She shared it with me," Mamá Teté pats my shoulder, sitting on the couch next to me. Tía Dulce sits in front of us. "But for some reason the Unknowns aren't letting me share the work with her, they insist on her taking a heavier portion of the load. Pero, she's my granddaughter. I see what weight does to her."

I hear Mamá speaking behind me as I reach the altar. The statue sets its eyes on me and does not let go. They are so beautiful. Their skin once made of cast and other materials now looks like real, melanated skin. It shines. The air around me is muggy and hot. My head feels light. I feel like I am also in trance. The objects around the statue blur so that my sight is only captivated by the clarity of them.

"Nuelis!" Tía Dulce says. I point towards the statue.

"They are so beautiful. So majestic," I whisper. The last word being the only thing I can boil it down to. "Tía, how'd you get that statue in here? It's so big." There's silence.

"Nuelis!" Tía calls me back. I look back at my elders and a heavy, deep sentiment falls over my body.

I look at Mamá Teté. Here I am thinking we are having a good date. Spending time alone. And she is telling Tía Dulce I can't do things on my own. She is saying I am not strong enough for the weight or the toll of all this. Even though I know she means it in the softest of ways, somewhere in the back of my mind, I am offended by her for the first time in a long while. Mamá Teté can be tough with her words and I have trained myself to understand them at the stake she means it, but right now I'm hot over what she's implying. All the blood in my body swims towards my head, and I feel a fire at my feet.

"Mirame, niña," Tía Dulce says, standing up and moving towards me. I want to obey, but my eyes won't move to look at her. My eyes stay on Mamá Teté, who stares at Tía and looks towards me in quick, stolen glances. The flames form under my body. But they won't burn me; they hold me. Keep me warm, alive, and safe.

"Look at me," Tía Dulce says softly. She takes my face between her hands. "You cannot go against who Culebra protects." Mamá Teté stands up, looking at me, and then turning her head from me with pride as she walks towards the counter. The agua florida fragrance from her skin makes me feel as if something has been taken from me. I want to leap towards her, but I hold my body, anchor it to the fire below me. My skin is boiling. I am fuming, upset at what feels like pretentiousness. My head suddenly feels like it's taken a blow. I walk to the couch and take off my black-and-red puffer coat. I fall onto the couch and take deep breaths.

It feels as if I'm alone. Like the Bruja Diosas have abandoned me . . . Mamá Teté has abandoned me . . . what else is there left? No, no. They haven't. They're right here. I just have to do this alone. The fire thickens.

Tía Dulce walks closer to me. "Sobrina, can you hear me?" she says. I blink. "You are a great, great fire. Your grandmother protects you on this side and the other. Your anger is being directed at the wrong person," Tía says. She runs to the back and quickly brings a cup of hot coffee to my face, and I drink it as fast as I would drink water on a really hot day. I notice she has bought back other things with her. When I am done, my hand allows the cup to fall on the floor without my permission. Tía kisses my forehead.

"Toma," she pours Brugal from a bottle into the cap. "Drink this," she says. I want to tell her I am only sixteen and that I shouldn't be drinking alcohol, but something in my stomach tells me I want this. An urge. A craving. I throw my head back and allow the rum to burn through my throat. The liquid quickly settles at the pit of my stomach.

Tía Dulce walks to the public altar, picks up a cigar, and lights it with the flame of a candle. She takes many puffs and blows it over the altar. Then she walks to me, kneels before me, takes a few pulls, and blows it on my face. The smoke smells exquisite, and it feels divine as it falls on my skin. I want to drink it. "¿Qué quieres más, Fuego?" I look at Tía, but it is no longer her, it is Miel.

"Chocolate negro," the words pour out of my mouth. I am not sure it is me that has answered. There is a cloak over my body, over my spirit, speaking for me. Miel stands up and runs to the back; a tail of gold flows behind her. I watch her come back through the blurriness that has taken over my sight. I take the bark of dark chocolate instantly when she brings it to my lips. It melts sweet and bitter on my tongue.

"I am not angry or lost or unwilling to provide answers. The girl is. We have been slowly bringing on her ascension because she is skeptical, almost scared of the visions—of the truths we have been sending her. She is frightened thinking she won't be believed, or she won't know what to do," a voice says.

"But visions?! Fuego, she is only a girl. Too young to be burdened with all of that," Miel shrieks. "Please, let us help!" It hits me that Miel is looking at me, and the initial voice has come out of my mouth.

"There's a boy in her school," the voice says from inside of me. I bring my hands to my mouth surprised, and then something instantly retrieves them.

"Oh that's just love, nothing to worry about. Don't we just love the act of loving?" Miel gets up, wrapped up in her glory and tale. Unsure of what she's speaking about because Mamá Teté hasn't had any time to tell her.

"No! Listen to me!" This time the voice is my own.

I close my eyes and see for what feels like the first time. Somewhere inside of my skin, inside of my soul, Fuego's wrinkled, umber hand grabs my own. Their eyes are a soft coffee shade and they look into me. *Can I do the talking?* they ask. I nod. They step into me.

"It is anything but love," Fuego says. "The girl is getting the truth: this boy is on a mission to try and fill a need. He won't stop until he gets it. It'll happen at the school."

"There must be someone we can reach to shift this," Miel sits. Her mouth hangs slightly open, like a circular question.

"Are you ready to go to war with all your love and perfume?"
The words exit my mouth like a machete, without warning, in a
hiss between my teeth. It's as if the words want to cut Miel. I try to
come up out of this warm and uncomfortable glory to tell Fuego
not to try to injure my elders, to tell Tía Dulce it's not really me.
But it is heavy, and I do not wish to go against an Unknown. "The
vision will be a reality. There will be blood. The girl—"

"You couldn't come to me with this Fuego?" a voice I recognize says. When I turn towards the counter, it's Mamá, but not
really Mamá. There are thick, green snakes with gold scales moving in a calculated motion around her neck. "I could've gone to el
Guia de las Tierras."

"You know how this works, Culebra," they say. "I chose her,
I come to her. I do not need permission from anyone else."

"The child is of me. I have protected her," Culebra yells, taking calculated steps towards me.

"And we thank you," Fuego says, gently. "But when it comes
to these matters—initiations—we are of different elements,
Culebra."

Culebra shakes her head, upset.

"The girl cannot keep making excuses for the boy," Fuego
continues. My body stands up and moves towards her. It stomps.
"Teach her to stop being so generous to those who are the danger. The fear in her isn't relevant, the anger is. She must stop
running away from her anger; like everything else, it is a life
force, and it will direct her into the path intended for her."

I feel wind rush from the bottom of my feet to the top of my
head. The blurriness slowly rises, the pressure over my spirit dis-
sipating. I take deep breaths until the air in my lungs isn't warm
anymore.

"Mamá?" I say, finally realizing it's just me now. Before my body aims for the floor, Mamá's arms reach out for me.

❨

First, I hear them. Mamá's voice shaped into explanations, Tía Dulce's giggles. There's a man in the room—his voice familiar. I open my eyes to the low, droopy ceiling of the botanica. When I turn my head to the door, I see Mamá Teté and Tía by the public altar. The candles and statues of the Bruja Diosas surround them. Mr. Leyva? I squint my eyes—it's him. I take a deep breath.

When I fully open my eyes, Mamá Teté, Tía Dulce, and Mr. Leyva are crouching over my face.

"Mr. Leyva?" I ask, as I sit up on the couch. He smiles, his straight white teeth covered by gold. Mr. L wears grills on the weekend and special occasions, he did say that one time.

"Before you ask, I was not stalking you on the weekend. My wife sent me out to buy some sage and other things, and I saw your grandmother. She says you fainted? Yoyo, have you been eating, resting? Or does this have to do with what you told me the other day?" Mamá looks at me. Her side-eye so strong she could practically send me back to the heavy place again if she really wanted to.

Before I can respond, Tía Dulce kisses my cheek. "She's fine now. How may I help you, Mr. Le-y-va?" She says his name slowly, looking him up and down. She rises in front of him, her arms readjusting her chest—doing the damn most. "Is it just the materials on this list you want?"

Mr. Leyva is blushing. He shakes his head and laughs a little. Tía Dulce is so, so extra. Mamá Teté tells me to put my coat on. This time it is she who suggests we order an Uber home.

The bodega owner, Maritza, is playing bachata a to lo que da. Mamá disappears into the back of the third aisle, and I know she is digging through the cardboard boxes for candles.

I stuff my hands into my pocket, my chin buried into the top of my neck. Today has been so important that it is full, full of tension, and I can feel it everywhere on my body. I am exhausted, as I should be.

"Here. Un regalito," Maritza says. She holds a Hershey bar towards me. "Sometimes we just need a little bit of sweetness in our life."

I nod and say thank you. She is way more generous than her husband, for sure. She moves on to the next customer, and I can't help but wonder if this woman has ever had a spirit ascend through her. That is also sweet. But even sweetness can be tiring, does she know? Opening the bar, I take a full bite from the top instead of breaking the bar into pieces, as I usually do. I bite into it, savor the piece of milk chocolate as it melts into my tongue.

"Morena!" Mamá yells from the back. I walk over to her, putting the Hershey bar into my pocket. "Help me get these to the counter." She cradles about four red candles and two purple, white, and green ones between her arms and her chest. I wonder why we didn't just get this at Tía Dulce's botanica, and then remember Mamá Teté had been in a rush to leave. I pull a couple, and when I reach out to pull a third, two candles fall and crash against the floor. Mamá looks at me with both frustration and regret.

"That's all right, Teté!" Maritza hollers, over the blasting bachata, from the front. "When glass breaks, negativity is released. You did me a favor!"

THE GAMES WE PLAY

Mamá makes a baño agrio for me. "You'll have to spread it over three days," she instructs. The baths are dark as the concoction flows from the top of my head to the bottom of my feet and down the drain.

"Mamá!" I call out on my way from the bathroom to the bedroom. I dry myself off, throw on some underwear, sweatpants, and an oversized white tee.

"Dime," she says. She stands at the doorway, inspecting me. "Much better, any lighter, yes?" I nod because I truly do feel lighter—like a boulder has been removed off of my back.

"Mamá Teté, what's up with this Fuego person? I know the basics, pero—"

"Well, first things first, this is now your Unknown and you don't regard them as 'Fuego Person,' Yolanda Nuelis. Un poco de respeto!" she says, sitting on my bed.

"You right." I sit on the floor by her feet.

"They are obviously a fire spirit. In their original human form, they were a wise, old man. Remember him from the stories I've told you?" she asks.

I nod.

"Everyone anywhere close or far to Fuego's village in West Africa came to them for advice. Anything from what to do with the sick cattle, to their grandchildren's futures. After their initial death, Fuego came back to the earth as a person in the New World during enslavement, in order to help Black people harness and bring with them the power they had in their original home."

I hang on to every word Mamá is saying.

"It is said that when the enslaved of Ayiti set flames to their French masters, Fuego was the one who implanted the idea and helped in making sure the fire led them to freedom."

I gasp in surprise, tears forming in my eyes. "Fuego helped create the first free Black nation in the world?" Mamá Teté and I have taken the bus into Haiti many times. She has old friends and even distant cousins there, who were forced out of DR and into Haiti or chose to simply go instead of putting up with the constant systematic discrimination once the Dominican government erased their birthright citizenship. It wasn't until she met my grandfather that she moved to San Pedro de Macoris to start a life with him, but she always remained connected to everyone at the border, and even though life was hard for them, she speaks of it also being magical—how everyone there chose to survive, creating languages out of dialect, sharing goods and resources with one another.

"That's right. The story goes that they tried to make it to the other side of the island, do the same work. But it was too late. They moved to San Pedro de Macoris and stood though and did all the preaching they could, before their human body gave out again."

"¿Qué más?"

"They helped a lot of people cope with the process of

enslavement. Not too many of the Unknowns made their way to Earth during that process—it is no easy task to birth yourself again just to watch your people suffer. But Fuego decided to do it without telling a soul. They didn't even tell their compatriot, Aire Fuerte."

"So they were a martyr?" My stomach turns.

"Yoyo, the Unknowns aren't fully human—they were once humans, can still take human form through us, but they are not us, and we are not them. There is no such thing as being a martyr for an Unknown. It is simply a duty they have with the bigger Unknowns, with the Universe, with the Creators, what have you." As she speaks, my mind goes into a million directions. If Fuego was this wise, this strong, this brave, and they chose me— what does that say?

I guess my face is saying it all because Mamá Teté snaps her fingers at me.

"Welcome back to Earth. " she laughs. "This is a powerful, deeply important Unknown, Morena. Your grandfather Papá Antonio was meant to be guided by Fuego."

"He was?!"

She nods with a smile. "But he didn't want to venerate the Unknowns. He said he saw how venerations could go sour way too many times in San Pedro, so he was scared to a degree."

I wonder if Papá Antonio would've survived a while longer had he taken to accept his connection to Fuego. I take a deep breath, feeling fresh grief around never being able to meet my grandfather in the flesh.

"No darling, it was his time," Mamá touches my cheek. Her round, dark eyes hold so much strength. I imagine her bones are made of wisdom. I can only hope to one day be like her.

"I have something for you," she says, taking out a small, red velvet pouch from her pocket.

I hug her before I take the pouch from her hand. I open the string and turn the pouch upside down. A gold necklace falls on my palm. The pendant is a thin plate shaped in the outline of the Fuego statue. "It was something I bought for your grandfather hoping one day he would heed to the Unknowns," she says. "I never got the chance to give it to him." Mamá Teté wipes the tears off her eyes. "Pero, now it's yours. Turn around," she says.

I listen and catch our reflection in my mirror.

"Ya," she says, when it's on. "Always keep it close to you." I turn back to her quickly and embrace her.

☾

"Girl, stop putting all that mess on my face!" I shoo Victory away. She's used face paint to trace a small number 22 on my bottom right cheek. It's a big game for the basketball team.

"Team spirit!" Victory shouts, mimicking the cheerleaders. And I roll my eyes.

"I don't want to hype him up, you know?" I try to hold it in, but bust out laughing at my own question.

"Why not? That's your man now," Victory smiles.

"Listen," I turn to her. "I have to tell you about this weekend. Mamá took me to the botanica, and I saw Mr. Leyva there."

"Mr. Leyva? The fuck?"

"Yeah, but that's not the important part." I begin to sweat although it be mad cold in these bathrooms. "I was chosen by Fuego," I blurt out.

Victory widens her eyes in excitement and hugs me tightly.

We hop around in circles, her arms wrapped around. "Girl, you acting like I just graduated or something," I laugh.

"This is a *big* deal," she reminds me, pulling back. "You better enjoy it and act like it!"

I nod. She's right. I don't need permission, but her reminder lets the feeling of delight wash over me. I've waited for this for so long, and it's finally here.

"They mounted me basically, and they confirmed my vision," I say, as I look in the mirror again.

"Girl," she replies. And it's all she has to say for me to know. My brain starts going through all the possibilities of what I can do now, to stop this finally. Like can I ask for the visions to be more specific, so that I can see what I must do instead of what Ben feels or plans to do? Or maybe I can use the power of fire somehow . . . but how?

"Let's go before we're late," Victory opens the bathroom door.

We run down the staircase laughing loudly, knowing there is no one else on this side of the gym. All fall and winter, we've been keeping ourselves together, but today, so close to winter break, we can finally live a little. We run from the Julia De Burgos wing into the gym, feeling the wind on our backs.

I've told Victory about the botanica. About Fuego. About how they chose me and what they said. I stop walking and allow that to settle into my body. Fuego can mount me whenever now, to deliver the downloads I must receive. What I need will come to me. I have a Bruja Diosa. The understanding of this makes my stomach flutter in delight, but also gives me nausea.

When we open the doors the basketball team is warming up. The humidity is enough to make my hair get frizzier immediately. I catch José wearing his LeBron 15s that he won last year through an online drawing. He's been wearing them for the last month in practice to break them in fully in preparation for this moment. The word "equality" is split on both the backs of the basketball sneakers in gold. He's also wearing black compression leggings and his burgundy and gold shorts and jersey. He's stretching and jogging in place, looking towards the other team. Victory tugs my arm towards the bleachers.

As I wave and smile at those on the top bleachers, I sit on the bottom one with Victory. Dayvonte sits next to me. "So you and homeboy a thing now?" he says, looking at my cheek.

"We a thing, ting," I smile. We give each other a pound, and then he switches over to Victory's side. She side-eyes me. We all know he's had a crush on her since forever. I mean, who wouldn't? Victory smells like shea butter and lavender all day, every day, and she has bomb ass vibes and style.

"Ain't you supposed to be on the team by now again?" Victory asks him.

"Ouch, Victory, that hurt," he says. Joking supposedly, but I can see it stung. "And my new girl, she a movie star," he sings. I bring my fingers over my mouth to cover up my smile. His lips quivering and eyes half-closed and all. I laugh loudly next to Victory as he hits a few more notes.

"Not you singing all up in my ear, Day. Damn!" Victory fake wipes her ear.

"Alright but tell me you like my voice or something?" Dayvonte says.

"It's aight," she responds.

My eyes move away from them as I examine the rest of the gym. It is lit as fuck! Everyone is super hyped. Posters everywhere to gas up the teams. The bleachers filled with people clapping and watching. Every space around the gym is crowded.

"LET'S GO, PIT BULLS, LET'S GO!" the cheerleaders chant for our team.

"LET'S GO, BEARS, YOU GOT THIS!" the other team's cheerleaders follow.

José stretches his fingers. Coach calls the team over and they jog towards him.

The lights turn off suddenly, so all the light you can see is coming from people's phones. With the lights so goes the noise. The gym freezes for a moment in time. Then they come on and off, on and off, on and off. I look to the right corner of the gym and see Cindy, the manager of the boys' basketball team, playing with the light switch, a hand over her mouth as she giggles. Vice Principal Choi jogs to her and whispers something, and Cindy walks to the bottom bleachers where the team sits while he stays by the switch.

The lights remain off for some time. When they do come on, Cindy turns to a hip-hop beat. The visiting team from a Brooklyn high school walks in.

"Oooooh!" Vic says, looking at one of the players and then at me. Dayvonte looks at her sternly, but with a smile in his eye. As they jog in, it's clear they've brought folks with them because a third of the bleachers stands up clapping and screaming with posters and blue-and-purple pom-poms. The gym goes quiet on me.

"Give it up for the Bears from Prospect High, everyone!" the Bears' manager calls from the bleachers. The other team forms a line by their bench and files by each other, high-fiving. Jay Rock's

"WIN" comes on. Everyone who came with them keeps cheering and stomping. We clap, out of courtesy, and because we ain't no haters, really. The song plays past its first verse and is then shut off.

"Alright Julia De Burgos, ya ready?" Cindy yells into the mic.

"YERRRRRRRRRRRRRR," we affirm back. She raises her hand up into the air, hyping us up, and we get up off our seats, stomping the soles of our shoes in unison and cheering until Cindy signals for us to bring it down. "Give it up for the Burgos PIT BULLSSSSSSS!" Cindy announces.

A$AP Rocky's "Praise The Lord" comes on. The second the beat drops, the doors open and our basketball team comes back in. Ms. Steinberg moves quickly towards Cindy, who is clearly letting her know she not about to change the song. Ms. Steinberg smiles at the crowd when she notices we looking at her and gives up. The boys run around the basketball court. Their hands smack the hands of the other team.

The entrance of the teams ends and the referees eventually walk into the middle of the court with the starting fives. The game starts. It's fire from the get because these schools have played before, and we won this past season. José sprints up and down the court. He's six foot four, and even against the other basketball players in similar height, he looks mad tall.

He looks up at the bleachers and our eyes meet. He waves at me, and I wave back. And then another player knocks into his legs accidentally and he goes down hard. I smack my palm over my forehead instinctively. *Fuck.* Dayvonte smacks his hat against his knee. Victory's hands are over her face. Coach Jorell places his hands over his head. The referee's whistle breaks the silence as he jogs to José, who is down. José kneels to tie his laces. "I'm good, I'm good," I see him say, looking up to the referee. He double knots his shoes and plays the whole thing off. Then, he looks at me and winks. It warms my heart and I smile.

"Twenty-two IS BACK!" Cindy yells into the microphone. "The champ is back! Jk, everyone. We all winners here!" she laughs. The game is close, 12 to 8, but I know it's killing José already to see our team losing. He runs to the other side of the court and motions to his teammate to pass the ball.

The crowd roars. I look up at the top of the bleachers and I'm overwhelmed by how much pride fills the space.

I look towards the entrance, and a couple men I do not recognize walk in. When they find a spot to sit or stand, they take out small notepads and pens. José mentioned scouts could come tonight to the game.

I turn my head back to the action to spot Ben moving through folks on the bleachers in our direction. "Hey, can I sit here?" he says, taking off his hat and stuffing it in his coat pocket. I don't say anything, but roll my eyes, and he still sits. He drops his tweed coat on the space next to me. He's wearing a gray cashmere V-neck sweater, with a round white T-shirt that pops at his neck. Can't ever just be left alone these days. Ed comes in with another man dressed in a black two-piece suit. They are carrying at least six cases of Gatorade each. "Feel free to leave them by the left end of the bleachers, thank you, Vladimir," he shouts towards the door. "See you in about an hour, Ed."

The men nod, but Ben still stands up and walks towards them. I watch him as he takes three cases from them. I'm annoyed with the obvious—he's trying to be seen. He walks towards Coach and leaves a pack by him. Then he begins to pass Gatorade bottles to all the students and staff standing nearby. Mr. Leyva looks at the bottle, holding a question, but shrugs it off and twists the cap and takes a gulp. Ben passes the remaining Gatorade bottles down the bleachers. Everyone is grateful. Halftime is called. Ben runs forward and people follow, asking what he's doing. He asks Cindy for the microphone. She looks annoyed, but still gives it to him.

"Hi everyone. Just wanted to quickly announce that there are Gatorades going around, and for anyone who wants a quick half-time bite, there are a couple of tables outside of the gym with sandwiches, pizza, and finger foods. Courtesy of my father, Joseph Hill, who is running for Congress next year."

As soon as he is off the mic, Ben is all smiles, giving high-fives mainly to those with the Bears and to those of us from here who seem to have forgotten what went down with the stickers. Victory looks at me, and we shake our heads. "You're welcome" and "no problem" exit his mouth every time he hands a Gatorade over. Definitely like a politician's son. A few teachers pat his back and Victory scoffs in disbelief.

"Dude is out of control," Dayvonte says. "But imma go grab me something to eat. You want anything, Queen?" he asks Victory.

"Don't be Queen-ing me, Dayvonte," Victory says.

Dayvonte gets up laughing.

"It's cold out there," I hear Ben's voice say, as he sits back down next to me. His back is erect and his chest is elevated.

"It's basically almost Christmas," I say blankly.

"Do you celebrate Christmas, Yolanda?" His body remains in place, but he twists his head towards me in a way that gives me the fucking creeps. His question carries an assumption. I turn my body to look straight at him.

"What's that supposed to mean?"

"I overheard your dad telling you your grandma could fix up one of her baths for you, the day we were suspended. That potion was supposed to alleviate what exactly?" His voice rises and falls. A rhythm that wouldn't be suspect in any situation but this one.

"Excuse me?" I tilt my head to the side.

"I know it's rude to eavesdrop. But potions and all that woo-woo stuff get my attention from time to time," he laughs. He looks straight at the court, and only looks at my chest to say the latter part of his sentence.

"It's not a potion. It's a bath," Victory says matter-of-factly.

He grins and bends his neck to the left, "OK, sure."

I want to reach out and pull his tongue out with my nails for being so damn sarcastic. Why can't he truly be who he pretends to be? Instead of going off on him, I turn to look for José as half-time ends. He looks across the court and tilts his head, telling me to come over basically, as he follows the team out of the locker room. I walk quickly across the floor.

"I like how my number looks on you," he brushes my cheek. I smile up at him and he grabs my head in for a kiss.

"OKAAAAAAAY!" Cindy says on the microphone. "I SEE YOU, Twenty-Two and YOYO." We can't help but laugh at her silly ass. The coach calls him over to the bench and I go back to my seat.

When the game starts again, I try to keep my eyes glued on José. He's dribbling, shooting, and running. I make a song in my head to relax: dribble, run, shoot; dribble, run, shoot; dribble, run, shoot. Something's gotta give. The world is out for the taking. Dribble, run, shoot; dribble, run, shoot.

"Glad to see the two of you happy," Ben says. I look at him and roll my eyes.

"Don't talk to me like we're friends, Ben." The words easily come out of me. He's getting on my last nerve.

"Oh, I am finally meeting the real you. Pretending to be put-together, but this is who you really are," Ben smirks. "You think you're too good for me, Yo?"

"It's Yolanda to you. Matter of fact, you don't gotta be saying my name at all," I snap.

The pressure comes, and I don't even fight it. Instead, I keep my eyes open.

It's snowing. I look down, and I'm wearing boots. I look up and the Julia De Burgos plaque tells me I'm in front of the school. Fuego floats around the school building, spreading salt and mumbling under their breath. I run towards them to get closer and listen to what's being said: "May everything that does not serve the dweller of this space be cleared with fire and salt."

Victory's hand over my knee brings me back. I look up at her and see she's agitated on my behalf. I feel a heavy weight start to grow between my hips. It feels like a painful numbing. I notice I am not breathing, and that a part of me feels threatened. I didn't say anything when Victory denied Mamá's bath being what it is—a curated list of ingredients meant to heal: a potion. And even though I don't have to say everything to Ben, it burns me that I denied it.

"I don't think I'm better than anyone, but no one is better than me either. That insecurity is all you," I say, picking up my coat—Victory behind me—and moving three levels up behind us.

"You good?" Jay asks as I sit down besides them. They look down toward Ben, who has picked up a conversation with Bianca.

"All good," I nod and smile.

"You know I got your back, Yo. No matter what, no matter

against who." Jay puts their arm around my shoulder and squeezes. They're wearing the team colors on their eyelids. I lean my head on their shoulder and take in the scent of jasmine.

"Thank you, Jay," I respond, feeling a sense of safety that makes my eyes water. "You don't miss being on the court?"

They nod. "I do. But I was tired of it running my life." They look out at the court.

"That's a dope chain! What is it?" Hamid asks, and reaches his hand over Jay to touch my chain. My hand stops his on instinct.

"Mind yours," I laugh. Hamid is cool, but I'm feeling protective. Like now, my body is truly a throne, a palace: a temple of my own since Fuego chose me.

BREAKS AND REST

School's out for winter break. I needed the break mostly from Ben.

I love staying home all day. Tomorrow is Christmas and although I used to split the holidays when Papi was around, I managed to convince him to bring my brothers and his wife, Norah, to Mamá Teté's house. I then got Mami to come through with Anthony. Mami was the one to put up the most fight. To her, Norah is still "that" woman who stole the man she thought she'd be with for the rest of her life. After going back and forth for a bit, Mami agreed to do it for me.

After my daily reading with the Sun, the World, and the Ace of Wands, I get out of bed smiling ear-to-ear. I don't even have to open the door to smell the sazón, the moro, and the mixing of all the goods we'll have tonight. The vibration of the loud palos Mamá Teté must be playing make my bunny slippers slide every time I try to get my feet in them. I laugh out loud as I finally capture the slippers with my toes. As soon as I open the door, Mamá Teté's there; her hair wrapped in a big purple headwrap, a dark green bata that can easily act as a dress. Her cucharón is in her right hand as her left hand asks a question. I playfully push past her to brush my teeth and get my processors.

The noise hits me all at once. Mercedes Cuevas y Los Paleros blast out the black speakers, so I know Mamá ain't playing today. The drums and the maracas force me to dance with my whole body. I bump into Mamá in the hallway, her cucharón still in hand with a bit of sazón now; she stuffs it into my mouth to taste. And we're off into a dance. Mamá goes down to the floor on her knees and kicks from below. When we dance to palos, there just really isn't anything our bodies can't do. Dance and music is how we best connect to the Bruja Diosas, and I feel so silly for not having thought of it earlier. As I dance, I feel a heat on my feet, the same heat I felt at Tía Dulce's botanica. I close my eyes and let my head hang and sway back. I reach for Mamá's hand, but with the dancing it slips.

You are highly protected, my child. You are fire. We are not afraid of high water, deep earth, or a storm of wind. We are fire. No one can put us out but us. Don't be afraid of catching the spirit, the spirit is always in you.

When the dancing is over, my body falls flat on the floor. I feel Mamá's hand supporting the back of my head as I fall.

It's three in the afternoon when I feel enough energy to stand. Mamá holds out a cup of coffee. She replaces the warm rag on my forehead with another. I hold the coffee mug in between my palms and inhale the sweet aroma of brown sugar, coffee beans, cinnamon, and nutmeg. Mamá cups my knee and looks at me proudly.

"You are Fuego's child. They're an old person who wears red and smokes tobacco. They love dark coffee."

"Like you are Culebra's child?" I ask. The sip of hot coffee burns my tongue and rolls down my throat. It feels like I've been gifted.

"Asi es. La Culebra chose me from birth, as I've told you," she says. Mamá often repeats this fact and I let her have it. It truly is a gift and an honor to be chosen that fast.

"Why did it take Fuego so long to choose me?"

"Every Unknown has their own timing. Plus, they probably chose you a long time ago. They just didn't want to scare you. One of the first things we are taught to fear as children is fire. How else could they have shown themselves to you without it?" she says matter-of-factly, and I nod knowing that she's right. I close my eyes in gratitude. *Thank you, thank you, thank you for sticking by me.* The gratitude fills me up to the point that it's almost overwhelming.

"Mamá, how long have the Unknowns chosen us, our family?"

"Bueno eso es desde hace mucho. The Unknowns existed before us. But when the world went into chaos, cuando los colonizers just started splitting us up and sending us wherever, the Unknowns had to tighten the reins on us, they had to work harder to protect us. My father was el hijo de Yeliel Yelcani. And when that saint mounted my father, everyone from near and far somehow knew about it. They would come with all types of offerings. And he would read them to shreds. Tell them what cattle were going to die. Tell them who their kids were going to leave home with. My mother on the other hand—just wanted to assimilate, be of the church. She hated it so much that the spirits sometimes mounted her just to get her to see how real they were. The worst thing you can try to do is deny the Unknowns the people they have chosen."

I take a deep breath and hug Mamá. I love when she tells me stories about my ancestors.

"Now to finish cooking."

Mamá is in the room getting ready, and I am fully done putting myself together. I am wearing a red turtleneck; a gray plaid skirt with green, red, and khaki; black tights; and black flats. In the mirror, I use my pick to expand my afro.

Mamá has worked hard today, so I open up the table. Mamá usually keeps it to a four-seater, but it expands for ten people. I open it and wipe it down. It's been years since the table has been this long. I bring out Mamá's large golden plates. I set ten of them down, then I place white disposable plates over them. On each side of the plate, I put down one of the thick red napkins. On one side, I put down a butter knife, and a fork. On the other, I place a big spoon and a smaller one. We don't really eat like this. Normally, there's a big cup with utensils and we choose from there. But Pearl and Valentine do it all the time, and it makes me feel fancy for a bit. I bring out the forks, knives, and spoons. Next, I set the mats for the hot plates for the food.

Mamá handled el pollo asado, el jamón, y el moro; I made the pastelon and some white rice. I leave some space on the table for the food others are bringing.

There's a knock on the door. And Mamá flies out the room, her dubi still on. She went to the salon yesterday to have her afro straightened. "¡Ay Dios! The table hasn't even been set yet," she whispers loudly.

"Don't worry, Mamá," I point to the table. She gasps and squeezes my cheeks. She goes back into the room to finish.

I open the door and it's Papi, Norah, and my brothers. Papi looks even thinner in the face than usual, but he smiles widely, bringing me to his chest.

"Ya, Papi, you're going to ruin my fro," I say playfully. I give Noriel a kiss on the cheek and get down on my knees to hug Nordonis. I stand to see Norah looking at me. I smile.

"Wow!" she says. Her light brown hair flows down the front of her coat effortlessly, and her green eyes scan my face. Everything about her face is so different from ours. "You look just like your father every day. That hair is just like his. The boys took after my own, gracias a Dios." Her comment feels like she tried to smack me sin mano, and I want to go off and tell her about how anti-Black it was. She opens her arms for a hug, and I just go in to avoid a fight. Her energy is so weird though. When I get out of her embrace, Papi is still looking at her like she said something stupid.

"What?" Norah whines at Papi.

"You could've kept that comment," is all Papi says.

Papi hauls the Christmas bags and puts them all under the Christmas tree. Norah places three desserts she made on the small window that separates the kitchen from the living room: cheesecake, flan, and tres leches. The boys are off in Mamá Teté's room doing whatever they want 'cause Mamá Teté spoils all of us.

A little bit later, there's another knock on the door. This time I know it's Mami, and my anxiety makes my heart rate accelerate. It's been years since they've been in the same room for more than two minutes.

Mami smells glorious. I don't even have to open the door completely to get a whiff of her rose perfume. When I open the door to her, she's wearing her long, loose curls to the side of her face. Her makeup is impeccable: white eyeshadow, making her skin pop, and the gold highlight at the top of her cheekbones is just everything. She looks almost like an ice queen.

"Merry Christmas, baby girl," she says, her arms weighed down by bags. Behind her, Anthony is holding a hotplate.

"Hey chica, ¿como está todo?" he says. He's more handsome than I remember. His cologne is potent. I smile at them. As we walk into the apartment, I see Papi escape to the bathroom. Anthony gives me a side hug as soon as he sets down the hotplate in the kitchen. Mami takes off her coat, gives it to Anthony, peels the aluminum foil off the hotplate, and rushes to place it on the table. Her steps are quick in her heeled boots until she sees Norah. She places the lasagna down.

"Hola Norah, how you doing?" Mami says, cutting into the pastelon. Making each slice of it perfectly aligned with the other. Norah responds with the same question. There is silence. I take the coats from Anthony and go to place them in Mamá's room.

The boys play with her dominos on the floor, while Mamá Teté finishes up by spraying agua florida on herself. She turns to me, her red lip in place, the blush at the top edges of her cheeks. She takes the pins from her hair, and her thick hair settles over her shoulders.

"Mamásita, where we going?" I say playfully.

"Oh stop it!" she says nervously. "Listen, I invited someone over."

"What?" I'm caught off guard, but it isn't me who asks this question. It's Papi behind me.

"I met someone at a misa a few months ago. Yolanda did their reading a few weeks ago, and we've been talking. I asked her, I mean them," Mamá blushes, "to come tonight. A good way to introduce them to everyone at once."

There's a third knock at the door. "That must be him," Papi says.

"They're not a him," Mamá says. There's suddenly so much silence it makes my chest hurt. I look down, and even my brothers have stopped playing.

"I'm happy to meet whoever it is Mami," Papi says, standing over Mamá. His golden sepia eyelids appear closed as he looks down at her intently. Mamá blushes, bringing a hand to his cheek and kissing him. "I just want you to be happy de verdad, Mami," he says. She taps his face before running for the door.

It is almost 9 p.m. when we sit at the table. I sit between Mami and Papi. Mamá sits at the head of the table, and to her right is Papi, and to her left is Marte. Noriel sits next to Marte. Nordonis and Norah follow. The other end of the table is Anthony, Mami, and me. Mamá asks us to hold hands.

"Earthly Mother, Father Sky, Unknowns, Benevolent Guides, Honorable Ancestors, Orishas, Santos, Higher Selves, Higher Guides, Guardian Angels, and all the good that guides and protects every single person at this table, I ask that you come forth. To bless this food, the ones that made it, and all of those that will receive it. I ask that on this holiday, you allow us all to surrender ourselves to the abundance of joy."

Mamá clears her throat and looks at me.

"We ask that you all wrap us up in a sacred, holy, and protective shield. One that will always guard us and keep us going despite the darkness. Please protect us from harm. Please deliver us into the greatness of each of our individual powers," I add.

Mamá winks at Marte, and Marte bows her head and stretches her jaw as if pleasantly surprised.

"Can I say a prayer?" Mami asks. Mamá welcomes it, and we pray a quick Padre Nuestro and Ave Maria. When the prayers are done, Anthony rubs his palms together, Papi looks over at him out of the corner of his eyes, and I squeeze his hand. We let go of one another and dig in.

"Este pastelon is very good!" Marte exclaims. "Very, very good."

"Ah, of course it is," I laugh. "Fui yo que lo hice." Mami, Papi, and Mamá Teté look at me, all at the same time, and the bright beam in the middle of my chest tells me they are proud beyond what I can ever imagine.

After the food, Mamá Teté opens the front door. It is her way of announcing to those who do not have a place to eat tonight to enter and indulge in what we have. Our neighbor, Elsa, comes by with her two young children, Leah and Samuel. They rush into Mamá Teté's room and play with my brothers. Elsa sits with us. Then Lonnie and his brother come in, and then Juan and his wife and children. By 10:30 p.m., Mamá Teté's apartment is filled to the brim. Mami and Anthony dance to bachata, and every time a salsa comes up, Norah convinces Papi to dance. While Mamá Teté and Marte talk with the neighbors, I squeeze into the kitchen and make some coffee. I take a small cup and piece of dark chocolate to my altar as an offering for the abundance of joy in the apartment and in everyone's heart. Then, I share some with the guests.

At midnight, everyone disperses, as if to give us space. By then my brothers have begged Papi at least twelve times to open gifts. So, Papi starts off by giving my brothers each a box. They rip through the paper. The sound of the ripping paper is linear, immediately telling me Papi has picked up the wrapping paper at the ninety-nine-cent store. I giggle to myself at his laziness. Marte brings out a small red box and hands it to me. I tell her she didn't have to, and I reach into the box anyway.

As I reach into the box, I feel out a circle. A ceramic item? When I pull it out, I see it's a statue of Fuego.

"Oh my God!" I cry. "My first statue!" A dark figure who is shirtless, smoking tobacco, a gold chain around his neck and a gold bangle around the left arm, with red pants. I have to bite my lower lip to keep from crying. This is truly a gift that will continue to pour more and more onto me and those around me. Papi taps my shoulder.

"You don't think I forgot my favorite daughter," Papi says, a huge grin on his face. I open a small red box. It's a double-finger gold ring that reads "Yolanda," that fits perfectly on my ring and middle finger. "Just in case you gotta knock boys out and remind them of who the fuck you are." We laugh. Like Mamá and Mami, he believes gold is one of the few items worth gifting, as it never loses value and you can always sell it if worse comes to worst. Mamá hands me a one-liter mason jar filled to the brim with my favorite bath. I hug her so tightly, feeling her heartbeat on my chest.

Mami takes my hand. "This is something from me and Anthony," she says.

"We took a wood carving class together and, carajo, I sucked. So I joined your mother, and we worked on a project for you," Anthony says. Mami playfully punches his chest.

I open the bag and bring out two white boxes.

"It's one gift, but it's in two parts," he adds.

I nervously smile. I hate assembling things. It's just not my forte, but I keep a smile on. I open the box, hoping my fears of having to put things together doesn't show on my face. I bite my lower lip as I feel inside for the gift. I bring it out to see a block of wood has been carved into my name, *Yolanda*. It's of a truly heavy bark, dark, and shiny. It's beautiful, but I look at Mami, confused. "It's a bookend, mi'ja, to keep all your books organized. Take the other one out."

Mami puts down her wine and helps hand me the box. When the other side of the bookend is out, I see it says *La Bruja*. Mamá Teté hands fly over her mouth in surprise, and when she catches herself she brings them down and pats down her blouse, smiling up at me. I put the bookend down and put an arm around Mami and another around Anthony—I hug them tightly.

"Thank you," I say. And it finally hits me. The beginning of my initiation is here, obvious to everyone. Yes, Mamá Teté already confirmed it. But now Mami gets it too. The realization makes my eyes moist with tears, and I throw both arms over Mami. I hold her close—hoping this never goes away, that she may see me forever. "You have a don, mi'ja. I know that," Mami whispers into my ear.

After everyone has opened their gifts, I walk to my room, a bookend under each arm. Noriel follows me and opens the door for me. I tell him that to come in, he has to take off his shoes. He does so without putting up a fight like he used to do when he was younger.

"How come we don't have a room here?" Noriel says, looking around, and sitting on my desk chair.

"Well, I've been around longer than you. Plus my parents

don't live under the same roof, you know?" I respond, placing the bookends on the floor.

"Papi didn't live under the same roof as my mom and us until the other day," he picks up a book.

"Yeah, that did happen." I watch him as he puts the book back with precision and looks at the thousands of lights coming out of Bronx apartments tonight.

He's quiet. He bites his fingers and picks up another book— this one a children's book in Spanish about loving your hair. A couple years back, I was the one that told my brothers where Papi really was. It was so unfair to keep going with the lie Norah had built for them.

"Do you want to talk about it, Noriel?" I ask. He nods. His eyes still "reading" through the book.

"What do you want to know?" I pull out a small stool I keep next to my desk and sit besides him.

"How come Papi didn't tell? Uncle Jeff and Uncle Mike didn't go to jail. I've heard Mami talking to her best friend, I know they were involved in what went down, too."

"Well, Papi doesn't believe in telling. Plus, our uncles had never been to jail before, and this was Papi's third run-in with the law, so you know he figured it would be better if he just took the fall for everyone."

"Like a hero?" he rolls his eyes.

"It's not heroic at all, bro. That's not what I am saying. What I am trying to say is that people have different values, belief systems, and all that. Papi didn't want to tell, he grew up in a time where snitching wasn't cool. No matter whether it was right or wrong, you just didn't tell. I am not saying it's correct, but I do have to respect his choices because he and I grew up in very different ways," I say. Noriel rubs his thumb on his palm. "We didn't have a dad that could take us to the park for the last few years, but our cousins did, you know?" I continue. "It's better three kids than seven." My brother rolls his eyes again and lets his forehead fall onto the desk. "It sucks. I know. But he's out now, and he's actually learned a lot in there. He's given me these books to read, and I think everything might turn out for the better. It was a lesson Papi had to learn, maybe."

"Will you let me borrow them, the books," he mumbles, "once you're done?"

"Of course." I slip my hand into his fist and squeeze. I run my other hand down his back, using my nails to softly create circles like Mamá does with me. He brings his head back up and puts it on my shoulder. He takes a few breaths, and then I feel his hot tears. Life can be so confusing sometimes. I hope I am making some sense out of all of this for Noriel. That my words feel like a soothing balm for this hurt we carry. I let him cry for some time in silence.

A merengue comes on, "Eta Que Ta Aquí" by Andre Veloz, and I pull Noriel up by the arm. "Let's go dance!"

When we get to the living room, Mami and Anthony and Mamá Teté and Marte are already dancing. Norah is on her cell phone, and Papi is watching *How the Grinch Stole Christmas* with Nordonis and reading the subtitles. "I don't know how to dance this," Noriel whispers into my ear.

"That's OK. I got time today." We hold hands and bring them up to the chest level. I place his right hand on my waist, and I place my own on his shoulder. I begin moving my hips side to side and shuffle my feet along, demonstrating for my brother.

"It's like a little march. You can do that right?" I say. Noriel begins tapping his feet, but I explain again, making sure he understands that it's more about the movement of the body during the march than the feet. He tries again, this time almost perfecting it.

"Now, let your shoulders sway with your hips," I yell through the music. He follows along, and the elders hype him up. He blushes, but continues to dance.

"OK! I see you marching for joy, for our ancestors, for our bodies, for the Earth, for ourselves!" I laugh.

Everyone else laughs. Mamá Teté pulls Papi away from the TV and brings him into the dance floor with her. Norah brings Nardonis in and teaches him how to dance merengue as well. He's enthusiastic about it as he moves his shoulders side to side. There's a smile on everyone's face. And I cannot help but think of the many times dance has saved us from madness. Of how dance allows us to rejoice even in the face of heartache. But most of all, I think of how beautiful my family looks as I catch our reflection in the living room windows.

☾

Ben's hand is stretched open as he holds out his hand to me. His nails are black as if he's been digging at the Earth all day. When I grab his hand, his palm is moist, like I am holding one hundred wet napkins. I let go quickly.

"Well, you coming?" he asks. I nod and take his hand again. We are walking to the library.

"There's a book I want to show you."

"What kind of book?"

"You'll see. It'll really allow you to finally understand me."

When he opens up the library door, he enters swiftly. My feet won't move. "Come in," he says.

"I'm trying," I say. But my feet are locked onto the floor between my feet. He takes a deep breath and exhales irritably.

"It's fine. I'll get it for you. Wait here," he says. The second he turns his back, the door slams hard and smacks me in the middle of the chest. I am knocked down, and I am left grabbing my heart as it pumps and bleeds, pumps and bleeds.

TRANSITIONS

It takes a couple weeks for me to get back into the swing of things at school. After two weeks off—eating every single one of my meals next to people I love, having long conversations with my elders, and visiting Mami and Papi and then coming home to help Mamá Teté—I am full to the brim with love. The world feels lighter. Like there might be a mountain the size of a planet on my back, but I have people who love me and so the weight of it is nothing.

The dreams come but they go, and so I don't let them stop me. For the first time since I got the cards, I am taking a break from reading myself every day. But when I help Mamá Teté with readings, my skills are still there, and so I don't suspect much is wrong.

By mid-January, our teachers are hanging posters on the hallways of Martin Luther King, Malcolm X, Rosa Parks, James Baldwin, and this year it seems they have even expanded their understanding of Blackness by throwing up some Indya Moore, Celia Cruz, and David Ortiz.

"Mr. Leyva," I say during passing periods, "what you think about this?"

"Well, I think that all year is Black History—" He looks at me hanging on to his every word until it connects that I am avoiding class. "Girl, go to class!"

I laugh and go about my way.

I spot José in the hallway, and he throws me a kiss that makes my laughter go on for longer. Victory spots us a few feet away and shakes her head playfully. As we enter AP Lit, she holds my hand.

"Girl, I am so tired of schools thinking we only Black during the month of February. I really, truly got a problem," she says.

"I know, it's kind of annoying 'cause it feels like we gotta juice the month for all its worth. It's the way it's always been though, you know?"

"So? All I care about is that tradition ending soon. I am going to start a petition to deliver to Principal Steinberg today." I nod. Victory is such a fire—with her, an idea quickly turns to action. "We not gonna keep doing this on my watch." As I walk to my seat, the bell rings.

On the screen for the Do Now it says to list five Black writers we know of. Ms. Kaur plays a low beat, and I know immediately it's TLC's "Waterfalls." I see her nodding her head like this used to be her jam. Can't fully imagine none of my teachers our age, although they are all relatively young. I write the following names: Alan Palaez Lopez, Angie Thomas, Elizabeth Acevedo, Akwaeke Emezi, Assata Shakur, and Malcolm X. Victory walks past me to throw something in the garbage, looks over my shoulder, and says, "That's six, not five, beloved."

I roll my eyes playfully. "You so annoying!"

"Sixty more seconds, people," Ms. Kaur announces.

When time is up, Ms. Kaur has us split into trios to share out our lists. I am partnered with Barbara, a twelfth-grader. I know her parents are Mexican because sometimes I get avena from them down the block at this tiny bakery. And Patrick, who is in my grade, he's Afro-Honduran, Garifuna, and he never lets us forget.

"I'll start?" Patrick offers, and Barbara and I nod. "Sulma Arzu-Brown, James Baldwin, Arturo Alfonso Schomburg, Richard Wright, and Angela Davis."

"Is Schomburg Black? I mean, isn't he just Latino?" Barbara asks.

"Yeah, well he was Puerto Rican, but racially—he was a Black man," I answer. Pearl was the one who sat Victory and me down in sixth grade when I started complaining about filling out ethnicity and race questions. None of it made sense to me.

"Ethnicity is for what is here," she said, pointing to her heart. "Your culture, your customs, your traditions, your music and beliefs, but race is this," she pointed to our arms. "Race is skin color. It's confusing because white men made it up. It's constructed by men, not nature."

"But he isn't like African-American?" Barbara says.

Patrick takes a long sigh.

Ms. Kaur is standing behind us now, listening. Barbara has no more questions, and Ms. Kaur stays quiet, not even trying to be a buffer.

"What's your list?" I ask to Barbara.

"Walter Dean Myers, Toni Morrison, Malcolm X, Angie Thomas, and the poet who visited last year." We nod.

"Joél Leon," Patrick says.

She nods, and I read mine.

When Victory's group shares her list to the whole class, a question around African-American and African comes up. Victory takes the floor to school folks. Tells them to stop acting as if

Mr. Ruiz didn't teach us about the African Diaspora and Pan-Africanism. "All we have is the shortest month of the year—February—and yeah, I think Black Americans fought for it for ALL Black people," she ends.

"Well, today we are going to be introduced to a new book. It feels hefty at first glance. Yet, I believe in all of your abilities to process the book." Ms. Kaur goes to the next slide of a book with water against an orange background. The book is called *Homegoing* by Yaa Gyasi. After a small introduction to the book, Ms. Kaur has us sign out individual copies. I run my thumb through the pages and get that good, old, new book smell.

"This class set was donated to our school library by Mr. Joseph Hill," she says, picking up a yellow poster paper. She opens it up for us. In the middle she has written "Thank you!" in her impeccable calligraphy skills. "I'll pass this around. Please write a small note."

Victory looks at me, taking the cap off her pen dramatically and placing it on the back of the pen. "Well OK then," she whispers mockingly.

"It's the performing for me!" I mouth, but quickly realize I've said it aloud. "Sorry," I look at Ms. Kaur.

At lunch, I enter the crowded lunchroom flattening my edges with my fingers and with my Telfar bag hanging off of one shoulder. I look around for José. As I do, I spot literally everyone but him. I sit where we normally do and wait.

It's not long before José walks into the lunchroom tensed-up. Despite his obvious mood, everyone still makes towards him and daps him or low-key side-hugs him. I laugh under my hand watching it all. He spots me and walks towards me with a brown paper bag in his hand. The other hand holds a packet.

"Mami got me a sandwich today," he says, and slides me a piece of it.

"Thank you!" I smile.

He puts the packet on his lap, even as he eats. And although I find that weird as hell, I mind my own business.

"I missed you, you know?" he says as he chews.

"I missed you too, weirdo, what's up?"

"I can't just say I miss you? Dang."

"Oh no, you can, but I can definitely tell"—I bring my fingers together and point up and down—"that something's up."

"Let's talk about it after school," he says. School is over in three hours. Not the end of the world, but just the fact that he says it gives me some anxiety. I already know I don't want to wait that long. I chew through the last bite of my sandwich half and gulp some water. He takes out chemistry homework and I do the same. We work through it.

"Listen," I say. I slide my hand into his. Look into his eyes. Worry. It's all in him. Worry.

"You can tell me—" The bell rings.

I spend the end of my school day waiting for the day to be over. I think of worst-case scenarios. And then convince myself that I am exaggerating. I text Victory, but she doesn't respond until the day is over. And by then I am already rushing out of the building to meet José by the entrance. I sit and wait for him.

"You all right?" I turn around to see Ben walking in my direction.

"Yeah, I'm good," I turn away.

"I've been seeing the school counselor," he says to my side, putting his hands in his pockets. "He says I should at least ask for forgiveness. I know you might be too proud to say sorry for the water bottle part," Ben begins. I take a long, exaggerated deep breath because my body needs it, but also to let him know I know this is all pretend on his end. I watch my exhale condense in front of my eyes. "I guess I am most responsible for all of this, right?" He takes his hands out his pockets. "So," he claps his hands together loudly, and then rubs them together. "I'm sorry, Yo. I really am." I don't turn to him. I won't give him the satisfaction of looking him in the eye.

"Actions speak louder than words, isn't that what folks say?" I say. "Yeah, that then."

He doesn't say anything, but I hear him walk away. Ben really thinks apologies are an easy way out. Growing up when I first learned the power of "I'm sorry," I tried to abuse it too, up until Mamá Teté forbid me from apologizing and only accepted changed behavior. I still struggle with it—apologizing a lot. I'm happy Victory checks me on it often, and the habit is dying down.

After he leaves, I continue to watch everyone come out and zip up their coats or adjust the hoods over their heads. We're supposed to have a snow day soon. It's 3:50 p.m. Ten minutes late. I put on my gloves. Consider going back and waiting for him next to the security desk with Mr. Leyva. It's 4:00 p.m. Now, I know I really am a tonta. Wow. I get up and convince myself to go. I wiggle my frozen toes inside my boots before I walk past the school gates.

By the time I am almost at the bus stop, I feel someone running towards me from behind. "Yo! Yo!" I turn around. "I'm sorry, I'm sorry, I'm sorry. I was caught up talking to Coach." He bends down to tie his laces. As he stands up, he kisses my forehead. Although I am angry for having to wait, I wrap my hands around his waist and hug him closely.

"I have to talk to you about that thing I mentioned at lunch," he says. "You want to go into The Lit. Bar? It's way too loud on the bus right now." I nod. Although it's cold outside, my palms begin to sweat. I can't help but project what's coming. The talk about next year. He's a senior after all; I should have seen this coming.

When we enter The Lit. Bar, it is cozy as fuck and smells like all the coffee beans in the world have decided to come together right in the middle of the Bronx. I look towards the Young Adult bookshelf and see the owner in the flesh! Usually when I come in with Victory or by myself, she isn't around. One time I did catch a glimpse of her heading towards the back—where her office is, I imagine. The owner is high-key Instagram famous and most definitely a neighborhood hero around these parts. She worked her ass off to bring this bookstore to the community. The themes on most of the shelves change every once in a while, and Black, Brown, and Indigenous writers are always in the front.

"Welcome to The Lit. Bar," Noelle says, turning to us. Her brown hair is wavy around her shoulders and the black, square frames of her eyeglasses fit her face just right. She notices I'm starstruck and smiles—so beautiful!

I stare at her until José responds with a quick thank-you. "No, thank you! I'm a fan of yours. Thank you so much for this store. Like forreal, forreal," I blurt out. Oh my God! I feel like such a lambona but whatever—I don't care! My cheeks are on fire and I can't stop smiling.

"I appreciate you saying that," she laughs. "It helps because it is not easy! Y'all here to hang out, books, or you want something from the coffee shop? Let me know now 'cause my girl is on break, so I'm going to be the one to serve you!" She turns to walk towards the area with the chairs and bar before I have a chance to respond. We follow her.

"I'll take a hot chocolate," I say, arriving at the bar. I can't stop speaking. "He'll take . . ." I look at José asking a question with my hands, because I most definitely forgot he can speak for himself. He chuckles watching me fangirl.

"I'll get a coffee—light and sweet," he says.

We sit at a round table and take off our coats, getting comfortable, and Noelle bring us our drinks.

"So college," he begins. He lays his hands flat over the table. I take a deep breath remembering why we're here. I've wrapped myself up in my own stuff to pretend I didn't know college was a thing looming over him. Isn't it too early to have gotten acceptances? No. He's a senior. His first acceptances have actually arrived later than other students. Or maybe he just never told me? *Breathe, girl*, I tell myself, *breathe*.

"I applied, and I've had some other really good schools, specifically for basketball, hitting me and Coach up, encouraging me to apply by giving me a full ride," he says. I hold my breath, feeling like the next step here is for him to tell me we're breaking up. But why am I thinking so far ahead for?

"So go! Of course, you've got to go!" I say, breathing out. A smile spreads across my face. Do I mean the smile? Absolutely not. It's a forced smile of course. I hate myself for it, but I can't do anything else. I'm not hating. I'm not. I smile again, this time with my eyes too, hoping the sadness won't show because my heart feels so still, it is practically numb, and if I let it continue its rhythm, I am scared I'll have to admit something I'm too afraid to own up to.

"Yo," he says. "I've had a plan this entire time. Play ball

through college, get a degree just in case I need a Plan B, right? And then take it from there." I look at the floor-to-ceiling wall shelves behind him. I read through the labels, trying to avoid his eyes.

"But it's hard to make a decision now." He runs his hands over my knuckles. I bring my eyes to him again. I take a deep breath and wonder how much of this is real? Mami has always said que los hombres son unos mentirosos. That they lie to get what they want. So this could all just have been a big ass show. If he knew he was going to leave for college, why did he pursue me? Why did I give in? I bring my hand out of his grasp.

"We're young. You're going to be a basketball star. You need to go," I say. I take a long swig of my hot chocolate. I cross my arms, unsure if I want to hug myself or stand up for the emptiness my chest feels. My confusion makes me angry at myself, angry at him. "It'll be fine," I add. Now tears are sitting at the brim of my bottom lids. Great, fantastic.

"Really, Yo? I'm trying to talk this out with you," he says. His eyebrows are raised in surprise.

"Really," I say. I take the last swig of my hot chocolate. My entire body feels like it's been set in flames. I slip my arms into my coat and bring my bag to my shoulder. I walk as fast as I can to the front of the store and smile at Noelle, hoping she didn't catch any of my conversation with José. I rush towards the bus stop and when I see there's not one coming, I head towards the train.

"Yolanda!" I hear his voice. "Stop," he grabs my elbow. And if I didn't know any better, I'd push him off with all the force in my body. "Can you stop? I am just trying to talk to you to figure it out. What else am I supposed to do?"

My chest begins to ache. The anger I feel towards myself is bubbling on the surface. I hate myself for having allowed a relationship into my life only to have to cut things off. I kind of hate him for coming after me. I take a deep breath, and all the hurt of loving people like Papi—only for them to eventually go—comes up to the surface.

"Make a fucking decision without involving me! I don't care what you do, just do it, and let it be what it is," I say. There's a harshness in my throat when I say this. I cover my mouth once I realize I reacted from a place of pain, but it's too late. When I look into his eyes, I see that all the worry has turned into hurt inside of him.

"All right fuck it then, forget it," he says between his teeth. Flakes begin to fall quickly; a flake settles on my nose, until it melts. "Forget you, Yo. Deadass." He turns his back to me and runs to catch up with the bus rolling into the stop.

MAKING UP

Parent-teacher conferences roll up faster than I had expected. Mami and Papi manage to agree on a date and come together. Lately, I am proud of the way they are communicating for my sake. My teachers give the usual downloads: I am full of grit, I use my resources, including my friends, to get topics I don't naturally grasp, my accommodation plan is still in place mainly keeping me in areas where I can hear things clearly.

Mami, Papi, and I walk from the ELA wing to the math wing, and I can't stop smiling. I can't remember a parent-teacher conference with the both of them. It was either one or the other or Mamá Teté usually, after Papi went in. Every time someone asks me if Papi is my dad, I answer yes with so much pride. No matter what, he's here, present, and alive. Mami holds my hand, and I turn to her and put my head on her shoulder. This moment is about her too. As we're turning the corner:

"Yolanda, how nice to see you again," Mrs. Hill says. Her voice is bright and cheery, like we're old-time acquaintances.

"Mrs. Hill," I acknowledge her. I look behind her, but Ben is nowhere in sight. José's mom, Penelope, spots Mami and rushes towards us—forcing Mrs. Hill to carry on about her business.

"Yonelis, que bueno que te encontre," she says with relief. They kiss one another's cheeks as if they've been friends since high school.

"¿Ustedes saben inglés, right? Can you translate for me? I want to make sure I am getting the right information," she says to Papi. José appears out of nowhere; the smile on his face drops when we meet eyes. We haven't spoken directly since our fight a week ago. José kisses Mami on the cheek and introduces himself to Papi with a handshake. Papi looks at me and then at José. I look away.

Papi talks to Coach, and José's mom stands by, waiting to be given the full translation. I walk away with Mami. I show her some of my writing on the board from AP Lit.

"I saw how you both looked at each other. Yolanda Nuelis, if you have a noviecito, you can tell me," she says. At regular voice volume!

"Shush!" I say. "He isn't nothing."

"So why are you so upset?"

"He was my boyfriend, OK? Now, I think he isn't. I mean I don't know. We had a weird fight and that's it. Drop it, Mami. Please." I look for Papi and find him talking closely to José, patting his shoulder and looking him in the eyes. Shake my head.

When I turn, I see Mami saludando a Valentine and Pearl.

Victory rushes to my side and looks me straight in the eyes. Her eyes look over at José and Papi and then me. "What's going on?!" she asks.

I bring up my shoulders—I really don't know— but tragame

tierra. I hug Victory. Mostly because I feel like I could melt at any minute. I hate that I was so cruel to José, but thinking of him leaving really got me in every single one of my feelings.

When Papi finally comes over, Valentine embraces him— pats his back over and over.

"My man, it's so good to finally see you. We're sorry we never got around to visiting—" Valentine begins, but Papi cuts him off.

"Man, I got my GED and my Associate's in there. Read books I would've never read in a million years outside. Got this one reading that Assata joint." Papi pats my head and then puts his arm around Victory in a hug.

"Congratulations, man!" Valentine says.

"They can't stop us from winning," Pearl nods. "They tried it though. They did try it."

Papi looks at me and Victory.

"That's right, but in my case—I 'did' the crime, ya know? Despite everything, it goes down like I did it," Papi says. His voice cracks a bit. "So I had to do the time. But I'll tell you something: I ain't ever going back."

Valentine looks at Papi closely. "You got a job yet?"

Papi gives him the whole spiel on the dealership, but not wanting to be around there anymore. He mentions having gotten a few construction opportunities.

"Come by my office, man," he says. "It wasn't a violent crime, right?"

"Nah man, nah," Papi responds.

"And you got that GED?" he asks.

Papi nods. "And that Associate's."

"Aight man, come by. I got you." They dap each other up. "Glad you're here, Nelson, forreal," Valentine says before he lets go.

Papi says he appreciates it. As we walk away, he pats the corner of his eyes.

Back in the car, Mami sits in the rear, takes a picture of my report card, and types away. I know that's going on Facebook for her little friends right away.

"So that José boy," Papi begins. I try to stop him, but Mami encourages him. "He says you ain't speak to him in a week, Yoyo? How come?"

"He got big things going on. I don't want to make it harder on him," I reply.

"It sounds like you're sad," Papi says bluntly. Mami giggles from the back seat.

"I'm not sad!" I lie. Of course, I lie. I got feelings—I'm a big girl, I know that—but I'm not about to admit it to my parents right now.

"OK. Well, you should talk to him. He's having a hard time figuring out what school he's going to say yes to. And half of the reason why is because he doesn't know if you want him to be nearby or not."

"It's his life," I suck my teeth.

"Don't play no mind games with that boy, muchacha." He stops at a red light and looks directly at me. "Don't be like your mother." And I wish he hadn't said that 'cause immediately Mami puts her phone down, and my body freezes and prepares for them to go at each other—as if it knows.

"Nelson, please don't start with me, OK?" Mami says plainly. Papi doesn't push it.

I take a deep breath, relieved at the fact that they've grown. Chill, body of mine, chill. We're good.

I go to Mami's because Mamá Teté has gone out to a retreat

with Marte. Mami has a date with Anthony as per usual, but I'm not complaining. I've already convinced myself to hit up José. The minute she leaves, I text him.

He's at her house in less than twenty minutes. He has a bowl of fruit in a paper bag that his mom made for him for getting an 88.9 average. "My mom says the entire bottom is Haitian mango slices she got from a friend who just came back from a trip, so you know the salad is lit," he says. I can't help but laugh and be grateful that he broke the ice.

"So she be caring about your grades?" I ask, locking the door behind him.

"She does. She says all she cares about is whatever is going to give me multiple options. That's why she doesn't even care about basketball to be honest."

As I try to think through all the options, I have to acknowledge the awkward energy in the room.

"So, I'm sorry," I say. All the blood in my body dances to my face. "I was feeling some things around you leaving, and instead of saying that, I did the most."

He smiles and throws his arms around me. He settles his chin on top of my afro.

We sit on Mami's couch. He opens up the fruit bowl. I eat most of the mango and papaya and he has whatever I let him have of the mango, and the pineapple and cantaloupe. "So talk to me," I say as I chew.

"I've got offers from eight schools. But I am only really interested in two. Duke, in North Carolina." He looks at me. "And then there's the University of Connecticut. Two and a half hours away, max. I can come every weekend. If it works out, you know?"

"But isn't Duke like really, really good? Especially for basketball?"

He shakes his head. "Yeah, but you're really good for me." My entire body heats up, and I feel as if there is a light inside me pushing out from all the corners of myself. He lays his head on my lap. I run my fingers through his hair, through the tightness of his curls. I have to remind myself to breathe in and out because some part of me feels like if I exhale, this might all stop. Is this what happens when people are involved in romantic relationships? This fluttering? This almost flying, because someone else in this big, old world thinks you're worthy of being vulnerable in this way too? He closes his eyes, brings his hand to his forehead. His face seems both alleviated and worried.

"Everyone on the team has a story of how they got into basketball, but I don't really have any. It was the easiest thing to do. I didn't have to fight to be good. Papi put me on the Dyckman teams since I was a toddler and I just did what I was told to do. I moved the way my body wanted to move and incorporated the moves of the game. Maybe that's why Coach talking about big plans, NBA this, NBA that, don't feel that serious to me. I be daydreaming sometimes like maybe I could be a cook, a poet, an entrepreneur or something if I tried."

"But don't you daydream about playing too? Like LeBron?" I fake laugh.

He shrugs. "I don't know. It feels like every decision I make now is around basketball. Basketball because college. Basketball before, maybe, NBA. Basketball so I can take my family out the hood once they finally gentrify the Bronx and these motherfuckers start pushing us out, like they do everywhere. Basketball because I can buy safety, maybe? It just takes the fun out of playing," he sighs.

"I hear you, José, but isn't that everything? Like we all want all of those things. Your future is a tiny bit more special though, because being this good at a sport means you can do big, big things."

"What I want is simple things, Yo. Access to safety, a home for me and my family, education, healthcare. That's basic shit all humans need. Why I gotta be exceptional to get that? Why I gotta be so good to get what I deserve? What we all deserve?" He looks at me embarrassed. "I went on a rant, my bad."

"Nah, you're right. I guess I got wrapped up in the hype of you being a big-time basketball player," I say, low-key embarrassed too.

"It's easy to do that. Even with the work you want to do, Yo. You can't be a regular community activist. You gon' have to take care of everybody, everywhere, do so much you are almost holy and shit. If not you won't get put on the pedestal, and if you don't get put on the pedestal, you don't get the funds from the people who should be helping folks survive in the first place, to help out the people you started out wanting to help."

He looks out my bedroom window. "I could go on forever because I've thought about it. No matter what either of us or anyone we've grown up with wants to do, to live a life that's comfortable—where motherfuckers ain't trying to just survive every day—we gotta be magical, Yo, deadass." He turns to me. His soft brown eyes hold some type of defeat in them. My heart aches for all of us.

We sit in silence for a while.

"I might never make it to the NBA," he says, breaking the

silence. "I talked to some players who are playing for colleges now, and they thought they were good, and then they got to college and realized they were one among many, and their chances for NBA dreams became slim. So they have to go into international leagues and shit."

"I feel like other than everything you said, you're also saying you're scared?"

He puts his face into my lap. "Yeah, I am. That's why I gotta make sure I have options. Like Mami says."

"Mothers be saying some shit sometimes," I laugh. Happy that the tension of the reality he mentioned, about us having to be magical, is dwindling.

"Yo—they do!" We laugh for like a minute like I've said the funniest thing, but I know that it's mainly relief. That we are here, able to be ourselves and honest with each other.

When the laughing settles, our eyes meet for a long time. He brings his face to mine and kisses me. I am all over him because God, I have missed him. He brings his free hand onto my chin, pulls away, and looks at me. I lean into him. My hands find their way under his shirt and all parts of him are strong, lean—a true athlete. We're kissing so hard my mouth almost hurts, but I don't want to let go. He takes off his shirt and suddenly I am pulling him into my room. The candles on the altar I keep at Mami's house are on. When I turn off the lights, the flames flicker on the ceiling. I watch them as we kiss and then remind myself to enjoy the moment and close my eyes. We sit on my bed and kiss some more. He puts his hand under my shirt. He asks if it's OK, I say yes. He grasps my breast over my bra. But then he's working to take my top off, and I think of my belly, of my chichos, of the heaviness of my breasts.

"Stop," I say. Pulling on a sweater I have nearby.

"OK," he says. He wipes the corners of his mouth. "You OK?"

I nod and slip my head into the hoodie. "I'm not as comfortable as you are with my body."

"I hear you," he responds. "And I know it don't matter what I gotta say 'cause it's your body and your feelings. But you're perfect. And I'm not just trying to spit game. I mean it. I feel really lucky that I can even sit next to you in this way." He puts his hand on my knee and looks at me.

"Where the hell did you learn to say all the right things?" I chuckle.

"I have an older sister. She raised me. She says I won't grow up being a fucked-up, privileged man like Papi or my uncles. So I've gone through lessons with her. You can't even imagine," he rolls his eyes playfully.

We laugh for a long while. Lay up against the wall, our socked feet up on my bed. We look at the altar like it's a fireplace. Sitting in silence, in the dark, has always felt good by myself, but with him it feels just right. I wrap my arm around his stomach and lay my head on his chest.

Gracias Bruja Diosas.

I look into the fire. It continues its dance, but the flames stretch up towards the ceiling.

You can tell him. "I have something to tell you, José," I whisper. He puts his head over mine, but I sit up, lean my head against the wall. He follows suit and turns his head to look at me.

"OK, so I have dones too. It's not just Mamá. Our tradition I told you about . . . I can see some stuff," I say. The minute the words are out, my chest feels less heavy. I take a deep breath.

"Can you see you at the Winter Formal on Valentine's Day with me?"

"You, Mr. Captain of the Basketball Team, go to those?" I say.

He laughs. Kisses my forehead.

"Yeah, I can see that," I say. "I can see that clearly."

"Brujas like you don't scare me, Yo," he says.

I hold in a happy dance. Promise my body we'll rejoice in dance after he leaves.

☾

I hear the sound of the zipper from a floor below him. I tiptoe closer to him. Ben opens his backpack. Fuego floats above him. As I trip over myself, Ben turns. He points the gun at me. Fuego starts a fire that melts the soles of his shoes and the gun in his hand.

I wake up in a sweat. It's only 8:00 a.m. Usually I wake at ten on weekends, but I decide to stay awake.

I go into the kitchen and unscrew the cafetera. Empty out the remains of yesterday's grounded coffee and make a new batch of coffee sprinkled in cinnamon and nutmeg. Then, I boil platanos and fry eggs, cheese, and salami. When a fork can go through the platano softly, I turn off the fire and spill out the water, but manage to leave a tiny bit. Next, I bring two tablespoons of butter into the pot. I mix and mash the platanos until they are soft. Mangú.

By the time I'm at the table, Mami has woken up. She walks into the kitchen and pours herself coffee. When she makes it to the table, she says, "Thank you for making breakfast, baby girl." She kisses my forehead as she walks to the bathroom. I take the opportunity to call Mamá Teté.

"Mamá," I say, swallowing a mouthful of mangú. "I don't

want to worry you, but I'm having more dreams, Mamá," I say. "Back to back too."

"So that's why you sound like you haven't rested, eh?" she asks.

"Yeah, most likely."

Mamá is silent for a long while, but I hear her breathing. I fix my eyes on my coffee mug.

"Meet me at the supermarket around noon," she says.

☾

At the supermarket Mamá Teté looks around and rushes me from aisle to aisle until we arrive at the produce.

"You're going to look through these coconuts. You're going to see the little faces on them. They'll talk to you, because you know, eres bruja, and you'll feel it, whichever one you bond with most, that's the one we're going to buy."

"Ummmm, OK."

Mamá leaves, mentions having to get some cheeses for a wine event she was invited to by Marte tonight.

I look through the coconuts as Mamá instructed. It isn't long until I notice that it's true—they all have hairy little faces. I take a deep breath and concentrate only on their eyes and mouth. The ones that are scared have faces that look like they've received horrifying surprises. They speak to me of the fall from the heights of the coconut tree that left them to the ground, which managed not to crack them, but moved everything inside them nonetheless. The happy ones have upright smiles. They speak of the gratitude they carry, about bringing nourishment and clear thoughts to humans, of the endless days they spent overlooking entire towns, seeing everyone below them move. The serious coconuts don't say too much. I go with the happy ones. They're really just the cutest. I choose one whose nose is obvious due to the way the bottom of the coconut pushes out.

At home, Mamá gives me a small cup of cascarilla. She tells me to dress the entire coconut with it.

"The coconut should be entirely white," she says. "Ask your guides and Fuego to speak to you. They will be clear. In seven days, you'll go to the entrance of the building, smash it, and listen for its sound."

COLDHEARTED LOVE

The gym is entirely transformed. The theme is Winter Love, although the students keep saying the theme is Cuffing Season. I see Mr. Leyva from a distance rocking a burgundy suit with a white button-up. He got his little dancing shoes on, too!

"OKAY, Mr. Leyva!" I yell. I lean back and cover my eyes, feigning being blinded by his grills.

"Yolanda, girl. You know we clean up nice," he says, his grills flashing. I pretend to be blinded again, throwing my hands over my eyes.

"You play too much!" he laughs. The words come out of his mouth in a rhythm that matches the merengue playing in the background. We fake pose around each other. And then I hear the jingling of his keys hanging off of his belt hook. Even on a day like today, he's carrying them.

I laugh so hard, my lungs have to fight for breath and tears come down my eyes.

"Captain, you looking real good too," Mr. Leyva says. I feel José's arms drape around me. He takes a second to spin in true pirouette form and suddenly we're laughing all over again. "Let me get a picture of y'all love birds."

José and I look at each other and decide this will be our first picture. We convinced our parents and his sister to not make tonight a big deal. José holds me from the back, his hands coming onto my hips. I tilt to the right side of us, so he can shine in the picture too. Mr. Leyva counts to three and we smile.

"Let's take a selfie though, Mr. L," I say. We take one, and then there's a bunch of other students in the frame.

As I put my phone into the small lilac Brandon Blackwood trunk Victory let me borrow, I run into her. She is dressed in all black like the rest of the camera and design team. Except Victory is wearing marbled stockings and a black dress with thick Doc Martens. "I see what you did," I say.

"You know I had to kill two birds with one stone: work and stunt," she says.

"Girl, I feel Big Bruja vibez," I say, fake flipping my hair. Victory did my makeup and gave me a dark lip that has got me feeling myself. She also stretched out my hair. It sits in a loose ponytail, reaching the middle of my back, and my edges are waterfalling down my hairline. I am wearing a violet strappy slip-on dress, gold accessories, and gold strappy heels I borrowed from Mami.

"You look good, sis. And he ain't looking bad either," she says. I follow her glance to José, who is in his slacks, shoes, button-up, violet tie, and a tweed blazer.

"Girl, please don't remind me." I bite my lip as I look at José. He's acting a fool with his friends, but he still makes me feel like I have a million fireflies going off and on inside of my stomach.

I turn towards the door, and the fireflies are gone for good. Ben walks in. He greets a couple of people. My stomach tightens.

I walk to the punch station and pour myself a cup. Before I can take my first sip, I feel the need to turn. I see Ben's got his eyes on me and is on his way over. Not today. I scan the room, and when I look back to his direction, I realize Mr. Ruiz interrupted Ben's journey. Ben looks at me over his shoulder.

"Ugh!" I say to myself. After a second, Ben continues walking towards me, and Mr. Ruiz follows. While I am glad Mr. Ruiz is acting as a buffer, I also feel self-conscious about the idea that adults think both of us are incapable of being next to each other.

"Ben. Mr. Ruiz," I say.

"Ms. Alvarez," Mr. Ruiz smiles.

"How long did that take?" Ben points at my edges. "It looks real, you know . . ." he grins as he supposedly struggles for a word, " . . . 'artistic.'" He uses air quotes. I want to peel the slight smirk on his face. Mr. Ruiz raises an eyebrow, but says nothing. In his silence, he fits right in with Ben.

"What is it to you?" I respond, my arms folded over my body.

"My lady," José slides toward us. Thank God, relief! "May I have this dance?" He bows at me, and I cover my face to laugh.

"You may," I bow back. We crack up laughing as we walk to the dance floor.

It isn't long until everyone is dancing. Despite the fans, the air is muggy and thick with heat. A few of the boys on the basketball team snuck in liquor in water bottles, and everyone seems to have taken a few sips. Every time dembow, soca, or afrobeats come on, the crowd goes nuts, and everyone is on the dance floor. The heat of the room is entering every single strand of my hair and gets it poofier and poofier.

I am grinding up on José when Mrs. Obi comes by, moonwalks, and shimmies herself in between us to pull us apart.

"Let's not do the most right now," she says. José and I laugh at her having zero expression on her face as she says this. I take the opportunity to go to the bathroom. On my way out the gym, I see Victory fixing up some hanging lights, and I stand by her until she's done.

The long hallway to get to the bathroom on the other side of the school is dimmed. Victory puts her arm through mine.

"Aside from today, I feel like I haven't been able to hang out with you in a while, you good?" I ask.

"Yeah, just all this damn studying. I feel like I can't even talk to myself sometimes."

"You're doing great, Victory," I mumble. Ever since I've known Victory, she works harder than everyone around her. But now the stakes are high—college. We open the doors leading us into the Julia De Burgos High wing. And the door to the staircase suddenly closes. By the time I am able to focus on that door, I only see a shadow.

"You saw that?" Victory whispers. I nod. I tiptoe to the door. Victory's eyebrows arch as she furiously mouths for me to stop. I don't listen.

I open the door, look up the stairs, and he looks right back down at me. The backpack I've seen in my vision dangles over the space between the stairs like a hanging fruit.

I lose all of my hearing and everything in my sight blurs but him. I run after him.

"Bro, what are you doing?" I yell after him. My chest is constricted, and my lower back numbs up with pain. When I finally get up to the third floor, I push open the bathroom door and stand in the doorway. He's closing his backpack.

"Trying to privately use the bathroom. Are you stalking me or what?" he asks.

"What's in the backpack, Ben?"

Locking my eyes into his, I realize the pain I saw in him is back. I haven't seen it in a while underneath the potent hate that leads him nowadays. The hate is so strong, it feels like it would take decades to undo. We don't have the time for that. I pull in his stare, manage to get him to lock eyes with me. When I have him, he attempts to dart his eyes away from me, but I struggle to keep him in place.

Fuego, come through, aid me in disarming this boy. May the hate in him be replaced with lighter energy. May—

"Yolanda, COME DOWN!" Victory yells. Just like that, the lock is loosened.

"Listen to your friend, bruja," he smiles. The way the word comes out of his mouth—rolling no r's—disgusts me. I look at him as I walk out and begin to descend the stairs. At the final flight, three floors away from him, I feel the heat around my head and the pressure build. The vision delivers itself into the center of my skull like a bad headache. It knocks me down to my knees. Before I see it, I feel a hand on my arm.

Victory grabs me and rushes us into the downstairs bathroom. Locks the door behind her.

"Victory," I whisper when we're alone. My head feels like a set of bricks on my shoulders. The entire bathroom is whirling around like a tornado. Victory becomes a breeze. Nausea sets in my chest. I crouch, pressing my palms into my knees. Taking deep breaths through my mouth. I pat my chest. I can't breathe. Every time air manages to get through my airways, it hurts.

"Yo, take deep breaths," Victory says. But her voice is distant like she is across the street from me, instead of right in front.

I watch her take my hands in hers, but I can't feel anything. I let go of her and quickly she repositions herself and begins rubbing my back. I close my eyes.

Ben's footsteps running up the stairs. Backpack. A brief, loud hissing sound. Rustling of paper. Gun. The pressure lifts up out of me, and I feel like I am descending out of a hot air balloon and falling onto Earth. I turn around and lean into the wall with my forehead. My entire body is sweating so much I feel as if I have peed through my tights.

"I saw it," I manage to say. "I saw it!"

"What?!" Victory yells.

"The vision," I gulp in a breath. "The one I told you about. The backpack. I saw what's inside. It's a gun. I . . . I been seen it, Victory. I just didn't tell you."

Victory shakes her head nervously. "I told you you should've been told!" She grabs her phone from the sink.

"What are you doing?!"

"You have to call 911." Victory begins dialing but stops at 9. "You do it."

"Why?!"

"Did you just see the weapon, Yolanda? Did you?" She grabs my face, and I feel her heart rate through her hands.

"It was just a—" I start, "a flash of the backpack, the gun." I take another deep breath. I think of the fact that we are still here talking. It's fine. We're fine.

"That's enough then. What else are you waiting for?"

"It isn't," I grab her wrist. "I didn't *see* anything. Let me just go talk to him."

"Have you really lost your mind, Yo?" she whispers loudly. It stings immediately. "You about to go out there and risk some shit just because you're forgetting who the fuck you are? You just have to be honest."

"I can't say it though! I can't!" I yell. "When has anyone ever listened to a witch?" I open the door to the staircase. My chest feels tight, but I rush upstairs, skipping one step at a time. I pray my heels don't break and neither do my ankles. He's coming down, as I am going up.

"Ben, please do not—" I begin as I continue going up the stairs to him.

"You're crazy, you know that?" He tries to continue down the stairs, but I block him with my arm. I notice he doesn't have the backpack on him. Just his coat this time.

"Why do you pretend to be OK here when you actually hate it so much?" I ask. I put my arms on the stairwell and he has no option but to stop. I take the opportunity to look into him. Try to begin the pulling and maneuvering through his eyes, but he bumps my arm with his knee, and runs past.

When I make it back to the bathroom, Victory is on her phone.

"He left," I tell her.

"I don't care. You have to call someone to help. There has to be proof that you tried to do something if it goes down, Yolanda! Please. I'm not letting you continue to do this anymore."

I bring out my phone. There's a blur, but I dial. I call the police as Victory watches me.

☾

By the time the cops are at the scene, Ben has gone home, the school has been emptied out, and Ms. Steinberg has tried to get me to repeat the story to her at least four times. Although I am told I have to give a statement, I ask for my grandmother to be present. She arrives with her purple satin scarf wrapped around her head and a bubble coat covering her bata. She asks for a minute alone with me.

"You say what you saw, you don't say how you saw it, you understand me?"

"Pero Mamá, I didn't see it. I *saw* it—" I say pointing to my head.

"Listen to me very clearly, Yolanda Nuelis, you think these cops, your teachers are going to understand how we see?"

"No but—"

"Pero nothing! You better start constructing what you saw." She opens her eyes widely at me, and I can't help but feel the uneasiness flowing through her. "AND STICK TO IT."

When the cops come back in, I explain that on my way to the bathroom, I saw him go into the staircase. I followed him. Watched him take out a dark object, shaped like a gun. When he heard me, he put it back in his backpack and we exchanged some words in the bathroom. I came back downstairs. Went into the bathroom with my best friend, and she decided to make the call.

"Are you sure it was a gun?" the first cop asks. He's got dark hair and green eyes. He stands as if the whole world is his space. I nod.

"Do you think this kid was trying to harm others?"

"I—"

"She can't tell you that, she's not in his head. But if he's got a gun, what do you think?" Mamá says in Spanish. The other cop translates quickly. He tells Mamá we'll have to go down to the precinct to give a proper statement.

The looks I get outside from the kids who manage to stay in

the area bring me so much shame. Some of them look at me with pity. Others roll their eyes, cut me, because I've cut short a night of fun.

"Yolanda," José yells. He approaches me, opens his arms for a hug.

"It's fine," I say in his embrace.

"Text or call me please," he says. Kisses my forehead, and I join Mamá in the backseat of an NYPD car.

When we get down to the station, Ms. Steinberg is there. She rushes to me.

"Yolanda, are you sure you saw a gun? They found nothing at school," she says. I take a deep breath. Mamá Teté tells her I need to settle down before I continue to talk to anyone.

Mr. Hill rushes through the front doors of the precinct. He walks straight to the counter. Fear envelops him. He puts his large hand on the countertop.

"Where's my son?" he demands.

"He's just right there in our room."

"No one has spoken to him, correct? He's seventeen, that would be illegal."

"No, Mr. Hill. Please come with us to the back." A police officer opens the door and lets him in.

I look at Mamá. I said I saw a gun. What if they don't find one? What if I'm wrong? What would they do to me for lying on one of them?

Fuego, are you there? I bite my lips to keep from crying. *Please, answer me.*

THE LET DOWN

They find nothing.

Even though I saw Ben walk out of school without a backpack, they claim he had one when they stopped the taxi he was in. They search every corner of our school, including the third floor bathroom.

Nothing.

I was wrong. The idea of the Bruja Diosas being nothing but a part of my imagination brings me to my knees. The simple thought that the voices in my head don't come from a higher source weakens me entirely.

I pray, I pray. I beg. For answers. For guidance. For anything. *The Bruja Diosas, Fuego, have failed me.*

Nothing.

All week, my teachers send me homework packets as if they've made a decision to keep me out of school before I've made up my own mind. I stay in my room for the most part. Mamá sometimes knocks. Papi sometimes opens the door, but I don't have it in me to turn to look at him. I don't want to talk. I don't want to look. I don't want to hear palabras de aliento, words that are supposed to make me feel better. He respects it. Sometimes he checks the bathroom to see if my processors are on me, or charging. They've been charging as of late, so he mostly leaves a note. Mami texts, and I tell her I am good, because it's better than imagining her come over. Victory tries to visit, but I lock my bedroom door.

I just want to be left alone. I wish I could crawl out of this skin.

During the downtime, I get lost reading *Homegoing* for homework and finishing Assata Shakur's *Autobiography* on my own. I begin to feel that my chances at making it through high school untouched by the fucked-up reality of this world was all a joke. Did I ever really have a shot?

I spend the days praying out of habit but not out of necessity. I start locking the door when everyone keeps coming in unannounced.

By the end of the week, Mami comes into the house, unlocks my bedroom door with a pincho, and takes the covers off.

"Get up!" she signals.

"STOP!" I yell. "STOP!" And I don't know how loud it is. But it's loud enough for Mamá Teté and Papi to storm in. Papi brings on the processors and holds them out to me until I put them on.

"Why can't y'all leave me alone?" I scream. Anger is so much easier to touch these days.

"We've let you be for five full days, Yolanda Nuelis," Mamá Teté says.

"We're going to a doctor. Put on some clothes," Mami says. She begins going into her bag.

"NO!" I yell. "I won't go. I'm not even sick."

"It's not a doctor, Yoyo," Papi says. He looks at Mami with

anger. "We've been mandated to take you to see a therapist before you can return to school."

"A therapist?" I ask in disbelief. My eyelids burn my eyes. *Julia De Burgos High has gone against me? They think I'm lost like this?* "Who mandated?" I ask, fighting my tears.

"There's nothing wrong with it. I've seen one before. Your mom saw one a few months after you were born. Sometimes we just need to talk to someone. Someone outside of our situation. Someone who can give us unbiased advice, you know?" Papi looks past me.

"I'm not talking to a white person. They won't—" I think of Ben and his privileges. The way everyone is looking at me like I've lost my mind off the strength of his supposed innocence. "They won't get it."

"It's one of us, Yoyo," Papi says. "I promise."

I slip into sweats, a long-sleeve top, and a hoodie. I wash my face, brush my teeth. I hear Mami telling Papi he babies me. Out of guilt. He says she adultifies me so that she can just live her life being a part-time mother. Mamá tells them both to shut up. I walk into the room and stare at both of them. I don't even have the energy to shake my head. After so many years, I guess nothing has changed.

☾

Mami and I drive into Harlem. We go up the steps to a brownstone. Immediately, the entire office feels like a home, but I fight the urge to immediately feel comfortable. I scope out the corners looking for cameras—none. We sit in the waiting area with cream walls and orange couches. There are names on the walls of at least five different therapists. I take out my Assata Shakur book, even though I've finished it, to avoid talking to Mami. I turn to the page and a line becomes a target for my eyes. "The rich have always used racism to maintain power," Assata writes.

"Yolanda Nuelis Alvarez?" they say into the room. When I look up, it's a beautiful Black person. Their dark beard is impeccable. A tinted lip balm roses up their lips. They wear a floral long-sleeved turtleneck under a black flowy dress. Their hair is twisted and falls over their shoulders. I stand up.

"Hi, what can I call you?" they smile.

"Yolanda, Yoyo, Yo. Anything really," I shrug, and fold my arms.

"Names are important. I think I'll go with Yolanda. I am Jonah. If you have to use pronouns, they/them is OK, but Jonah is better." They look at me like I'm a baby bug or some shit.

"She/her is fine by me," I say.

"Amazing. Would you like to come with me to my office?"

I look down at Mami, who smiles and nods, reaching over for a magazine on the table in front of her.

Jonah's office is in a small room. There's a brown leather couch, and I immediately recognize it is where I will sit. Jonah sits on a light-blue, modern-looking chair with a high-back frame, positioned in a corner between a window and a bookshelf.

"Why don't you start telling me a little bit about yourself and why you're here?" Jonah moves a pad and a pen from their desk. "Before you start, I should probably mention anything you say here is confidential. Unless you are thinking of harming yourself or others. That I am required by law to tell authorities in place, including your caring adults. Anything else it's between you and me."

I nod.

"Are you OK if I take notes? Mostly for me."

"OK," I say.

"Anywhere you want." They signal for me to begin by lifting their hand palm up.

"I'm sixteen, but I am guessing you knew that. I am in tenth grade, and I go to Julia De Burgos High. I run the Brave Space Club," I begin. "Well, if nothing has changed after last Friday."

"What happened last Friday? Is that why you're here?"

"Yes. Well—" I bring my legs up to the couch. Cross them around me. My mind takes leaps. I look at the clock on the desk: 1:30 p.m. Can I trust this person? I bite my lip. What if Mr. Hill is paying them off? What if they just want to take notes about how my brain works? I shake my head—no way. No way am I gonna go down this conspiracy-theory rabbit hole. I didn't ask Mami who exactly mandated that I be here, but I trust I have to do this. I breathe deeply.

They breathe.

"I am only here to hold space for you," they say. We sit in silence for a bit.

"I thought something was happening. But then it didn't," I finally say, at 1:36 p.m. "By the time I figured out I was wrong, it was too late. My best friend had me call the police. And the whole school was harmed."

"Harmed? What do you mean by that?"

"The school went under lockdown. The dance was canceled. People were really scared. Kids called their parents. The police scares people, you know? Ben was picked up and taken to the precinct."

"Who is Ben?" they ask.

"This new kid. He's the son of Mr. Hill, who is running for

Congress. He's white and comes from money, and has been an asshole since day one," I say. "Even when I couldn't accept it. Even when I was giving him the benefit of the doubt. But I guess I was wrong about him having a gun."

"And how do you feel about that?" they ask.

"Crazy. I feel crazy."

"What did you feel the moment you believed you saw a gun?"

I take a deep breath and prepare to keep bending the truth to protect myself. "I was scared. But I felt it—I felt that he had it— that I wasn't wrong." I know it makes no sense without saying the vision part—without saying the word—but I say it anyway.

"Yeah, I can only imagine," Jonah says, looking at my hand on the armrest. "Yolanda, I am a holistic therapist. That means I consider lots of things about my patients. For example, religion, spiritual practices, and traditions. Your mother mentioned your spiritual practices on the phone."

"I bet she had lots to say," I snap.

"No," Jonah lightly shakes their head. "She was actually making sure I respected and honored your belief system."

"Oh," I whisper. "Well, that's good."

I scan the bookshelf by their desk. On the very bottom, I spot their altar. Three small shot glasses of water in a row. Pictures of those who must've passed. A plate with apples and corn. *You're safe.*

"I've been having visions since Ben came to Julia De Burgos. The visions reveal parts of who he is. I wanted to try and give Ben a chance or stop him from releasing his anger on us myself. One of the visions that I've been getting in small bits is one of him with a backpack. Inside the backpack is a weapon. I had more visions about the gun and I gaslit myself until I saw it again at the dance. I told two of the adults in my life I was having visions. I thought it would help." Tears start swelling my eyes.

"I see. Can you tell me about the last vision?"

I bring my knees up to my chin. Hug myself. Close my eyes. Pray to the Bruja Diosas only by moving my lips and asking for their guidance inside my head. I take a deep breath when the top of my head feels light and heavy all at the same time.

"Everything is going fine. Like a regular school day. People have just switched classes. After five minutes into the period, I go to the bathroom. I walk into the stairwell to go up to the third-floor bathroom; it's the cleanest. I see Ben crouched in the corner of the stairwell, but he doesn't see me. I walk closer to him. He goes into his backpack. My own heartbeat creates a suspenseful, dark rhythm. He brings out a gun."

I open my eyes. "That's it."

Jonah takes a deep breath.

"I know I'm crazy. Just give me my diagnosis," I laugh awkwardly.

"Why do you think you're crazy?"

"Visions, dreams. Some would call that hallucination."

"Do you think they're hallucinations?" they ask. Their unbiased questions begin feeling heavier.

"Don't you?"

Jonah thinks for a while, their pen pressed up against their chin. "I think a lot of people of color, specifically Black people, have been made to think they're crazy for having visions. I just witnessed you call up a vision. Were you praying?"

"Yes, to the Bruja Diosas and my Unknown. They haven't been too clear with me since I started getting these visions."

Jonah asks me to explain who they are. I say they are my ancestors, my guides, my saints, my higher self. It's just a name I gave them as a child and it stuck.

"Why do you say they haven't been too clear?"

"All of it is confusing. What I feel. What they show me. What I think I should do. What I am scared of," I shrug. "When I have the visions, it doesn't feel like the way communicating with them used to feel in the past. The visions always feel dreadful. I feel my chest constricting, like I can't breathe."

"I hear you, and I wonder if we can look at this through another perspective. Maybe they are communicating as best they can about a truly difficult thing. I also don't think it's fair to say they've abandoned you, Yolanda," Jonah responds.

"When the cops were called, I was so scared. I have only seen cops in action when they've arrested my dad, or when they stop people at train stops. I've just never had a positive interaction with them. And so when Victory called them and I knew they were coming, I had the same feeling again of not breathing, or feeling like I was going to die. After the cops came and the school was turned upside down, Ben had left. But they found him and searched him, and they went into his locker. They went to his home. It was searched too. Nothing. At the precinct, everyone looked at me as if I had lost my mind, or had made the whole thing up. I prayed for the Bruja Diosas to tell me the truth. But my chest constricted and I thought I was going to die then too. I couldn't breathe. I felt alone, by myself. I felt so alone. Why had they sent me that vision if it wasn't true?" The words are coming out of my mouth quickly and with tears and snot. Jonah offers tissues.

"Sweet Yoyo, you had a series of panic attacks. Fear, confusion, mental and emotional pressure—married to the negative energy of others around us—can definitely cause them. I don't know what your guides are trying to communicate, but I wouldn't discredit them. What I will say is our people have survived due to our spiritual connections. I am not sure it is time to give up on your Bruja Diosas yet."

I take a deep breath. Jonah is the first person I have ever talked to directly about my Bruja Diosas, other than Victory, Mamá Teté, and somewhat my parents. Mami always tells me to exaggerate about being sick to doctors, and never say too much to people about what I see and hear. Will I be a study case? Will I be locked away, examined, and probed? Suddenly I start feeling as if Jonah can see right through me. I bury my fists in the space between my thighs. I bring my shoulders in, and tuck my head onto my chest. I feel my cheeks flushing and then my ears are hot. *Take a deep breath. We're here. All is well. We're here. We haven't ever left your side.*

"Deep breaths," I hear Jonah say. They move to my couch. I look up at them. My eyes are swollen, but there are no tears anymore. They smell like every essential oil in the world, yet the citrus kicks in the most. When I was younger, I used to smell the skin of oranges just because it brought me joy. Mamá Teté tells me Bruja Diosa Miel loves oranges on the altar. Maybe I'll add some to mine.

25

BACK TO BACK

Jonah signed off on the mandated therapy form. They told me if I wanted to continue seeing them, I could, but they also understood if I wanted to take a break. I spend the rest of Friday and Saturday binging series after series. All I want is my brain off. If I had an off button, I would press it. On Sunday, I finally get up and shower. After I dress, there's a knock on the door—Victory.

She sits on the bed next to me. A part of me wants to scream at her, tell her I wasn't ready to call the police. But I miss her more than I regret calling the police.

"What are you watching?" she asks.

"Some good old videos of animals being animals in the wild," I say. She nods. We spend three hours watching the wolves birth and care for each other.

We end up falling asleep in my bed.

There's a gray cloud hanging over Julia De Burgos, but everyone is moving as if it is not there. When I look towards the front door, I see Ani, the bodega cat, come in. I follow her throughout the day as she catches roaches and dust bunnies. By the time I get bored of watching her, I step into the third-floor bathroom, but she follows me in and cuts me off before going into a bathroom stall. She charges at a rat. She wrestles with it behind the toilet. She comes out, her tail high in the air. And settles the dismembered body at my feet. I watch her as she hops onto the sink and washes and scrubs her paws with fennel, oregano, and salt.

A knock at the door wakes us up a little past four. "¡A comer!" Mamá says. I take a deep breath in, taking in all the sazón in the air.

"I bet she made us locrio. She knows I love that shit!" Victory says excitedly, getting up. But I catch her arm and adjust my processor.

"It's been nice being together today," I say. I let go of her arm and spin some of my curls from around the stickiness of the processor. "Like I feel way more hopeful about going back to normal, you know?"

She smiles. "Yeah, I know what you mean." She hugs me, and it feels as if her arms are helping put me back together.

☾

On Monday, after I get ready for school, I walk to the living room. Mamá has made me scrambled eggs with mashed yucca and served me a glass of OJ. I sit, and she settles down on a chair across from me sipping her café. From time to time, I smile at her as I chew. I give myself permission to daydream about the kind of bruja I will be when this is all over: confident, grounded, and direct. I imagine myself never slouching, always sitting upward, walking down the street with posture that reflects my power, not having to always hide.

"You OK?" Mamá asks, bringing me back. I haven't been the nicest, and although I know she understands, I want to give her back her granddaughter.

"Mamá, what comes first, the manifesting or the healing?" I ask. I want a world where I don't have to think of people like Ben, who want to bring others down just so they can stay on top. I want to create that world, but there is something in me that tells me I have to turn into myself first.

"The healing, mi'ja. Ponte las pilas," Mamá Teté nods, with her cup hanging off of her finger. "You can't build a sound house on top of debris and rubble."

"But I can clear out what is no longer of use *and* build a foundation for the house," I wink at her.

"You've got to want the healing all that much more. It takes great power to do both at the same time." Mi vieja looks at me, taps my nose, stands up, and bends to kiss my forehead. "All this work," Mamá's voice breaks, "it was never my intention to pass the heaviness of it down to you."

I look up at her and smile. The tears rush down the wrinkles of her face. I wipe them. "I know, Mamá. But I got it. Don't worry. Forreal, I got it."

☾

"You OK to go in by yourself?" Papi asks. I nod. I've forced him to get to work late this morning, so he can drive me in after the first period has started. I didn't want to be all up on that crowded bus. I don't want to see everyone just yet. I want to slip into school unseen.

I throw my hood over my head, kiss Papi, get out of the car, and cross the street and walk into the school gates. It's the longest walk I have ever been on although it takes less than sixty seconds. The minute I step into the school, Mr. Leyva is at the front desk.

A big machine, similar to the ones I've seen at the airports, stands between myself and the hallway to get into Julia De Burgos.

"Yoyo, you're back," Mr. Leyva says. "I guess you haven't met our new friend, the metal detector? It's state-of-the-art. Donated to us. The procedure is you take all your metals off, put them into the plate, and you step on through. I'll give them back to you on this side."

I smile. An uncomfortable smile. I wonder how long it takes people to get into the school building now. I think of how much more they'll hate me now. I empty my pockets of my cell phone, my Fenty gloss, my keys, and I take off my earrings. I throw them in the tray, and they land hard, making more sound than I intended.

I step into the metal detector. I close my eyes. I've been step-ping into these since I was six. To go to court with Mamá Teté; to visit Papi in jail. I take a full step forward, taking a look back to see the green light for myself. I put my earrings back on and fill my pockets.

"We've missed you around here, Yoyo. I know it's going to be a little off today, but don't you ever forget that I have got your back," Mr. Leyva says. I give him a half smirk. "That ain't enough, girl. Come on, you know we can talk," he pushes.

"Mr. Leyva, I just feel tired. Tired of this boy being part of my day-to-day things, you know?" The bell for first period by, but Mr. L doesn't rush me to class. Instead he brings me by the office, pulls out a chair, and puts it next to his own—the one that always stays in the hallway for security.

"He's a character, Yo. I don't think you're wrong about what you're feeling about him. But I am worried about you, aside from him," he says.

What if I told Mr. Leyva the full truth? What would it look like for him to know, know?

"His energy is off, Mr. L," I begin. "There's something dark in him. I know you always tell me to see the good in people, and I do see some of it in him, but overall, just bad. And I've told you about the visions. I hate that I was wrong, but I am still not happy he's here." I shake my head and get up.

"I see you, Yo," he says as I walk away.

"I know, I know." I stop and stand in the middle of the hall-way, looking back at him.

There's a silence between us so deep, but I feel comforted by it. I want to tell Mr. L that he's done right by me, but my chest hurts at the thought of saying the words.

"And all I know is that this boy is lucky he met you this year. Because trust, last year, you would've gone about this completely differently," he continues.

"You right about that," I laugh.

"Girl, you remember the time you yelled so loud into a junior girl's ear, she thought you'd made *her* deaf?"

I laugh uncontrollably.

"And you were like 'who's the deaf girl now?' Girl, I could've kicked you, talking that mess in front of her parents like it was nothing."

Now I am laughing so loud, I have to cover my mouth. So hard I have tears coming down my eyes. I can hardly breathe.

"Oh snap, that was funny," I gasp.

"I'm glad I was able to give you that medicine. Sometimes we just need a full belly laugh."

"Yeah," I say, smiling big in approval. Pick up my Telfar bag. I should probably get to class, but a part of me wants to stay with Mr. L all day.

"I'm always going to be here if you need another reminder of who you are, or a laugh, Yoyo."

I have to clench my jaw to keep from crying.

"I appreciate you more than you'll ever know, Mr. L. You a real one," I smile.

"I know, Yo. I appreciate you, too," he says, "Now go on, girl. Get to class."

◖

Math goes fine. My seat is in the very front, so I feel everyone's eyes burning into my back. My teacher slips me a note saying to come to her for office hours, and I nod. Even after a few minutes of laughing, the weight comes back like it never left. I take deep breaths mainly to stay with the class, but also to keep the panic attacks away.

By period two everyone somehow knows I am here today. In the hallways, it's like they all have chosen to give me space. I am no longer a sardine, packed tightly by my peers. I am a shark that can swim right into my next class. I smile at Mrs. Obi. She holds my shoulder as I rush in and looks at my eyes. I hear her question: *Are you OK?*

I nod. I settle into my seat. Wait for the inevitable. Having Ben slouch next to me. I wait. Wait. Breathe. Wait Breathe. Wait. But he never shows. All period I feel as if I am waiting for him. More for me than for him. But still waiting. I want to see what my body will do. Every day I am learning more about myself, about the things that make me tighten and loosen. By the time the lab comes around, a number of people have found creative ways to approach me, lend me a smile, a fist bump, or "just to say hi." I feel less alone.

But seen.

I don't know if it makes me tighten up or loosen up.

José gets into chemistry halfway through the lab. He gives Mrs. Obi a pass, and she directs him to work with me. My heart drops, and I bite my lip to keep from smiling or crying. I look back down at the beaker.

"Hey," he says. He drops his backpack next to me. I give him an upward nod, eyes still on my beaker. Waiting for the colors to change. I explain briefly what the lab called for, what it is I am waiting on.

"Yoyo," he whispers. Even though all I want to do is hug him, there is a part of me that feels conflicted. The colors have changed. The process is complete. I raise my hand for Mrs. Obi to confirm.

"Great job, Ms. Alvarez. You can go to the next station. José, feel free to practice this one on your own again." I stand up, my binder and pen in hand. I catch his eyes and then walk away.

For lunch, I decide to skip the cafeteria. I take the stairs, skipping a step, breathing, reminding myself that the vision is in the past and I was wrong. I knock on the library door. Mrs. Aguilar gives me a big hug and tells me I have first dibs on seating. I take the one-person couch that looks out the window. I take out my *Assata* book. But I can't concentrate much. I think of the many times Victory and I chose this seat. I'd fit myself between her legs and she'd braid my hair. I would always fall asleep until she asked me to bring the jam jar closer to her. Sometimes if we were laughing too loudly, Mrs. Aguilar would come over and remind us we weren't at a beauty shop, but she'd never kick us out. Once, she even asked Victory to braid her hair.

My phone buzzes in my pocket. *I heard you're in school. Where are you?* Victory texts.

Even though it was nice having Victory over yesterday, I still feel some sort of resentment. In some way, Victory forced me into telling. She shouldn't have. She took away my right to make my own decision. But what could she've done? Let me continue having the visions and the nightmares without warning anyone? She had me call the police though. Without considering the repercussions, without considering my feelings. And now folks are traumatized and we have metal detectors.

☾

By Friday, things start feeling normal again. I'm eating in the cafeteria with José and Victory. We don't talk about anything past classes and surface-level things. Mrs. Obi has asked me to lead the social justice meeting after school, and I accept. I tell her I can't do anything heavy yet. And she says we don't have to and assures me Ben isn't allowed in Brave Space anymore. She says to start off we can have a circle and then watch a movie.

Mrs. Obi has ordered pizza and a few apple pies from the bakery down the block. Everyone eyes the goodies on their way to the circle. I hold Penny.

"I know I haven't been here in a while. I want to thank everyone for holding it down. I figure we keep it light today. Let's share one another's zodiac signs. If you know your moon and all of that, share that too! I'll go this way."

"Sagittarius sun, Scorpio moon. You know what they say about the scorpions!" Rashaud says.

"Heyyyy," Cindy hypes Rashaud up. "Scorpio sun, Aquarius moon."

"Gemini sun, Capricorn moon, and Aquarius rising," Victory says looking right at me.

"Aquarius rising, Taurus sun, Leo moon," José adds. By the time Penny gets back to me, I add that I am a Gemini rising, my sun is in Libra, and my moon is in Aries. The door opens, and everyone turns to it. His head peeks in.

"Hi Ben," Mrs. Obi breaks the silence. "We're in the middle of a meeting."

"Can I join?" He raises an eyebrow.

"Please meet me outside, Ben," Mrs. Obi stands up and walks to the door. She steps out and closes the door behind her. My chest begins to constrict. I bring my palm to my neck; both are sweaty. I try to take deep breaths and they escape me.

"We're going to be watching *Walkout*," Victory takes the lead. I rush into Mrs. Obi's supply closet. Jonah told me to use the five senses strategy. Five things I can see. Beakers. Dye. Chemistry textbooks. Vans on my feet. Mrs. Obi's pink wig she wore on Halloween. Four things I can touch. Looseleaf. Paper plates. Wooden color pencils. My black jeans. Three things I can hear. Cars. Movie. Steps towards the closet. I take another deep breath. The door unlocks. José. He walks in. Two things I can taste. "The first bite of the apple pie is yours," he laughs, trying to break the tension. He brings a spoonful of apple pie to my mouth. Apple pie. I chew softly and swallow.

"You OK?" he whispers, his chin over my head. I nod, wiping the sweat off of my forehead. I kiss him. As if we were in my house alone. Second thing I taste is his tongue. I kiss his neck. One thing I can smell. I inhale the lavender scent from the fabric softener his mother must buy. He pulls away. "We'll have to wait for all of that," he says, pointing back towards the classroom. I nod. Hold my wrist. My heart rate is significantly down.

The movie ends up being a favorite. Cindy says she was unaware of Latines going so hard for education rights. Mrs. Obi mentions Sylvia Mendez, whose case opened school integration before the Little Rock Nine in the late 1950s.

"Does integration work, Mrs. Obi? I mean, most of our schools are segregated still, but there must be schools out there that are integrated. My cousin goes to a charter school in Brooklyn. He says it's cool to go to school with all types of people," Jay says.

"I bet they're more rigorous. The classes, I mean, right?" Mariamma asks.

"I can't speak to that," Mrs. Obi says. "I think we'd have to think about it in terms of academics, but also in terms of emotional and social health." When she notices no one is satisfied with her response she offers, "We're integrated enough though if you think of it. We come from so many different cultures."

Victory waits for me by the door. We know each other so well—we don't even gotta talk to know what's up. We both walk to our lockers. Pick up our things and meet outside. We empty our pockets. Two dollars and seventy-five cents together. We walk to the bodega. She orders a grilled cheese and a large hot chocolate with two cups. We split both things in half and eat on the bus. My stomach filled with something already. Air. A premonition. I chew and bite, chew and bite, swallow, trying to push it down. I do this in silence. All the way home.

She squeezes my hand before she exits on the Grand Concourse. I give her a small nod.

You scared me when you called the police. I know you know this already. But I just have to get it out so maybe I can stop feeling like this. You didn't think about my history with the cops. Maybe they had to be called. But you didn't give me time to think. I type out the message and send it to her.

You're right. I'm sorry. I believed you though. I still believe you, she responds.

(

I stop at the supermarket on my way home from school. I can't get the bodega cat dream out of my head, and I know that probably means I have to do something with the herbs Ani washed the blood off her paws with.

Please have the herbs, please have the herbs, please have the herbs, I chant in my head as I walk in. The supermarket is packed with people rushing through the aisles with overflowing carts.

"They're saying we'll be inside for months!" I hear someone say. I walk past the aisles with toiletries and candles and notice there is no more toilet paper on the shelves. As I move to the bread aisle, there are only three bags left. Many areas of the Bronx, including this one, are still food deserts, so sometimes Mamá and I have to drive elsewhere to get the herbs and things we need for food or baths. As I walk into the aisle with vegetables, the misty ventilators sprinkle water on my face. The fennel sits out, and I realize my chant has done better than I expected. I grab one bunch of fennel; it sits cold on my hand. *Thank you for making your way to me.* I scan all the green produce and find no fresh oregano, but settle for some dried leaves from the next aisle.

Walking home from the supermarket, I bundle my gloved hands into my coat pockets and let the cold air press up against my cheeks. I blow out my breath just to see it condensed in front of me in the darkness of the winter evening. Little kids skip in front of their mother, as she yells for them to be careful and not bump into me. I smile, but really just want to freeze up time, preserve this space and their innocence.

When I open the door to Mamá's apartment, the warmth announces my safety. I take off my coat, step out of my boots, and wash my hands in the kitchen sink. I open the door to the fridge to get water and notice our fridge is fully stocked. Mamá must've used our food stamps to get ready for the virus they keep saying is going around.

After I drink my water, I prepare myself to begin making the bath. *Honorable Ancestors, Fuego, Mysteries, Bruja Diosas, Mother Earth, Father Sky, all that love and protect me,* I pray. I close my eyes. *Guide me as I make this bath. I don't know what it's for, but facilitate its job.* I bring a big caldero of water under fire. While that boils, I chop up the fennel from trunk to leaves. When the water is bubbling, I throw the fennel in, sprinkle the oregano, and pour in the sea salt Mamá stores under the sink.

"What are you cooking up?" Mamá calls out, stepping out from her bedroom. She turns on the television in the living room before coming into the kitchen. She's been taking naps and praying at her altar more and more these days.

"A bath I had a dream about," I respond, stirring the pot. Mamá stands over it and inhales.

"Fennel is known to protect from evil. Oregano to heighten psychic abilities. Salt wards off anything that doesn't serve us," Mamá says. "It's a smart bath." She winks at me and pulls out the strainer. She places it above a big mason jar as I pour in the contents from the caldero.

The news broadcaster announces that COVID-19 rates are rising rapidly, and the governor will address the state tonight. Mamá sucks her teeth. "May The Unknowns and all that is good protect us," she says.

I take the jar into the bathroom and take off my uniform. I step into the shower and clean off the day. Then, I scrub the tub clean, imagining I am scrubbing off all the negativity that has clung on to my community. I rinse off the grime, put in the plug on the bathtub drain, and let the warm water run. I pour in the bath, slowly watching the water turn green. I let my mind run with that color.

Other than the kiss with José and the bus ride home with Victory by my side, the anxiety keeps getting the best of me. I take a deep breath and step in. I sit and hug myself. *I thought I was a bruja, but could I just be crazy, could I just be making this up?* My mind starts to run away from the moment, but I breathe and try to catch up with myself. Even if it all feels like it's slipping my grasp, *I am glad to be here. I am glad to be here. I am glad to be here.*

After dinner, Mamá dips her fingers into lavender oil and gives me a head massage. She then takes Florida water and pats my entire body. It's been years since she's tucked me in, but I let her. She looks towards my altar. The flames are flickering, the candles about to run out.

"You got extra candles around?"

"No, I'll buy some tomorrow," I say.

"Don't forget to put up your candles for your Unknowns and your ancestors. You know—"

"They can be vengeful. I know Mamá," I say. "Cion Mamá."

"Que todo lo bueno te bendiga." I take off my earpieces and give them to her.

In the silence of the night, I watch the flames dance, try to stay alive, and eventually run out of something to burn through.

26

THAT'S REAL

*T*hey're looking right at me. My Unknown. Let me show you something, they say as they take my hand. We run and are in a village, no clothes on the people. There's joy and an abundance of everything that's needed. There are true leaders in the community, not leaders sucking up the power of the community. Give me your hand . . . we run and appear to be in Egypt. I see the pyramids being built by brick and magic. We fly from Egypt to West Africa, witness the crossing of Africans aboard their own ships. Heading to the New World on their own. Heading to the Polynesian Islands. We see them as they land at their destinations and offer yams and trade other things with Tainos, Arawaks, Māoris, Samoans, and Tongans. We stay. We build bridges. For an old person, my Unknown can jump. For a girl with more chest than muscles, I can fly.

We watch colonizers arrive. Destroy. Plummet all there is. Do something, I say. Let's do something, I beg. They take out their cachimbo, place tobacco into it. They snap their fingers and flame forms. They place the flames in the tobacco and puff. They smoke; they exhale out. If not in this life, they say, then in the next. We are strength. It's not a curse. It's a gift, my child.

Give me your hand, they say.
I don't want to, I respond.
Please, child of fire, your hand.
I give it to them. We run through the lanes of history. Arrive to
the present day. We jump the train because we've got no money,
no Metrocards. The cops see us, they chase us, tell us to stop for our
own good. I slow down, and they zap my feet to encourage me to
run faster. People are who they show you the first time, child. Run.
Run. Run. When we arrive at the end of the train tracks, they hold
both of my hands. We float up from the underground into the street;
I close my eyes; I open them when my shoulders don't feel pressure.
I open my eyes and we are in the sky. Swimming through the places in
between planets, dancing through the distance of galaxies. Around
me is all of us, all of us. All. Of. Us.

☾

When I wake up, Mamá is sleeping at the foot of my bed. I tap her
and she jumps up. There are dust bunnies and crumbs all over
her purple bata.

When Culebra visits Mamá's body, sometimes she crawls like
her snake.

"*Culebra protects you,*" I read Mamá's lips, as she kisses my
forehead. I run to the bathroom, place my processors on, and tell
her about my dream.

"Your Unknown will always be by your side, Yolanda Nuelis,"
she says.

☾

Mrs. Obi's class isn't hitting right today. Like the rest of my
classes. Since returning, school feels like I am sleep-walking at

best. The only time I feel like my old self—the me I was before Ben ever entered Julia De Burgos—is when I cross paths with Mr. Leyva. The pull to want to be home under the covers is so strong. The only thing I'm grateful for is that Ben is not in class again today. I sluggishly raise my hand, my left cheek cradled into my other arm. Mrs. Obi walks over to me as everyone works at their stations.

"May I go to the bathroom?" I ask. She puts her hand on my forehead and nods. As I grab the plastic beaker that serves as the pass, I can't help but feel guilty.

I roam the first floor, but I don't find Victory or anyone of interest really, so I open the door to the staircase. Slowly, I climb two steps at a time as I go up.

When I take a moment to catch my breath, I hear the low hiss. The low hiss that has come to me so many times. I imagine the zipper of his backpack as a vicious snake. Its body pumping as it reveals the deadly thing.

I continue going up the stairs, two steps at a time, but quietly. I force my breath to come out silent. My body is pumping and rushing with adrenaline.

I peep through the rails of the stairs, and he is sitting down against the metal gate on the stairwell that blocks access to the top floor. He is giving his back to me, but I close my eyes and envision what he is going through in his backpack as I hear the sounds: binder, book, loose papers, Glock, bullets, Glock. *Bruja Diosas, Fuego, Mysteries, Honorable Ancestors, Higher Self, Guardian Angels, Guides, please come through.*

My eyes furiously open. "Ben?" I say aloud. He turns around rapidly. His eyes are wide with surprise, his jaw low on his face, revealing a bit of the inside of his mouth, and I know I've startled him. I look down towards his hands, and there it is—the gun.

At this moment, I wish I would've been wrong all along. That my visions were off.

He closes his mouth and swallows. Then he turns to me completely, and still sitting, leans his elbows onto his knees. The gun dangles. "Yolanda, Yolanda. You just don't seem to be able to stay away."

Before I can speak, he pulls the front part of the gun down between his legs and it makes a clicking sound. He isn't even trying to hide it. I hear the Bruja Diosas in my ear like my Mamá and her friends get when they're in an intense argument: all talking over one another, all with their input on their tongues, yelling, panicking. *Protect yourself, stand your ground, breathe, leave!* I feel like I am melting—my feet onto the steps I'm standing on, and my hands onto the railing.

"Why the fuck do you keep following me? Don't you know anything about consent? No means no," Ben smiles. His cheeks flush and he keeps his smile on for longer than makes me comfortable, like he is trying to convince me everything is as it should be. I don't let go of his eyes. I try to enter him. His mind, his soul is thick with rot though—too heavy for me to flow easily into.

I want to tell him the truth: that I've seen this moment so many times. His smirk. The way he handles the gun. The power he holds like a trophy.

All I've been trying to do is stop this moment, or avoid this moment somehow. And here I am, frozen.

My tongue sits numb in my mouth. A mountainous rock. He turns around, reaching for something else in his bag. And I turn, planning to run back down.

He bangs the metal against the stairwell. Freezing me again. "No, no, no, no, no, no, no," he says. "Didn't you want to spend time with me?" He stands up and takes a step downwards, the Glock firmly in his grip. His eyes move and fixate on everything but my eyes. My body already knows what it feels like to be looked at, and it gives me a second to remember my own powers.

"What's so special about you anyway?" he laughs as he turns the stairwell and approaches me. He looks at my eyes now, and I reach. My stare begins to dig until I hit bone. I attempt to flip his blood, bring it up to his sockets. He is now only four steps away from me.

"Don't look at me," he demands. But I don't let go. His voice is shaky and falls into a hole of shame. I don't let go. He takes three steps towards me. He now towers over me. "Don't look at me," he repeats. When I don't let go of his eyes, his fist knocks my face before I get a real chance. I trip on a stair and fall onto the landing. I attempt to pick myself up immediately.

Being on my knees gives me the opportunity to live. On my knees, my eyes manage to make their way down the stair railing, and I see José's eyes. He's peeking up, and he meets mine and brings his pointer finger to his lips. *Be quiet.* He disappears.

Bruja Diosas, Fuego, Honorable Ancestors, all of you, please help me, help me.

Ben circles around me. The gun in his hand like it is a part of it. The cologne that bounces off of his blazer, along with the scent of detergent, makes me queasy. There's a hot pool of saliva under my tongue. I wonder why he sprayed cologne today; who was he trying to impress? It's the kind of scent that clings to the cotton of your clothes even after the hours have gone by.

"We could've been friends, Yolanda. We could've just been friends. But you wanted to act like you were too good for me," he laughs.

"I tried," I manage to snarl.

"You're right," he nods excitedly. "But you just wanted to pretend it didn't happen, huh? The coming over to my house just to leave me. The water bottle. The constant edging me out of the club." He grabs my hair and wraps it around his knuckles. "Let's go downstairs; let's go see the ones who couldn't make a little space in their miserable lives for me."

He forces me down the stairs. 1, 2, 3, 4, 5, 6, 7, 8, 9, 10, 11, 12. If he kills me and not any more people, that'll be better than countless dead and multiple wounded. 13, 14, 15, 16, 17, 18, 19, 20, 21, 22, 23, 24. I don't want to die. I haven't done much with my life. Not much at all. 25, 26, 27, 28, 29, 30, 31, 32, 33, 34, 35, 36. I should've stayed away from it.

"Just shoot me. Make your statement and call it a day," I say.

He puts the metal to my forehead and pushes hard into my bone. "Yeah, that's what you want?" My heart practically leaps out of my chest with every beat. My legs feel nonexistent, and I want this all to be a lie. This waiting is worse than death, and I wish he would shoot or leave. On the first floor, the door opens. I see a hand. "Don't come in!" I yell, before Ben smacks my lip with the bottom of the metal. I taste my own blood.

A loud thud behind us, coming out of the third floor, distracts Ben, and I look down towards the first floor to see Jay open the door slightly below. Turning my head around is painful as my hair is still in his grip, but I do it anyway. And I manage to see José bring down a crowbar to Ben's left hand. It forces Ben to cry out in pain. He lets go of my hair, but his other hand still holds the gun.

"Mr. Leyva!" Jay calls out downstairs. They leave a foot on the door. They look conflicted, as if they do not know whether to leave or come up and help us.

Ben takes this opportunity to use his healthy hand. The sound of the bullet escaping the gun pierces through my head. It shatters something inside as it wounds the wall. A cloud escapes with the sound, making it seem like he and I are in a dream. I cough. Through the fog, I see Jay falling to the ground. I try to run towards, but Ben reaches into my hair again.

"Get the fuck away from her, you fucking gringo de mierda," José says. He holds the crowbar like a bat. I imagine José went around and up through another staircase. Why didn't he call anyone?

"You piece of shit," Ben growls at José, kicking him and swinging my head with his movements.

A door swings open. I look downstairs to where Jay has fallen and see Mr. Leyva has entered.

"Ben, please put down the weapon," he says. Ben and José are struggling. Then I hear a loud thud, and see José stumble onto a wall. Ben tightens his grip on my hair, and I feel some of it break off. I can't breathe.

"Ben, I repeat. Put down your weapon," Mr. Leyva says. Approaching slowly. My chest contracts. *No, no, no. Don't come,* I mouth to him.

The speaker comes on. There's a clearing of the throat, "Teachers, staff, and students: Code RED. Adults, procedures must be followed," Ms. Steinberg says calmly.

Ben smiles. "What a shame, what a shame," he says. As José attempts to stand up, Ben hits him again with the bottom of the gun and then kicks him down. Then, he points the gun to José. "I was just beginning to have fun."

I turn my eyes up to look at Ben; his face is flushed, and I can't tell if he's excited or nervous. *Bruja Diosas, Fuego, bring him in.* I try to pull in the blood around his eyes, but he's jittery. I can tell from the way his lips can't stay neutral, they won't choose between a sinister smile or a frown. Mr. Leyva doesn't look like he wants to do anything, and the indecision paralyzes him. His arms are out as if they are shields and not a look of surrender. Ben's green eyes are relaxed as he takes turns looking at José, Mr. Leyva, and me.

The slow waves of these seconds press my brains into my skull. *Protect us, Bruja Diosas. Fuego, please. Protect us.*

Ben points towards José and pulls the trigger. The loud bass of the bullet shocks something in my chest, forcing me to close my eyes. When I open them, I see the bullet has shattered a concrete wall, and José escapes into the doorway. In frustration, Ben lets go of my hair, and I try to run past Ben and towards the doorway as well, but he reaches his arm around my body and brings his hand to my shoulder, his fingers reaching into tender places. The painful pinch forces me to my knees, but he forces me back up and uses me as a shield.

"Get the fuck away from her!" José yells from the other side of the door. He slams the crowbar into the door. Ben laughs. When José looks towards us, I see the powerlessness in his eyes. It tears something in me to see him so defeated.

"What do you want from us?! Why are you doing this?" I yell and cry. I step on his foot with all the weight I can conjure from my body. He turns me around, giving his back to Mr. Leyva as he points the gun to José. Grinding down on his teeth and looking straight into me, he moves his hand from my shoulder to my cheeks and presses down on them with so much force I think he'll puncture them.

Bruja Diosas, Fuego, I pray. Everything slows down. I spot

Mr. Leyva behind Ben running up the staircase, two steps at a time. Ben bangs my head against the wall. One, two, three times. I feel the warmth on my scalp first and then I smell it—blood.

José rushes in and swings the crowbar at Ben. Mr. Leyva is so close, his hands reaching out for me.

I look into his eyes and there is a smile, a peace, a love. It overwhelms every cell in my body. In my confusion, I know what comes next will break me.

Bruja Diosas, Fuego . . .

Ben pushes me onto the neighboring steps. He turns as I fall, and before the blow from the crowbar touches him, he pulls the trigger. The piercing sound of the bullet doesn't stun me this time.

When my skull falls heavy against the steps, everything, the whole world, goes dark.

27

UNDER ATTACK

DEATH TOLL AT 1 AND COULD RISE

By Kathy Nacorri and Pedro Rodriguez

Ben Hill, the 17-year-old gunman accused of opening fire with a Glock 17 at his former high school in the Bronx, New York, has been arrested and is awaiting charges. Hill is the son of candidate Joseph Hill, running for New York's 12th Congressional District. Although candidate Hill has yet to comment on the shooting, an insider has revealed he will be stepping down.

Ben Hill was arrested at the scene, Julia De Burgos High School, in the South Bronx.

Authorities said the suspect concealed a gun weeks prior to the incident inside a broken ceiling tile of the public school's bathroom. A student, who will remain anonymous, tipped police on having seen a weapon, but after a thorough sweep by the NYPD nothing was found and no charges were pressed.

Until recently it was unknown to the public that Hill had recently been expelled from Butler Prep and another private institution for disciplinary reasons, including hate speech, aggression towards students and faculty, and bullying. Private schools in the area were advised against enrolling Ben Hill. Thus, at the end of October, Hill was enrolled in Julia De Burgos High School, an act many viewed as a wonderful demonstration of progressive values by the Hill family.

What We Know:

- Three students and one staff were directly involved. One is dead and one is in critical condition.
- Suspect identified as Ben Hill is awaiting charges. He may appear in court by this Friday.
- Hill, 17, was believed to have used a Glock 17, a popular weapon used by the NYPD and believed to have been found in the Hill home.
- Bronx County Sheriff's Office is set to hold a news conference at 9:30 a.m. ET on Friday.
- A YouTube user named "Benjamin Hilton" reportedly posted "Becoming a Professional Public School Shooter" on the site on September of last year.
- The President has tweeted: "Ben Hill did not belong in the Bronx AT ALL! What was he doing there? What was his Dem dad covering up? The Liberals are desperate and dangerous." He will address the nation at 10 a.m. ET.

As of now, we know the gunman had no accomplices, federal and local authorities stated.

There's nothing to say.
   Esto no silve pa'na'.

28

GRIEF

The second I wake up, many of those I love in the world rush over to me. Their eyes examine me as they stand in a circle formed around the hospital bed I lay in. They're all wearing baby blue masks. A wave of relief rushes through me like when I arrive at Mamá Teté's after a long day. But—

It comes back to me like a rainstorm: Jay falling onto the ground. Mr. Leyva. The crumbling of my body. The shots. José takes my hand. His forehead is stitched up, his eye black and blued.

"What about Mr. Leyva?" I ask. My voice creeps out of my rusty vocal cords. His nostrils flair and he throws a hand over his face. Mamá Teté asks him to take a moment.

Mamá Teté purses her lips and begins by talking of ancestors. Her soft voice builds a quilt of stories around me. She calls forward memories of her telling me about Papá Antonio and his role as an ancestor, she mentions the historical figures we've lost who act as protectors from another realm. For a minute, I am lulled. But there's a question pressing the back of my brain.

"Where is he, Mamá?" I say louder than before.

"He has transitioned, mi vida. Mr. Leyva is now an ancestor himself," Mamá replies. She throws her arms around me. She's crying by the time I yell at her. I scratch my way out of her hug. Mami and Papi hold on to one another as they look at me helplessly. I tell them all to leave my room. And like ants in a row, they march out, looking back at my fury.

"Wait!" I say as the last person, Victory, is about to go. "Is Jay OK?"

She breaks down.

"Oh my God!" I yell, smacking my fists onto my thighs. The tears rolling down my eyes feel like acid on my cheeks.

She catches her breath. "They're still with us. We're hoping for their recovery, but the shot touched a major artery on their upper arm."

She goes at some point.

Recovering.

Recovering.

Recovering but not gone, not an ancestor.

I spend dark, long hours alone. Nurses come in after tiny knocks to check my vitals and leave after giving small talk a try.

Good people die. The world keeps moving somehow. The Unknowns. The Bruja Diosas nowhere to be found for answers.

The doctor comes into the room sometime at dusk. I open my eyes from a nap to see her eyes glued to the chart they keep by my bed. Her jet-black hair sits in a low, long braid going down the back of her white coat. I read her name tag. Doctor Taveras.

"Hi," my voice raspy. I cough and clean out my throat.

"Oh hi there, Yolanda. I didn't want to wake you." She places her hand on my knee, looking at my vitals on the screen beside me.

"Do you know anything about my friend?" I say, trying to lift my body up.

She shakes her hand and presses the buttons on the side of the bed, which do the work for me. "Jay went through a lot, but they're going to be OK," she nods.

"Can I go see them?" I ask.

"I think you should really just rest," Doctor Taveras says.

I stare at her—refusing to layer up my face with any type of emotion. Truly I am not about to beg.

Her olive-tone skin flushes. "OK, I can bring you over to Jay's room. But just for a minute, OK?" She taps her pen on my chart.

I nod. I am helped onto a wheelchair even though I tell them I don't need it. My body is sore, my neck is stiff, and I feel woozy. Mamá Teté tells Doctor Taveras that she bought her a tres golpes on our way out. She smiles in gratitude and pushes me out the room and down the hallway.

"Before we go in, I just want to prepare you," Doctor Taveras says, kneeling besides me. She gives me a mask and tells me to wear it in there since Jay is in critical condition, and we must all be safe now, especially with COVID-19 spreading. "They're still weak and on heavy pain meds. Please don't be surprised if they're not up."

I nod. She opens the door and rolls me in. Jay's mother and grandmother are on the end of the bed with a rosary in hand. Their bed is surrounded by flowers and get-well balloons like mine.

"Hi," I say, "I'm Yolanda. Jay's classmate."

"You doing all right, child?" Jay's mother asks.

"I'm OK," I nod. I keep my eyes on her, too aware of Jay's bloated face from my peripherals.

"Go on now," she gestures. Jay's grandmother pats her eyes.

I turn to Jay. There is a tube inside their mouth. Their head is bandaged. The moment they fell to the ground, and a flash from Mr. Leyva comes back to me, and I have to bring my hand to my mouth to stop myself from screaming. My eyes well up with tears.

Jay, please stay. You have a whole life. Please do all that fighting now. Do it to stay. Please, I pray. I reach out into their hand and press down.

"It's all right now," Jay's mother puts her hand on my back and begins to rub. "Jay must think you're pretty extraordinary to put themselves in harm's way."

I smile only to be polite.

This can't be it. Truly, this cannot.

29

THE STAGES

It's been a week. Most days it seems like I'm in purgatory. The questioning has been nonstop and not knowing what my answers are doing for us makes it all feel like I'm choosing between heaven or hell. No one will leave my side. I've eaten more soup than I'll eat for the rest of my life. It's the easiest thing for anyone to stuff into my mouth.

When I am finally released from the hospital, my sight turns to shit. Doctor Taveras told me the post-concussion symptoms might last for a while. She says I should be going in for physical therapy right away, but the way COVID-19 is going through the hospitals, I probably won't be starting up until it settles. The lights bother me. Great, I'll be the basically deaf and practically blind girl. ¿Qué importa? Who needs their senses? Este mundo esta matando a to' el mundo. Since the day it all went down, they're talking about shutting schools down officially, and mandating people to work from home in New York. A part of me wishes the governor would've acted quicker. Maybe that would've stopped all of this from going down. But there's no use in wishing

or hoping or nothing. The virus is spreading, and people are starting to die. The sirens from the ambulance are nonstop. When I
put on my processors, I hear them all the way up here, all day,
every day.

Mamá follows me everywhere. People come visit, and she
makes everyone spray themselves down with disinfectant spray
she got her hands on before she sends them to wash their hands
thoroughly. When Papi can't make it, he checks in at every second. Mami spends half of the week sleeping on Mamá Teté's
couch just to be able to know what's really going on with me.
Victory's parents drive her here and she sits with me most days.
But we don't share words. We just sit. Breathe the same air. José
comes in and out, bringing food I don't eat.

I stand to use the bathroom, but most of the day I stay in bed.
My daily steps on my Health app have gone from 15,000 on a normal day to maybe 200.

On the fifth day of this, Victory puts her phone down and
eyes my room. She looks over at my night table.

"Do you want to read the cards?" she asks, as she stretches
over me and grabs them. I take a deep breath. The day I took the
deck to school for the first time seems so far from now, although
it was just a few months ago.

"Fuck the cards. Take them," I say.

"Yoyo, you don't mean that," she says.

"But I do," I snarl.

She puts the cards down on the space between us and sits up
against the headboard of my bed. I slouch my body down on the
bed like a snake crawling from a tree to the ground, cover my face
with my quilt, and wish her away.

"I've known you long enough to know that you're angry," she runs her fingers through my hair. I try to let the soothing her fingers give my scalp be enough; I try to allow it to be a nice thing I need. "Higher forces never abandon us. We do that, humans do it, Yoyo. Don't shut them out."

I want to remind her that she wasn't there. I wish I could tell her that what happened will never affect her the way it'll affect me. But instead I remain quiet. I don't have the energy to get into it with anybody, and she is just trying to do the best she can.

When I don't respond, I hear her take out her laptop. Her fingers begin dancing across the keyboard.

"Our school is trending," she says. I imagine her in full glee. All she does is curate content for her social media page, so this can be content for her or whatever—yay.

I don't say anything.

"There's a hashtag," she states. The tone in her voice seems half excited. She wants whatever this hashtag could do to mean something. But it could never mean a thing—it could never undo what has happened. And based on what I know, the accountability of shooters who look like him hardly means a thing. How can Victory not see this?

"FUCK YOUR HASHTAG!" I scream so loud my throat instantly burns. I throw the quilt off of my face. "A hashtag can't do nothing for me, nothing for our school, nothing for Jay, and definitely nothing for Mr. L!" My body is crumbling again.

"Yo, I didn't say it could. I just mean we're trending and maybe—" she starts.

"And? Trending should make me feel any better? That's the

thing with some of ya'll, you really fall into the dumb shit they try to sell us," I yell.

"What?" she says, confused.

"Just go, Victory," I whisper.

"I want to be with you," she says. Her fingers twist into one another.

"But I don't want to be with you! GO!" I yell.

As she packs up, she looks back at me. "I miss him too, you know," Victory cries. "He meant a lot to all of us, Yo. And I'm sorry about the way things went down. I wish they wouldn't have." I pretend not to hear her. When she puts her coat on, she swings her bag over her shoulder and walks to the door. "I love you, girl," she says, putting on her mask. When she closes the door behind her, I glance down at the cards. I throw them into the air and watch them all come back down to the ground like confetti.

⟨

The thing about grief and depression is that sleep is such a relief. The only relief. So, it comes easier than anything else. And it's hell when, at other times, sleep won't appear, and empty thoughts drag you through the night. Tonight it's past 3:00 a.m. when I am finally able to drift into sleep.

Fireworks are going off. But it isn't the Fourth of July. The Bronx is angry. Our buildings are burning, crumbling into the streets and the crowds that stand outside. Run, I keep hearing whispers in my ear. Run. So I do. I turn into neighborhoods that aren't burning. I realize the world is just ending for some of us. The anger confuses me, but I turn and run back to the place I call home. I cross suburbs,

other cities, but I can't find the Bronx. I wail and yell. Bring my
hands to my face in panic. The smoke whooshes through my nostrils.
I look up and Fuego is floating near a space where the smoke comes
from. I run towards him, their body a north star.

☾

Victory doesn't return my texts for two days. I know I did the
most, but I couldn't take it in the moment. I couldn't. I wanted
silence and she wanted to fill up the space with the outer-world
shit I don't give a hell about.

Mamá comes in from a reading. Ever since the shooting, she's
been going to clients' homes for work. She knocks on the door,
taking off her mask, and I put down my book.

"Yolanda," she sits on my bed. "Mr. Leyva's funeral is in three
days. We are going to go pay our respects."

"Ha! ¿Funeral pa que? ¿Una celebración de que? The
Unknowns have no mercy," the words spill from my mouth, thick
and fat with regret.

Mamá Teté takes a deep breath. "I know you're going through
a lot. But I plead you to stop doubting the Unknowns and your
Bruja Diosas, Yo—"

"Mamá, they have left me, they have left everyone at that
school. Why did they just let it happen? You know what?" I stand
up. "Do they even exist?! 'Cause I can't see them."

I brush my arms through my altar. The statues, the crystals,
the photographs, the candles—all explode onto the floor like
missiles.

Mamá begins to pray under her breath. Her eyes are lit in
a fury.

"Get out!" I demand. And she leaves. I fall to the floor. Bang my fists against my thighs. I feel a fire on my chest. I let my head touch the cold floor. I notice my bookends, Yolanda La Bruja, and I can't help but laugh and cry. I crawl over to the books and bring the only thing that has reminded me that my anger, my grief is normal—Assata's autobiography—to my chest.

30

ON THE INTERSECTION OF HOPE AND DEATH

"You died.
I cried.
And kept on getting up.
A little slower.
And a lot more deadly."

—Assata Shakur, *Assata:
An Autobiography*

Police block off traffic four blocks north, south, east, and west of the Ortiz Funeral Home. So basically Fordham Road is closed. But the whole city has been quiet since COVID measures started to be put in place by the mayor. No ladies on the corner selling empanadas or hot chocolate out of coolers. No kids hanging at the Burger King or the corner pizza shop after school. No one going in and out of sneaker stores trying to get the best deals on whatever sneakers is most hot right now. No loud music blasting out of speakers coming from cell phone stores or bodegas. It's eerie to see the Bronx so silent, so still.

There are cardboard boxes and wood planks over some businesses down Fordham Road. A few days ago, a woman called Breonna Taylor was killed by police in her own home, in the middle of the night, woken out of her bed. There have been so many protests for her—people have hit the street despite the fear of catching the virus—to speak up against her unjust death. For today, Mr. Ahmed, the owner of Bronx Soles, and Ms. Lee, the owner of the jewelry spot, have convinced the remaining stores to close and pay respect to a man who contributed to all their rents. A loyal customer. A loyal friend. Even though people are shook about COVID, they show up— masked up, some with plastic glasses and visors over their eyes. There was no way folks who knew him were going to miss his homegoing.

This is all for Mr. Leyva.

Papi has parked the van in a lot on 183rd Street, and we've walked the whole way—him, Mami, Mamá Teté, and my little brothers. Papi holds my left hand and Mami stands on my right. Mamá is at the back of me. Over the N95 masks on our faces, we have white cloth masks with Mr. Leyva's last school photo, distributed to us by his family.

"You ready for this, Yoyo?" Mami asks. There is a strain in her voice. Like she wants to do more than she can to protect me from the grief, from what it brings out in me. I nod. Of course, I am.

"They asked for you to say a few words after his family members. I told them no, you aren't ready—" Papi starts.

"I can do it, Papi," I say. He's been extra-protective of me lately. Even when all I do is stay in my room, he sleeps over Mamá Teté's when Mami stays at her place, just to watch over me. I guess the only thing they've decided on as a team is this sleeping schedule.

The camera crews are everywhere. Channel One, News 12 The Bronx, Univision, Telemundo, BET, MTV News, CNN, Fox News, more folks I have never seen, but they're here. The shooting has been everywhere. On all the front papers. On headlines all over the TV. I like to think it's due to Mr. Leyva. Maybe even due to José's wounds, Jay's wounds, and my own. But nothing is ever about us. Why would this be any different?

I throw my black hood over my head. We have to walk around crowds of people, all of them wearing black or dark colors, some of them holding white candles. Some of them are holding red ones. I imagine they must've known Mr. Leyva. Known enough to know, he built his whole wardrobe around red. The color of love, and not of blood.

"Alvarez, girl, I am so proud of you. Despite having a tough start, you came in here and turned all the dark into gold. You glow, girl!" He was so corny with that line! The memory pierces my focus.

Mr. Leyva was always cheesy, always loving, always hopeful. I feel the tears generating. My back begins to tighten and then my chest. I turn around and Mamá's arms are already open; she receives me amidst the crowd.

"You cry, Yoyo. You cry on," she whispers. The crowd is loud. The sirens are everywhere.

"We have to keep moving, mi'ja," Mami says. And so I let go of Mamá and keep walking. Papi offers apologies and excuses as he opens the way for our family.

"Yonelis!" Someone calls for Mami. It's José's mother with José and his sister. They squeeze through the crowd towards us. José is wearing a white button-up shirt and pants with a black coat. He looks handsome as he does before big games. His eyes are small and swollen, like mine. He greets everyone along with his mother and sister. And then his mother holds my face and says, "Que Dios te bendiga, niña."

Getting into the funeral home is an entire mission, but we manage to do it anyway. Despite wanting to stay anonymous, it seems people know my face and my name. Inside the funeral home, there are rows reserved for Julia De Burgos students and family. My family and José's squeeze in there. I see kids from my school, and it becomes nearly impossible not to break down. I bite my lip just to keep myself stable.

At the podium a woman coughs lightly into the microphone. She's wearing all-white and her locs are in an updo. Her deep melanated skin shines under the lights.

"My husband was a good man. A man of principles. Morals. You know my family always got on my case 'cause I chose me an older man. I was twenty-five and here was a thirty-six-year-old treating me like a queen. We been together twenty years. When I told him I couldn't have kids, it just wasn't in the cards for my body, he said, 'Baby, that is perfect, 'cause I have four hundred and fifty students a year.' His kids at school was always his kids. He been in education way before I ever met him, and showing up for his kids every day was what was most important to him. So it don't surprise me at all that my man went this way." Mrs. Leyva puts her hand over her mouth, takes exasperated breaths, and laughs.

"The first time we met. It was pouring outside. I had no umbrella. My momma always told me to check the weather. But I was young, you know? I wasn't going to carry around no umbrella. So at like six in the afternoon, the rain just started pouring. It was in early October, so already I was chilly. He was walking behind me and said, 'Aye little lady, look like you drenched.'

"I looked back and he had a huge red umbrella, it looked like a damn tomato. I kept walking like, 'No, stranger.' And then I slipped going into the train station. He helped me up, scribbled his number on a twenty-dollar bill, and told me to take a cab home. I called him two days later and the rest was history." She laughs some more.

"I don't want his homegoing to be sad," her voice cracks. "He loved music and chocolate and smoked a cigar every time we were on vacation. My man lived a good life. Doing what he wanted. Looking after your kids, protecting them from systematic enemies, and from enemies that wanted to hurt them like this kid, who I won't waste a breath for by saying his name. May the Universe grant that little boy whatever it is he needs. I want you all to remember my husband, Roy Leyva, as the man he was: patient, funny, and loving. It's all he would've wanted. Thank you for being here."

The pastor gets back on the mic. "Beautiful words, Linda," he says. "Next, we will hear some words from some of Roy Leyva's students."

The man who goes up is dressed in all white and says he was a student of Mr. L's fifteen years ago. His hand trembles as he unfolds a piece of paper he takes out of his pocket. He clears his throat and tells us Mr. Leyva was the only person who believed in him. In high school he went two years without anyone finding out he was homeless, hopping around people's houses, and it was Mr. Leyva who told on him. He was angry that first day, but Mr. Leyva had saved his life. On random nights, he would just sleep on the MTA. Today, he stands before us as an engineer. Making more money than he ever thought, working three weeks on and three weeks off on ships because Mr. Leyva told him he was going to amount to something. Declared that his passion for math and science was going to lead him to the ocean. Mr. Leyva was his only caring adult. The one who showed up for his teachers at parent-teacher conferences. The only one who showed up to his college graduation. The man who walked him down the aisle when he got married three years ago.

I begin to sob. Loudly.

"You must be Yoyo La Bruja, the secret weapon, the master of clapbacks," Linda turns around as the man finishes and reaches for my face. "My husband thought the world of you, girl. I heard you might not want to go up," she says. "But you ain't go no business letting him down." Her smile is weak but bright, and it pains me to think of the pain she's feeling.

I laugh through my tears. Mami wipes my tears with a thick napkin. "It's hard. I know, but you've better go get up on there," Mrs. Leyva motions with her head. And I get up, softly.

I step out of the pew and walk up the stairs to the stage, looking down to my black boots, attempting to avoid looking into the coffin. My heartbeat accelerates when I stand behind the mic and look up at the crowd. There are so many people. I know Mr. L would be so hyped to see the turnout for him, despite all the shit going on in the world right now, despite the fear of COVID. I bring down my masks.

"I've lost my way, I think," my voice is rusty. I clear it. "The last two weeks have felt like I've just been trying to float in thick, thick honey. Except it's not honey because it isn't sweet.

Shootings happen all the time where we live, especially in this country nowadays, and it hurts that it's always us on this end. Why are we supposed to put this country on a pedestal when it always fails to 'protect' us? Sometimes it's like, why am I tripping? I should be used to this, it's the way it's always been. But all of this hit home way too close for me.

"Mr. Leyva. He saw me. From the moment I entered Julia De Burgos, he held me. He was always there my first year when I got kicked out of classes for yelling at a teacher for not hearing me, or for not speaking clearly enough for me to hear them, or for hitting a classmate for making fun of my processors. He was there for me when the reality of my dad being in jail wouldn't allow me to concentrate on school on random days. He was there for me when I was happy, filled with joy over one thing or another. He was there for me when I was having trouble with my best friend or with just anyone, even him. He would listen to me. I don't remember a time he wasn't there for me when I needed him. When I didn't want to listen to his advice and I wanted to be petty, he always looked at me serious as hell and said, 'You are what your ancestors prayed to the earth for, you will not fail due to silliness.' And I believed him, so I remade myself. By the power of all that guides and protects me, I decided to be better, to live in my truth a little bit more. Mr. Leyva wasn't just a dean. He wasn't just an adult we saw in school. He was an extension of all the good in the world that has always existed.

"If I am honest, I am a spiritual person, my grandmother says the Bruja Diosas chose me before I chose this body. But since Mr. Leyva, I can't get up to pray, to eat, to do anything. I can't believe he isn't here. He isn't here to push us, to tell us about the lights that always guide us, to believe us, to see us. I am so sorry to the Unknowns, the Bruja Diosas, and all that surrounds me. I haven't been kind. I've thought up some terrible things. I have told my grandmother just this morning that I don't believe anymore because the Unknowns I believe in wouldn't have allowed for Mr. Leyva to go this way. This is the first time someone I care for deeply died.

"Mr. Leyva was so committed to small joys, and I want to hold on to that. Every day he had the same hot chocolate for lunch. Even if he had one thousand things to do—and he always did because our school always, always needed him—nothing could keep him away from that warm cup. I respect that. Because it was his small thing, his small moment no matter how bad things were or how excited people were around him. Mr. L never forgot himself; he put himself first. He cared for us because he really cared for himself. He had so much space to hold us because he held himself. And he knew himself so much that he never took anything personal unless he knew he had to own up to something— then he'd say, 'I apologize,' or 'I'm sorry.' I feel so fortunate to have known someone so kind and true to themselves like that," my voice cracks.

"What happens to us after we are gone? Are we really just ancestors to the ones we leave behind, until our souls decide they want more life? 'Cause I miss Mr. L so much, I want to be selfish, I want him to be around a little longer even if we can't see him," I cry. I take a deep breath, look into the crowd at all of my classmates, my family, and Mrs. Leyva. I close my eyes, wiping my tears off of my face. When I open them again, everything around me has become a blur.

Except him.

I see Mr. Leyva by the doorways. Smiling. Wearing the white suit he's wearing in the casket. The melanin in his skin is glowing.

"What do you wanna be?" The words blow in my ear and without a doubt, it's his voice.

My knees go weak and for a quick second, I think I'm going to fall or float away. It's the first time I've heard his voice since he transitioned. And I don't know. I don't know what I want to be anymore. I wipe my tears and breathe.

"I wanna be the truth." The answer spills from me in a soft whisper. "I wanna be the truth. I wanna help the future young people be the truth, too. I want to follow in Mr. Leyva's steps. We need people who love us when we're dumb, lost, and stupid. I was so comfortable living in rage when I entered high school. Because I didn't have my dad. Because my mom had to humiliate herself daily just to make a living. Because I still have to wear these things to listen and people didn't know how to mind their business yet. But by the grace of the love Mr. L and my family gave me, I allowed for the Unknowns and the Bruja Diosas to speak to me. I don't want to end my life. I want to breathe air into what's left. I want to light up my path in little ways each day." I speak into the microphone, and trust the blurry audience is still listening.

I laugh, tears coming down my face, as I look up and still see Mr. Leyva as crisp as ever among the blur. He brings up his hands which hold a cup of hot chocolate. Everyone shifts in their seat, sniffs around them. They whisper about the scent of chocolate.

He nods. Brings his hand to his belt hoop. It is as I always remember it to be, heavy with keys. He unclips them, sticks out his arm, and descends towards me. The cloud over my eyes begins to lift. I look around and confirm no one else can see him but me. My lips tremble at how serene he looks. We are standing so close, face to face. The urge to hug him chokes me, but my body can't move.

He drops the keys at my feet.

"You got the keys, girl. Open every door to yourself. To shift the world, even just a little, you've got to know the truth about you," he says. Then, he's gone.

(

"LOCK HIM UP! LOCK HIM UP! LOCK HIM UP! LOCK HIM UP! LOCK HIM UP!" It's what the crowd is chanting when we step out of the funeral home. As we maneuver through the crowd, to try to get to the car, I look at Papi clueless. I haven't been watching the news.

"They're talking about the active shooter at your school," Papi whispers to me in my ear.

"There's a protest," Victory says. Victory and her parents were also at the funeral, standing by the entrance. "They're trying to say he had mental health issues."

"Should we go?" I ask. José looks at me and nods.

"No, no, no, Yolanda. We are going home. We don't have to actively look for problemas," Mami says, reaching for my hand. We are basically at a deadlock on the streets. Between the protesters, the folks who are exiting the funeral home, the closed streets, and the police, there's no space to move, no space to breathe. I look at Victory: there is an entire revolution glimmering in her eyes. We haven't spoken since I kicked her out, and I want more than anything to be with her, to prove I am sorry. José stands tall, ready to do whatever it is he is called to do. We are all standing here because Mr. Leyva was taken from us. Our ancestors are reaching out from our bodies at this moment because they too are frustrated.

"Mami!" I yell over the sirens, the chants, and the uproar. "I have to go. He hurt us."

"Dejala," Mamá Teté puts an arm around Mami. "She's protected, Yonelis."

As soon as Mami nods her head in agreement, José, Victory, and I start maneuvering our way through the crowd. By the time we are by the bottom of the 4 train on Fordham Road, we finally reach the front of the protest.

"Hey, hey, NRA! How many folks were killed today? Hey, hey, NRA! How many folks were killed today?" the crowd chants. I feel pulled in every way. The whispers in my head are faint due to the external noise of the chants. Five senses. I see the back of a neon-orange hat, a woman blowing her nose, a child raising their fist, someone dropping their glove, silver shoes. I hear the chants, hip-hop spilling out of someone's speakers fueling our spirits, the train roaring into the station above us, and there's laughter. I smell day-old garbage, hot dogs from the stands, and coffee. I feel Victory and José's hands. Each of them holds one of my hands in order not to lose one another. Victory's hand is moist and José's is dry, and somehow they manage to balance the turmoil going on inside of my head. I taste blood in the back of my throat, and I know it's from all the clenching I've been doing lately.

The kids holding the megaphones look our age, but the ones to the side of them look a bit older. I imagine them to be college students. One of them looks over at us.

"Hey are y'all from Julia De Burgos?" they ask. We nod.

Before we know it, everyone knows we're here. They usher us to the middle of the crowd, behind the banner that says, "DON'T SHOOT." We walk down Fordham Road towards Kingsbridge. It isn't long until we find out that they have walked from Julia De Burgos, in the South Bronx, to here, and that we are marching towards Van Cortlandt Park to meet other small protests in the area.

"Hey, you're Yolanda. right?" one of the older kids asks. She has her locs up in a messy bun. A blue one falls down her face. She's rubbing lotion into her deep brown hands. The brown leather coat she wears is over a gray hoodie with a panther that says "People's Food Program." I nod.

"I go to Fordham University. I'm from 194th and Briggs. When I heard what had gone down, it broke my heart. But mostly the fact that you ran the Brave Space Club got to me, because I feel the same kind of hate on my campus. Everyone pretends to be progressive or whatever, but they never show up to our events or stop to question what we're doing. Anyway, we went down to your school and tried to get an interview with you. But I guess we were doing too much. Too soon."

"Yeah," I say. Take a deep breath.

"If you're up for it, would you say a few things when we get up to Van Cortlandt Park?" she asks. "We're trying to read a poem at every stop. We read 'Puerto Rican Obituary' by Pedro Pietri when we first started. A middle schooler from MS 111 is about to read 'I, Too' by Langston Hughes. When we get up to Bedford Park a woman from Brooklyn will read 'If They Should Come for Us' by Fatimah Asghar. Would you want to read something when we get to our final stop? It can be your work or someone else's."

"Can she think about it?" Victory interrupts. "Let you know when we're getting close?" I am glad she's near me. Because my head is starting to feel foggy.

"Of course, little sister," she says. "Just let me know. My name is Horus."

The streets grow more and more crowded as we go on. The group grows. Everything also gets louder. Everyone is chanting one behind the other to every single call and response. I don't even have to say anything for Victory to know I feel heavy. I look around, and it's all us—Black and Brown youth. That makes me feel like what's happening is revolutionary.

By the time we get to Mosholu Parkway, the crowd has quadrupled, and it's louder and angrier.

By the time we reach Van Cortlandt Park, there are news reporters and government officials in front of the tortoise statue and steps. Ms. Steinberg speeds up ahead of the group. She seems to be speaking to them and then immediately they move away from the statue. A group of white kids bring out a banner. They climb the steps, as everyone watches. With a string they tie the banner and it unfolds for all of us to see. "WHITE SUPREMACY IS NATIONAL TERRORISM." They stay put around the tortoise and hare statue. They know no one is going to touch them. They don't even move when the cops try to push them to remove the banner. "You can't touch us, we're underage and this is a peaceful protest," they shout back when the police try to intimidate them into moving.

Those who continue moving start chanting. "NRA, what if your kid didn't come home today? NRA, what if your kid didn't come home today? NRA, what if your kid didn't come home today?" The police have been tailing us all along, and I don't know if it's for protection's sake, or to have a watchful eye on everything.

I tap Horus and nod. I follow her as she climbs onto the stairs. Once at the top, I am shook at the sight. Every bit of the field is taken up by bodies.

Congresswoman Estevez climbs three steps. Behind the mic, she removes her mask and speaks into it. She introduces the organizers and invites Horus up, who introduces herself as one of many community organizers from the Bronx who helped put this together. Behind her are two police officers; they stand each on one side of her as if they're indeed protecting her. Their hands rest over their guns. Horus signals for me to take her place. My heart accelerates as I approach the mic. I take a deep breath. I see José in the crowd, I see Mrs. Obi and her husband, I see Hamid, I see Mariamma, I see Amina. I hear cars, I hear birds, I hear crying, I hear laughter. I touch Victory's hand, I touch the mint inside my coat pocket. I smell Victory's cocoa butter when she hugs me, I smell tea tree in her hair. I taste the mint, I taste the water she makes me drink.

"They're only here to make sure nothing happens," she says, reading my mind. "I know it's not comfortable. Please look at me, we're safe." I try to believe her.

"Hi," I say. My voice booms and echoes off of the speakers they have set up facing the crowd. The crowd is predominantly us. But everyone has joined. Black and Brown elders, even white families with their dogs and small kids. And ninety percent of the crowd wears masks. "I am Yolanda Nuelis Alvarez. I attend Julia De Burgos High in the South Bronx, and I am in the tenth grade." The entire crowd mumbles. Everyone knows it's me. The one he had held hostage until they were able to take him down.

"Thank you for being here. I know things are really hard for most of us right now," I say.

"This is community, muchacha! En la buena y en la mala," someone yells from the crowd.

"Speak, baby, speak!" I catch an elder say. The crowd claps.

"Everyone keeps saying how sorry they are; they look at me like I've lost this huge part of myself. I guess I have. But also I've gotten a lot of affirmations on what I want to do when I'm older, based on this experience. It's why I am reading one of Assata Shakur's poems titled 'Affirmation.' My dad gave me the book. He was in prison for some time. And when he came back home, he said there was one decent guard, who, after he had read most of the books in the library, sneaked in *Assata* for him. My dad has got me reading it now. And it's great. So here it is," I say. I take a deep breath. Try to focus on the poem, instead of the amount of people in front of me. Tell myself it's going to be great, it's going to be great, it's going to be great.

"I believe in living.
I believe in the spectrum
of Beta days and Gamma people.
I believe in sunshine.
In windmills and waterfalls,
tricycles and rocking chairs.
And i believe that seeds grow into sprouts.
And sprouts grow into trees.
I believe in the magic of the hands.
And in the wisdom of the eyes.
I believe in rain and tears.
And in the blood of infinity.

I believe in life.
And i have seen the death parade
march through the torso of the earth,
sculpting mud bodies in its path.
I have seen the destruction of the daylight,
and seen bloodthirsty maggots
prayed to and saluted.

I have seen the kind become the blind
and the blind become the bind
in one easy lesson.
I have walked on cut glass.
I have eaten crow and blunder bread
and breathed in the stench of indifference.

I have been locked by the lawless.
Handcuffed by the haters.
Gagged by the greedy.
And, if i know anything at all,
it's that a wall is just a wall
and nothing more at all.
It can be broken down.

I believe in living.
I believe in birth.
I believe in the sweat of love
and in the fire of truth.

And i believe that a lost ship,
steered by tired, seasick sailors,

can still be guided home

to port."

The crowd cheers. My body begins to feel effortlessly light. I shiver inside my coat and reach for Victory's hand, who is right near the side of the stage they've created. I believe, I believe, I believe, I believe. The words play on loop in my head.

"Can I borrow your megaphone?" I ask Horus. She gives it to me.

"I believe in living!" I shout, my free hand in a fist swiping through the air.

Horus directs them, reading off her phone. "I believe in birth!" the crowd shouts back.

"I believe in the sweat of love and the fire of truth!" I shout.

"I believe in living!" the crowd says again with Horus.

"I believe in birth!" I say back. My voice is breaking.

"I believe in the sweat of love and the fire of truth!" the crowd repeats after Horus.

"I believe in living!" I shout. Tears and snot running down my face. Victory cries with me. I pass off the megaphone and hug her, hug her tightly, almost wanting to put her body into my own. Wanting to bring everyone I know and love into a safe place inside of ourselves, where nothing can hurt us. It's not even that I am sad or broken in this moment. It's that this crowd feels like a world in which peace can work out. Stricter laws on guns, mental health services provided to all, an end to shame around needing help, an honest conversation about the malady that is white supremacy. It can exist. It doesn't have to be this complicated.

Crystal Walker, a Lake View survivor, gets on the stage. She repeats the chant and thanks me for having moved the crowd with Assata's poem. Victory and I step down from the stairs and join José.

"Let's start off with a moment of silence for those who have lost their lives to gun violence," she begins. I take a deep breath, close my eyes, bow my head. Victory and José hold each of my hands.

I feel a fire that runs up and down my crown to my feet, and back again. I take a deep breath. I am angry and wish there were no need to hold moments of silence. Instead I'd be cheered down the graduation stage by Mr. Leyva. That instead of this protest, we were back at school cheering on our team at a game. I take a deep breath. *Bruja Diosas, please help me hold my anger. Fuego, come through at a more constructive time. Please. Not now.* I look up.

"We just held a moment of silence for two minutes. Two minutes for the hundreds of lives lost at schools in the past few years alone due to guns. It should be noted that it has taken some just seconds to do away with the lives of multiple people while injuring others. Seconds," Crystal begins.

"We shouldn't be here. We should be at school. We should be learning. We should be reading. We should be figuring out how we can change the future, inside classrooms. But instead we are escaping them. Escaping them because they have become unsafe spaces. I guess for some of us, they have never been quite safe, but they serve some sort of purpose. They are now a place where we go to learn how to evade a school shooter. They are now a place where we have drills on how to save one another's life.

"Guns. It's been three years since a white, middle-class boy, with clear mental health issues, brought one to school and unleashed his hatred on my friends, on my teachers. Three years have passed since seven teenagers, a mother, a father, and a teacher lost their lives. Three years since I had to pretend to be dead to keep my breath. I wish I could tell you that I have somehow figured out the lesson in all of this ugliness. That I figured it out. That I don't have nightmares. That I no longer cry. That I don't cringe when someone's a little too nice. That I don't bend out of shape to befriend people at work who I don't want to be friends with, but I don't want them to be lonely enough to do something horrific. But all of that would be a lie.

"I speak to you today not because I want to appeal to the NRA, not to give anybody in the world more tragedy porn. But to let every single one of you know that there is something gun violence and oppression cannot take away from us.

"That is our soul, our grit, our power. Every day, I am woken up by the mere fact that I survived. I received a second chance—and those who didn't, they push me, even on bad days when my PTSD almost chokes me. So whatever systems are out there planning for the demise of people like me, you might take us out one at a time, but we will never cease to exist."

THREE
MONTHS
LATER

June 2020

31

NOT A RETURN,
AN ELEVATION

José's father lent him his car, and we've decided to cross the
bridge, head to New Jersey, and look at the city from there. I
hold his free hand as he drives. Noname blasts from the stereo.
I open the window and feel the warm air brush my skin. Spring
has come and is actively leaving. Summer at the very tip of our
breath. I look over at José. His Yankee fitted low as he drives, he
looks over at me and moves his hand to my knee. It's such a beautiful thing to be young and free. Freedom in these limbs wasn't
always a given. Despite the grief, I have to enjoy it. I open the car
roof and stick my head out. The day is so bright and warm. I let
my arms go and take the wind with me.

At the park, we settle on a bench looking into New York. I sit
on the head of the bench, my Vans grounded to the part I should
be sitting on. José goes into his backpack for the coconut water
and bodega sandwiches he's bought for us. As he's moving, I lean
against his shoulder and rub my nose against his shirt. The faint
lavender scent is still detectable despite his cologne.

"José," I start. "You wanna know something? I am so proud of you. You've worked so hard to get into the best colleges. The best teams. You an actual big deal!" He puts our stuff down and leans his body into the space between my legs. He kisses me, and I cradle his jawline in my hands.

"You deserve the big dream. It's so attainable for you," I say. "It's a huge miracle, you know, that you weren't injured considering how close you were to everything that day. It means this dream is for you, and no one can take it from you." I take a deep breath.

"I know, babe. I like that," he laughs. "I like that you're proud of me. It means a lot." He plants a peck on my nose. He settles on the bench and pats the space next to him. I lower my body. Begin undressing the aluminum foil off of my sandwich. *He's not going because he loves you. Give him permission to go although you rule no one but yourself.* The voice, my voice, is here again.

"I don't think you should choose Connecticut. I think you should choose Duke. You're really good, José. It's where you belong." He finishes the mouthful.

"That was before us, before you," he says, taking a gulp of the coconut water. "Plus, I already turned it down."

"José, they would take you back in a heartbeat, and you know it."

"No, Yo—"

I turn to him. "Listen, if this year has taught us anything, it's that we are blessed. That there is a plan out there for all of us. It is not every day that a boy from the Bronx is recruited by Duke. Also, I want you to live out your college experience. I am still going to be here, in high school, working hard too." I throw up my arms. "Whatever is intended for me, you know? It's not going to be easy for us to keep this up long distance, going through different experiences. And I don't want to work hard ever again. Not after what we have been through," I laugh, looking towards the river that separates two masses of land. When I look at him, there are tears in his eyes.

"You're letting me go?" he asks.

"For now, my love," I say. And now it's my eyes dressed in blood as I try everything not to cry.

The water between New Jersey and New York divides the states perfectly. The water provides us with space. I have heard so many times that true love is letting something that needs to be free, go. I think that's what I am feeling.

If it's meant to be for us, en un futuro.

☾

Jose and I drive by Julia De Burgos to pick up our things. Students haven't returned to the building since the day it happened, and today everyone has been giving time slots to pick up their things.

"Bruja Diosas, Fuego, Universe, grant me the strength," I say aloud as I walk through the gates of Julia De Burgos. José nods.

There's a mural on the entrance of Julia De Burgos. Mr. Leyva on one side. Wearing red jeans and a black sweater. His hair is salt and peppered into a perfect cut, the shape-up impeccable. His left fist is held high, and a cup of hot chocolate is in its grip. He smiles the side smile he always flashed when he couldn't agree with the teachers and sided with students.

Victory jumps out of her father's car and runs to me. "You're here? Why didn't you tell me you were coming?" Her eyes are flushed. Her skin looks duller than usual. I've been so distant, even when she's held me, that I've missed how this was affecting her.

"I didn't want to worry you," I say. "I'm lying. I just forgot. I'm sorry. I also forgot you, right?" I open my arms and she hugs me. "I'm sorry," I cry into her shoulder. And she doesn't have to say anything for me to know that it's OK. We stand at the mural crying and in each other's arms for what seems like forever. I've cried so many times in the last few months. But this time it feels different, like a part of me is finally accepting that what happened, did go down. That something has shifted and I can't continue to drown in what once was.

"Happy birthday!" I say, letting go of her and taking a small box out of my bag. "It's a Gemini ring for my favorite Gemini!"

She smiles. Tears rolling down her eyes soak her baby blue mask. "You remembered."

I walk to my locker, my heart beating out of my chest. My locker feels like such a foreign place. I haven't opened it since the day everything changed. I reach out for the lock, circular, the metal heavy and cold in my palm. I turn it to the left three times and then to the right once until I find the eleven. I turn it to the left two times to find the twenty and then to the right until I find thirteen. It was the day Papi went to jail.

The lock clicks, and I take three deep breaths. The picture of me and Victory smiling, cheetah tape circling it. There's a post-it with a corny joke Mami wrote to me one morning. My favorite picture of Mamá Teté blowing me a kiss. The Polaroid of me and Papi. In the middle, my name written in bubble letters by Mr. Leyva on my first day of sophomore year. He said it was a gift, to remind me that he was good at tagging up back in his day, but also to remind me he was young too once, so what he advised me was always for my own good. I run my hands through the paper. The dents on the page from the weight of the pen make me shiver.

"Let me find out! You did graffiti when you were in high school, Mr. Leyva?" I had asked him.

"Yep, I was a fool. Got busted spray-painting train carts and building walls. But I always went back to it," he responded.

My tears feel like hot liquid iron on my eyelids. My black-and-red puffer coat I wore on the day it happened hangs from the top hook, like a flower. Below it, my binders still lean on each other the way I left them. There's a note sticking out from between two binders. I already know it's from Mrs. Obi. I had asked her to bring me a book I had in here.

Dear Yoyo,

What a year. I'm sorry I didn't get to say goodbye in person. The truth is I don't have the courage to tell you I won't be running Brave Space with you next year. In fact, I am taking a break from the classroom. I've decided I want to be a mom. After I saw you reading Assata's autobiography, I got my own copy. There is a line in there in which she says, "I am about life. I'm gonna live as hard as i can and as full as i can until i die. And i'm not letting these parasites, these oppressors, these greedy racist swine make me kill my children in my mind, before they are even born." All my life I've thought I don't want to bring life into this world because it's so hard for us, Black women. And because of you, the way you stand in your truth, even if that is 1% because of me, then I can be a good parent, you know? The world needs more Black and Brown faces that know what joy is, love hard, and unapologetically live—big or small. They won't keep me from birthing that anymore.

I know it must feel like life never gets easy. Like at every turn there is a heartache or an issue that questions your humanity, Black girl. I promise you life will continue to feel that way. The world we live in isn't filled with ease, even though that's what we deserve at this point, but our ancestors are always on their feet, working hard to protect our right to be free, and when we get it, that space, even when it's tiny and short-lived, sweet child, it feels like everything. People say we are magical. Yet it is those short moments of winning that light us up enough to keep pushing.

When I went off to college, my mother gave me a book by Toni Cade Bambara called The Salt Eaters. It's frustrating and sometimes hard to get through, but there's a quote I have always held onto: "Are you sure, sweetheart, you want to be well? . . . It's a lot of weight to be well."

The world will tell the like of us, Black and Brown women deeply connected with the Earth and the things that pull at the Earth's orbit, that we know nothing and are even a little crazy. Because we call it like we see it, because we talk shit about capitalism although we have to live by its rules, because we are OK plunging into the darkness and our subconscious to come back alive with more life, more to give to ourselves and the world. But remember you are well. It is the world that is sick.

My card is in the envelope. Please, Yoyo, stay in touch.

Love you & live free,
Keehan Marie Obi

I take a deep breath. My eyes well up, and I allow the tears to flow down my face. My chest feels so light. Mrs. Obi will be a bomb ass mother. One who shows up for her kids and pushes them to be the very best version of themselves. I peel off the pictures and Mami's note, fold them into the envelope with Obi's letter. I take my big black-and-red puffer coat and stuff it in the bag. I throw the binders in the recycling bin; there is no lesson for me in them.

"Oh, you out here, out here?" Victory laughs as she walks out of the Julia De Burgos building. The sun is high and bright in the sky. Summer is officially here.

"I know you didn't think I really forgot," I say, holding a bouquet of sunflowers and daisies. It's my girl's birthday. I gotta go in. She rushes towards me. "You know I go hard when I try." I hand her the flowers, and she throws her arms around me.

"You ready?" Papi yells out the driver's seat, as he drives up in his car. I open the back door for her. Victory raises her eyebrow and pretends to clap as she enters.

"Welcome Ms. Victory. Happy birthday. What can we play for you on this journey to Van Cortlandt Park this sunny afternoon?" Papi says as I sit in the passenger seat. He remembered his lines, and I flash him a quick thumbs- up.

"Let me hear that 'Gbona' by Burna Boy, Mr. Alvarez!" Victory snaps and crosses her legs.

Papi puts on the song and turns the volume all the way up as we drive up north. The song bounces off the speakers loudly.

Victory dances in her seat and Papi downloads the song on to his phone. "This beat makes me want to dance!" Papi says.

"That's what he's saying, Mr. Alvarez!" Victory yells. "The drum does something to the people." Victory continues moving in her seat and we laugh.

☾

"Alright, you've arrived, ladies," Papi says when we reach 242nd Street and Broadway. He pops the trunk, and I bring out a basket I prepared before I left with José this morning.

"Nah, a basket?!" Victory yells. Papi laughs as he steps into the car and drives away.

"It's a real ass date, girl. For your birthday. We deserve!" I say. We begin walking on the concrete path into the park. Victory puts down the jean jacket hanging off her bag, and I untie the hoodie off my waist. As we arrive on the lawn, there's a baseball team practicing in masks, a soccer team kicking the ball around, people working out and running around the track, and a small protest of middle school students marching around. Victory and I look at each other and scream joyfully. Even though neither of us say, I know we are thinking the same thing: Nothing like the Bronx. Nothing like community.

"What tree is calling out to you, girl?" she asks me.

"Nah, you choose," I say.

"I like this one," she points to a few feet away. It's a healthy white ash tree. As we sit, I put the basket down. I open the lids. I bring out a white blanket from my bag.

"You had a whole blanket in there?"

"Yeah, I planned for this!" We take off our shoes and sit. "I got us a bottle of kiwi and strawberry spritz. Caprese sandwiches, kettle chips 'cause you know we need a side, mango slices 'cause dessert, and Hershey kisses 'cause more dessert!" I say, pulling out each item. Victory smiles brightly. I bring two glasses out and serve us—feeling fancy AF. When I look up, a series of tears are running down Victory's face.

"You OK?" I ask, offering her a napkin.

"Give me a minute," she says. She covers her face with her hands and the napkin. "It's just a lot," she starts when she catches her breath. "This year has been a lot. And I've been pushing through this semester like it's nothing, but I was scared all the time. I'm just grateful to be here. I'm grateful you're safe." The tears stream down the hills of her cheeks again.

"I know. I hear you. It has been hard," I respond. I scoot over to her side, and she lays her head on my shoulder.

"I get it. Life isn't"—she brings out her hand—"a walk in the park. It can't be rainbows and butterflies all the time. I know that. But I am tired, girl."

I take a deep breath. "It's hard to keep surviving, you know?" I say.

She nods.

"But I am grateful we did." She lifts her head up. "And now: IT'S THRIVE TIME!"

"To thriving," I bring up my glass.

"To thriving," she repeats. We clink our glasses and take a sip.

I bring out our sandwiches and chips. As we chew into them, I catch Victory up on what's gone down with José.

"I love that you did that for the both of you," she says. And I smile. I did do that, huh? I'm going to miss the hell out of José, but I know he's going to be able to live up to his best potential at Duke. And I know I'll see him from time to time, too.

"What are you planning to do with all of summer?" I ask.

"DO NOTHING!" Victory exclaims. "I just told you I AM TIREDT, OK?! I am going to rest. My parents are going to take two weeks off in August. I'm pretty sure we'll travel down to Atlanta to visit family or something. But girl, I am going to take that in. Sleep under trees, on porches, on a hammock in a clearing, by the water. I am going to rest and be free at every second."

I snap my fingers. "Go aaawwwffff, sis!"

"The work is not going to stop and junior year might drag us, right? 'Cause that's what colleges focus on anyway." Victory takes a swig of water from her water bottle. "How about you?"

"I leave to Dominican Republic tomorrow with Mamá Teté," I smile. "To complete my initiation." Victory does the snapping now. I tell her Mamá Teté surprised me with the tickets out of nowhere, mad last minute.

"It's been a long time coming and a HELL of an initiation," she inhales.

"Talk about it."

As we finish the last bites of our sandwiches, I lay down and look up at the trees as they attempt to sway and cover up the sky. I place my hands on my stomach and take a deep breath. I exhale and feel my hands fall as my stomach deflates. *Alive.*

Victory lies down next to me. She holds my hand. And I squeeze it. Everything inside of me feels overwhelmed by the love I feel for my friend. No matter where life goes, how many things get in the way—Victory and I are a forever thing. A fat cloud passes by.

"Girl, you've been reading the cards again?" she asks.

I look over at her. Her fro is spread around her face on the blanket. The green of the grass and the white of the blanket com-plementing all the deep melanin of her skin.

"Yeah, I picked them up again," I sit up. "Want to do a read-ing together?"

Victory sits up quickly. "You mean to tell me, you Yolanda, first of her name, is about let me, a regular, degular, unwitchy being, touch your beloved cards?

"You doing too much now!" We laugh. I eagerly go in my bag and bring out the bundle of cards wrapped in a red scarf.

"Fuego, Bruja Diosas, Honorable Ancestors, Higher Beings, Universe, God, Goddess, Mother Earth, Father Sky, I ask that you come through and guide us through this reading. Please show us what we must see today for the higher good of all involved," I pray.

"Ase!"

I unwrap the cards and set the stack of cards on Victory's hands. "You shuffle. The cards should feel your energy." I smile. She shuffles awkwardly, but she shuffles, and then splits, and then reshuffles again. She spreads out the cards in front of us.

"Think of a question," I say. Victory closes her eyes. "Focus all of your energy on it. Let yourself feel it." She opens her eyes and brings out her hand over the cards.

"Ooooof, it's that one," she points at a card towards the left.

"Pick it up then!" I laugh. She slowly picks it up without turning it. "It's OK," I whisper. "Look at it."

"La Estrella!" she yells. "Is that good? It looks good right?"

"Look at it. What is it telling you?" I smile.

Victory takes a deep breath and taps her right cheek with her pointer finger. "It's been rough, but a new time is coming—full of trials, yes, but sweetness. Abundance. I have to keep pouring into myself outside of studying and doing all the things I think I have to do. I have to take care of me and everything I am deserving of will follow."

I nod. "That's a great first reading, V!" I bring the cards back together and wrap them up in the red scarf again.

ON MY WAY

"I am about life. I'm gonna live as hard as i can and
as full as i can until i die."
— Assata Shakur, *Assata: An Autobiography*

Papi taps my shoulder, scaring the living crap out of me. I
don't have my devices on. Lately, I don't wear it much unless
I am going outside. Not listening to the regular sound of everything around me—the train, the neighbors, the conversations
through the walls—allows me to settle into the rhythm of me.
Allows me to remember what's mine and what is not.

"You don't have to do this, Yoyo. You don't have to go," I read
Papi's lips. I get up and walk past him to the bathroom. I put on
my processors.

"We can have a beautiful, beautiful summer. Un verano en
Nueva York!" he says. He takes a few salsa steps in front of me, his
hands moving and shaking with invisible maracas.

"But I do have to go, Papi," I say. I cup his face with my palm.
"Papi, we'll go together as soon as your parole is over. I promise

even though I'll be grown as hell, and I won't really have to travel with my dad." He laughs. Sits on a chair next to my altar.

My altar is back to normal. Red candle for Fuego is lit. White candle for Bruja Diosa Clarity lit as well. Another white candle for my ancestors. Five glasses of water. One for my grandfather. One for the ancestors I do not know, but I feel them pumping through me. One for the Bruja Diosas que me protegen, including Fuego. One for Mr. Leyva. One for autumn. The tarot cards are stacked and topped with a quartz crystal.

I open the maleta. I am bringing one of my own for the first time. Usually it is not mine alone since it is stuffed for things to give away to family and friends back on the island. Mamá sent a caja a month ago with all of that. Says we can do things comfortably now. We don't always have to go around carrying loads.

"What are you most excited for this summer?" Papi asks.

"The beaches, the food, Helados Bon, but mostly, Papi, I want to learn, I want to go to las Misas, to the gatherings. I want to dance and feel and scream and cry. I want to know what it really has taken for these gifts to be preserved and passed down."

"You already do. Mamá made you before your mother and I thought you up, you know?" Papi says.

"Yeah, she never lets me forget. But I want to know, know."

"Mi'ja, all you need to know is already in there," he says pointing to my chest. "You are a bruja. The world once burned and killed people like you and Mamá. And if they couldn't, they used you all for the power, or straight up had ya'll looking crazy. Because they were scared, and couldn't take the profound knowledge y'all hold. If I would've listened to Mamá, I would've avoided so much mierda. Pero that's how life goes. We have to learn by our own accord. But you, you my heart, are connected even when you try to move away. The Unknowns have got your back. And I can't wait to hear how they show up for you. Quisqueya, man, it is truly a wonderful place. Sometimes when things got hard out here, and I fought myself to avoid asking Mami for help, I couldn't help but assume this land don't got no space for magic, magic. Like sure, it still works, but in Dominican Republic it's just in your face, you can't escape it. Like it's another element," Papi says.

"Papi, Mamá never talks about Papá Antonio. Was he a brujo? What happened to him, really?"

"It was in his blood like it is in me. He didn't keep his word to the Unknowns is how I've always seen it. He was a good man and a really great father. You would've liked him," he says, moving some hair out of my face. "You should know: there's good and bad. But you choose how you want them to move. Whichever way you decide, that's the work they're going to do. And you have to keep your word always—"

"Or else blessings become downfalls," I spill.

"Exactly, Morena. Exactly that."

☾

Mami and Anthony drive us to the airport. After Mami gives Mamá Teté the address of her relatives in La Vega and has her swear to take me and let me stay a while, Mami hugs me.

"I'm sorry if I am not the greatest at this," she says.

"At what?" I ask, looking up at her.

"At mothering. I see how you are with your grandmother. And even though your father has been gone for so long, you have a great relationship with him. I wish I could be more," her voice breaks.

"Mami, I love you. No matter what. I appreciate you trying your best. It's been enough for now." I hug her. My heart tears for her though. Mami's aura has always been kind of floaty. Although she doesn't tell me, I know it has to do a lot with her upbringing. Her own mother not being affectionate and all, leaving for the United States and only sending for her when she was sixteen. Mami was raised by a family who could offer her a roof and food on a regular basis, and after they died, she was sent off to her tías, her mother's sisters, who were only five years older than her.

"I was created inside of you; I continue to be guided by you and your adelante spirit. That's more than I could ever ask, Mami," I say. She kisses my forehead before we finally go through the security gates.

☾

"Good afternoon, passengers. This is your captain speaking. First, I'd like to welcome everyone on JetBlue Flight 333. We are currently cruising at an altitude of thirty-three thousand, three hundred feet at an airspeed of five hundred and fifty miles per hour. The time is 1:35 p.m. The wind is on our side today, and we are expecting to land at Las Américas International Airport at approximately 5:55 p.m. The weather there is clear and sunny, with a high of eighty-three degrees for this afternoon. If the weather continues as is, we will get a magnificent view as we descend. In about ten minutes or so, the cabin crew will be coming around to offer you a small snack and beverage. I'll come on here again before we reach our destination. In the meantime, sit back, relax, and enjoy the rest of the flight. You're in great hands with our crew. Thank you for choosing JetBlue."

Mamá Teté runs her hand over mine. She has given me her

window seat, and she sits on the aisle. There are empty seats up and down the plane. People aren't traveling due to COVID. It makes sense. Mamá Teté says she wishes circumstances were different, but we had no choice but to return to DR.

"I am going to show you everything I know," she says. "De todo un poco. And hopefully a whole lot if we get the time."

"Isn't that what you've always done?" I ask.

"Yes, but now you've grown, that you've been through some stuff, you understand, really understand, that the light and the dark exist together. Now, I can show you how to do it all in the name of love, and not offend the Unknowns." Mamá Teté smiles so grand, from ear to ear, in a way I have never quite seen. Her face shifts. Yet, she is soft, joyful, elegant.

"Culebra?" I ask.

"Sí, hija de Fuego pero igual mia. First things first, you can't play with the Unknowns—what you call Bruja Diosas."

"I know."

"Second, our goal is always to take back what's rightfully ours. Our joy. Our abundance. Our connection to the elements. We are free spirits who have been robbed. The practice is to take that back."

"And third?" I smile.

"Rest up. Just because the world can't break you, doesn't mean you won't bend out of shape. We need you to be as aligned as possible."

"Anything else?"

"It'll come. Patience, you fireball. That reminds me. STOP leaving your candles on when you aren't home. Fuego loves to play with flames even when it's for something light."

I laugh until I begin to feel tired. I close my eyes, knowing when I awake, I will be back on solid ground.

AUTHOR'S NOTE

Many of the Brujería and "magical" references in *The Making of Yolanda La Bruja* are inspirations or nods to the names, spells, histories, and symbolisms of syncretic religions practiced in the Caribbean by Afro-descendants. My references and nods are all fictional. Afro/Black-Caribbean religions' practices and belief systems are sacred to our communities and this novel has been written with deep reverence.

ACKNOWLEDGMENTS

None of this would be possible without the love of the Most High, my honorable ancestors, and my divine team. They fortify and guide me, and I am forever grateful they chose me to deliver this story.

I extend gratitude to all the Black, Brown, and Indigenous spiritual and religious practitioners across time, space, and belief, who act in accordance with the good of all involved, and have helped, directly and indirectly, sustain us all.

To my grandmother, Gladys, who taught me the power of prayer. To my late father, Miguel, for the lineage. To my baby, Shadhey, whom I know would've grown up in this world to be as fierce and brilliant as Yoyo, for everything she taught me.

To my nieces and nephews for never letting me forget to take time to be playful and listen.

To my mami, Tati, and my dad, Felix. Your love is a saving grace. When I quit teaching and returned home to the Bronx, the roof and food you provided for me allowed me to finish this book and go all in and pursue this writing life. To my godfather, Andres, for making the best café con leches and bringing them to me in my room while I worked.

To Chinenye Eto for providing top-notch emotional support during all the processing, tears, venting, and outbursts of joy from the moment this manuscript went out on submission. You lucky.

Now to those whom this physical book wouldn't be possible without:

To all of the youth I've had the privilege to teach. Especially: elementary school students at Academic Leadership Charter School (Bronx, NY), middle school students at Brooklyn Prospect Charter School (Brooklyn, NY), and at Everett Middle School (San Francisco, CA) Thank you for trusting me. Honorable mention: Sidney Chapman at Everett Middle School (2018–2019), who read through the classroom library and said she was bored and wanted to read what I was writing. Many thanks to her for truly being the first reader of *The Making of Yolanda La Bruja*.

To Elisa Avila, my aunt, who was patient and loving during the period I went back to San Pedro de Macoris, Dominican Republic, to learn more about my father's lineage and their connection to the tradition.

To Kulwa Apara for editing this book in its first phase. Your edits and labor on the first 50K words pushed me to completion.

To Mechi Annaís Estévez Cruz for revising this book in its final stage. All of your probings allowed me to go deeper into the characters' arcs in this book. Your support as I continued to revise during a very tough year was deadass everything.

To my beta readers: Jehan Giles, Rocio Martinez, and Shyla Espejo. Your words affirmed me at a moment when I was ready to put this story away. To Pamela Reyes, who believed in the story of "la brujita esa." To Nia Ita Thomas for being a sounding board and looking over early chunks of this novel. To Sonia Alejandra Rodriguez, who workshopped the first ten chapters with me after our time together at VONA.

To my agent, Patrice Caldwell. When I wrapped my head around what an agent was and why I needed one, all my research and requirements led to you. Thank you for believing in me and my stories. I am so honored to be represented by such a powerhouse! To Trinica Sampson for always supporting and answering all the questions and being a step ahead.

To my editor, Nick Thomas. I am so grateful for all the care you poured into *The Making of Yolanda La Bruja*. Your belief in this story really means a lot! Your notes were validating and always felt aligned with where I wanted the story to go. Thank you for reminding me of the power of positive feedback. To Irene Vázquez, Assistant Editor and Publicist, who read *The Making of Yolanda* first at LQ—thank you for vouching for us!

To Daniel José Older, my instructor at VONA's YA workshop in 2020, who uplifted Yolanda. But also because back in 2018, before meeting him—when I couldn't go to workshops or be given access to an MFA—I reworked the opening of this book thanks to all the gems he dropped on Skillshare. To Elizabeth Acevedo, for encouraging me during my querying process and for providing feedback on my letter & first chapters.

Thank you to Wilgrid Peralta for her generosity in allowing me to interview her about the tradition.

Thank you to everyone at Levine Querido for believing and uplifting *The Making of Yolanda*:

Arthur Levine (President and Editor-in-Chief)
Antonio Gonzalez Cerna (Marketing Director)
Maddie McZeal (Assistant and Managing Editor)
Arely Guzmán (Assistant Editor)
Freesia Blizard (Senior Production Developer at Chronicle)

Shout out to Chindo Nkenke-Smith, who designed the cool jacket and case of this book. To Blane Asrat for the beautiful cover illustration. And Lewelin Polanco for the care in the interior design of this book.

Thank you to each and every person who engages with this book.